London Gambit

TRACY GRANT

Dedication

*For Richard Havel, a wonderful uncle who has always
supported me and my writing, with everything from
attending graduations and countless book readings,
to being there when my daughter was born.
Thank you, Uncle Dick!*

ACKNOWLEDGMENTS

As always, my fervent and heartfelt thanks to my agent, Nancy Yost, for her support of Malcolm and Suzanne, and of me, and for her input and advice on this book and from the start of the series.

Thanks as well to Natanya Wheeler, for a beautiful cover that evokes the mood of the book and series, captures one of the early scenes to perfection, and looks about as close as I can imagine to Suzanne Rannoch, and also for shepherding the ebook expertly through the publication process. Thanks to Sarah Younger, for looking after the book so well on the print side. And to Adrienne Rosado and everyone at NYLA, for their support throughout the publication process.

Thank you to Catherine Duthie and Kate Mullin, for the invaluable feedback on the manuscript. To Eve Lynch, for the careful copy editing and answering countless questions about the finer points of grammar and style.

To all the wonderful booksellers who help readers find Malcolm and Suzanne, and in particular to Book Passage in Corte Madera, for their always warm welcome to me and to my daughter, Mélanie. Thank you to the readers who share

Suzanne's and Malcolm's adventures with me on my Web site, Facebook, and Twitter. To Suzi Shoemake and Betty Strohecker, for managing a wonderful Google+ Discussion Group for readers of the series, and to all the members of the group, for their enthusiasm and support. Thank you to Gregory Paris and jim saliba, for creating my Web site and updating it so quickly and with such style. To Raphael Coffey, for juggling cats and humans to take the best author photos a writer could have (and to my daughter, Mélanie, and our cats, Suzanne and Lescaut, for being so wonderfully cooperative over a two-hour photo shoot).

Thanks to Raphael, Bonnie Glaser, and Veronica Wolff, for nurturing Mélanie so Mummy could get a few more words down. To my colleagues at the Merola Opera Program, for understanding that being a novelist is also an important part of my life. To the staffs at Pottery Barn Kids, Peek, and Blue Stove at Nordstrom, all at The Village in Corte Madera, for a friendly welcome to Mélanie and me on writing breaks. And to the staff at Peet's Coffee & Tea at The Village in Corte Madera, for keeping me supplied with superb lattes and cups of Earl Grey, and keeping Mélanie happy with hot chocolate and whip cream and smiles as I wrote this book.

Thank you to Lauren Willig, for sharing the delights and dilemmas of writing about Napoleonic spies while also juggling small children. I'll always remember sitting on your sofa and discussing Jane's Pink Carnation book while our daughters bonded over *Pirates of Penzance*. To Penelope Williamson, for support and understanding and hours analyzing Shakespeare plays, new works, and episodes of *Scandal*. To Veronica Wolff, for wonderful writing dates during which my word count seemed to magically increase. To Deborah Crombie, for supporting Malcolm and Suzanne from the beginning. To

Tasha Alexander and Andrew Grant, for their wit and wisdom and support, whether in person or via email. To Deanna Raybourn, who never fails to offer encouragement and asks wonderful interview questions. And to my other writer friends near and far, for brainstorming, strategizing, and commiserating—Jami Alden, Bella Andre, Allison Brennan, Isobel Carr, Deborah Coonts, Catherine Coulter, Alexandra Elliott, J.T. Ellison, Barbara Freethy, Carol Grace, C. S. Harris, Candice Hern, Anne Mallory, Monica McCarty, Brenda Novak, Poppy Reiffin, and Jacqueline Yau.

Finally, thank you to my daughter, Mélanie, for inspiring me, encouraging me, and being amazingly tolerant of Mummy's writing time. I am so excited you are beginning to make up stories yourself!

DRAMATIS PERSONAE
*indicates real historical figures

The Rannoch Family & Household
Malcolm Rannoch, Member of Parliament
Suzanne (Mélanie) Rannoch, his wife
Colin Rannoch, their son
Jessica Rannoch, their daughter

Laura Fitzwalter, Marchioness of Tarrington, Colin and Jessica's former governess
Lady Emily Fitzwalter, her daughter
Raoul O'Roarke, Laura's lover, Suzanne's former spymaster, Malcolm's father

Miles Addison, Malcolm's valet
Blanca Addison, his wife, Suzanne's maid and companion
Valentin, footman
Michael, footman

Lady Frances Dacre-Hammond, Malcolm's aunt
Aline Blackwell, her daughter
Dr. Geoffrey Blackwell, Aline's husband

The Davenport Family
Lady Cordelia Davenport
Colonel Harry Davenport, her husband, scholar and former intelligence officer
Livia Davenport, their daughter
Drusilla Davenport, their daughter
Archibald Davenport, Harry's uncle

The Mallinson/Carfax Family
Hubert Mallinson, Earl Carfax, British spymaster
Amelia, Countess Carfax, his wife
Lady Lucinda Mallinson, their youngest daughter

David Mallinson, Viscount Worsley, the Carfaxes' son
Simon Tanner, playwright, David's lover

Edward (Teddy), Viscount Craven, David's nephew
George Craven, his brother
Amy Craven, their sister
Jamie Craven, their brother

Cecilia Whateley, sister to the Carfaxes' late son-in-law
Eustace Whateley, her husband

Lady Isobel Lydgate, the Carfaxes' daughter
Oliver Lydgate, her husband
Ellie Lydgate, their daughter
Billy Lydgate, their son
Rose Lydgate, their daughter

Mary Fitzwalter, Dowager Duchess of Trenchard, the Carfaxes' eldest daughter

Marianne Fairchild, a cousin of the Mallinsons'

The Laclos/Caruthers Family
Bertrand Laclos, French émigré
Rupert, Viscount Caruthers, his lover
Gabrielle, Viscountess Caruthers, Rupert's wife and Bertrand's cousin
Stephen, their son
Nick Gordon, Gabrielle's lover
Gui Laclos, Gabrielle's brother, betrothed to Mary Trenchard

Waterloo Veterans
*Arthur Wellesley, Duke of Wellington, British ambassador to France
*Lord Fitzroy Somerset, his secretary
*Emily Harriet Somerset, Fitzroy's wife and Wellington's niece

Captain John Ennis, former intelligence officer
Anne Ennis, his wife
Kit Ennis, their son
Tim Ennis, their son

Ben Coventry, former enlisted man
Sue Kettering, his mistress
Jemmy, their son

Colonel William Cuthbertson

Viscount St. Ives, Life Guards
Sylvie (de Fancot), Viscountess St. Ives, his wife

*Auguste-Charles-Joseph, Comte de Flahaut, former aide-de-camp to Napoleon Bonaparte

*Margaret (Mercer Elphinstone), Comtesse de Flahaut, his wife
*Hortense Bonaparte, Flahaut's former lover, stepdaughter to Napoleon

Others
Jeremy Roth, Bow Street runner

Marthe Leblanc, dressmaker and former French agent
Charlotte Leblanc, her daughter
Sophie Leblanc her daughter

Louis Germont, clerk in the French foreign ministry

Manon (Caret), Lady Harleton, actress and former French agent
Crispin, Lord Harleton, her husband
Roxane, Manon's daughter
Clarisse, Manon's daughter

Jennifer Mansfield, actress and former French agent
Sir Horace Smytheton, her lover, patron of the Tavistock Theatre

Lisette Varon, former French agent

Maria Monreal, former British agent

Julien St. Juste, agent for hire

What is honor? A word. What is in that word honor? What is that honor? Air.

Shakespeare, Henry IV Part 1, Act V, scene i

PROLOGUE

London
June 1818

He was safe. No, not that precisely. The world wasn't safe anymore. But he was safer than he'd been on the streets of London, where he'd dodged blows and seen a brawl break out. Safer than he'd been at Harrow, or he wouldn't have had to leave. Safer than he'd been jolted in a farm cart on the drive here. Safer than he'd be at home. No, not that. He didn't have a home anymore. Safer than he'd be in his uncle's house.

He eased the door shut and stepped into the cool, damp darkness. Shadows offered safety, he reminded himself. He could think here. Decide what to do next. He took two steps forwards, then slumped against the wall and slid down to land on the floorboards with a thump. He'd bumped his knee jumping from the cart, and his elbow running from the brawl.

He reached inside his coat, pulled out a hunk of the dry bread the man with the farm cart had given him, chewed a bite. His eyes were heavy. If he could just sleep for a bit, he'd feel better. Then he'd be able to figure out what to do. At least this place had been his father's. That made it safer somehow. He let his shoulders sink further against the wall.

Something scuttered across his foot. He started, screamed, jumped to the side, wide awake. He put a hand on the ground to keep his balance and touched something. Something soft. Hair. A dog. No, a person. God, someone else was asleep in here. He snatched his hand away. Something dripped from his fingers. Something sticky. He caught the coppery tang, but it was a moment more before he realized it was blood.

1

Malcolm Rannoch swung down from a hackney in Rosemary Lane. The light mist that had been falling when he left Brooks's had whipped up into genuine rain, but the street was still crowded. Men and women lounged in doorways, three boys clustered round a sputtering fire under an overhanging roof at the street corner. The sight of a gentleman in a black evening coat, cream-colored pantaloons, and a silk hat stepping from a hackney drew a number of surprised, cautious looks. Malcolm nodded, smiled, and slipped through the crowd to the door of the warehouse.

Jeremy Roth opened the door at once in response to his knock. "Thank you for coming." The Bow Street runner's gaze was level as usual, but his dark eyes betrayed his concern. "I'm sorry to have disrupted your evening. Especially on young Colin's birthday."

Roth and his own sons had been at Colin's party at the Rannochs' Berkeley Square house earlier in the day. Malcolm waved a hand. "We took the children to dinner at Rules after the party. Colin was sound asleep two hours since. I was at an election strategy meeting at Brooks's. I was bewailing our dim prospects for meaningful gains with David and Rupert and Oliver when I got your message. You saved me from sinking further into wallowing in regret."

Roth stepped aside so Malcolm could enter the warehouse. Two lanterns had been lit, shedding flickering yellow light over the high beam ceiling and smoke-blackened walls. Even before he noticed the blanket-covered form on the ground against one wall, Malcolm caught a whiff of the sickly sweet stench of blood.

Roth nodded. "Someone seems to have broken in. There's a hidden compartment in the wall near the body that we found open and empty, so I'd had hazard a guess the dead man broke in to steal something and had a fight with a confederate who took whatever they were searching for."

"Or someone else broke in in search of the same thing and surprised him."

Roth raised his brows. "Possibly. The body has begun to stiffen, so it looks as though he was killed between six-thirty and ten-thirty this evening. Given the break-in, I'd hazard a guess it was on the later side. But that isn't why I sent for you." He jerked his head to the far end of the room. A small figure sat at a round table, shoulders hunched, feet not quite reaching the floorboards. "He wouldn't tell me his name," Roth said. "But I recognized him."

Malcolm recognized him as well. The body language and the gleam of the fair hair in the lamplight. What Roth didn't say, but what hung between both of them, was that Roth had met the boy three months earlier when he'd come home from Harrow, angry and sulky over his mother's death closely following his father's murder.

"I thought about sending for Lord Worsley," Roth said. "But the boy's adamant he doesn't want to see him. And given that he obviously ran away—"

Malcolm touched his friend's shoulder. "Quite right."

Roth's gaze lingered on the boy. "He was quite resourceful. Used the last of his money to pay someone to carry a message to the nearest constable. I'm not sure I'd have shown such presence of mind at nine."

"Nor I. The constable sent for you?"

"A combination of the dead body and the boy's accent and his refusal to volunteer further information. Fortunately I was the one who took the message. At least I could identify him." He hesitated a moment. "I could send for Worsley now—"

"No. David may not forgive either one of us, but between Teddy refusing to talk and a murder investigation, it's as well I got here first."

The boy lifted his head as Malcolm crossed the warehouse. Edward St. John Craven. Viscount Craven since his father had been murdered in Hyde Park three months ago. That, followed by his mother's death less than a week later, had shaken Teddy's world. Though he didn't know that his mother had taken her own life or that she had hired the man who killed his father. At least, Malcolm hoped to God Teddy didn't know. Given all that had happened, his running away from school wasn't that surprising. But something must have driven him to take such an action now.

The constable, a fresh-faced lad with white-blond hair, was leaning against the wall near the table, but as Malcolm approached, he gave a quick nod and moved towards Roth. He appeared to have brewed Teddy a cup of tea over a spirit lamp. It was in front of the boy, a faint curl of steam rising over the cup.

"Good evening, Teddy." Malcolm dropped into the rickety chair across the table from his friend's nephew. "I hear you showed great presence of mind discovering the body and alerting the authorities."

Teddy's chin jerked up. He looked as though he was about to deny his own identity and then realized the impossibility of doing that with someone who had known him since babyhood. "I had to. I mean, I couldn't just leave him lying there." His gaze shot towards the blanket-covered form, then away.

"Quite right."

Teddy's hands curled round the cup, though he didn't lift it to his lips. "Do they know who he is?"

"Not as far as I know."

Teddy nodded and stared down into the depths of the teacup. It was white, with a blue transferware pattern and a chip at the rim.

"You showed a great deal of initiative, not just in sending for a constable, but earlier," Malcolm said. "I often felt the impulse to run away from Harrow, but I never actually put it into action."

Teddy's gaze jerked to his face. "I couldn't stay. Not after— And I can't go back."

A thousand petty cruelties and unthinking tyrannies shot through Malcolm's memory. "For what it's worth, I think your uncle David will understand that better than anyone. Except perhaps for me. We neither of us had a very easy time at Harrow. To own the truth, I'm not sure I want my own son to go at all."

Teddy's brows drew together, as though Malcolm's words shook the order of his world. Which, in a way, they very much did. "So you'll send Colin to Eton? Or Winchester?"

"I rather think we won't send him to school at all. He can go on doing lessons at home with his sister."

Teddy's eyes widened. "But—"

"David didn't want to disrupt your life. But if you explained matters to him, I suspect he'd be quite amenable to a similar arrangement."

Teddy shook his head, so vigorously his fair hair flopped across his forehead. "I can't. He can't know. I couldn't tell him—"

Malcolm looked into the anxious young face. "Is it something to do with your mother?"

Teddy's eyes widened. "How do you know?"

"I was a schoolboy once. I can remember what would have angered me enough I'd have been tempted to run away. And what I wouldn't have wanted to share even with a sympathetic uncle." The sting of casual comments came back to him through the years. Those comments had started questions he hadn't fully articulated for years and hadn't answered until a few months ago when he learned the actual identity of the man who had fathered him. Though that answer had raised a whole new set of questions.

"It was vile." Teddy's hands curled into fists on the splintery wood of the table. "They can say what they like about me, but my mother wasn't—she wouldn't—"

"Impugning the honor of someone's mother is a sadly commonplace insult," Malcolm said. "It doesn't mean anything except that your tormentors displayed a lack of imagination."

Teddy's brows drew together. "Do you really think so?"

"As I said, I was a schoolboy myself." Save that in Teddy's case, as in Malcolm's own, those casual aspersions on their mothers' honor had a grain of truth. In Malcolm's case, Arabella Rannoch's reputation had accounted for the rumors. But there was no reason to think anyone, outside a very small, trusted circle, should know about Louisa Craven's tragic love affair. It certainly shouldn't be common knowledge among schoolboys at Harrow. Who knew? Who had talked?

"I couldn't tell Uncle David," Teddy said. "I couldn't repeat those things about my mother. And then they said—" He drew a sharp breath.

"Teddy?" Malcolm watched the boy's conflicted face. "Did they say something about someone else? About your father? Or Uncle David?"

Teddy's face confirmed the latter. Schoolboy slights again welled up in Malcolm's memory, still fresh as the blood from a blow to the nose. This was at once more and less fraught. Because while Malcolm hoped to God Teddy never learned the truth about his mother, at some point he was going to grasp the truth about David and Simon Tanner, and it was vitally important that he do so in the right way.

"I'm sure anything that was said to you is something Uncle David has heard before and is well used to deflecting," Malcolm said.

Teddy's gaze slid to the side. "Yes, but—"

"Teddy." Malcolm spread his hands on the table. "Your uncle David is a good man. Young as you are, I think you're old enough to understand that. And I think you know Simon Tanner is a good man as well."

Teddy's gaze snapped to Malcolm's face. "They said—"

"It doesn't really matter what they said. It matters what you think of David and Simon."

Teddy's brows drew together. He was silent for a long moment, then nodded slowly.

"Why did you choose this part of town to hide in?" Malcolm asked.

Teddy cast a glance round the warehouse. The lamps Roth had lit cast giant shadows on the rough walls. "I couldn't think where to go at first. Then I thought the warehouse might be a good hiding place."

"You were coming *here* deliberately?"

Teddy nodded. "It's my father's."

Malcolm cast a glance round the warehouse. "Whateley & Company," he said, reading a placard fastened to one wall.

"My uncle. Eustace Whateley. He's married to my aunt Cecilia. My father's sister."

"And your father was his partner." Something of the sort came back to Malcolm from their research into Craven's affairs after his murder.

Teddy nodded. "He didn't talk about it much. I don't think he liked that Uncle Eustace was in trade. I don't think Aunt Cecilia likes it much either. But I came here once with him. I thought it would be safe. And I suppose—"

Malcolm caught a flash of yearning in Teddy's blue eyes. "It reminded you of your father?"

Teddy nodded.

"Nothing wrong with that. It's good to find ways to hold on to people we've lost."

Teddy gave a tentative smile. "What happens now?"

"If I have anything to say about it, you don't have to go back to school. But I very much hope you'll let me take you home."

"To Uncle David."

"And your sister and brothers."

"And Uncle Simon."

Malcolm reached across the table and touched his fingers to Teddy's hair. "And Uncle Simon."

2

Suzanne Rannoch lifted the hood of her cloak and stepped from the carriage. The cobblestones were rain-slick beneath her satin evening slippers. She pulled the black velvet of her cloak close over the pomegranate gauze and sarcenet of her gown. The sign over the building before her swayed in a gust of wind. A gold needle and thimble, indicating a dressmaker's. The dark windows, now shuttered, would display gleaming bolts of fabric, bright lengths of ribbon, and sample gowns during the day. Suzanne had called here often enough for a fitting or to order a new gown. But tonight she didn't go through the blue-painted front door with its shiny brass knocker. Instead, she opened a door to the side of the windows that had been left unlatched for her and climbed a narrow flight of stairs, lit by a single glass-enclosed candle. The stairs gave onto another door. She rapped three times.

Almost at once the door opened. A tall woman with reddish-brown hair stood before her. Marthe Leblanc. For all they had been through, she looked little changed from when they had first met in Lisbon, over five years ago.

"Thank you for coming." The relief in Marthe's voice showed how concerned she had been.

"Of course." Suzanne met the other woman's gaze. They said a woman had few secrets from her dressmaker. That was doubly true when both had been French agents working together against Britain while living among the British.

Marthe stepped aside and gestured Suzanne into the sitting room. "I've ruined your evening. And it's your little boy's birthday."

Suzanne smiled at her friend. "You're sweet to remember. After Colin fell asleep, Malcolm went to a meeting at Brooks's, and I looked in at a rather dull reception I was regretting I'd agreed to attend." She moved into the room. It smelled of potpourri and Marthe's violet scent. A lamp was lit on a table covered with a flowered silk shawl. "What is it?"

"I had a message from Bertrand. He's bringing someone in tonight. And it sounds as though medical help is needed."

Suzanne's gaze went to the brassbound box on the shawl-covered table, similar to her medical supply box at home. Bertrand Laclos rescued those who needed to flee France, which had once meant Royalists and now, three years after the Battle of Waterloo, meant Bonapartists who had been proscribed by the restored Bourbon government.

"I don't like to involve you," Marthe said. "You have more to lose than the rest of us."

Suzanne undid the ties on her cloak. "I'm better positioned than many of our friends. My husband knows the truth of my past now. Bertrand brought one of his refugees to our house less than two months ago. We were in the midst of giving a ball. Malcolm took it quite in stride."

"I know how you worry for him."

Malcolm's face shot into her mind, laughing with their son and daughter on his lap at Rules three hours ago. Leaning in to kiss her before he went to his meeting at Brooks's.

She saw his dispatch box, which she had once ransacked for information, and which now held the travel documents prepared should they and their children have to flee Britain at a moment's notice. Malcolm had been nothing but sanguine about the preparations, but she could not but be aware of what she had brought him to. "Malcolm can take care of himself, as he'd be the first to say."

"Your husband is a remarkable man."

"I'm more aware of it every day."

Marthe had two young daughters and a sympathetic solicitor who wanted to marry her and who hadn't the least idea she had been a French agent. Suzanne, protected by her husband's fortune and his position as a Member of Parliament and the grandson of a duke, was in an enviable position, all things considered. Set against that, the fact that she was tearing herself in two over what she'd done to Malcolm shouldn't be held to matter.

An owl hooted outside. Marthe gave an answering call and a few moments later opened a concealed door in the paper-hung wall. Bertrand Laclos staggered into the room, his auburn hair dusted with gray powder, his nose and jaw disguised by expertly applied putty, half supporting, half carrying a fair-haired man wrapped in a greatcoat.

"Take him into the bedchamber," Marthe said, hurrying to open the door.

Suzanne snatched up the medical box and ran after. "He was shot on his way to meet me at Calais," Bertrand said, once he had laid the man on the clean sheets in the bedchamber. "I didn't realize how bad it was until we had set sail. I cleaned and bandaged the wound as best I could, but we were delayed in the Channel, and I fear he's turned feverish."

Suzanne put a hand on the man's head. It was burning to the touch. He seemed to have passed out, which was just as well, given the pain he'd been in. "Bring some brandy in case he wakes," she told Marthe, opening the supply box.

"He kept talking on the crossing," Bertrand said. "He seemed to be trying to tell me something, but I couldn't make head or tail of it."

"Who is he?" Suzanne peeled back Bertrand's makeshift dressing.

"His name is Louis Germont. At least that's the name he gave me. I don't ask questions. He was a clerk in the foreign ministry, suddenly facing questions about his past."

The man who called himself Louis Germont appeared to be in his late twenties. His blond hair was cut fashionably long and the softness of his hands said he did not live by manual labor. He woke in the midst of her cutting away the makeshift bandage from his infected flesh. Marthe came in with the brandy and poured some down his throat. He grimaced but stayed still with the stoicism of a trained agent. By the time Suzanne had a fresh dressing secured over the wound, he seemed to have lapsed into unconsciousness again. But when Bertrand and Marthe had left the room, Suzanne heard him mutter something unintelligible. "It's all right," she said, smoothing his hair as though he were one of her children. "You're safe."

His fingers closed round her wrist. "Have to warn."

"Have to warn who?"

"Message." His fingers tightened on her wrist. "Someone needs to know."

"We'll make sure the message gets through." With her free hand, Suzanne pressed him gently against the pillow, afraid he would pull on his wound. "When you feel better you can tell us—"

"Heard them. No doubt." He twisted from side to side against the pillow, lapsing back into his feverish delirium. But before he lost consciousness, she heard him murmur quite clearly, "The Phoenix."

Suzanne drew a harsh breath. She was still sitting on the edge of the bed in Marthe's neat spare bedchamber, with the blue-flowered quilt and the cross-stitched sampler hanging over the bed. But her world had tilted on its axis. For a moment she thought she was going to be sick.

Because she knew what The Phoenix meant. It was a code name. Not for an agent. For a plot.

A plot to rescue Napoleon Bonaparte.

3

The footman who admitted Malcolm and Teddy to the Craven house in Brook Street was the same man Malcolm had shouldered past three months ago when he ran up two flights of stairs to be greeted by the report of a gun that signaled Louisa Craven's suicide. The footman looked older now, the bones of his face sharper, his eyes more deeply set. The last three months had left their mark on all of them.

David stepped out of the library before Malcolm could address the footman. "Malcolm, did we forget something at Colin's party—" David stopped short, catching sight of his nephew.

"Teddy was obliged to leave school unexpectedly," Malcolm said. "He's had quite an adventure. I'm sure you're eager to hear of it, but perhaps you could have some food sent in directly."

David gave a quick nod and turned to the footman.

"Sandwiches and lemonade," the footman said. "Right away."

"Thank you," David said. "And have Master Teddy's bed made up for him."

David reached out and touched Teddy on the shoulder, quickly, a little awkwardly. Footsteps sounded on the stairs. "Jamie's finally down for the third time," Simon said, his gaze over the rail on David, the only one visible from his vantage point. "I thought he'd never—" He broke off as he came round the bend and saw Malcolm and Teddy.

To Malcolm's relief, a smile crossed Teddy's face. "Uncle Simon. I'm glad you're here."

"So am I," Simon said. "I don't know why you left Harrow, but I suspect you showed a great deal of good sense."

They repaired to the library. Malcolm let David pour him a whisky, which gave Teddy a couple of minutes to settle in. The footman came in with hastily cut roast-chicken-and-watercress sandwiches and a large glass of lemonade. Teddy took a swallow as grateful as a man gulping a drink, wolfed down half a sandwich, and at last looked at his two uncles and launched into his story. Once he began to speak, he talked quickly and surprisingly coherently, putting in enough detail to flesh out his story. He had the makings of a good agent. He confronted the accusations about his mother in a firm voice, but skipped over any comments on David and Simon.

David's face went shuttered as he listened, a clear sign to Malcolm of the depths of the emotion he was feeling. At the mention of the dead body in the warehouse, his eyes widened and he shot a quick glance at Malcolm, then turned back to Teddy. Simon listened in silence, a little drawn back in his chair, though Malcolm saw his friend's fingers curl round the carved arms of the chair. By the end of Teddy's story, Simon's knuckles were white.

David got to his feet and dropped down in front of Teddy's chair when the boy had done. "You handled it well, Teddy. Better than I would have done at your age."

Teddy's gaze skimmed over his uncle's face. "You're not angry?"

"I wish you'd sent to me rather than running away. I'll own to feeling a distinct chill at what you went through. But I can understand why you ran away. School can be the loneliest place on earth."

Something lightened in Teddy's eyes. "That's it precisely. It seems odd, because one never has a moment alone. But—"

David nodded. "I was lucky to meet Uncle Malcolm."

"Which meant we were lonely together," Malcolm said.

Teddy looked from Malcolm to David. "I can't go back."

Malcolm drew a breath. *Oh, David, don't be stupid.*

David touched Teddy on the shoulder. "You don't have to, for this term at least. I'll send an express to the headmaster in the morning. They'll be concerned."

Teddy's face relaxed a trifle. "I can help teach George and Amy."

"You'll do lessons yourself, scamp." David ruffled his hair.

"Yes, sir," Teddy said, but he grinned, looking more like a nine-year-old boy than he had all evening.

Bridget, the nursery maid, who struck Malcolm as a sensible young woman, rapped at the door to say that Master Teddy's bed was made up, and if he promised not to wake them he could peep in at his brothers and sister before he went to bed. Teddy grinned, took a last sip of lemonade, and got to his feet. He hesitated a moment, then gave David a quick, awkward hug. "Thank you, sir." He stepped back. "Thank you, Uncle Malcolm."

"I'm glad I was there," Malcolm said.

"Me too." Teddy turned to Simon. Simon gave a quick grin and an answering smile broke across Teddy's face.

"Well done," Malcolm said, when the door closed behind Teddy and Bridget.

Gaze fixed on the closed door, David grimaced and ran a hand over his hair. "I didn't know—I thought it was better to disrupt his routine as little as possible."

"It was a good assumption," Simon said.

"I forgot what a hell school can be." David strode across the room, picked up his whisky, and tossed down a swallow. "He can stay here until the next term. But what the devil are we going to do then?" He glanced at Simon. "Do you think he'd do better at Winchester?"

"Based on my experience?" Simon got to his feet and splashed more whisky into his glass. "No. Save that I wasn't very happy in my grandfather's house, I'd have much preferred to forgo school altogether."

"That's all very well for you, but—" David bit back his words.

Simon regarded his lover, the decanter held in one hand. "But Teddy's destined to be a viscount, not a Radical playwright?"

"Of course not. Damn it, Simon, you know—"

"We don't plan to send Colin to school," Malcolm said.

"You've already decided that?" David asked.

"To own the truth, I don't think Suzette would stand for it," Malcolm said with a grin. "I see no reason to put my son through what we went through. Besides, I'd miss him."

David took another swallow of whisky. "I just want him to be prepared for the life he's going to lead."

Simon went still for a moment. There it was, Malcolm saw. The life of a peer that Teddy was destined for, that David himself was destined for. The life that threatened to divide Simon and David. But Simon merely took David's glass and splashed some more whisky into it. "One could argue a life that gave him a bit more perspective would better prepare him for the life of a viscount. We can find him a good tutor. And George, and Jamie when he's old enough. Amy too."

David stared at Simon. "How long have you been thinking this?'

Simon shrugged and went to refill Malcolm's glass. "I think my feelings on public school are fairly clear."

"You never said."

"You had a good point that it made sense to disrupt Teddy's life as little as possible. Besides, you're their uncle."

David opened his mouth as though to argue, then took a drink of whisky and dropped down on the sofa. "Who was this dead man found in the warehouse?"

"He appears to have broken in," Malcolm said.

"To steal money?"

"Unclear. Just as it's unclear if he was killed by a fellow conspirator with whom he had a falling out or someone else who broke in."

David and Simon stared at him. "You think two different people broke into Whateley & Company tonight?" David asked.

"It looks possible. What do you know about Whateley & Company?"

"Very little," David said.

"Eustace and Cecilia Whateley came to our ball in April, but I can't say I got much sense of either of them," Malcolm said.

"I've only met them a handful of times. Cecilia seems kind, if a bit colorless. I remember Whateley more from Harrow than recently."

"So do I," Malcolm said. Eustace Whateley had been a couple of years ahead of him and David. "He always seemed to have a bit of a chip on his shoulder. But I don't think I had the least appreciation of how hard it was to be at Harrow as a banker's son whose grandfather had been a tin miner."

"Refuses to hide the fact that he's in trade," Simon said. "I rather admire that. Not easy when one's married into the beau monde."

David swirled the whisky in his glass. "To own the truth, I rather forgot Craven had invested in the business. But then Craven was enough of a snob not to make a big point of it." He looked at Malcolm. "You're going to assist Roth in the investigation?"

"He's asked me to. When it comes to the beau monde, it's often easier for Suzanne and me to make inquiries than for Roth to do so. And someone will have to talk to your father."

Simon gave a wry smile. "Better you than me." He got to his feet. "I have to be at the Tavistock early. With *Measure for Measure* about to open even Manon isn't balking at morning rehearsals. I should be getting back to the Albany."

David and Simon had shared rooms since their Oxford days, but after Louisa's death, David had moved into the Craven house while Simon still, at least nominally, lived in the rooms they had once shared in the Albany. Simon, usually careless of appearances, was careful to preserve them for the children's sake. The arrangement, Malcolm thought, couldn't be comfortable for any of them.

Simon bent and gave David a quick, hard kiss. There was a time when they'd have avoided such displays, even in front of Malcolm. It was almost as though the changed circumstances made it more important to establish the reality of their relationship.

"This can't be easy on either of you," Malcolm said when Simon had left.

David grimaced. "Simon's a marvel. He's the only one—including Bridget—who can get Jamie to sleep. We all nearly went mad one night when he had a late rehearsal." He took a drink of whisky and stared into his glass. "It's odd, I don't think they saw Craven or even Louisa that much, but they sure as hell notice their absence."

"There's a difference between absence and knowing one will never see one's parent again," Malcolm said, remembering his own mother's absences.

David tapped his fingers on the sofa arm. "Bel would have taken the children, but it would have strained her to the breaking point with her own three, especially since Rose had the measles last March. Mary's got enough to deal with, with her own husband's death and the baby about to arrive. Georgiana's out of the country. Mother and Father—They found their own children challenging enough. And Eustace and Cecilia barely knew them."

"You don't have to convince me," Malcolm said. "I agree it was the best choice." He leaned back in his chair. "I always thought you and Simon would make good parents."

David shook his head. "I never thought—Simon didn't ask for any of this."

"I don't see him complaining."

"He's being a saint. I hope—I keep thinking we'll get back to something like normal."

"I think every parent thinks that. Until they realize the new reality is normal." Malcolm hesitated. "I don't know that anyone would say anything if Simon stayed here. Rupert and Bertrand live together."

"Rupert is married to Bertrand's cousin. An uncomfortable situation for all of them, but it has advantages."

"True. But if Simon stayed here—"

"There'd be talk." David drained his glass. "The children—"

"The children love you both. They'll sort it out eventually."

David shot a look at him. "Not everyone does."

"I'm sorry," Malcolm said. "I don't mean to belittle the challenges."

David got to his feet and refilled his glass. "A few of our friends accept us. Others—notably my parents—choose to be blind to what's in front of them. Some others really are blind, I suppose, or simply don't have the imagination to see it." He poured more whisky into Malcolm's glass. "But still others are only too ready to gossip. And many to condemn."

Malcolm looked at his friend, his chief confidant since they'd both been schoolboys Teddy's age. He had shared things with David he hadn't even shared with Suzanne. And yet—"You don't talk this way often."

David shrugged as he clunked down the decanter. "Nothing to be gained by dwelling. But it's still a hanging offense."

"My God." Malcolm set his glass down hard on the chair arm. "We live in an appalling country."

His wife would have said *You only just discovered that?* But David shook his head. "You don't mean that. There are challenges, but they don't outweigh all the things to honor and admire."

"A country that condemns two of the finest people I know for loving each other has a lot to answer for." And he was a member of that country's government. As was David, though they both sat in the Opposition.

David sank down on the sofa. He moved as though his bones ached. "It's not as though every other country would welcome us with open arms. One grows used to living with secrets."

Malcolm took a swallow of whisky that burned his throat. He knew a great deal about living with secrets since he'd learned his wife had been a Bonapartist agent. But for once he couldn't confide in David.

Bertrand looked up as Suzanne came back into Marthe's parlor. He had removed the putty from his face, though traces of powder still clung to his hair. He was alone in the room, sitting on a stool, hands linked round his knees, gaze mild. "Did he talk to you?"

Suzanne drew a breath. She'd always wondered how much Bertrand knew. They'd never discussed it, but given what he'd seen in Paris three years ago, not to mention in her own house last April, he probably knew or guessed a great deal. "Only incoherent ravings. I'm not sure what to make of it."

Bertrand regarded her for a long moment. "People talk to me," he said. "I see no reason to share what I overhear. But I thought perhaps you were the right person to talk to our friend here."

Suzanne met Bertrand's clear gaze. It looked very blue just now, while at other times it seemed just as green. "You're a remarkable man, Bertrand."

"Most people are remarkable when one gets to know them." He unfolded himself from the stool and got to his feet. "I'm sorry I missed Colin's birthday party."

She swallowed, warmed by the memory of the crowd gathered in her drawing room that afternoon, torn by the possible future. "We missed you. But I knew it must be something important."

He moved to her side and squeezed her hand. "At least Rupert and Gaby and Stephen could represent the family." A smile crossed his face. "Odd that, having a family. Still takes my breath away."

Suzanne returned the pressure of his hand. "Mine too."

Half an hour later, in the privacy of her lacquered sapphire barouche, Suzanne pressed her hands to her face. The watered silk walls and mahogany fittings of the barouche enclosed her in luxury. The luxury that typified her husband's life. She had a few moments of privacy before they got back to Berkeley Square. The most privacy she was going to get to think through the night's shocking revelations.

Bonaparte. St. Helena. Freedom. *Dear God, no* had been her first thought on hearing the wounded man's hoarse words. Surely it couldn't all begin again now. The plotting, the scheming, the fighting. The killing. The conflict that had come close to tearing her in two those last weeks before the battle of Waterloo.

And yet—closely following on the dread had been a stab of wonder. She saw the redcoated British troops milling about in the Bois de Boulogne, thronging the quais and boulevards of Paris. The inscription *Liberté, Egalité, Fraternité* scraped from the Porte Saint Martin. The cells of the Conciergerie crowded with her friends. Those who hadn't fled into exile or gone to their deaths. Neither her father nor her spymaster, Raoul O'Roarke, had ever forgiven Bonaparte for making himself emperor. Even before that he'd been a flawed leader for what remained of the dream of the Revolution. But if one had ever doubted he was infinitely preferable to a return of the monarchy, the years since Waterloo had proved the point.

If there was a chance to get him off St. Helena, to change the government of France—how could she live with herself if she tried to stop it? And if she told her husband what she had learned, she would be doing just that. Because Malcolm would be honor-bound to go to his spymaster, Lord Carfax.

And Carfax would do anything in his considerable power to stop such a plot.

And yet, if she didn't tell Malcolm, if Malcolm learned the truth—*when* Malcolm learned the truth, because if there were a plot, at some point he would hear of it. Suzanne shivered. Her husband had come to understand her divided loyalties in the past. He accepted them when it came to protecting her comrades. He'd even assisted her. But an active, present-day plot—a plot that was almost certain to involve people she knew and cared about.

Including Raoul.

Her fingers closed on the velvet folds of her cloak. She saw Raoul O'Roarke as she had last seen him, six weeks ago, sprawled on their drawing room carpet, arranging Malcolm's prize chess pieces into an imaginary court with five children clustered round him. His face had been alight with laughter, relaxed as she had seldom seen it in all the years he'd been her spymaster, the shorter time he'd been her lover, the years since in which they'd been comrades.

But she knew, none better, how he could lose himself in the moment and then change back into a hardened agent when the task required it. It was the only way for a spy to hold on to sanity, he had often told her.

Close on that memory came another. Malcolm and Raoul laughing together over a Shakespeare folio. That same evening? Or the night before? A trivial night, talk and laughter, dinner and lottery tickets and charades with the children. Except that she'd caught something between Malcolm and Raoul. For a moment they'd been more than agents who had been on opposite sides. More than husband and wife's former lover. They'd been father and son. Which, in fact, they were, though Malcolm hadn't learned it until recently.

Suzanne chewed on the finger of her silk knit glove. If Raoul was involved in the plot to restore Bonaparte, if Malcolm had to expose him to Carfax—

It wasn't just herself she was protecting. It wasn't just her own allies. It was her husband. Because she knew instinctively such a choice would tear Malcolm in two.

4

It was months since Suzanne had returned home knowing she had to lie to Malcolm. The acrid bite in her throat was at once familiar and alien. Valentin, their footman, greeted her with a smile that was so normal it almost brought tears to her eyes. "Good evening, madam."

"Is Mr. Rannoch home yet?" Suzanne asked, as Valentin lifted her evening cloak from her shoulders.

"I don't believe so, madam."

It was just as well. She needed to speak to Laura first. Suzanne climbed the stairs, reminding herself this was nothing she hadn't done before. She'd always known that sooner or later she'd have to dissemble with Malcolm over something. She just hadn't realized how high the stakes would be. She moved past the salon and drawing room on the first floor and climbed the next flight of stairs to the second floor and the bedrooms.

A light showed beneath the door of Laura's bedchamber between the night and day nurseries. Suzanne rapped at the door. She had promised Laura a report on the evening, in any event. Laura Tarrington had been their children's governess for over a year. Now, after the unexpected events of the murder investigation three months ago, she was a friend who lived with them along with her own daughter.

Laura set down her book as Suzanne came into the room. "How was the party?"

"I saw Cordy and Harry, scarce more than an hour after we left them at Rules, and relived the highlights of Colin's party. I talked to Bel about her ball. I made myself agreeable to Lady Grandison whose husband might support Malcolm's emancipation bill in the next session. Otherwise—overcrowded rooms. Passable champagne but it hadn't been chilled enough. The same lobster patties everyone else has been serving this season. A string quartet playing Mozart at a tempo that would have grated on Malcolm's nerves."

Laura smiled. "And you wonder why I don't go out more? Having missed the first four years of my daughter's life, why on earth would I prefer such an entertainment to spending the evening with her?"

Suzanne set down her reticule. "It's a fair question."

"Oh, you're a very different case. You have your husband's career to consider. One does all sorts of things in the name of politics."

"So one does."

"Suzanne?" Laura's gaze flickered over her face. "What else happened tonight?"

Suzanne dropped down on the edge of a chair separated from Laura's by a small table, still sifting through what she could say. "When did you last hear from him?"

Laura met her gaze, her own unblinking. "What makes you think I've heard from him at all?"

"For heaven's sake, Laura. I'm not blind."

Some of the tension drained from Laura's face. She gave a reluctant smile. "Whatever may be between us when he's in

London, it doesn't mean I know Raoul's whereabouts when he's gone. You haven't heard from him?"

"The occasional letter I've shared with you. He thinks he can spare Malcolm's and my feelings by staying out of our way. Which is rather sweet, though quite impossible considering how intertwined all our lives are."

"But I'm sure you have a way to reach him in case of emergency."

"You mean in case I'm accused of treason? I do. But I think you have a route as well."

"Why?"

"He'd want us to have more than one way to contact him. And, among other things, he'd want to make sure you could reach him quickly if you were with child."

Laura's fingers tensed. "Surely you realize Raoul and I, of all people, would be careful."

"I do. I'm also well aware accidents can happen, and no one knows that better than Raoul. And I think he'd have wanted to write to you."

Laura gave a reluctant smile. For a moment something flashed in her eyes that made her seem almost like a schoolgirl. "I had a letter last week. He didn't say where he was. I have a way to get word to him, though I don't know that it's faster than yours." She scanned Suzanne's face. "How serious is this?"

Suzanne's fingers closed, unbidden, on the folds of her gown. "I'm not sure."

Laura leaned across the table between them and touched Suzanne's arm. "You're sure enough to have gone pale. I'd ask you what I can do, but if it's this serious I doubt you can tell me about it."

Suzanne looked into the eyes of her friend, the woman she trusted with her children, the woman with whom she shared secrets that could destroy both of them and nearly every-one they both loved. The instinct to confide was so strong she could feel the words forming on her lips. But the spy's instincts held her in check. Spies weren't supposed to have friends. But no matter how many rules of the game she broke, she wasn't so entirely lost as to abandon it entirely. "You know how well I trust you, Laura. But—"

"It's all right, Mélanie." Laura, like Malcolm and Raoul, now often used the name Suzanne had been born with rather than the one she'd adopted as part of her masquerade when she married Malcolm. "Don't forget I was a spy myself. You wouldn't be yourself if you confided too easily." Laura picked up a doll dress that was dangling off the arm of her chair. "And Malcolm would say the same."

Suzanne's fingers locked together. "Malcolm—"

"Loves you for being true to yourself." Laura twitched a bit of blue ribbon smooth on the doll dress.

"I'm not sure he'll feel that way when he learns the truth. If he ever learns the truth." Perhaps it would have been best to leave it at that. Perhaps she had already said too much. But she found herself adding, "I'm protecting him as much as anyone."

"I don't doubt it." Laura set the doll dress on the table between them. "Though you hate it when he tries to protect you."

Suzanne bit back the retort that sprang to her lips. "This isn't—It wouldn't be fair to ask him to choose." She swallowed, an ache in her throat that could warn of a coming fever. "Though I don't know that he'll see it that way."

Suzanne went down the passage to her own bedcham-ber. A lamp was lit on the pier table. The glow caught the white of the covers in the cradle over Jessica, her seventeen-month-old daughter. The deep, even sound of Jessica's breathing confirmed that she slept. Berowne, their cat, was curled up on the bed, his silver gray fur gleaming in the lamplight. Suzanne touched her fingers to Jessica's hair and stroked Berowne. The room was empty otherwise, but the black evening coat Malcolm had been wearing when he went out was flung over the back of the frayed green velvet chair. A sliver of light showed through the gap where the door to the night nursery was ajar.

Suzanne crossed the room and pushed the door further open. Her husband was between the beds where their five-year-old son Colin and Laura's four-year-old daughter Emily slept. Malcolm was on the edge of Colin's bed, smoothing their son's hair. Colin had the new stuffed horse they'd given him for his birthday in the curve of one arm and his beloved stuffed bear in the other. Suzanne stayed still. Tenderness washed over her, as it did at unexpected times. Perhaps it was the angle of Malcolm's head or the way his hair fell over his forehead, but Malcolm looked unexpectedly vulnerable. Her throat tightened the way it did when she looked at the children and willed time to stop, trying to commit the moment to memory. It was these unexpected moments that had so very nearly been her undoing a hundred times or more in the years of her deception. The preciousness of life sneaked up on one, not so much in times of danger, when one would expect it, but in seemingly trivial moments. The sort of moments that went to make up a life and a marriage and a family.

Malcolm turned, as though aware of her regard. A smile crossed his face as he met her gaze. He touched his fingers to Colin's hair one last time, then to Emily's, got to his feet with his usual catlike grace, and crossed the room to her. He took her hand, lifted it to his lips, and drew her into the bedchamber. "I can't believe he's five," he murmured.

"Nor can I. It seems only yesterday he was squirming in my arms." She glanced at the cradle. "Of course if he were still that little, we wouldn't have Jessica."

Malcolm closed the door with his free hand and instead of releasing her pulled her into his arms and kissed her with unexpected urgency.

It was a relief to lose herself in his kiss and then to slide her arms round him and bury her face in the starch and lavender smell of his cravat. He rested his chin on her hair for a long moment, then at last drew back enough to look down at her. "How was the Grandisons' reception?"

"As dull as I feared. Fortunately I had distraction. I received a message from Marthe. Bertrand needed my help settling someone." Nothing odd in that. It wasn't the first time it had happened. Better, Raoul had taught her, to stick as close to the truth as possible. She kept her voice level and her heartbeat even. If she hadn't learned to control it long since Malcolm, would have suspected her years earlier.

Malcolm twined one of her side curls round his finger. "Someone you knew?"

"No, but he'd been wounded on the way to meet Bertrand in Calais. I helped with bandaging."

Malcolm nodded. He now knew the location of a number of former Bonapartist agents who were settled in London. In fact, he had helped her settle several of them. He accepted helping them and keeping their secrets without question. A sign of how far he had come since their marriage. Of how far they had come. Mostly she thought it was a good thing. But every so often she felt a faint twinge. Was she encouraging him to compromise so much that one day he would look back and hate where he had ended up? Hate the wife who had helped him get there?

"My evening was interrupted by a summons as well," Malcolm said. He drew her over to the green velvet chair and sank into it, holding her against him as he proceeded to recount the message he'd received from Jeremy Roth and finding Teddy Craven at the Whateley & Company warehouse.

"That's why you were sitting with the children," Suzanne said, lifting her head from her husband's shoulder to look into his familiar gray eyes.

Malcolm nodded. "One tries so damnably hard to protect them. Sometimes I look round and the world seems full of traps. Growing up is challenging enough for children who are protected and nurtured. For those with added challenges—"

"We both faced a lot of challenges, and we managed to muddle through more or less," Suzanne said.

He slid his fingers into her hair. "You're a marvel, my darling. What you went through—"

"But I had more love and security in my early years than you did. More perhaps than Teddy Craven did. I don't think Louisa and Craven were the warmest of parents."

"No." His fingers stilled in her hair. "Simon and David can do a great deal for the Craven children." A smile curved his mouth. "I never thought to see Simon an expert on putting a two-year-old down. Apparently he's the only one who can get young Jamie to sleep."

"I'm not surprised," Suzanne said. "I remember how easily he held Colin when we first met him."

"Yes, but it's a bit more challenging when one can't hand the child back."

"Is he still going back to the Albany every night?"

Malcolm nodded. "I saw him leave. David was franker than I've ever heard him about the challenges of a relationship that has to remain secret. About his parents' veiled disapproval. And the people who think worse." His brows drew together. "I don't think I properly appreciate how it is for them."

"We've talked about the pressure on David to marry." Suzanne was confident David could withstand that pressure, but Malcolm, she knew, had doubts at times. He was less of a romantic, he said, though Suzanne vehemently denied she was a romantic. Perhaps it was that Malcolm was more clear eyed about just how strong the pressures of being born an aristocrat could be.

"Yes, I worry about what that could do to David. But they're so comfortable with each other and we—not just the two of us, but Bel and Oliver, Harry and Cordy, Rupert and Bertrand, Crispin and Manon—are so used to seeing them as a couple that I think I forget sometimes that to the rest of the world they can't be." She felt his fingers tighten. "David reminded me that it's a hanging offense. According to laws imposed by the Parliament I'm a part of."

"Not laws you had anything to do with passing."

"Still."

"You could introduce a bill to repeal them. It won't get anywhere, at least not now. But then neither will your capital punishment bill. And it would lay groundwork. Jeremy Bentham argued for repeal of the anti-buggery laws thirty years ago. And others have more recently. Juliette Dubretton—"

"Not to mention my wife."

"That provoked more comments than some of my articles," Suzanne said. "But a parliamentary bill would cause more talk. You'd have to consider the position you'd be putting David in though."

"You mean because there'd be talk if he supported it? There'd be talk about me as well. There already is. Has been since David and I were boys, though it took us both a while to understand it."

Suzanne pressed a kiss against Malcolm's throat. "Yes, dearest, but you aren't at risk of getting caught. At least not unless there's a great deal going on in your life that I'm not aware of."

"Given my difficulties sharing myself with you, I really can't imagine doing so with another person, sweetheart. Of either gender." He turned his head and kissed her temple. "David would brave the talk. He has the courage of a soldier. But I think what's even worse for David is that the world expects him to marry and produce an heir. Which would be solved if we simply got rid of inherited privilege, as my wife advocates."

"You advocate it too. In writing. Very cogently."

"And yet I've benefited. Though the man from whom I inherited all this"—he glanced round their room, where so many intimate moments in their life had taken place, in this exquisite house they had inherited from Alistair Rannoch—"has no biological connection to me. What a world we live in." He laced his fingers through her own. "A bill is a good idea. But it won't begin to do enough." His gaze darkened. "I knew I couldn't leave the intelligence game, not completely. And I had no illusions I'd be able to get very much done in Parliament. But I thought at least I'd be my own man."

Suzanne lifted her head to look at her husband, so stubbornly idealistic for all he'd deny it. "And you are, darling."

"To a degree. Better than in the diplomatic service, where I had to argue for policies that half the time I didn't believe in. But I'm still arguing within the terms of a debate set by someone else. And the damnable thing is sometimes I get so caught up in the debate I don't see the parameters enclosing it."

"Sometimes—" She drew a breath. There were still things she tried not to burden him with.

"That's how you feel as a Republican living as the wife of a duke's grandson?"

"Sometimes."

He tightened his arm round her. "Sometimes I think Davenport has the right idea, living a life of scholarship."

"I think Harry would go mad if he couldn't help with our investigations."

"There is that. It's just hard not to feel tainted by the game. All the games." Malcolm stared down at his arm, curved round her own. "I've never heard David talk with such anger as tonight. In truth, we've scarcely talked at all about— about how it is for him." He was silent for a moment, one of those shifts when he talked of something he'd hitherto held close. "I remember one night the summer before we went up to Oxford. We'd gone to the theatre—*As You Like It*. And I glanced over and saw David watching the actor who played Orlando. Just watching him. But something about the look in his gaze—I'd realized years before, sitting in a maths class, watching David have that same look in his eyes as he glanced at another boy. But this time David turned his head as though he realized I was watching him. I think he was embarrassed at first. But then he seemed to understand that I understood. And that was that."

"You never talked about it?" Suzanne asked.

"Not in so many words. When he met Simon. Well, first I pretended I was deaf and blind and tried to give them as much time together as possible. But I remember telling David a few months later when it was pretty clear which quarter the wind sat in—not that it hadn't been clear from the night they met—that I was happy for him. That he had something I never thought to have. David started to protest and then said 'Thank you.' He complains sometimes about the pressure on him to marry, but even that he tends to avoid. I never heard him rail at a world that's so savagely, insanely set against him. Even tonight he was telling me how much there is to honor in Britain. Christ."

"Given everything he sacrifices for Britain, he probably has to believe that or he'd go mad."

Malcolm looked at her for a moment. "Insightful as always, Suzette. Perhaps that's it."

"Simon talks a bit more."

"To you in particular."

"The outsiders banding together. But even Simon doesn't complain. Nothing like as much as he has cause to."

Malcolm frowned at a patch of shadow on the carpet. "I wish I could have found the right words to say to David tonight."

"It's not as though you can fix it, Malcolm."

"No, but—" He shook his head. "I couldn't of course tell him that I have a whole new appreciation for the challenges he and Simon face keeping their relationship secret now I know my wife's story."

Not for the first time, Suzanne wished Malcolm could talk to David about her and the challenges of their marriage. It would be desperately good for him to have a confidant. But she knew he feared David's reaction to the truth more than that of any of their other friends. David, Malcolm said, was an Englishman to the core, with very precise ideas about what that meant. She drew a breath. "David—"

"Believes there's much to honor in England. The country with laws on its books that would hang him and Simon. The country—"

"I betrayed."

"You aren't an Englishwoman. But I wouldn't be surprised if David thought I'd betrayed it now if he knew the extent of my actions."

Her qualms of earlier in the evening came flooding back. "Malcolm—"

"I'm not saying I regret anything, Mel. Quite the reverse in fact. You've opened my eyes to things I should have seen earlier. David and I have always seen the world in different ways."

"The last thing I ever wanted was to come between the two of you."

His arm tightened round her. "You haven't, beloved."

"What did you learn about the dead man in the warehouse?" she asked.

"He appeared to have broken in to steal something. There was a hidden compartment in the wall that had been pried open near where he was lying."

"Empty?"

Malcolm nodded. "It looks as though he had a confederate who turned on him and took what they had come to steal, or a second person broke in in search of the same thing."

"Something of Craven's?"

"There's no way to tell at this point."

"Jeremy wants you to assist him with the investigation?"

Malcolm nodded with the abashed look of one who didn't quite want to admit he was pleased. "Someone will have to talk to Carfax, given that Craven was his son-in-law, not to mention one of his agents. It's only sensible for me to do that.

And I can probably help with Eustace and Cecilia Whateley." He twisted his head round to meet her gaze. "That is, we can, if you're willing."

Suzanne felt a genuine smile break across her face. "Unlike you, dearest, I'm not going to even pretend I'm not pleased to have another investigation."

Paradoxically, some of their most intimate moments had come in the course of investigations. And, a small voice said inside her head, hopefully this investigation would distract Malcolm while she looked into the rumors about the Phoenix plot.

Malcolm smiled. "I own there's something appealing about a puzzle. Though I could wish it didn't involve Carfax, however tangentially."

"Carfax is in the middle of too many things for that."

Malcolm gave a wry smile and pulled her in for another kiss. "I told Roth I'd call on Eustace Whateley tomorrow. He was at Harrow a couple of years before David and me so I can use the old school tie."

Suzanne drew back to look at her husband. "Was everyone even remotely on the fringes of the beau monde at school with you, darling?"

Malcolm gave an abashed grin. "Most boys whose parents want them to grow up to be gentlemen go to Harrow or Eton or Winchester. So if they're remotely close to my age there's a one in three chance. Whateley's father was a banker who wanted his son to move up in the world, know the right people, speak with the right accent. Looking back, I'm afraid he suffered more ribbing from the other boys than I appreciated at the time."

No wonder thinking among their set could be so uniform. "I don't want Colin to go away to school, Malcolm."

He kissed her forehead. "I know. I shocked David today by telling him as much. One of the ways he and I see the world somewhat differently."

"I imagine Simon was all for it."

"Mmm. Though careful to acknowledge the decision is David's."

She put her hands against his chest. "I suppose I'm afraid—"

"That I'll change my mind?"

Memories shot through her mind. Malcolm and David laughing over a school memory with a schoolmate. The almost palpable connection one could feel in the air when one learned two men had attended the same school. The unthinking way Malcolm would refer to someone as a Harrovian. "It's a tradition."

"You keep expecting me to revert to type."

"And you keep confounding my expectations. I'm sorry, darling. But—"

"Once a revolutionary, always a revolutionary?"

"A palpable hit. So I'm the one who's reverting to type?"

"We're all perhaps partly a prisoner of our world. Though you have more flexibility than most. Look at how well you tolerate the world you married into because you were trying to change it."

She choked. "Talk about flexible thinking, dearest. But you can't deny it's part of who you are. I wouldn't want it not to be. It's part of the man I love."

"Fair enough. I won't deny it. But I won't send Colin away to school. Even if you decide you want him to go."

"I wouldn't—"

He kissed her nose. "My point precisely, beloved."

Suzanne laughed and reached up to wrap her arms round his neck. "Fair enough. Unless his thinking is as flexible as yours, Eustace Whateley isn't likely to talk more freely if I go with you." She frowned, staring at her husband's cravat. "Darling. I never told you, because I was trying to keep her out of it as much as possible. Last April when Bertrand and Raoul brought Lisette to us and Lisette lost the letter in the garden. It was Cecilia Whateley who accidentally picked it up." The letter Lisette Varon had been transporting had been from Hortense Bonaparte, Josephine's daughter, to her former lover, the Comte de Flahaut. They had all had some anxious moments when it was missing.

Malcolm's brows rose. "Interesting."

"Apparently Cecilia was in the garden to speak with a man she'd loved before her marriage. Just to talk, she told me. I don't think she even looked at the letter. At least that's what she said, and I've been telling myself it must be true. I don't know if it makes her more or less likely to confide in me now."

"Difficult to tell," Malcolm said. "Though it means you're already beyond social formalities."

"There is that. But it also may mean she's wary of me. I'll see if Cordy has any connections to Cecilia. Despite the lack of girls' schools, Cordy's connected to nearly as many people in the beau monde as you. It's almost as if the two of you spent your lives preparing to run investigations into their numbers."

Malcolm grinned. "One has to put the social tedium to use somehow."

5

Suzanne again stepped out of her barouche before Marthe's establishment, this time in the fitful morning sunlight. She had breakfasted with Malcolm, Laura, and the children, and seen Malcolm off to call on Lord Carfax, but it was still early for a lady to be calling on her dressmaker. Early but not impossibly so, should anyone notice her barouche and wonder at her presence. She put a hand to her lips, tasting the tang of Malcolm's goodbye kiss in the entrance hall. He hadn't blinked when she'd told him she was going to call at Marthe's to see how the man Bertrand had smuggled into London the previous night got on. It was what she'd have done in any case, without any worry about Phoenix plots and Napoleon Bonaparte. Even her sharp-eyed maid and companion Blanca hadn't seemed to notice anything out of the ordinary. She had to remember not to overthink things.

She smiled at Randall, their coachman, as he handed her from the carriage. This time she went through the main door of the shop for the benefit of anyone watching. Marthe's assistant was behind the counter, but it was Charlotte, Marthe's elder daughter, now ten, who came forwards to greet Suzanne.

"Madame Rannoch. Maman said I was to bring you back for your fitting as soon as you arrived."

"Thank you, Charlotte." Suzanne smiled at the girl. Charlotte's gaze held both seriousness at the gravity of the situation and a sparkle of excitement. Were all spies' children destined to be drawn to the intelligence game?

Charlotte led Suzanne into the back room where her seven-year-old sister Sophie was winding lengths of ribbon. But instead of taking Suzanne to a fitting room, Charlotte opened a door that lead up to the family quarters above. Suzanne gave the girl a quick hug and climbed the stairs to Marthe's sitting room. She found Bertrand there with Marthe, which was not surprising. More startling were the looks of concern on both their faces.

"What is it?" Suzanne asked, closing the door behind her. "Has he taken a turn for the worse—?"

Bertrand and Marthe both turned towards her. "He's gone," Marthe said.

"*Gone?*" Suzanne saw Louis Germont's feverish face against the white linen of the pillowcase. "But—"

"I checked on him twice in the night," Marthe said. "He seemed to sleep, though his skin was hot to the touch. I gave him the comfrey you left, and he seemed easier. Then I slept for about three hours. When I went in this morning, his bedchamber was empty, and the few things he brought with him were gone."

"He appears to have gone out the window," Bertrand said. "I found some fragments of thread that look to have come from his trousers. And, as Marthe said, he packed his things. So he didn't simply stumble out in fevered delirium."

"How much do you know about him?" Suzanne asked Bertrand.

"Not much, as I told you last night. He approached me through an old friend who is still employed in the foreign ministry. Germont really does appear to have been a clerk in the foreign ministry." Bertrand leaned forwards, brows drawn together. "Is there any chance he could have been faking his injuries?"

"The wound was real enough. And if there's a way to counterfeit a fever, I have yet to learn of it. It would be very handy on occasion. But it's amazing what one can force oneself to do if the need seems pressing enough." She'd once broken into an English general's billet, stolen a coded dispatch, climbed a tree to elude pursuit, and decoded the document all the while vaguely aware of her fever spiking. She'd seen Raoul direct an entire skirmish after taking a bullet to his side, only to collapse from loss of blood when the fight was won.

Bertrand, who had nearly died of injuries in Spain and been wounded numerous other times, nodded.

Suzanne hesitated. Damnable she hadn't been able to learn more last night. "I couldn't make out what he was talking about last night, but from what I did hear he may have thought he had a message he needed to deliver." She couldn't say more. Not yet. Not to Bertrand, whose lover sat in Parliament with Malcolm, nor to Marthe, who was building a secure life here. "Did he know anyone else in London?"

"He didn't know anyone in Britain," Bertrand said. "Supposedly. I'm questioning a lot about him now. Suzanne—"

"I'll talk to some of my contacts." Which was true, as far as it went. It just didn't include precisely what she would talk to them about. "I'll let you know when I know more."

"Suzanne," Marthe said, "you don't need to—"

"I'll be careful," Suzanne assured her friend. "I wouldn't have survived this long if I hadn't learned to be very careful indeed."

Bertrand, who she suspected understood more than Marthe, gave a slow nod.

"Ah, Malcolm." Hubert Mallinson, Earl Carfax, looked up from the papers strewn over his desk and regarded Malcolm over the top of his spectacles. "I was wondering when you'd get here."

Malcolm pushed the door of Carfax's study to behind him and moved to one of the two straight-backed chairs that faced the desk. His spymaster. His best friend's father. A force in his life since boyhood. The man who could destroy his wife. "How much do you know?"

Carfax set down his pen and leaned back in his chair. "My grandson ran away from Harrow and took refuge at Whateley & Company. He stumbled over the dead body of a man who seemingly broke into the warehouse."

Malcolm dropped into a chair. It would be wasted breath to ask where Carfax got his information. "Young Teddy showed great presence of mind."

"Something to be grateful for. He seems to have more wit than his father. According to the word I have from David, he's doing as well as can be expected this morning. David makes for a far better father than Craven."

"He's good with the children. So is Simon Tanner."

Carfax frowned, the way he always did over Simon. "Yes, I have to admit David's taking them on was probably the best solution." A shadow crossed his face. He was always gaunt and always hard to read, but since his daughter Louisa's death and the revelations about her life, he seemed to have sunk in on himself. His wit cut sharper, but sadness lurked in the back of his unfathomable eyes.

Sympathy, so unexpected when it came to Carfax, welled up on Malcolm's tongue. But as always, it was hard to know how to express it. Save that he knew Carfax, like he himself, would prefer not to dwell in uncomfortable areas. "How much did you know about Whateley & Company?"

"As little as possible." Carfax adjusted his spectacles. "As I've told you, I found Craven's doings of little interest."

"He was your agent."

"He reported to me," Carfax said. "I made use of his information from time to time."

"You could say the same for me."

"Craven didn't have a tenth of your wit. Though he was easier to control. At least I thought he was."

"Between his working for you and his being married to Louisa, don't tell me you didn't investigate him."

"If I'd investigated him a fraction as well as I should have done, don't you think I'd have made sure—" Carfax drew a sharp breath. "It's folly to refine upon the past."

"But speaking as one with perhaps more experience of regret, it's also impossible not to do so," Malcolm said.

Carfax gave a wry smile. "As often as I've lamented your conscience, perhaps I should have been taking lessons." He tapped his fingers on the chair arms. "I looked into Craven's associates when he offered for Louisa. Craven's younger sister Cecilia married Eustace Whateley, the eldest son of a banker whose father began life working in a Cornish tin mine. It only took two generations for the Whateleys to marry into the beau monde."

"I thought you admired enterprise."

Carfax snorted. "Whateley got the idea for the shipping company and talked Craven into investing. Craven always had pockets to let."

"Hence his willingness to work for you."

"Quite. Until—" Carfax drew a breath but apparently he wasn't ready to refer, even obliquely, to the ten thousand pounds he had paid Craven to accept Louisa's illegitimate child, and the tragedy that had ensued.

"What was Whateley & Company's business?"

"Imports from the Continent. With the blockade, they turned to tea and iron."

"Above board?"

"More or less. There was talk Whateley had invested in a slave ship, but it seems to have been an attempt by his rivals to tarnish his reputation."

Malcolm grimaced. Britain had banned the slave trade over a decade ago, though the slaves held in British colonies in the West Indies had yet to be emancipated. He was drafting an emancipation bill for the new parliamentary session.

"Lamentable," Carfax agreed. "And messy. But even assuming some believed the smears, unless you think abolitionists broke into the warehouse for proof—"

"It's possible, but it doesn't seem likely." Malcolm sat back in his chair. "Do you think Craven could have kept papers in the warehouse?"

A shadow crossed Carfax's face, though from the flash in his eyes Malcolm knew his spymaster had wondered about this since he first heard of the break-in. Carfax leaned forwards and adjusted his pen on the desktop. "Obviously I didn't think so, or I'd have seen to it the warehouse was torn apart after Craven's death."

"You didn't?"

"You think I'd have missed something?" Carfax demanded.

"It doesn't seem likely."

Carfax tugged a piece of paper smooth. "Are you going to ask the other obvious question?"

"Were you behind last night's break-in?"

"The murdered man doesn't sound like the sort I'd hire."

"You hire all sorts. And either he was working with someone else who killed him, or someone hired by a different person broke into the warehouse and killed him."

"A messy business either way. You know I try to avoid mess."

"And we both know the most seemingly simple mission can turn messy."

Carfax took his spectacles off and folded them. The gaze he turned on Malcolm was—perhaps deceptively—unarmored. "I didn't hire either of them. I didn't have the least idea that anything of import might be hidden at Whateley & Company. To my chagrin." He set the spectacles down. "Do you believe me?"

"I'm not sure," Malcolm said.

Carfax gave a wry smile. "I'd be disappointed in you if you said otherwise. I trust you and Suzanne will again be assisting Jeremy Roth."

"You want us to? Because you think there's a connection to Craven?"

"I'd be a fool not to realize there might be. But whether there is or not, there was something in that warehouse that someone thought worth killing for."

"Suzanne. Laura." Lady Cordelia Davenport threw down her pen and hurried towards Suzanne, Laura, and the children. "What a welcome interruption. I'm trying to reply to a letter from my mother, which always seems to bring on a headache." She stopped to ruffle Colin's and Emily's hair as they ran towards her daughters Livia and Drusilla, who had a wooden castle, the twin of the one Colin had in Berkeley Square, set up on the hearthrug.

Suzanne set Jessica down so she could toddle after the older children. The three women moved to a cream-and-tan satin sofa. "What's happened?" Cordelia asked in a low voice, one eye on the children. "It's plain from both your faces that something has."

Suzanne had stopped in Berkeley Square on her return from Marthe's to collect Laura and the children. She needed to make inquiries into Louis Germont and the Phoenix plot, but she also needed to follow up on the events at Whateley & Company. She and Malcolm had updated Laura that morning and now she and Laura told Cordelia about the events of the previous night. At least those that concerned Teddy Craven and the break-in and murder at Whateley & Company. "Poor Teddy." Cordelia's gaze moved to the children again. Emily was putting a new crown on a princess doll while Livia and Colin raised the drawbridge, and Jessica and Drusilla galloped horses round the castle. "Poor little Teddy. Do you know, I was relieved both my children were girls, and it was partly because it meant I wouldn't have to send them to school."

"We aren't sending Colin," Suzanne said.

"Yes, now with your example I've realized that's an option if Harry and I ever have a son. Odd, considering how I always was known for flouting convention, that I didn't consider some of the more sensible ways to flout it." Cordelia looked at Suzanne for a moment. "I suppose you're helping Inspector Roth again? Is it quite horrid of me to be excited at the prospect of an investigation?"

"I felt much the same," Laura said.

"So did I," Suzanne said. "How well do you know Eustace and Cecilia Whateley, Cordy?"

Cordelia wrinkled her nose. "I didn't number Eustace among my conquests unfortunately. Or fortunately. There's a limit to how far I should push Harry's extreme tolerance when our investigations involve my ex-lovers. But Cecilia Whateley—Cecilia Craven that was—came out the same year I did. One sees those girls over and over. At Almack's. At one another's coming out balls. At the Queen's Drawing-rooms. Driving in the park. It's a bit like being in the same class at Harrow or Eton. Or Oxford or Cambridge."

"Sometimes I'm grateful to have grown up in India," Laura murmured.

"A debutante season can be its own sort of hell," Cordelia said. "Though I confess to feeling the appeal. One's so sheltered, but one still has so much more freedom than in the nursery."

"Cecilia Craven was a friend of yours?" Suzanne asked.

"Not precisely." Cordelia adjusted one of the profusion of tasseled sofa cushions. "I thought she was a bit stuffy—which is to say, she wasn't nearly as wild as I was. But our mothers were friends, and I saw her enough to be more than acquaintances. She was quite taken with a young lieutenant that first season. I can't remember his name, but I can still see them dancing together with eyes for no one but each other. It made an impression because—" Cordelia's fingers tightened on the gilded arm of the sofa. "It was the way I looked at George in those days. I don't know what happened, but he shipped out for the Peninsula at the end of the season and the next spring she married Eustace Whateley."

"I take it she didn't have a large dowry," Laura said. "I assume that's why she married a banker's son. Unless she was madly in love with him, and it sounds as though she was madly in love with someone else."

"For someone who didn't grow up in the beau monde, you know us well, Laura," Cordelia said. "Yes, the Cravens have an old name, but the fortune was depleted. Something I know more than a bit about myself. I remember Eustace Whateley watching Cecilia on the dance floor with her lieutenant that spring. Thinking back now—I imagine it wasn't unlike the way Harry later looked at me. I was at their wedding. No expense spared, thanks to his father. Cecilia was as pale as her gown. Eustace looked—terrified."

"Of marriage?" Laura asked.

"Of what he had to lose, I think. Or perhaps of never really having it in the first place. I hope they've managed. It's not easy when one person's more in love than the other."

"I talked to her at our ball in April," Suzanne said, and quickly described Cecilia's accidentally picking up the letter. Laura already knew much of the story. Cordelia knew about the letter but not that it had been from Hortense Bonaparte.

"Hearing what you say now, I wonder if this lieutenant was the man she was talking to that night," Suzanne concluded.

"It sounds like it," Cordelia said. "I wish I could remember his name. But I do know Cecilia enough that I can take you to call on her and give it the illusion of a social call."

Suzanne smiled. "I thought you'd never ask."

Laura picked up her gloves. "While I can take the children to the park."

"You're not a governess anymore," Cordelia said.

"Of course not. I'm a mother who missed out on too much time with my daughter and enjoys being with her and her friends, of whom I also happen to be exceedingly fond.

Does it really surprise you that I find the children better company than most of Mayfair society?"

"On the contrary," said Cordelia, once known as a social butterfly. "It shows admirable sense. Only an investigation could tear me away."

6

Whateley's Bank was in Fenchurch Street. Malcolm had almost started his search at the Whateley house in Upper Grosvenor Square or at White's. If Whateley were as eager to be seen as a gentleman as his father had been to groom him as one, he might avoid his offices as much as possible. But the clerk took Malcolm's card, vanished into an inner office, and returned a few moments later to say Mr. Whateley would see him.

He conducted Malcolm to an office with windows looking out on Fenchurch Street. Polished walnut furniture that was handsome but functional, an Axminster carpet, and bookcases filled with enough ledgers to show this was a working office.

"Rannoch." Eustace came forwards to shake his hand. He was a well-built man with dark hair and mobile features. A rower at Harrow and he'd kept himself fit. "I've been expecting you."

"You always were quick, Whateley, but—"

"Your friend Roth was by the house late last night to inform me of the break-in. He said you'd likely be by today. I know you've worked with him before. To own the truth, I was relieved. Much rather talk to you." He waved Malcolm to a chair covered in tufted burgundy leather. "Coffee? Or something stronger?" He gestured towards a table by the window. A set of decanters glittered in the fitful morning light.

"Thank you, no."

"I keep them mostly for clients." Eustace gave an unexpected grin. "Cecilia would frown to hear me use the word, especially with you. But might as well call a spade a spade. Not as if you don't know full well where I came from and what I do."

Malcolm dropped into the chair. "Coming from a family that built this"—he gestured to the building round them—"is something to be proud of."

"Spoken like a man whose family go back to the Conquest." Eustace sat, not in his desk chair, but in a burgundy leather chair that matched the one Malcolm had taken. "Roth said you took young Teddy home. He didn't volunteer further details. I don't think he felt it was his place."

"Teddy ran away from Harrow. Some unfortunate comments about his parents, apparently, particularly his mother."

Eustace grimaced. "Appalling how cruel the young can be. Though perhaps it's simply that when one's older one can pretend some of the subtler comments go over one's head."

"Was it very bad for you at Harrow?" Malcolm asked. Putting Eustace at ease was not a bad tactic, but the question was genuine not planned.

Eustace shrugged. "Was Harrow easy for anyone? Even the bullies were mostly bullied at one point, though it took me years to realize it. I suppose there were a few of the golden sort who were good at sport and decent at academics and had impeccable lineages and managed to sail through, but mostly I think it's a place one remembers more fondly in retrospect. Or is glad to have survived."

"Are you glad?"

"That I survived?"

"That you went."

Eustace crossed one leg over the other and contemplated the glossy polish on his black kid shoe. "It gave me the right accent. It taught me how to navigate a ballroom. It allows me to converse with my clients while preserving at least the illusion of equality. It got me admitted to White's. And Brooks's. Don't laugh, Rannoch. Only men who don't need clubs can sneer at them."

"I wasn't. I'm very grateful not to need them. Though as a politician I have a more than passing need for Brooks's."

"Yes, I suppose you do." Eustace curved his fingers round the tufted leather of the chair arm. "And of course, without all that, Cecilia would never have looked twice at me, no matter how paltry her dowry, no matter how padded my father's bank account."

"It's not easy to marry into the British aristocracy," Malcolm said. "My wife reminds me of that."

Eustace shrugged again, a defensive gesture that put Malcolm in mind of Harrow and a boy with a chip on his shoulder that the younger Malcolm hadn't precisely understood. "Father had his heart set on my marrying at least an earl's daughter. Liked the idea of his daughter-in-law being styled Lady even if I lacked a title myself. But in the end I think he was very pleased that I was brother-in-law to a viscount."

"And you?" Malcolm had only seen the Whateleys in company at large entertainments, and almost by definition fashionable couples didn't spend a great deal of time in one another's presence.

Eustace dragged the toe of his other shoe across the carpet, tracing a line of gold in the rich pattern. "I could hardly fail to be pleased, could I? It's not as though I didn't share my father's ambitions, though, having been to Harrow and Cambridge, I had a more realistic sense of what was possible. Men making their way in the world don't have the luxury of falling in love."

"Love isn't always so easy to control."

Eustace gave a short laugh. "You underestimate ambition, Rannoch. Ask your friend Oliver Lydgate. Though he didn't even have a fortune to offer Bel."

Oliver Lydgate had been friends with Malcolm, David, and Simon from their days at Oxford and was married to Lord Carfax's third daughter, Isobel. They were close friends of Malcolm and Suzanne's. Suzanne, Malcolm, suspected, would quickly leap to the defense of the Lydgates' marriage, but Malcolm steered round the question.

"And your own wife?" Malcolm asked.

"What about Cecilia?"

"Would it have been so difficult to fall in love with her?"

"Thinking about the Lydgates?" Eustace raised a brow. "I suppose Isobel must love Lydgate. Hard to see why she married him otherwise. But I don't think Cecilia would have welcomed a declaration of love from me. In fact, it would probably have sent her screaming in the other direction. In our case the transaction was very simple."

"Was a partnership with her brother part of it?"

Eustace grimaced. "Not at first. In fact, if you'd told me when we first met that Craven and I would ever be partners—"

"You have three times his understanding," Malcolm said.

"He had a knack for landing on his feet. Cecilia had to marry into trade, and he managed to snag Carfax's daughter. And her father's influence into the bargain. And there's no denying some of that influence rubbed off on him, especially after he got his position at the Board of Control. When he came to me suggesting a partnership, I had to listen. It would have been bad business sense not to. Much as my desire was to laugh in his face."

"The company was Craven's idea?"

Eustace raised a brow. "You assumed I was the one who lured Craven into trade? No, I assure you. He told me with his contacts at the Board of Control he thought we could do well."

"Carfax implied otherwise. He must have been mistaken. When did it begin?"

"Nine years ago. No, closer to eight. Cecilia and I had been married a year. Roger was a baby. Craven and Louisa had been to dine with us. One of the rare times they did. Craven made a decent case. He'd thought it through, I'll give him that. I'd put up the capital—even as Carfax's son-in-law he always seemed to have pockets to let—and run the business, and he'd steer contracts our way. It was a good opportunity. The bank was doing well. I needed a new venture to put capital into, and I confess I was a bit bored."

It was the rationale another man might have given for taking up painting. Or taking a mistress.

"Did Craven visit the warehouse often?"

"Almost never. We mostly met at White's."

"He must have come occasionally. Teddy knew about it."

"Yes, Craven brought the older children by round Christmas time last year. They were on their way to a pantomime. But it was hardly one of his regular haunts."

"Do you think he could have hidden anything there?"

Eustace's gaze shot to Malcolm's face. "Is that what you think the thief was after?"

"You must have wondered."

"I went to the warehouse last night with Roth. As I told him, I can't tell anything's gone. And I didn't know about this compartment the thief seems to have opened. My first thought was that one of our clerks had stowed something there. There could be a number of reasons for someone working in shipping to want a hiding place."

"You think one of your clerks was smuggling?"

"I didn't until last night. I pride myself on my skill in hiring my employees. But it was the first explanation for the compartment that leapt to mind. Why on earth would Craven—"

"How much do you know about Craven's work for his father-in-law?" Malcolm asked.

Eustace's hands closed on the arms of his chair. "Oh, lord. Malcolm, are you saying Craven was a spy?"

"More a low level agent. At least as far as Carfax tells it."

"Christ." Eustace passed a hand over his face. "Am I a coward to confess the thought of Carfax being so close to anything I was involved in sends a chill through me?"

"No, you're pragmatic. Though for what it's worth, Carfax claims to have little interest in Whateley & Company. Of course, with Carfax one can never be sure if one can take him at face value."

"Does he think Craven might have been hiding information in the warehouse?"

"He says if he did he'd have gone after it himself. Which makes sense. So I don't think he did. Unless he's the one behind the break-in. Or perhaps one of the break-ins."

"Good God." Eustace put his head in his hands. "This isn't my world, Malcolm. I run a bank. Safe, sober investments. A trade venture to keep things exciting. And now I've got Carfax breathing down my neck."

"Carfax won't be interested in Whateley & Company. Unless you've got something to hide."

Eustace shot a look at him. "Is that a question?"

"Should I be asking questions?"

"You're investigating, Malcolm. I don't see how you can help but ask questions. Whateley & Company are as dull as you and Carfax assumed before the break-in. But of course you don't have to believe me. I daresay I wouldn't in your shoes. Not without further investigation."

"Can you think of anyone else who would want to break into the Whateley & Company Warehouse?"

Eustace gave a wry smile. "I'd like to say we were so successful our competitors couldn't wait to steal our secrets. But in general trade's a boring business. Moving goods, storing them, selling them. Trying to eke out a few more pounds. I can't claim to have any secrets worth stealing except the value of sticking at it, day in, day out."

"Has anything unusual happened?"

"Unusual how?"

"Have you seen anyone hanging about the warehouse? Had any unusual visitors?" Sometimes the trick was to look for a break-in the pattern.

"No. Well, not except—"

"What?"

Eustace shook his head. "One couldn't remotely call it hanging about. He strolled right in. It was just so odd to see him here. We're related in a sense, but it's not as though we've ever spent a great deal of time together. So receiving a visit from him was unusual."

"Who?" Malcolm asked.

Eustace paused, and for a moment Malcolm would almost have sworn he was enjoying this. "Your friend Oliver Lydgate."

"Lady Cordelia. Mrs. Rannoch." Cecilia Whateley approached them with the careful formality of Mayfair drawing rooms.

"Surely you can still call me Cordy, Cecy." Cordelia leaned forwards to kiss the other woman's cheek.

Cecilia accepted the greeting with good grace, but then stepped back and smoothed her skirt. "We aren't girls anymore, Cordelia."

"All the more reason for us to enjoy what remnants of our girlhood we can."

Cecilia gave a strained smile and gestured them towards the matched lavender-striped settee and armchairs. "Inspector Roth was here last night. He told us about Teddy and that Mr. Rannoch took him home. Have you heard how he does today?"

Suzanne shook her head. "But Malcolm said by the time he left Brook Street Teddy was in better spirits."

"Those poor children." Cecilia shivered. "To lose both parents. I can scarcely comprehend it. Eustace and I could have taken them in, but I can see Louisa's family wanting to keep them."

Something about the way she said "Louisa's family" told volumes about Cecilia's relationship to her brother's in-laws. In the ornate social strata of the beau monde Cecilia had married below her station while her brother had married above his.

"I think it's good that the children are able to remain in their home," Suzanne said. "They've lost so much, they need whatever semblance of stability they can muster."

"Yes, of course. And Lord Worsley is so good with them. Though it will certainly be a challenge for his wife when he finally marries. Beginning marriage is challenging enough without starting off with four children."

Cordelia tugged her second glove from her fingertips. "I think anyone who loves David will understand that that also means taking on the children."

Suzanne suspected her friend had the same image in her mind she did. Simon with young Jamie draped over his shoulder.

"I hope so," Cecilia said.

A footman came in with a tea tray. Cecilia busied herself pouring tea into gilded cups. "Eustace went with Inspector Roth to the warehouse last night. Mr. Roth told Eustace Mr. Rannoch was assisting him with the investigation. I assume that's why you're here, Mrs. Rannoch." She handed a cup to Suzanne. "I may not be at the heart of Mayfair society, but I do know your husband has assisted Bow Street in the past. And that you assist him."

Suzanne took a sip of tea and choked on the idea of assisting Malcolm. Still, it was very useful their reputation had preceded them. As long as it didn't put Cecilia too much on her guard.

"Cecilia—" Cordelia said.

"To own the truth, I'm relieved." Cecilia handed a cup to Cordelia. "If I must talk to someone, I would much rather talk to you. Not that I have anything to say. I have little to do with my husband's affairs."

Suzanne wondered if the word choice was deliberate. But then perhaps Cecilia had used "affairs" because she didn't want to use the word "business" or anything more closely approximating that. "And your brother?" she asked.

"Edward didn't confide in me either."

Odd to hear Craven referred to by his given name. Even Louisa had called him Craven. A reminder that he had once been a boy as young as Teddy. As young as Colin or little

Jamie. "But you knew he was your husband's partner in Whateley & Company."

"Oh, yes." Cecilia twitched her ruched cambric skirt, as she might to pull it back from a puddle of muddy water.

"All sorts of gentlemen make investments," Cordelia said. "Many not as sensibly as your husband."

Cecilia squeezed a wedge of lemon into her own tea. "Eustace is clever. Cleverer than Edward was. I'm not ashamed. I knew what I was getting when I married him. I'm fortunate to be so comfortably situated."

"It sounds as though someone was at pains to remind you of that," Suzanne said.

Cecilia took a sip of tea. "By the time my grandfather and father paid off their gaming debts, what was left of the family fortune was entailed and settled on Edward. And heavily mortgaged into the bargain. Cordy remembers our season. Any number of men were willing to dance with me, but when it came to marriage, most weren't willing to risk it. Sensibly. It isn't easy to live on nothing."

"I know what it's like to have no dowry," Suzanne said. Which was true. It was also true she'd never expected to have one. "I'm very fortunate Malcolm came to my rescue." Which was also true, though at the time she wouldn't have used quite those words.

"There are very few men like Malcolm Rannoch," Cecilia said.

"Men who could marry anyone and choose a penniless émigrée?"

Cecilia shrugged, fluttering the rouleau of muslin at her throat. "Most marriages are bargains one way and another. Eustace and I each gave the other something. We went into it with our eyes open. I'm very well aware of what he's done for me. It doesn't mean I need to take an interest in his business dealings. In fact, I think he prefers it if I don't do so. My role is to lend social polish to our partnership." She leaned forwards to refill the cups. The muslin frill on her sleeve fell back at just the right angle to display her pearl bracelet. "It would be much the same if I'd married a soldier or a politician. I wouldn't expect him to want help with battle tactics or parliamentary speeches."

She set down the teapot and reached for another wedge of lemon. Her smile indicated she wouldn't dream of being so ill bred as to allude to the fact that Suzanne helped draft her husband's speeches. And of course, that very careful lack of allusion couldn't help but bring it to the fore. Without meeting Cordelia's gaze, Suzanne knew her friend was either bristling or stifling a laugh or both.

"Still, your husband must talk sometimes," Suzanne said, with the smile of one wife to another. "Men do. Isn't listening part of a wife's role? Do you know if he had any enemies?"

"Enemies?" Cecilia choked on her tea. "Eustace?"

For a moment Suzanne pitied Eustace Whateley. His wife might almost have said she couldn't imagine him doing anything interesting enough to create enemies.

7

"Malcolm." Oliver Lydgate looked up from his newspaper in a quiet corner of the Great Subscription Room at Brooks's. "David came to see us this morning. He told us what you did for young Teddy last night. Thank you."

Malcolm dropped into a chair beside his friend. "I think of him as my nephew as well."

Oliver folded his copy of the *Morning Chronicle* and put it on the table between them. "Bel went back to Brook Street with David, though she says she sometimes fears seeing her simply reminds the children that their mother is gone."

"Bel's nothing like Louisa."

"Thank God." Oliver gave a wry smile. "Is that why you're here? Normally you avoid Brooks's like the plague unless we have a meeting."

"I wouldn't quite say that. But there is something insular about it."

"Spoken like a man who never doubted he'd become a member." Oliver, the son of a penniless Devonshire country lawyer, was always frank about his origins and the life he'd married into. His brows drew together, dark against his pale skin "Has something else happened with Teddy? I've been afraid—"

"No. Not with Teddy directly." Malcolm stretched his legs out. "Roth's asked me to assist him with the investigation into the murder of the man Teddy found at Whateley & Company."

Oliver grimaced. "As if those children haven't seen enough death. I can see Roth wanting you involved, especially with the connection to Craven. Have you talked to Carfax?"

"First thing this morning."

Oliver gave one of those grins as engaging as when he'd been an undergraduate. "Better you than me. I prefer to face my father-in-law with a drink in my hand if I have to. Do you think the break-in had something to do with Craven?"

"We're not sure. But we have to at least consider it."

Oliver watched him for a moment. "How can I help you?"

Malcolm had spent most of the drive from Fenchurch Street debating how he would frame his next question, but he still wasn't quite sure. "Eustace says you called at the Whateley & Company warehouse a week ago."

Oliver's gaze showed no surprise. "Yes, I did. There were some details about Louisa's marriage settlement that I wanted to make sure he understood. It's difficult for Carfax to talk about and David has his hands full, so I offered to talk to him. Sometimes being a barrister can come in handy. Is that so surprising?"

"I think Eustace thought it a bit odd you went to the Whateley & Company warehouse instead of the bank."

"For some reason I thought I was more likely to find him at the warehouse that particular day. I can't remember why precisely. Malcolm, what on earth did Eustace say to you?"

"Just that it was a surprise to see you at the warehouse. I was asking him about anything to do with the warehouse that seemed unusual."

"And he thought—what? That I saw something that made me hire the man who broke in and was murdered? Or that I came back myself and murdered the man? I was here with you last night."

"The man was probably dead before any of us got to Brooks's."

Oliver gripped the arms of his chair. "For God's sake, Malcolm—"

"No one's suggesting you had anything to do with it, Oliver."

"But you're here, asking questions."

"It struck Eustace as unusual enough that he mentioned it. I wouldn't be doing my job if I didn't follow up."

Oliver leaned back in his chair. "Fair enough. I just—"

Malcolm watched his friend for a moment. "The investigations I undertake have a tendency to involve friends and family. You and Bel haven't been caught up in that before. I'm sorry. It's not a comfortable situation. As David discovered during the investigation into Trenchard's murder."

Oliver stared at him. "You can't seriously mean you suspected David of murder?"

Malcolm frowned at the toes of his boots, memories of three months ago shooting through his mind. "Seriously? I couldn't ever truly bring myself to believe it of him, but that may have been a failure of imagination. Logically I knew I had to consider him as a suspect. So I forced myself to do so."

Oliver nodded. "Funny, thinking back to those nights at Oxford. Drinking wine in one of our rooms. Scribbling in a coffeehouse. Rehearsing. Quoting Shakespeare or talking about how we'd change the world. Even then I knew the future was filled with uncertainties. But I'd have sworn I'd always trust the three of you with my life."

"I'd trust you or David or Simon with my life," Malcolm said without hesitation. "That's a very different thing from what questions I have to force myself to ask."

Oliver nodded slowly. "You always were ruthless at exploring a thesis."

Malcolm felt his shoulders relax against the chairback, releasing a tension he hadn't realized he'd been holding. "Did you notice anything when you were at the warehouse?"

"You mean anything that could connect to this break-in?"

"Anything at all out of the ordinary. Sometimes the most trivial detail can prove to be a vital clue."

"I'd never been there before, so I didn't really have a basis of comparison. The warehouse looked ordinary enough. Crates piled round. Sheaves of foolscap. Eustace and I went into a small office to the side. I haven't had a great many dealings with him. But we've met at the occasional gathering of the greater family. Which both of us married into. We share a certain fellow feeling as outsiders. At the same time—" Oliver's fingers curled round the arms of his chair. "I'm quite sure Eustace resents me. For marrying up in the world and not even bringing a fortune to balance the scales."

Malcolm stared at his friend. Like David's outburst about the secrecy he and Simon lived in, Oliver had just put into words something he rarely alluded to. Malcolm drew a breath. "You and Bel—"

Oliver stared at a hunting print that hung on the wall across from them. Redcoated figures sending sleek horses over a fence. Blue sky, rolling green grass. A world of exclusivity and privilege. "Bel does a thousand things for my parents, mostly without letting them see it. She brought out my sisters. Her fortune provided their marriage portions. And paid for my brother's commission. Without her fortune—and family name—I'd never have been able to stand for Parliament. We wouldn't have our house. I most likely wouldn't be a member of Brooks's." He glanced down the long room at the men playing whist or reading newspapers. "I'd probably be a country lawyer like my father. Or a solicitor with tradesmen for clients. Not a barrister with chambers in the Temple who sits in Parliament."

"Bel married you because she loves you. It's quite different from the marriage Eustace and Cecilia seem to have. Eustace was at great pains to make it clear it was a business arrangement. Perhaps somewhat too-great pains now I think about it. I'm not sure if the business arrangement is on both sides or simply on Cecilia's. At least in Eustace's view."

Oliver gave a wry smile. "One never knows entirely what goes on in another's marriage. Even when it comes to friends. You're fortunate, Malcolm. The man who claimed not to believe he was capable of love and found the perfect wife."

"I know full well how fortunate I am." There was a time, six months ago, fresh from the revelations of Suzanne's betrayal, when Malcolm would have struggled to keep the irony from his voice. Now it was no struggle. He'd known, almost from the first, that he and Suzanne had to find a way to make their marriage work, for Colin's and Jessica's sakes. But somehow they had got to the point where his good fortune at meeting Suzanne still took his breath away. Paradoxically, perhaps even more so now that he knew the truth of her masquerade. A change in mission strategy, a shift in the war, greater qualms on her part about embarking on such a long-term mission, and they would never have married. He wouldn't have her, or Colin. Jessica would never have been born.

"You deserve it," Oliver said with a quick, warm smile. "I, on the other hand, probably have more good fortune than I deserve."

Something about his tone and the look in his eyes and his earlier comment about marriage took Malcolm back to the moment in the Peninsula when he'd slit the red wax seal on David's letter and first read the news of Bel and Oliver's betrothal. He'd been happy for his friends, glad they had both found someone, glad, selfishly, that their marriage would bind them both more closely in the small circle of his closest friends. But beneath the joy had been undeniable qualms. One could put them down to his own doubts about the institution of marriage at the time. Save that he had read the same qualms between the lines of David's careful letter. Isobel had been out for a few seasons. She was pragmatic, not the acknowledged beauty her elder sisters were, and ready to get married and have her own establishment. Oliver was penniless and ambitious, for all the right reasons, eager to enter Parliament and fight for the same things Malcolm and David believed in. As an alliance it made sense in many ways. Save that Malcolm suspected Oliver's heart was still engaged elsewhere, and that Bel knew it. Which also might not have been an insuperable bar. But once or twice the look in Bel's eyes had made Malcolm suspect she was not as pragmatic when it came to Oliver as she let it appear to the world. A companionable, even a passionless marriage could succeed on its own terms. But where the balance of passion was unequal—

"I know full well Bel has given me more than I've given her," Oliver said.

"I've said the same about Suzanne," Malcolm said.

Manon Caret's dressing room smelled as it always had, from the Comédie Française to the Tavistock Theatre. Of grease paint and powder and her signature tuberose-and-violet scent. Manon's hair glowed as bright a gold as when Suzanne had first met her, a young agent in training, in Paris with Raoul, drinking in the talk of the seasoned agents. The only mark of the change in Manon's life was the slender band of gold on her left hand that Crispin Harleton had placed there five months ago.

The ring flashed in the lamplight as Manon spun round and sprang to her feet at the opening of the door. "*Chérie!* Just what I need after an exhausting afternoon on the scene with Angelo. My first Isabella. Opening night tomorrow, and I'm still not sure I can be a convincing nun."

"You're always saying you want new challenges."

Manon laughed. "Have you brought the children?"

"And Laura and Cordy. They're outside with Roxane and Clarisse." Suzanne hesitated. She should take advantage of their time alone. She told herself she wanted to ease into the topic, but the truth was she found herself wanting to prolong this moment with her friend and the illusion that life was normal. Or as normal as it ever could be for a pair of ex-Bonapartist agents living in London, married to English aristocrats.

"Marriage plainly continues to agree with you," Suzanne said. It was true. Manon's color was high, her gaze bright, and the strain about her eyes that had been there before she left France and when she first came to England quite gone.

Manon laughed as she swept a pearl-beaded robe and a feather-trimmed velvet cloak off the frayed tapestry settee. "I was so afraid it would change things and then I told myself that was silly, what would it really change except that we'd live in Crispin's house instead of him spending nearly all his time in our lodgings. And then in the end it did change, far more than I dreamt. But not at all in the way I feared." She held a spangled scarf against her for a moment, her usually shrewd gaze filled with a wonder Suzanne had only seen in her friend's eyes when Manon was on stage.

"Marriage can do that," Suzanne said. She could still hear Malcolm's voice repeating his wedding vows and feel the gut punch of realization of how seriously he took their marriage of convenience. It had been more complicated for her than for Manon, but then she hadn't been in love with Malcolm. Not then.

"Of course there are challenges. It's taken some of the servants a bit of time to get used to seeing me as their mistress. Crispin actually dismissed one of the footmen, though he claimed he'd had trouble with the man before. But mostly the challenges are from his own set. I'm quite sure he doesn't receive as many invitations as he used, though he claims he's quite pleased not to have to sort through so many gilt-edged cards and feel duty-bound to spend dull evenings."

"That sounds very like Crispin. And I suspect it's the truth."

"So do I, though sometimes I'm afraid I'm just trying to comfort myself." Manon waved Suzanne to the now cleared settee. "Last week we made the mistake of driving in Hyde Park just before the hour of the promenade. We encountered Lady Wychcombe. Not the first time I've received the cut direct, but the first time I've done so with my husband."

"Oh, Manon. I'm sorry." Not for the first time Suzanne was aware of the advantages of her fictional aristocratic past.

Manon shrugged as she turned up the spirit lamp. "I wouldn't care for myself, but the girls were with us and it's difficult for them to understand. Though I'm afraid they are acquiring an all-too-shrewd knowledge of the codes of the ton. I've never see Crispin so fierce. If Lady Wychcombe were a man, I think he'd have called her out. Of course others have been quite accepting. It helped that you hosted our wedding breakfast."

Suzanne dropped down on the settee. "I never stop feeling guilty about my supposed past."

"You shouldn't. It's very helpful for your friends." Manon reached for a blue enamel kettle. "Why are you here, *chérie?*"

"Isn't seeing my friend enough?"

Manon's blue gaze settled on Suzanne's with the sharpness of an agent. "You didn't bring the children in with you. Or Laura or Cordelia. So I suspect this isn't a social visit."

Suzanne swallowed, her mouth dry. "Not entirely."

Manon set the kettle on top of the spirit lamp and turned to the shelf above the settee. "Is it your husband?"

"No. That is, not directly." Suzanne locked her hands together. Manon had been her confidante six months ago when Malcolm learned the truth of her past, supportive, but also clear eyed about the risks to Suzanne and to her marriage. A number of things had changed since then, including that Manon was married to the man she loved, but she was still a realist about the pitfalls of relationships, particularly for former spies. "Malcolm continues to be remarkable in his understanding," Suzanne said. She already felt she was doing Malcolm enough of a disservice. She could at least be clear about this.

Manon took a tin of tea off the shelf. "That can be a strain in and of itself."

"No. That is, yes, sometimes, but that's not—" Suzanne drew a breath. She was almost afraid to put it into words. "Have you heard anything about the Phoenix?"

Manon dropped the tea tin. "Damnation. I was hoping you wouldn't hear."

Certainty settled like a lead weight in the pit of her stomach. Until now, Suzanne realized, she'd been living with the hope that she had misunderstood. "Are you—"

"God in heaven, no." Manon picked up the tea tin and carefully put two spoonfuls into a blue transferware pot.

"But you've heard—"

Manon cast a quick glance about the dressing room. A spy's instincts never left her. "Sancho Fuentes came to see me a fortnight ago."

Sancho had been a daredevil in the Peninsula. He'd settled in London, where his work was still on the shady side of legality. Their paths hadn't crossed often since he'd come to Britain but the memory of his ready laugh and good-humored face brought a lump to Suzanne's throat. "Sancho is—"

Manon picked up the steaming kettle and poured water over the tea leaves. "He told me he'd heard rumors of a Phoenix operation. I swear, I've never seen him so nervous, even under fire. He kept looking round my dressing room as though he expected someone to pop out from behind the dressing screen. He wanted to know if I'd heard of it, and if I was involved. I asked him if he thought I'd gone mad." She set the kettle down and snatched her hand back, as though the droplets had burned her.

"Did he say where he'd heard the rumors?"

"No, and I didn't ask. I didn't want to know. I don't want to know." Manon straightened up and regarded Suzanne. "I deplore what's happening in France as much as any of us. Sometimes I can't even read the French papers, they make me so angry. But it's different now. I have a life here. It was perhaps very selfish of me to have married Crispin, but having done so I at least have enough conscience to know I couldn't put him through his wife plotting with his country's enemies." She shot a look at Suzanne. "It was different for you. Malcolm was an agent. You married him to spy on him. Crispin didn't choose this game. I cut him off from family and school friends. I can't risk embroiling him in treason."

Suzanne saw Malcolm's dispatch box and the papers in the false bottom that were there should they need to escape. "I understand."

"Besides, I couldn't risk what my daughters have found." Manon bent down to open a cupboard hidden beneath a hatstand and retrieved a pitcher of milk and a bowl of sugar. "Of course I risked an incalculable amount for them when I was spying in France. But now—they have a father, a home. We may never fully belong, but they have roots here." She reached back into the cupboard for a plate of almond biscuits. "And—" She shook her head, an odd smile dancing in her eyes. "We aren't telling many people yet, but I wanted you to know in any case. Crispin and I are going to have a baby."

Suzanne sprang to her feet and hugged her friend. "Dearest, I'm so glad."

Manon colored. "I swore I would never do it again, but then I swore the same thing about marriage and look where I've ended up. It wasn't an accident, believe it or not. Crispin would never ask it of me and he loves the girls as though they were his own, but I knew he wanted us to have a child together." Her hand moved to her abdomen, in that unconscious gesture that was so common in pregnancy. "And I found—I understand why you wanted to have Jessica. I didn't need to have another child, but I wanted a child with him."

"The girls are going to be splendid big sisters."

"Yes, they're in transports. And Crispin's beside himself. I had to talk him out of his inclination to wrap me in cotton wool, but other than that he's been quite sensible. And I already know what a wonderful father he is." Manon dropped down on the settee and drew Suzanne down beside her.

"Did you tell him about Sancho's visit?" Suzanne asked.

Manon froze in the midst of lifting the teapot. "Are you mad? Crispin may not be an agent or the sort to fuss about Crown and country, but he is an Englishman. Why would I put him in that position?"

"Did you tell anyone?"

"Of course not." Manon poured steaming tea into two blue-and-white cups.

Suzanne added milk to her tea. "You didn't think of telling me?"

"I was trying to protect you, sweetheart." Manon clunked down the teapot. "I couldn't put you through that. The strain of whether or not to tell your husband. It was bad enough that I had to keep it from Crispin. With Malcolm it would have been ten times more complicated."

Suzanne took a sip of tea. Odd how comforting she now found the very English drink. "There's always the possibility that we could have told them so they could try to stop it."

Manon regarded Suzanne over the rim of her teacup. "I thought of that. But it's one thing not to assist the plan. It's another to actively stop it. Especially as we don't know who's involved."

Suzanne took another sip of tea, a little too quickly. She must have not added enough milk, because it singed her mouth. An unvoiced name hung between them. "Did Sancho say if Raoul was involved?" Suzanne asked.

"No." Manon took an almond biscuit and broke it in half. "But he wouldn't necessarily know. Another reason I thought it best that you weren't involved. Do you know where he is?"

"Not precisely. But I've sent word to him. So has—someone else."

"Laura." Manon took a bite of the biscuit.

"You don't miss much, do you?"

"When Raoul was here in April and you had us to dinner, it was quite plain there was something between them, for all they didn't even touch hands. Perhaps because of it. The way he followed her with his gaze—I haven't seen him so in earnest since—you."

Suzanne reached for her cup again and blew on the steam. "It's quite serious, I think. For both of them."

Manon's gaze moved over her face. "I'm glad for him. He deserves a bit of happiness. But not perhaps the most comfortable situation for you."

Suzanne took a sip of tea. So rare to be able to speak with unvarnished honesty. Manon wasn't Malcolm. If she was jealous at all she could admit it. "I care about both of them so much."

"Caring doesn't make jealousy go away."

"Oh, I don't deny the occasional twinge. How could I not feel it? I think one always would with a man one was intimate with, and Raoul and I—There's no denying what he was to me. But to be brutally honest"—in a way she couldn't be with Malcolm—"I'm surprised it hasn't been worse. And—" She hesitated, not sure how to articulate what she was feeling, even to herself.

"It doesn't really change what's between you and Raoul."

Suzanne's gaze flew to her friend's face. "I'm not—I don't—"

"I know. You love him but you're not in love with him. And I'm not saying you want to share his bed. But what's between you both will never go away. I imagine your husband understands that."

Suzanne's fingers tightened round her cup. Raoul was now a frequent guest in their house, something she would never have thought possible. One could even call him one of the family, hard as that was to imagine. But she and Malcolm still tended to speak of him obliquely, more in terms of factual details than emotional responses. When it came to Raoul, Malcolm's own feelings were still a tangle that Suzanne felt she had no right to attempt to unravel unless Malcolm chose to confide in her. He accepted Raoul as part of their lives. He even, she thought, cared for him in his own way. But what he understood or didn't understand about her own relationship with her former spymaster she couldn't begin to say. "I'm not sure what Malcolm understands when it comes to Raoul," she said. "Save that Malcolm is the most forbearing man imaginable."

"He loves you," Manon said, as though it explained everything. Which was funny, because Manon used to claim not to believe in love. "And he knows he's the one who shares your bed and gave you his ring and is the father of your children. Based on last April, I'd even say he likes Raoul. None of which lessens the damnable mess you'll be in if Raoul is involved in the Phoenix plot."

Suzanne saw Raoul's bleak gaze that day in Brussels three years ago when she'd told him she'd no longer be his agent. *It's over,* she'd said to him then. *We lost.*

It's never entirely over, he'd replied. *But we were certainly dealt a decisive blow. Not only has the game changed, it will be played on an entirely different board.*

"He wouldn't risk himself in a quest he thought entirely foolhardy." Suzanne hunched her shoulders, fighting off what she feared was to come. "But if he thought there was a chance of success—we both know he's capable of taking the most hair-raising risks."

"And he doesn't have a family to worry about. Or didn't until recently." Manon added more tea to both their cups. "How much would concern for Laura and Emily hold him back?"

Suzanne saw Raoul last April, lifting Emily up to pluck a leaf from one of the plane trees in the Berkeley Square garden while Laura stood beside them. In that instant they'd looked like a family. And then there was Malcolm, who she knew was Raoul's family in every sense of the word, and herself and Colin and Jessica, who she thought he considered his family as well, though she could say none of that to Manon. "They mean a lot to him," she said. "But it hasn't stopped him from running equally appalling risks in Spain now."

"Have you told your husband?" Manon asked, though her gaze said she already knew the answer.

Suzanne gulped down a swallow of tea. "How could I? Not without knowing—"

Manon nodded. "I think Raoul would be the first to say you shouldn't protect him. But I can see how difficult it would be. That's why I didn't want you to know. Once he knew, Malcolm would be honor-bound to tell Lord Carfax."

Suzanne nodded and took another swallow of tea. What she couldn't tell Manon was that she couldn't be sure what Malcolm would do, not just because of what Raoul meant to her but because of what he meant to Malcolm himself. All she could be sure of was that either choice would tear her husband in two.

"Damnable," Manon said, "the coils we find ourselves in, even years after the fighting supposedly stopped, years after we actively left off spying." She took a quick sip of tea. "I can help you. Help you get information at least. I can go that far."

"You don't have to," Suzanne said.

"I know. But you aren't going to be able to let this go, are you?"

"How can I?" Suzanne asked. "I need to know. If Raoul isn't involved, I need to tell Malcolm."

Manon reached for her teacup. "And if he is?"

Suzanne drew a breath that made her corset laces bite into her flesh. "I don't know."

8

Jeremy Roth dropped into one of the Queen Anne chairs in the Berkeley Square library with the ease of a friend and accepted a cup of tea from Suzanne. He moved as though his bones ached. "I've been scouring the docks and Seven Dials with two of my constables. Difficult to get anyone to talk, but we've finally identified the dead man. At least, an associate of his just came to view the body and says it's Ben Coventry. He served in the Peninsula in the 95th. Took a musket ball to his right leg at Waterloo. Since then he's lived by his wits, mostly as a petty thief and sometime smuggler from what I could tell. No one seemed surprised to find him caught up in something criminal, though they were surprised he got himself killed. Apparently he was both brave and resourceful."

"Do you think it's a genuine identification?" Malcolm asked. "Or a feint to cover up the identity of the real victim?"

"Difficult to tell," Roth said. "But several people said the description sounded like him, and the man who identified him got teary-eyed. Which doesn't preclude him being a good actor." Roth set down his cup and stretched his legs out in front of him. "It appears his closest relationship is with a woman named Sue Kettering, who works at an establishment called the Gilded Lily in St. Martin's Close." He glanced at Suzanne, then gave a rueful smile as though acknowledging the folly of being overly delicate. "No one, of course, wanted to admit it to me straight out, but reading between the lines it appears to be a brothel. Yet Coventry seems to have had an ongoing relationship with Miss Kettering."

"Not uncommon," Malcolm said in an easy voice. He didn't want to risk a look at his wife, but he wondered what her reaction was. He could not but be aware of the revelations of six months ago and the fact that she had once been employed in a brothel herself.

"No." Roth reached for his teacup and turned it in his hand. Eggshell porcelain rimmed in silver. Delicate and refined. Like the face Suzanne showed to the world. Malcolm wondered suddenly what it meant to his wife to make a life for them in Mayfair. He had no doubt now that the family they had built was genuine, but had the trappings of the beau monde driven her mad with their hypocrisy, a silver-rimmed shell round whatever was real between them? Or, after a past that had at times been appallingly raw, had she been building a haven for herself as much as anything? "Murder's still an unusual occurrence in London, thank God. But now we know the man's identity, the chief magistrate's attitude to the investigation is rather less urgent than when the Duke of Trenchard was murdered."

Roth's ironic tone held a knife-sharp edge. Malcolm could still remember Roth's hard gaze sweeping over him in the guttering light of a Spanish farmhouse. That had been their first meeting. Roth had been assigned to assist Malcolm on a mission. Malcolm had been disguised as a wine merchant, but had dropped the persona to strategize with Roth.

His clothes might have been worn and mud-spattered, but his accent had been Oxbridge with a hint of Scotland. Roth had quickly grasped the details of the mission and responded with strategic suggestions that were shrewd and to the point. But his mocking gaze said he had sized Malcolm up as an aristocrat and suspected Malcolm was playing at being an agent. It wasn't until the end of the mission, by which time they had each saved the other's life, that Malcolm felt he had won Roth's trust.

"They aren't suggesting you drop the investigation, are they?" Suzanne asked.

"Oh, no." Roth took a sip of tea. "Murder is still murder. And the property of gentlemen of substance is involved. That should be enough to ensure some interest from the London authorities." He returned his cup to its saucer, as though being careful not to clunk it down. "I could go talk to Sue Kettering in my official capacity, of course. But given how difficult it was to even uncover her name, I doubt she'd say much to a Bow Street runner. I wonder if we wouldn't do better—"

"With someone undercover?" Suzanne asked.

Roth met her gaze and smiled. "You're under no obligation, of course. But you can't blame me for thinking of what's best for the investigation."

Suzanne's smile deepened. Even Malcolm couldn't read any hesitation in his wife's expression. "An evening out away from Mayfair and a chance at a genuine mission in disguise? I could kiss you, Jeremy."

Roth laughed, something he would never have done at such a comment six, even three, months ago.

Malcolm reached for his teacup and managed a smile.

Malcolm looked across the barouche at his wife. The interior lamps reflected off the watered silk seat coverings, casting a soft glow, but Suzanne had applied her lip and cheek rouge and eye blacking with an unusually heavy hand that created a harsh effect. The thick layer of powder on her normally luminous skin implied that she was covering up imperfections in the complexion beneath.

She turned her head and met his gaze with a mocking, knowing smile, as though already sinking into her persona. She had worn that same auburn wig for a visit to a dockside tavern in Paris, a night that ended in a murder and set them off on one of their most challenging investigations.

"Are you sure about this?" he asked.

"Darling, you enjoy a mission in disguise as much as I do. You just aren't as quick to admit it. How often do we have a chance to do this since we've come to Britain?"

"I didn't say I didn't enjoy it."

"It's probably a good deal less dangerous than when we broke into Carfax's study three months ago."

"I wasn't thinking of the danger." He hesitated. He was still learning to navigate the waters of her past. "You could be pardoned for not wanting to visit a brothel."

"It's hardly the first time. Remember Le Paon d'Or?"

Malcolm had a vivid image of his wife firing her pistol at the man who had him at sword's point. "That was before—"

"You knew I'd been a whore myself?"

"Stop it, Mel. You shouldn't say such things about yourself."

Her brows lifted with amusement, but her gaze was hard. "Would you rather I said prostitute?"

"It's not the word, it's the tone." He reached for her hand. He wanted to fold her in his arms, but he knew she'd regard that as too simple.

She let him take her hand, though her shrug was a defensive gesture. "It's part of my past, Malcolm. Not a part I particularly enjoy remembering but not one I want to deny either. You may not have known it at the time, but Le Paon d'Or did stir some memories. But nothing I can't handle."

He saw the gleaming paneling and velvet upholstery in the brothel in Brussels. "Le Paon d'Or was—"

"More elegant? It's true. The Gilded Lily sounds more like the brothel I was in in Léon. All the more reason it's a good thing I'm here. I do think I'm rather more equipped to navigate it than Jeremy. Or even you, darling."

He tightened his fingers over her own. "That's without question."

The smile she gave him was as brilliant as diamonds. Or a polished knife blade. And somehow at once ruthlessly honest and resolutely armored. "We both know one can never move on if one can't confront the past."

Scenes from his own history clustered in his memory. Coming back to Britain had meant confronting his past, part of the reason he'd resisted it for so long. But he wasn't at all sure he'd managed to adequately do so. "Easier said than done, sweetheart."

"No one said this was easy, dearest." Suzanne turned her gaze to the dark shadows beyond the gleaming glass of the carriage window. "Here we are."

Suzanne accepted Malcolm's hand and climbed down from the carriage into the shadows. Randall had let them off on the edge of Seven Dials, close enough to Covent Garden that if anyone glimpsed the barouche they would just think he was finding an out-of-the-way place to wait while his employers were at the theatre. Dangerous to take the carriage into Seven Dials itself, and counterproductive to their masquerade if they were seen descending from it.

She stumbled as her foot hit the cobblestones and had to clutch Malcolm's arm. The cobblestones were uneven and slick with damp and oils and God knew what. Plenty to account for her unsteadiness. She gave Malcolm a quick smile designed to indicate her slip had been mere foolishness. It couldn't have anything to do with tonight's mission. Danger was more likely to quicken her blood than turn her stomach. And if their destination could not but stir memories, it was, as she had said to Malcolm, hardly her first visit to a brothel since she'd left the one where she had once made her home. It wasn't even her first visit with Malcolm.

Though it was the first since he'd known the truth of her past.

Randall snapped the carriage steps back into place. "You're sure you'll be all right?"

"It's a short walk," Malcolm said. "And we can look after ourselves."

Randall grinned. "Can't argue with that, sir."

"Go back to Berkeley Square," Malcolm said. "We'll find our own way home. It should be quieter in the streets by then."

They had taken the carriage less because they needed transport for the short distance than because walking through Mayfair dressed at they were would have stirred unwelcome comment.

Suzanne took Malcolm's proffered arm, and they moved into the winding labyrinth of Seven Dials. Shadows closed in round them like the curtains of a stage set. Butting up on Covent Garden and the theatres like Drury Lane and the Tavistock, where the streets would now be thronged with fashionable carriages like theirs, Seven Dials was its own world. The streets round Covent Garden were narrow and winding in their own right. (Suzanne, an expert at navigating uncertain terrain, still vividly remembered getting hopelessly lost on her first visit to Britain on her way to meet Raoul in a coffeehouse.) But in Seven Dials the buildings were even closer set, blocking out the sun in daylight hours, seemingly almost designed to allow thieves to shake pursuit.

The streets were coming to life for the evening. Torchlight flickered over smoke-stained stone walls. Dice rattled. Shouts and the smells of ale and sausages filled the air. Once they narrowly avoided the contents of a chamber pot dumped from an upper story window, another time a stream of urine. Two men shouted offers to Suzanne, despite the fact that she was holding Malcolm's arm. The occasional well-dressed young man appeared amid the crowd thronging the streets. Suzanne wondered how well their disguises would hold up if they encountered anyone they knew, and what story they would come up with otherwise.

A sign with a faded, gold-tipped lily clutched in the hand of a fair-haired woman with a filmy white gown slipping from her shoulders marked the Gilded Lily. A couple staggered out the door, the man clutching a bottle of gin in one hand, his other arm thrown round the woman's shoulders and his hand halfway down her laced bodice. The smell of gin and fetid breath slapped them in the face.

They stepped into hot air, loud voices, the slosh of liquid. Not entirely unlike the crush at a Mayfair entertainment, save that the voices were a bit louder and the smell of unwashed bodies a bit stronger; the flickering light was the greasy glow of tallow candles, not the soft brilliance of wax tapers; and the drink of choice was ale rather than champagne. Malcolm released her arm and wrapped his own arm round her shoulders. Partly, perhaps, because it presented a less decorous picture more in keeping with their masquerade, but also, she thought, because he was having one of his Hotspur-ish protective moments. And, for once, she was grateful. In fact, she knew a traitorous impulse to turn in his arm and bury her face in his shoulder. Her past washed over her. Coarse words, groping fingers, soul-destroying powerlessness. For a moment, the urge to run was almost overmastering. And so she did the only thing she could when fear threatened to overwhelm her. She tossed her shoulders, sending her spangled shawl slithering down her arms, and marched into the fray.

Rough plank tables were scattered about the room. A staircase led up to the next floor. A couple were on their way upstairs and another were coming down, the man buttoning the flap on his breeches. The girl had dark hair and thick face paint, but she didn't look much over fifteen. Maybe less. A flash of light from the swaying iron chandelier caught the bleak look in her eyes. Suzanne willed her footsteps to be steady on the ale-soaked floorboards.

The Gilded Lily appeared to be a tavern with rooms upstairs in which the girls could service clients, rather than an organized house like the one Suzanne had worked at in Léon. Malcolm steered her towards a table. She received two more offers before she had seated herself and settled her spangled skirts. Malcolm ordered ale from the pockmarked waiter who approached them, and asked after Sue Kettering. His voice had a Scots lilt to it, which came naturally to him and worked well when he was playing against aristocratic type.

"Leaky Sue?" The waiter raised his brows. "What do you want with her?" His gaze slid to Suzanne. "Looks as though you're already well-provided for."

"She's a friend of a friend."

"Is that what they're calling it these days?" The waiter gave a short laugh, but when Malcolm slid a coin across the table to him he said he'd see what he could do.

Suzanne let her shawl slither down over the chairback and leaned closer to Malcolm. She tugged the spotted handkerchief he wore in place of a cravat loose and planted a kiss on his throat. It wouldn't do for it to look as though they were at the Gilded Lily on any business but pleasure. He turned his head and kissed her forehead. A bit too tenderly. But then tenderness, thank God, could be found in any setting.

A baby's cry rose over the buzz of talk and clink of tankards. Suzanne looked round to see a fair-haired girl in a grimy pink dress, with tired eyes set in a teenaged face, tip a glass of gin down the throat of the baby in her arms.

Two tankards of ale slammed down on the table. Suzanne turned back to see not their waiter but a woman with hair of a brilliant auburn not unlike her own wig. The woman wore a low-cut scarlet gown and smelled of gin and violet scent. "I'm Sue Kettering. What do you want?" She glanced between them. "I don't do threesomes."

Malcolm, to Suzanne's relief, didn't blanch. But then, his abilities as an agent always trumped his delicacy of mind. "I'm a friend of Ben Coventry's."

Raw grief shot through Sue Kettering's blue eyes. Almost immediately, wariness closed over it like a shutter pulled taut against prying outsiders. Or snipers. "I've never seen you before."

"My name is Randall. Charlie Randall."

"Ben never talked about you."

"We served in the 95th together. I was there when he took a musket ball at Waterloo."

She dropped down in a chair opposite them. "He didn't talk about the war much."

"One doesn't. Even with those one is closest to." Malcolm took a sip of ale. "I stayed on in Paris after I was demobilized. Good pickings for a man who knows where to look. That's where I met Suzette." He glanced at Suzanne.

Suzanne flashed back the smile of a woman besotted but not quite to the point of forgetting to look after herself. "And he persuaded me to come to this damp, gray island," she said, her French accent pronounced. "I'm still not sure when I became so soft in the head."

Sue Kettering gave a short laugh. She had strongly marked brows and high cheekbones that lent a sort of elfin prettiness to her face. "Men. They'll do that to you if you aren't careful. Many's the time I told Ben I never wanted to see him again—" She slammed a fist over her face.

"I was trying to find him when I heard of his death," Malcolm said. "I'm so sorry. He was a good friend."

Sue wiped her hand across her eyes, smearing her eye blacking. "He was a bastard. But he had a way with him. And he didn't cut and run, I'll give him that." She hunched her shoulders and pulled her tattered lace shawl closer about her. "He'd disappear for weeks at a time. Months sometimes. But he always came back. So's I suppose you could say he was loyal to me. And Jem—" She bit her lip.

"You have a child?" Suzanne asked. "*Mon Dieu*, it's so difficult, isn't it? I swore I'd never again be tied to a man and then before I knew what I was about I've gone and tied myself to him all the same through *nos enfants*. We have a boy who's two"—their story had to have the children born after 1815—"and a baby girl."

Sue hesitated a moment. "We—I have a boy. Jemmy. He's just past two. He doesn't know about Ben yet. Can't work out how to tell him."

Suzanne slid her hand across the table and touched Sue's own, too thin and with the paper dryness of harsh soaps laced with lye. "Sometimes honesty works best, *chérie*. Even with little ones. I had to tell *mon fils*—my brother took a knife to the ribs in a tavern brawl."

"Pierre was reckless," Malcolm said, with a shake of his head that told volumes about the supposed Pierre's character. "Ben wasn't." He turned back to Sue. "I heard he took a knife to the back. He wasn't the sort of man to let someone sneak up on him. What happened?"

Sue cast a quick glance about the room. "I don't know."

"But you must have ideas. Someone said he'd gone soft—"

"Soft!" Sue's voice squeaked. "Ben was a lot of things, but he was canny as ever." Her gaze slid to the side. "Damn it, he told me he'd be careful. He said it was worth it."

"What?" Malcolm's voice was gentle and compelling as only he could make it.

Sue cast another glance about, then leaned forwards across the table. Her breasts threatened to spill from her low-cut bodice, but there was nothing seductive about her attitude. "I don't know. Not entirely."

"But?" Malcolm asked in the same inexorable voice. "He was my friend. He saved my life in the Peninsula when a French patrol surprised us outside Salamanca. I want to find out what happened to him. I'd like to see him avenged."

Sue's gaze shot to his face and lingered there. She bit her lip. "It was just fetching something, he said. A bit of paper someone was willing to pay more for than any ink and paper should be worth. But if it was worth that to them, his not to question. He said no one should be there. Not even guards. Safer than stealing silver and more blunt to be had. I don't understand who killed him."

"Nor do I," Malcolm said. "Who hired him?"

"He said I was better off not knowing."

Suzanne snorted. "That sounds like a man. They say they're protecting you and rush headlong into trouble."

Sue met her gaze. "In a nutshell."

"But you're clever." Suzanne smiled at her with fellow feeling. "You must have heard or seen something."

Something flashed in Sue's eyes. Suzanne recognized the triumph of not letting oneself be coddled.

"One night. About a week since. I'd gone back to his lodgings with Jemmy for the night, and I got up because Jemmy was fretful. I heard the voices first. The man had a gentleman's voice. That caught my attention—not the sort of man Ben usually entertained."

A portly man with breath that smelled of gin and garlic staggered into their table and stuck a hand down Sue's bodice. Sue pushed him away without looking at him. "I couldn't make out most of the words, but I caught something about 'mission' and 'warehouse' and something like 'wait lee.' Then they came towards the door, so I had to nip out. But I ran to the window and saw the man leaving. The torchlight caught him for a moment. Plain dark coat. But from the way he moved—I'd swear he was a soldier."

Suzanne felt the stillness that ran through Malcolm, though his face betrayed nothing. "What makes you think that?"

Sue tugged at her shawl and gave a faint smile. "I've dealt with a fair number of soldiers, one way and another. During the war they were the ones most likely to have blunt. There's a certain way of carrying their shoulders, a certain swagger. You get used to spotting which are the best prospects. I'd swear this one was an officer. Or had been."

"Do you think he was someone Ben had known in the Peninsula?" Malcolm asked.

"Not sure. Like I said, Ben didn't talk much about the war. But they seemed on good terms. More familiar than you'd expect a gentleman to be with a man like Ben if they didn't know each other."

"When you heard them talking," Malcolm said. "Did you hear anything that could give a clue to who he is?"

Sue frowned and slid the fingers of one hand into her hair, heedless of her curls. "I've been going over that, even before. Before we got the news about Ben. I think I heard Ben call him something that sounded like 'En' or 'Ens.' Sorry it's not more."

"That could be very helpful." Malcolm's smile warmed with encouragement. "Did you happen to get a look at his face?"

Two men at the next table were arguing over a girl. Sue leaned forwards across the table. Her frown deepened. "His hair had a reddish glint, I think, beneath the hat. Side-whiskers. A bit taller than Ben, but shorter than you, I think. Oh, and he walked with a limp."

"You have a good memory," Malcolm said.

Sue gave a lopsided smile. "Like I said, you get used to sizing a man up in my line of work. And remembering details so you know who to approach again, who to avoid." Her gaze flickered over Malcolm's face. "Do you think you can find this man?"

"I still have a lot of friends who were in the army. Even some officers."

"And then what?"

"I'll try to get answers." Malcolm reached into his pocket and pulled out a red velvet purse, heavy with coins. He put it on the table.

Sue's eyes widened. "I didn't ask for money."

"No, but it's the least I can do for Ben's woman and child. Call it repaying a debt I owe him." One would swear from Malcolm's voice and posture that he was remembering a real friend to whom he owed his life. Being an actor and an agent were so intertwined.

Sue reached for the purse "You have children of your own." Her gaze moved to Suzanne.

"We're flush right now," Malcolm said with an easy smile. He reached across the table and touched Sue's hand. "We'll call again when we have news. If you remember anything else or need to reach me for any reason, you can send a message here." He pulled a card from his pocket, not one of his calling cards but a plain white paper with a coffeehouse address scribbled on it. "Can you read?"

"A bit." Sue peered at the card and sounded out the words. "Enough for this."

"Good." He squeezed her hand. "I won't fail you."

9

"You could make anyone trust you, Malcolm," Suzanne told her husband. "Even in the guise of a ruffian."

Malcolm gave her a sideways grin as they picked their way down the winding street outside the Gilded Lily. "There's honor among thieves. Trust is often the best way to get people to talk. That applies even when one is in disguise."

"But not everyone can come across as quite so compellingly honest as you, dearest. Some things come from within."

He tightened his grip on her arm and steered her past two men arguing loudly in front of a smoke-blackened building with broken windows. "I hate to think of her stuck there. With a child."

"You can't save everyone, Malcolm."

"No, but you can make a start. Or you risk losing your own humanity."

"She's a survivor. But she won't find it easy to break free of that life. Not without help." Suzanne drew a breath. The pressure of unspoken words hurt her lungs, though she couldn't have said whether she wanted more to speak or to be silent.

"The brothel in Léon was a bit like that. Only we all worked for the house, instead of renting rooms."

"Sweetheart." She could feel his gaze upon her, though she didn't dare meet his eyes. "You don't have to tell me anything. You don't ever have to speak of it again as far as I'm concerned. But if you ever want to talk, I'll always listen."

She jerked her head up at that and met the compelling honesty of his gaze. He was open to anything and somehow that cut her to the quick. "I don't know that I want to talk about it. But it's a part of who I am. We can't either of us deny it."

"I know who you are," he said quietly.

She turned away and fixed her gaze on the grimy cobblestones, the chipped gilt on a fading shop sign, the cracked glass of a broken street lamp. Anywhere but on the tenderness in his gaze, which threatened to bring tears to her eyes. For some reason, since Malcolm had learned the truth, she'd quite lost her ability to hold tears at bay. "The worst was being powerless. Even as a child I hated feeling powerless. Apparently the easiest way to cajole me out of a tantrum was to make me feel I had a say in what was happening."

"Jessica takes after you."

"Yes." She managed a smile, then forced her thoughts back into the most uncomfortable corners of her past. "Logically, there are things I've done as an agent that I should be more ashamed of. But I chose to do them. I may have mixed feelings about the choices, I may even regret some of them. But they were *my* choices."

"It wasn't through any choice of your own that you were powerless. And it's a testament to your spirit that you survived. With your fighting instinct intact."

"Some of the other women were kind. Tried to take me under their wing. I suppose you could even say some of the men were kind. Or at least there were a few who looked at me as a person. But mostly numbness was the best I could hope for."

Memories clustered behind her eyes. She forced herself not to shy away because really what was the point? She was stronger than that. Cobweb-hung expanses of ceiling. Stale mattresses. Probing fingers. "Women like Sue deal with the same and more every day for years. I only had to endure less than a year."

She could feel the tension running through Malcolm. She tightened her fingers round his arm. "Save your energies for people you can help in the present, darling."

He again released her elbow and wrapped his arm round her, this time not at all in the service of their masquerade, she thought. She allowed herself the luxury of leaning in to him. He pressed a kiss to the top of her head.

They turned a corner into a more brightly lit street. The cracked pavement before them was blocked by three men sprawled in front of a gin shop. A boy who looked not much older than Colin, clad in tattered breeches and what appeared to be his father's waistcoat, slipped from the gin shop carefully holding a sauceboat full of gin, and picked his way round the sleeping men. Malcolm drew Suzanne into the street, just as the door of the gin shop jerked open and someone threw a young man with a well-cut coat and high shirt points into the street. "Damn it, I didn't know she was your girl," the young man yelled. He stumbled backwards over one of the sleeping men, who sat up with a curse. The boy jumped out of the way, managing not to tip the sauceboat of gin.

The young man scrambled to his feet. Suzanne kept her gaze fixed straight ahead as they hurried past. She had no desire to find herself looking into the eyes of someone she knew.

"Was that story you told about the ambush real?" she asked Malcolm when they had slipped back into the shadows.

"Yes, actually. Safer to use real stories when one can. Save that it was Jeremy Roth who saved me, not Ben Coventry."

"From a French ambush."

"Surely this isn't the first time you've considered that your people tried to kill me, sweetheart."

"No, but—"

"Different when you know the specifics? People died on both sides."

It was what she had told him. It was what she had to hold on to. "One more reason to be grateful to Jeremy Roth."

"For what it's worth," Malcolm said, "I grow cold at the thought of how often my own people must have come close to killing you."

"But I wasn't—"

"You were a spy. I was a spy."

She drew a breath, gaze on the blue-black web of the cobblestones. Malcolm's matter-of-factness never failed to shake her to the core. "What do you think about the soldier Sue says she saw Ben Coventry with?" she asked.

"It's plausible. I don't see any reason for her to have made it up. I'm not quite as confident as she is that she could recognize a former soldier, but as a former soldier himself, one can see Coventry being hired by a fellow military man. But as to what an officer or former officer wanted with the contents of Whateley & Company—"

"I don't recognize the man she described." And in the Peninsula, Vienna, and Brussels, Suzanne had met more than her share of British officers. "Do you?"

"Not off the top of my head. I'll talk to Harry."

Harry Davenport, Cordelia's husband, had been in military intelligence until he sold out after Waterloo. "If I know Harry, much as he enjoys translations, he'll be delighted to dip his toe back into intrigue."

Malcolm grinned. "We couldn't blame him without seeming hypocrites, could we?"

"Not in the least. It's just nice to see you admit it, dearest."

"I never claimed not to enjoy it, sweetheart. Perhaps to question my sanity for enjoying it, but that's another matter."

"Oh, well. If we had any claims to sanity, I abandoned them long ago. And I think a sane husband would be deadly dull."

They had left Seven Dials behind and were walking down Piccadilly, quieting down now that the post-theatre rush was over. The street lamps glowed with familiar warmth in the misty air. Suzanne lifted her face to the damp air. A burden she hadn't known she'd been carrying had lightened in her chest. She felt an absurd desire to laugh, despite the Phoenix plot and its attendant questions, despite her concerns about Simon and David. She was walking with the man she loved, their night's mission had succeeded, and the air was a little clearer between them. Sometimes one simply had to draw a breath and savor the moment.

"What?" Malcolm asked.

"Nothing. Merely that tonight went well. At least we've taken a step forwards."

"All one can ask for."

She pressed her cheek against his shoulder as they turned into Berkeley Street. Almost home. Jessica would want to nurse. But first she wanted to look in on Colin. Every mission, however seemingly routine, she had to start and end with seeing her children. And Emily. Having another child in the nursery meant—

Something hard closed round her arm. The next thing she knew she was spun round and whirled to the side. The hard pressure at her temple was unmistakably a pistol.

10

"Don't move, either of you," said a low voice. "Don't turn round, Mr. Rannoch, and your pretty wife won't be harmed. This is just a warning. To show what will happen if you don't drop your investigation."

"Which?" Malcolm's voice would have sounded unconcerned to any ears but her own. "We have several."

"Don't be clever, Mr. Rannoch. Leave the Whateley & Company break-in alone."

"We weren't the ones tasked with investigating it," Suzanne said.

"Tell your friend Roth it's nothing more than the petty robbery it appears. Should be child's play for people of your talents."

Suzanne let out a groan and collapsed backwards in her captor's arms in a seeming faint. The man staggered under the force of her dead weight. The gun slipped away from her temple. She spun round in his now slack hold and kicked him in the groin.

The low-voiced man yelped and fell to the cobblestones. Malcolm pounced on his chest. The man dealt Malcolm a blow to the side of the head with the butt of his pistol. Malcolm grabbed for the man's throat. Suzanne started forwards when someone else grabbed her from behind.

She let out an involuntary cry. Malcolm glanced round. Only a split second, but it was enough. The first man pulled away from him and ran down the street. The second man flung Suzanne to the ground and ran after.

Malcolm pulled her to her feet. "Are you all right?"

"Only a bruised ego. Damnation—"

"There were two of them. With a gun." He pulled her tight against him. "I never get tired of seeing you in action. But I thought we agreed we were going to remember we were parents before we did anything foolhardy."

"That wasn't foolhardy. I calculated the odds carefully. I didn't break away until the pistol was away from my head."

"It was carefully calculated in the way a desperate charge is. And bloody brilliant." He kissed her hair.

"Malcolm." She drew back and looked up at her husband. "Someone threatened us at gunpoint over the break-in at Whateley & Company."

"And presumably not Carfax, who's the most likely person connected to Whateley and Craven to be involved in intrigue."

"So what the devil have we stumbled into?"

"Precisely."

"Darling." She looked at him in the light of a street lamp. "You wouldn't suggest we stop."

"Of course not. The threats may just be bluster. But we have to take precautions."

Laura stared across the day nursery at Suzanne and Malcolm. "Good God. I know there's always risk, but I wasn't expecting—"

"Nor were we, obviously." Malcolm dropped down on the settee beside Suzanne, opposite the chair where Laura sat. His tone was easy, but he stretched his arm along the back of the settee, touching Suzanne's shoulder. He always turned protective in the wake of danger. "Especially once we got out of Seven Dials. I'm not quite sure what we're in the midst of, but it seems more complicated than we at first supposed."

"Sometimes my life seems very tame," Laura said. "I've never had anyone hold a pistol to my head. Not literally."

"I have." Suzanne tightened her arms round Jessica, who was industriously nursing, oblivious to the danger her parents had been in. Her failure bit her in the throat. "I should never have let him get the jump on me."

Malcolm's fingers tightened round her shoulder. "You weren't expecting it. We neither of us were. I'm cursing myself for a fool, but there's no sense wasting time on regrets. We'll be prepared next time."

"You think there will be a next time?" Laura asked.

"I'm not sure." Malcolm tugged off his neckcloth and stared at the spotted fabric. "Always difficult to tell how much of these sorts of threats is bluster. But we should take precautions. Addison or Valentin or Michael can go along on any outings with the children."

Many mothers would have panicked at the suggestion that their children needed guarding, but Laura was not most mothers. She gave a matter-of-fact nod. From her first days in their household, she'd grown accustomed to the fact that occasionally extra protection for the children was required.

"I don't think we need fear anything tonight," Malcolm continued. "Even if they are in earnest, it's too early for them to realize we aren't heeding their warning. But I'm going to speak with Addison." He touched his fingers to Jessica's head and Suzanne's cheek and smiled at Laura before he left the room.

"He's remarkably calm for a man whose wife was held at gunpoint," Laura said.

"He's learned," Suzanne said, as Jessica squirmed round to nurse on the other side. "Five years ago he'd have been much more inclined to wrap me in cotton wool. He's realized I can take care of myself. Or that it's useless trying to keep me out of things. Or both."

Laura hesitated a moment, fingering a fold of her dressing gown. "I don't suppose—"

"That this has to do with why I needed to contact Raoul? No. At least, not as far as I know. It's a bit difficult to determine what precisely is going on. But the man who grabbed me quite definitely mentioned Whateley & Company."

Laura nodded. "You don't live an easy life."

Suzanne looked down at Jessica. She had lapsed into sleep, one arm still curved over her mother's breast. Something about the boneless weight of her body brought a lump to Suzanne's throat. So much trust in that utter relaxation. "Coming from you, that says a lot."

Laura shrugged. "I risked exposure. But governesses lead a fairly sheltered life. So do British women in India though I had more freedom than most. Except for when I was in Newgate, the danger was more from what I feared might happen."

"Nine-tenths of an agent's life is often numbingly dull. Even on the most dangerous assignments. It's the ability to get through those times without being tripped up by one's own boredom that makes a good agent." Suzanne stroked her daughter's hair, still feathery, though it was beginning to fill in. "Not that I was ever bored as Malcolm's wife. But there were days at a time when I forgot."

"What your mission was?" Laura's gaze and tone, as always, held no judgment.

"And what I was doing to them. Malcolm and my children."

"Your children are fortunate to have you. So is your husband." Laura glanced at three dolls, grouped together round a small doll table. Emily liked to set up tea parties. "I'd forget too. For long stretches of time. I'd sink into being Colin and Jessica's governess. I'd find myself caring about you and Mr.— Malcolm. Then I'd get a message from Trenchard. And feel a chill of dread. Though, I suppose—"

"It awakens one from the monotony?" Suzanne asked. "There's nothing quite like the rush of danger." She looked down at Jessica, her head fallen back against her mother's arm. "Being a mother doesn't change that. But it does make one more aware of the risks."

Blanca Mendoza pushed shut the door of Suzanne and Malcolm's bedchamber and leaned against the panels. "Mr. Rannoch and Addison are talking about things like 'points of vulnerability.'"

Suzanne looked up from Jessica, asleep in her arms, at the woman who was nominally her maid and companion and in point of fact her companion in deception from the moment they had stumbled out of the trees in the Cantabrian Mountains and met Malcolm Rannoch and Miles Addison, who had eventually become their husbands. "We need to take precautions. But I think the threats were more bluster."

Blanca waved a hand. "We're more than a match for hired ruffians. We've faced worse before."

"You weren't pregnant before." Suzanne looked from her daughter in her arms to her friend, whose stomach was just beginning to grow rounded beneath the folds of muslin nightdress and silk dressing gown.

"But you were." Blanca dropped down on the dressing table bench, facing Suzanne who sat on the bed. "Twice. You had people throwing rocks at you when you were about to give birth to Jessica." She folded her hands over her stomach and fixed Suzanne with a hard stare. "Is this really about the break-in at the warehouse of Lord Craven and his brother-in-law?"

"A man was killed."

"People don't usually make such a fuss over the death of a hired thief."

"That rather depends on what the thief was hired to take."

Blanca sat back on the bench, arms folded over her chest, emphasizing the curve of her belly. "You're worried."

"Of course." Suzanne willed her hands to be steady round Jessica. "This touches on David and Simon and the children. I'd be worried in any case, and they've already been through so much."

"That's all it is?"

"Isn't that enough?" She and Blanca had shared so much. But she couldn't trust Blanca with the Phoenix plot. Blanca wouldn't want to keep it from Addison. Suzanne wasn't even sure Blanca would keep it from him. In Blanca's mind they had got past the tangled mess of the past with their men. Whereas Suzanne knew all too well they would never truly be beyond it.

Blanca continued to watch Suzanne with that sharp-eyed gaze that had detected both her pregnancies, her love for her husband, and her anguish at the spy game almost before she was ready to admit any of them to herself. "I know that look in your eyes. The way you've been picking at your food. You were like this at Waterloo. You're like this whenever you're at the breaking point."

"It's only six months since my husband learned I was a French spy. It's only three months since one of our closest friends was accused of murder and the sister of another of them killed herself. David and Simon are under unbearable strain, and the business at Whateley & Company is only going to make it worse. Raoul's in Spain running God knows what risks. And Malcolm and I went to a brothel tonight, which, though it may sound petty beside all the rest couldn't help but stir up the past." Suzanne rocked Jessica in her arms. "Isn't all that enough?"

"Just because I'm having a baby doesn't mean I can't help," Blanca said. "You should be the first to understand that."

"Perish the thought. I don't know how this investigation will twist and turn, but I imagine there will be plenty for us all to do."

"Just because I'm married to Miles doesn't mean we can't talk."

"Of course not, *querida*. When has my being married to Malcolm ever interfered with our talking?"

Blanca pushed herself to her feet, but stood for a moment looking down at Suzanne and Jessica. "Secrets are dangerous, Mélanie."

That, Suzanne knew, was all too true. But they were also the currency of a spy's life.

"Everything secure." Malcolm closed the bedchamber door. Suzanne was by the cradle, adjusting the covers over the sleeping Jessica. He went still for a moment, taking in the tenderness in the way his wife's fingers smoothed the blanket and stroked Jessica's hair. "Valentin and Michael are taking the first watch, then they'll wake Addison and me. I told Addison he and Blanca need all the sleep they can get before the baby comes."

Suzanne smiled and moved to her dressing table. "At least they've watched us since Colin was born. Helped us." She dropped down on her dressing table bench and began to apply cream to her heavy face makeup. "They'll be better prepared than we were."

Malcolm grinned as he shrugged out of his coat. "In some ways, no one could have been less prepared than we were." He'd gone from expecting never to be a parent to realizing he'd be a father within six months. Even then he hadn't really understood what that meant until he watched Colin slide from Suzanne's body and Geoffrey Blackwell put the squirming newborn in his arms.

"Making it up as we go along. Rather the story of our lives." Suzanne rubbed at the blacking on her eyes. "Laura took the news about the investigation well. Not that I expected otherwise."

Malcolm tossed the coat onto the green velvet chair. "I don't want to take advantage of her, but she could be an asset in the investigation."

Suzanne smiled. In the dressing table looking glass, her face was very pale, wiped free of makeup, save for black smudges that made her eyes stand out, the blue-green of a turbulent sea. "I suspect that Laura, like Cordy and Harry, would welcome the challenge. We're none of us made for a settled life."

"Which is why we're all friends." Malcolm unbuttoned the scarlet waistcoat he only wore when in disguise. "Poor David. He's the only one of us who I think actually relishes peace and quiet." He tossed the waistcoat after the cravat. "Well, perhaps

Bel does too. Not sure about Oliver." He frowned, remembering his talk with Oliver at Brooks's that afternoon.

"Darling?" Suzanne asked. "Do you think Oliver was holding something back when you talked to him today?"

"I'm not sure." Malcolm dropped the waistcoat on top of the coat and stared at the silver buttons. "His story made perfect sense. But—" He twitched the waistcoat smooth, seeing his friend's face, hearing Oliver's easy tone. A bit too easy? "I may be jumping at shadows. God knows it's easy enough to do so in an investigation."

"And you're so ruthlessly determined to be fair-minded, I think you're sometimes harder on your friends than on anyone," Suzanne said.

"A point. There was a time I'd have sworn I knew Oliver and David and Simon better than anyone. But at that time I never dreamed we'd all be involved in a murder investigation." And in the investigation three months ago, he hadn't even been entirely sure of David's innocence.

Suzanne rubbed at the last of the blacking and got to her feet. "Do you mind? I can't do the laces on my own."

The spangled, claret-colored gown she'd worn to the Gilded Lily left little to the imagination in front but fastened down the back with dozens of impossibly tiny strings. He'd got reasonably adept at unlacing her gowns in the years since their marriage, though even now his fingers shook when he touched her. Moments like this were often the prelude to a kiss and more. Memories tugged at his senses as he undid the laces. Burying his face in the crook of her neck, her body arcing against him, sweeping her up in his arms. He felt a tremor run through her. At the same time, the smell of the cheap violet scent she'd doused herself in for the visit to the Gilded Lily, so different from the subtle blend of her usual perfume, washed over him, reminding him of what they had seen, what she had told him, and what intimacy had once meant to her. He drew a breath, schooling his body to listen to the dictates of his mind. Tonight of all nights was no time to ask anything of her.

She jerked beneath his touch, pulling one of the strings from his fingers.

"Sorry," he said. "Clumsy."

"No." Her voice was at once husky and taut as a thread pulled to the breaking point. "Malcolm, don't. Don't let what we saw tonight, what I told you tonight, taint things. Don't see that instead of seeing me."

She spun round in his arms. Her face wiped free of makeup, her dark hair spilling loose over her shoulders, she looked younger than usual, but her eyes, still shadowed by the faintest smudges of black, were the eyes of a woman who had seen things he would never be able to fathom.

He lifted a hand and brushed the backs of his fingers against her cheek. "I'll always see you, sweetheart. But I can't bear to think—" That what happened when he took her in his arms and carried her to their bed had anything to do with what happened on the stale mattresses at the Gilded Lily. That the solace he took from her had anything to do with what men had once paid her for, what men still bought from women like Sue Kettering.

"Don't let it." She reached up with both hands and pulled his head down to her own. "We have to reclaim what we have for ourselves. Or the monsters win."

Surrendering to her kiss was never a challenge. He slid his fingers into her hair, and when he moved his mouth from her own it was only to brush his lips against her temple, the hollow of her cheek, the corner of her mouth. He scooped her into his arms. She crooked her arm round his neck, and he carried her to their bed to make new memories.

11

"Good God." Harry Davenport flung his pen down to clatter beside the scribbled-over sheets of paper and haphazardly piled classical texts on his desktop. "You have all the fun when we aren't along."

"Suzanne predicted you'd say that." Malcolm dropped into a worn velvet armchair beside the desk in his friend's study.

Harry leaned back in his chair, hands folded behind his head. "How serious is it?"

"Difficult to say. Usually threats like this are bluster. But as I haven't the least idea who we're dealing with or what someone thinks is so important at Whateley & Company, it's difficult to predict. If I had to hazard a guess, I'd say it's a cheap trick to get us to back off. By someone who thinks we'll be willing to let it go because, after all, the murdered man was only a thief from Seven Dials." He could hear the roughness in his voice as he spoke. "Never mind that his child and the child's mother will miss him as much as those of any aristocrat. Perhaps more so."

"They should have read some of your speeches before they tried such tactics on you," Harry said.

"I think we can handle any risk," Malcolm said. "But I'll understand if you and Cordy don't want Livia and Drusilla to play with the children until this is resolved."

"Damned if I'm going to give way to threats. We can protect the children. Anyway, if anyone is seriously watching you, if the children stopped spending time together, it would be a clear clue something was up."

Malcolm nodded. It was what he had expected Harry to say. "Do you recognize the description of the soldier Sue says she saw with Coventry?"

Harry rubbed the shoulder of his bad arm, which hadn't healed properly after a break in the Peninsula. "It could be John Ennis. He was in the 95th but was seconded to military intelligence. He took a bullet to the leg at Waterloo. Walks with a limp. His hair gleams red in the right light."

"I don't recall ever meeting him."

"He wasn't in Lisbon much. Devil of a hell-raiser. Gambling. Fraternizing with the local women. Even fought a duel once and nearly got cashiered, but he had a cousin who hushed it up. I could imagine him knowing a man like Ben Coventry seems to have been."

"Have you seen much of him in London?"

Harry shook his head. "He isn't in London. He married—a vicar's daughter of all things—and settled in Shropshire. I suspected he'd got some poor girl with child and that he'd be off again as soon as he could contrive a posting anywhere else. But he sold out. Invested his money in a farm. Raises sheep or pigs or something. Can't quite imagine it."

"He didn't hire Ben Coventry from a farm in Shropshire."

"That's just it. Alec Drummond said a week or so ago that he ran into Ennis at Tattersalls. Up from the country with the family on a rare visit, apparently. I didn't think much of it, except that it was hard to imagine the John Ennis I knew paying family visits of any sort. But I imagine he's still here. He's likely going to Wellington's Waterloo banquet." The Duke of Wellington was holding a dinner for Waterloo veterans on the anniversary of the battle. "If he's still in town—"

"Quite."

A man with reddish glints in his dark hair stood between two trees in Green Park, supervising the energetic wrestling of two small boys who seemed to be competing not so much over who could pin whom to the ground as who could get dirtiest. A young woman in a print dress stood nearby. The man looked up at their approach with a start of surprise and then a quick, easy grin. "Davenport. Good God, it's been a long time." He came forwards, clearly favoring one leg, to shake Harry's hand with no hint of discomfort.

"Ennis." Harry returned the handclasp. "I don't believe you know Malcolm Rannoch?"

"Only by reputation." Ennis shook Malcolm's hand. "Your name was legendary on the Peninsula, Rannoch."

"You mean curses about meddling diplomats?"

"Hardly." Ennis grinned. "At least not most of the time." He turned to the boys and scooped one up in each arm. "My sons Kit and Tim. Dust your coats off and make your bows, boys. Then, contrive not to kill each other for a few minutes and mind Sally while I talk with my friends."

The boys, who looked to be about two, complied with this request and darted off to their nurse. Ennis shook his head. "I suppose I had as much energy once. It's difficult to imagine."

"I often think I'm fortunate to have girls," Harry said. "Not that they lack energy, but mostly it's a bit more focused. Though that may simply be their personalities."

Ennis turned his gaze from his sons to Harry. "I heard about you and Lady Cordelia. I'm glad."

"Thank you. Though I expect you think I'm mad."

"On the contrary. I think Waterloo changed a lot for all of us."

Harry inclined his head towards the boys. "Fatherhood seems to suit you. How's—it's Anne, isn't it?"

"You always had a good memory, Davenport. She's well. Though you're undoubtedly having as hard a time imagining me settled into connubial bliss as—"

"As you had imagining it about me?"

Ennis grinned. "Perhaps." He folded his hands behind his back. "I don't know why Waterloo should seem so different from all those years in the Peninsula. It's not as though I didn't know battle was hell. But I'd never been through a battle on that scale. I'd never seen so many of my friends die. Friends with wives and children. Girls they planned to marry. I'd never made plans for anything. I'd never thought of the future. And then suddenly we could. All that carnage, but it was over. We'd won."

It was a touchingly naive assessment of Waterloo. Malcolm choked on the thought of what Suzanne would say, but he could well understand the need to hold on to something in the wake of the battle.

"I came home on leave," Ennis continued, his gaze going to the boys, now rolling across the green under the gaze of their nurse. "I'd known Anne since we were children. Her father's had the living near my parents' estate since I was in shortcoats. But it was as though I'd never properly looked at her before. My tastes—Well, as Davenport could tell you they ran in a rather different direction. My ideal woman was someone who couldn't be pinned down because she couldn't pin me down." He shook his head.

"Given my own marriage," Harry said, "I'd be the first to admit people change. Lately, I'd even be inclined to say the change can last."

"I thought I'd miss it," Ennis said. "Oh, not other women so much—" He gave an abashed grin. "Well, perhaps a bit. But the danger, the excitement. For the first few months a part of me was waiting for the boredom to kick in. But then Anne was with child and the twins were born—" He shook his head. "It's hard now to remember my old life."

Davenport was watching his colleague with half sympathy, half calculation. "And yet you do see people from your old life."

"From time to time. When I'm in town, which isn't often. Anne wanted to visit an aunt who's been ailing and I thought we could combine it with the Waterloo dinner."

"And you saw Ben Coventry."

Ennis's gaze locked on Harry's. For a moment, Malcolm had no difficulty imagining Ennis in military intelligence.

"Surely you know he was found dead two days ago," Harry said. "You must have been a bit suspicious about why we wanted to talk to you."

"Coventry is dead?" Seemingly genuine shock filled Ennis's gaze.

"Of course," Malcolm said. "The murder of a duke is all over Mayfair before the body goes cold, but the murder of a thief in a warehouse goes almost unreported."

"Ben was murdered?" Ennis's eyes had gone even wider.

"Stabbed during a break-in at the warehouse of a shipping concern known as Whateley & Company," Harry said. "But I imagine you know more about that than we do."

"Why on earth would I know about some trading company and what Ben might be doing there?" Ennis's gaze went to his children again but this time it seemed less in order to enjoy their antics than to make sure they were safe. "I'd only seen him a handful of times since I sold out. I know he had some connections that might be called unsavory, but he was a good man. A brave man. Saved my life at Bussaco."

That last carried conviction but Malcolm could read mendacity in his denial of knowing what Coventry had been doing at Whateley & Company, and he knew Harry could read it too.

"Coventry's mistress saw you leaving his lodgings a week ago," Harry said.

"That's impossible. I—" Ennis bit back whatever he'd been about to say.

"Was sure you weren't followed."

"No. Of course not. I wasn't there."

"John." Harry stepped in front of Ennis and swung round to face his friend. "You're good at cover-ups. But not good enough to play this game with two seasoned agents. You hired Coventry. We want to find out who killed him and why. You were his friend. You should want to find that out too."

Ennis drew a harsh breath. His gaze went back to his children. "It was supposed to be simple. Coventry survived Moore's retreat from Coruña and all those years in the Peninsula and Waterloo. Who'd have thought he'd find an enemy he couldn't defeat in a shipping warehouse?"

"He appears to have been taken by surprise," Malcolm said.

"Coventry wasn't the sort of man who gets taken by surprise. He almost seemed to think it wasn't enough of a challenge when I told him about it, but he said the blunt would come in handy. There was a woman—I suppose this mistress you mentioned. He wanted to get her out of the situation she was in."

"There's a child as well," Malcolm said. "A boy. About the same age as your boys."

"Yes, he mentioned that. The whole thing seemed ridiculously straightforwards. Just go in, grab the papers—"

"What papers?" Harry asked.

Ennis shifted his weight from one foot to the other. "I don't know what they contained precisely. Just that they were concealed somewhere in the warehouse."

"And just why," Harry asked, "did you want your old friend to steal papers that contained you know not what?"

Ennis's hands curled into fists. "It was a favor."

"For?" Harry's gaze was hard, though not without sympathy.

"Damn, Davenport. You know a gentleman doesn't betray—"

"A gentleman honors his friends. That includes learning who murdered them. I'd say that ranks above protecting a confidence."

Ennis glanced away again, this time facing away from his children. "You don't understand. You're a good man, Davenport, but you never took some things seriously enough."

"Try me."

Tension shot through Ennis's frame. Suddenly, he looked as though he stood on the parade ground. "I can't—"

"Perhaps if I left—" Malcolm suggested.

"It's not that, Rannoch. It's duty."

Harry regarded his former comrade for a long moment. Even Malcolm couldn't quite read what was in his friend's gaze. "And your duty to your wife?"

"What does Anne have to do with—"

"Odd how a marriage works." Harry's voice was meditative, but his gaze remained hard. "If it's a good marriage, one tells one's spouse things one would probably tell no one else. And yet one doesn't tell everything. I'd wager there are things you haven't told your Anne. Such as what happened after Badajoz. Or the real reasons behind your duel with Guthrie Fanshawe."

Ennis stared at Harry, as though he had stripped off his skin to reveal an entirely different person beneath. "You wouldn't."

"I don't want to," Harry said. "But I would. I told you, we aren't playing a gentleman's game."

Ennis drew a shuddering breath. "Damn you, Davenport," he said again, this time not in the tone of one speaking to a friend.

"Who was it?"

Ennis cast another quick glance at his children, then turned back to Harry. "Fitzroy Somerset."

For a moment, Malcolm saw Fitzroy Somerset patiently writing out orders by candlelight the night before Waterloo, felt Fitzroy's weight in his arms when he'd carried his friend from the battlefield, saw Fitzroy holding the hand of his young daughter. Wellington's military secretary, Fitzroy had lost his arm at Waterloo but had returned to his post with surprising speed. His good humor was equaled by his unwavering sense of honor, which to him was far more than a word.

"Fitzroy asked you to break into Whateley & Company?" Malcolm said, hearing the disbelief tremble in his own voice.

Ennis turned his gaze to Malcolm. "He's a friend of yours? If you know him, you'll understand that when Fitzroy asks you for a favor you don't ask questions. You assume it's important. You don't question that it's the right thing to do. Fitzroy would never do something dishonorable."

Harry raised a brow, but said, "Just what did he say to you?"

Ennis scraped the toe of his boot over the damp ground. "He came to see me in Shropshire. He said he had an unusual job that needed doing, and he thought I might know someone who could help. A tactful way of referring to the type of people I used to associate with. Some papers that needed to be recovered. He couldn't tell me more, but he pledged me his word that no one would be hurt by taking them, and irreparable harm could be done if they were not recovered. I didn't press him for more. One doesn't."

"How did he say the thief should recognize these papers?" Malcolm asked.

"That they'd be hidden. And in the form of a letter."

"From Fitzroy himself? To Fitzroy?"

"He didn't say. In fact, he seemed relieved when I told him Coventry couldn't read much beyond his name."

"Did he indicate anyone else might be after these papers?" Harry asked.

"Why on earth—"

"Because whoever killed Ben Coventry may have been someone else who broke in in search of these papers."

Ennis stared at him.

"A hiding place was open beside Coventry's body," Malcolm said. "But it was empty. Difficult not to draw conclusions."

"My God." Ennis spun round. "I have to warn Fitzroy."

"No." Malcolm closed his hand round Ennis's arm. "I'll do that."

"People never fail to surprise you," Harry said as he and Malcolm walked away.

"Ennis?"

"A bit. More the marriage than his hiring Coventry. But I was thinking of Fitzroy."

Malcolm stared at the sodden ground in front of him. "It doesn't make sense."

"You're the one who always says one can never know what a person will do under every circumstance. It sounds as though he has his reasons. Knowing Fitzroy, I suspect they were good ones."

"That's just it. If Fitzroy wanted something stolen that was top secret, why wouldn't he simply ask me? Or you? He must know breaking into a warehouse and searching for hidden papers would be child's play for us. Why go to an old friend in the countryside and bring in a hired thief?"

"Because if the whole thing went haywire he didn't want us caught up in it," Harry said. "He was trying to protect us."

That eased some of the tension in Malcolm's chest. "I could see that. Fitzroy's just the sort to try to spare his friends."

"Of course it could also be because he doesn't want us to see whatever is in those papers," Harry said.

Malcolm nodded. "And either way, the question of what is in the papers remains."

12

"Malcolm." Fitzroy Somerset looked up with a smile as Malcolm entered his study. He'd greeted Malcolm with the same smile in makeshift headquarters in the Peninsula, in the cheerful chaos of Brussels, at the inn where Wellington and his staff had bivouacked the night before Waterloo. "It's been too long."

"We'll see each other more when you're in the House." Malcolm dropped down in a ladder-back chair opposite the desk. "Even if it's across the chamber."

Fitzroy flushed. He was still based in Paris as Wellington's secretary at the British embassy, but he was in London for the Waterloo anniversary, and he was standing for a seat in Truro in the forthcoming general election. He was standing as a Tory, opposed to Malcolm on most issues. The often-vituperative rhetoric of the House could not be more different from Fitzroy's usual measured approach to interactions.

"It's all right," Malcolm said. "Being a diplomat and an agent taught me that one can be friends with the enemy."

Fitzroy fiddled with his pen. He'd got very adept at writing with his left hand since he'd lost his right arm at Waterloo. "It's not—I'd never see you as an enemy, Malcolm."

"My dear idiot, of course not." Malcolm leaned back in his chair and crossed his legs. "It's been plain for years that we see the world differently. It doesn't change our friendship."

Fitzroy's brows drew together. "We favor different tactics, perhaps. We both want the same thing for our country."

Fitzroy was committed to supporting the system Malcolm's wife and father were equally committed to bringing down. That Malcolm himself opposed more and more the more he saw of the world. The more he talked to his wife and father. But that didn't change the fact that Fitzroy was one of the most decent men he knew.

"Harriet saw Suzanne in the park with the children," Fitzroy said. "And Lady Tarrington."

His voice held just the faintest question about Laura but didn't pry. Fitzroy wouldn't.

"Laura's a good friend," Malcolm said. "She's had a difficult time of it."

"I have friends who knew her in India as a girl. Damnable what she's been through. It's wonderful you can help her."

"She's enjoying her daughter, and our children adore her."

Fitzroy spread his fingers on the desktop. "Harriet said young Colin had taken the reins."

"Yes, he has remarkably steady hands for five. Your own three must be quite a handful."

Fitzroy grinned. "And to think I used to think there was no chaos like a group of aides-de-camp."

Malcolm grinned as well, sharing the solidarity of their time in the Peninsula and their lives now as the fathers of young children. It was tempting to prolong the moment. But experience told him it was also the perfect time to ask his question. "Really Fitzroy," he said, in the same cheerful tone, "if you had to hire someone to steal documents, didn't it occur to you to give the work to your friends?"

Fitzroy went still. Malcolm kept his gaze level. "Davenport and I've just been to see John Ennis. We know he engaged Ben Coventry. We know you asked Ennis to do so."

Fitzroy tensed as though he scented enemy sniper fire. "Ennis wouldn't—"

"Probably not under normal circumstances. He was dealing with two agents and Davenport knows him enough to have leverage."

Fitzroy's one hand slammed down on his papers, white knuckled. "You don't know what you've stumbled into, Malcolm."

"No, not in the least. That's why I'm asking you."

Fitzroy lifted his gaze to Malcolm's face. The gaze at once of a friend and of a soldier. "Let it go, Malcolm." Amazing that soft voice could carry such force.

"You know me, Fitzroy. You know I can't."

"No good will come of this. And it could do incalculable harm."

"The man you hired is dead. Harm's already been done."

"And I don't want it to get worse."

Malcolm folded his arms. "It's Wellington, isn't it? Christ, has he written more indiscreet letters? Whom to this time?"

"Damn it, Malcolm, why must you jump to—"

"Because the duke's a remarkable man, but pretty women are his weakness."

"No."

"Fitzroy—"

"Why are you so sure this is even to do with the duke?"

"Because you're not the sort to have personal secrets."

"So sure, Malcolm?" Fitzroy asked. His hand was taut on the desk. His gaze turned harder than Malcolm had ever seen it, even in the field. "You're always saying one can never tell what people may be capable of."

"Fitzroy, if you're in trouble—"

"You'd help me get out of it?" Fitzroy's finely molded mouth twisted with unwonted derision. "You of all people should know you can't promise that, Malcolm. We've been comrades. I hope we're friends. But the election proves we aren't allies in everything we do."

The question Malcolm hadn't been sure he'd be able to ask shot from his mouth. "Did you hire the men who attacked Suzanne and me last night?"

The recoil in Fitzroy's eyes betrayed shock. Or a good counterfeit of it. "Good God, Malcolm, what happened? Is Suzanne all right?"

"Suzanne's fine. We've both faced worse. But the men made extravagant threats if we didn't stop the investigation. You haven't answered my question."

Fitzroy stared at him across the desk. For a moment Malcolm could feel the weight of his wounded friend in his arms as he carried Fitzroy from the field at Waterloo. "How can you possibly think I'd have done such a thing?"

"I wouldn't have thought it," Malcolm said. "But as you just pointed out, we aren't allies in everything we do."

"Rannoch."

Malcolm turned on the steps to see John Ennis hurrying towards him. "Ennis. Come to warn Fitzroy?"

Ennis's gaze darted over Malcolm's face. "You've already seen him? And he wouldn't tell you anything?"

"Let's just say I still have questions."

Ennis gave a curt nod. "I did come to see Fitzroy. But I was also hoping I'd encounter you." A muscle tensed beside his jaw as though even now he was debating the wisdom of saying more. "I don't understand this. But Ben was a good man, and he was killed on a job I engaged him for. I owe it to him to do what I can to learn the truth. So if this will help—"

"Yes?" Malcolm said, in the steady voice he used to draw out confidences.

"When I went to see Coventry. The night his woman must have overheard us. Coventry had gone round to Whateley & Company to do some reconnaissance. He still seemed to think it was a fairly routine job. But he said there were some surprises. I should have suspected—"

"What?" Malcolm asked.

Ennis drew a breath. "Coventry said Whateley & Company were shipping more than tea and iron. He got a look in one of the crates, and he said they were shipping guns."

13

Suzanne froze in the midst of fastening her garnet pendant round her throat, gaze fixed on her husband's own in the looking glass. "Oh, darling."

Malcolm pulled his razor along his jaw. He'd moved his shaving things into the bedroom so they could talk while they prepared for the opening night of *Measure for Measure* at the Tavistock. "It's hardly the first time I've crossed swords with one of my friends in the course of an investigation."

"No, but Fitzroy is—" Suzanne hesitated. Difficult to put into words the bonds forged at Waterloo. She would never fully know what Malcolm had gone through that day, but she knew the bonds she had forged sharing it with David, Simon, Cordelia, Blanca, Addison, and Rachel Garnier nursing the wounded in Brussels. And Fitzroy's steady temper and a sense of honor in its own way as strong as Malcolm's own made them particular friends.

Malcolm stared into the looking glass he'd propped atop the chest of drawers. "Fitzroy and I disagree about a number of things. And I know how loyal he is to Wellington." He dipped the razor in a bowl of water.

"You think Wellington ordered him to orchestrate the break-in at Whateley & Company?"

"Possibly. Or Fitzroy's trying to protect the duke on his own." Malcolm angled his face to the light and drew the razor along his jaw on the opposite side. "The more interesting question is what was concealed at Whateley & Company that the duke or Fitzroy or both of them is so determined to uncover. Fitzroy bridled at the suggestion that it was a love letter, but he would have done whether it is or not. Though you'd think the duke would have learned his lesson."

"That's a lesson men find it difficult to learn. Some men."

Malcolm shot a smile at her over his shoulder. "Thank you."

Suzanne reached for her pearls and fastened them over the pendant. "Do you think Craven had papers that contained a secret about Wellington?"

Malcolm set down the razor and picked up a towel. "That's the likeliest explanation for how such papers could have come to be in the warehouse, though it's still difficult to see how he came by them. Easier to see Carfax having such papers in his possession. And I suppose it's barely possible he could have had Craven hide them for him, but I'd be surprised Carfax trusted Craven that much."

Suzanne smoothed the sea-green tulle of her gown. "If the papers are a love letter or letters—It's possible Craven got them from the lady in question. Or Eustace Whateley did."

Malcolm emerged from scrubbing his face with the snowy towel. "You think one of them shared a mistress with Wellington?"

"Is that so surprising?"

"Given that we know Wellington was involved in some fashion with Lady Frances Webster who's also been linked to Byron—If that's the case, I wonder if Carfax suspects."

"It's only a theory, darling." Suzanne got to her feet and went to her husband's side. A trace of shaving lather clung to the corner of his mouth. She wiped it away.

Malcolm caught her hand and drew it across his mouth. "It's a good theory."

"It doesn't explain Ennis's claim that Coventry said Whateley & Company were shipping guns."

"No." Malcolm's gaze grew serious. "God knows there was profiteering during the war, but more likely from contracts being steered one way or another than actual gunrunning."

"Suppose someone in the military had got hold of excess weapons and was selling them under the table and paying Whateley & Company to do the shipping?"

Malcolm frowned. "Possible. But while I can see Fitzroy covering up a love affair of Wellington's, I can't see him involved in gunrunning."

"Nor can I." Suzanne tightened her black satin sash. "But he could have engaged Ennis as a favor for a friend without knowing the specifics. Men can be very loyal to those they've fought with. And Fitzroy is the sort who might trust a comrade's word of honor."

"In which case it could have nothing to do with Wellington. But if Whateley & Company were shipping the weapons why break in and steal papers? Presumably whoever was behind the gunrunning was in league with Eustace Whateley."

"Perhaps that's it." Suzanne shifted the puzzle pieces in her mind. "If Fitzroy was investigating possible gunrunning and looking for proof—"

"Why in God's name wouldn't he have told me?"

"You aren't a diplomat anymore, darling. Or an official agent. If Fitzroy suspected a fellow officer but wasn't certain—"

"He might have hesitated to tarnish someone's reputation, especially to one outside the family."

Malcolm had been almost, but not quite, one of the "family" of Wellington's aides-de-camp in the Peninsula and at Waterloo. But a lot had changed since then. "That could fit Fitzroy. So could protecting Wellington. I need to talk to Eustace Whateley." He looked down at Suzanne for a moment. "I don't think Fitzroy would have hired people to attack us. At least not to attack you. But depending on who else is involved in this—"

"We're taking precautions," Suzanne said. "That's all we can do at this point."

"That, and learn what was in the papers," Malcolm said.

Suzanne glanced round the grand salon of the Tavistock as theatregoers thronged it for the interval, then turned to smile at Laura. "I'm glad you came with us."

"So am I. It's a brilliant play, and Manon is brilliant in it. I'm less sure about the show here. Or at least, I might not mind watching it, but I don't know how I feel about being part of it."

Laura's, or rather Jane Tarrington's, return from the dead had caused a good deal of talk, and Laura still went out in society little enough to attract a good deal of interest when she did venture out. "You're a rarity," Suzanne said. "Some people would play upon that to hold society's attention."

Laura shook her head as David's sister, Isobel Lydgate, came up to join them. "Simon looks rather the way I feel when I'm giving a ball," Isobel said. "Though I suppose that's a frivolous comparison."

"I'd say it's very apt," Suzanne said. "How are the preparations for tomorrow night?" A few weeks ago, Suzanne had helped Isobel write out the cards of invitation for her ball, but in the press of the past few days, she'd almost forgot that the ball was the following evening.

Isobel gave a wry smile. She was impeccably gowned in pale blue crêpe, her thick fair hair swept into a smooth knot, but strain showed between her brows and about her eyes. "Oliver says I worry too much. I haven't got your wonderful sangfroid when it comes to entertaining, Suzanne."

Suzanne put an arm round her friend. "Meaning you still have illusions that perfection is possible, whereas I've long since accepted that it isn't. The trick is not minding when something goes wrong."

Isobel shook her head, dislodging a strand of her straight hair. "So says the woman who gives the most exquisite parties in Mayfair. But as Oliver said to me when we left for the theatre, we're as ready as we're going to be, so there's no sense in staying home and being nervous. Not that we'd miss Simon's opening." She turned her gaze to Laura. "You are coming tomorrow, aren't you, Laura?"

"I promised Ellie and Billy and Rose I would, so I can't very well back out now."

"Thank goodness for my children's powers of persuasion. You know Billy still tells everyone who'll listen that he's going to marry you."

Laura laughed. Isobel had always treated her more like a friend than a governess, and Laura seemed more at ease with her than with many of the mothers she'd known in her governess days. "I thought Billy had transferred his attentions to Emily."

"He'll probably have to fight Colin for her if he does," Suzanne murmured.

Laura shook her head. "Amazing what—Simon." Her face broke into a smile as Simon approached them. "The production is quite splendid. I'm intrigued to see how you handle the ending."

Simon grinned. "Brandon accused me of going soft in rehearsals."

"So you see Isabella accepting the duke's proposal?" Suzanne asked. At one time she'd have disagreed with that ending. Now she found she rather hoped for it.

"I think so. On her own terms."

"She's a fortunate woman if she can dictate them," Isobel said.

"I think the events of the play teach her that she can't hide from the world," Laura said. "And—Oh, there are James and Hetty. I should speak with them."

Laura moved off, head held high, to speak with her brother-in-law and sister-in-law. Isobel's attention was claimed by Emily Cowper. Suzanne turned back to Simon, who had retrieved two glasses of champagne from a passing waiter. "Isabella will be able to do a lot as a duchess," Suzanne said, accepting one of the glasses. "And I've always thought—well, since I had Colin—that seeing her brother and Julietta's baby makes her want children."

Simon gave a wry smile. "There is that. I suppose children are on my mind these days."

Suzanne studied him. They'd had less chance for private conversation in the months since he and David had taken the children. Usually both their children were with them, even when other adults weren't. "It's quite an adjustment, adding children to a relationship. And you and David have started with four."

Simon dug his shoulder into the gilded paneling of the wall behind them. "In some ways we're closer than ever. In others it seems we barely talk anymore."

"Parenthood can do that to you. You exchange greetings over the nursery breakfast or pass a crying child back and forth."

"Yes. But—" Simon drew a breath.

Suzanne searched her friend's face. "It's different because they don't seem like your children?"

Simon lifted his glass and contemplated the bubbles. "In some ways I'm amazed at how much they do. How naturally Jamie snuggles in. How I find myself thinking about them during rehearsal. How hard it is to remember a time when we didn't have them. But—" He hesitated again. "David can be clear about his commitment to them. Can say they have a home with him forever. All I can say is that I'm their uncle's friend."

"Your commitment to David gives you a commitment to them."

"Difficult to articulate that to the children when I can't articulate my relationship to David to them. And—" His eyes darkened. As steadfast as his commitment to David and David's to him—Suzanne knew few married couples with relationships as deep and enduring—Suzanne knew that Simon worried what the pressures of David's role as future Earl Carfax would do to the bond between them. She'd never heard him quite articulate it—as though he feared to put it into words. That he'd come close as he had to doing so was a sign, she thought, of the level of trust between them.

"I can't tell you how often I've envied how at ease you and David are with each other," Suzanne said. A truth she wouldn't speak to many.

Simon's mouth twisted. "That's the years."

"Those years are what go to make up a marriage. Because that's what you have, you know."

"Not in the eyes of the world. Or David's family. Or most of our acquaintance."

"Surely it's what it means in your and David's eyes that matters."

Simon met her gaze. It was one of those moments when she was sure he saw more about her than she'd confessed to him. More perhaps than was safe for either of them. "You can't really believe that, Suzie mine. You can't really believe two lovers can exist in a soap bubble. Or even if lovers could, parents certainly can't."

She laid a hand on his arm. "Of course the world touches all of us. But it doesn't have to define us or our options."

"It's not my options I'm thinking about. It's David's." Simon drew a breath. "Having children brought you and Malcolm together. I saw that. Much as I love them, the children remind David of all the reasons we can't be together."

"They'll sort it out for themselves. They'll understand."

"You think so? Why on earth should they be different from so much of the rest of the world?'

"Because the two of you are raising them."

Simon gave a faint smile. "A good answer. Though you may be putting too much faith in our childrearing skills. Not but what getting Teddy out of Harrow would be a step in the right direction."

Bertrand joined them to offer his congratulations to Simon with every appearance of being no more than an enthusiastic theatregoer. But when Simon moved off to speak to Sir Horace Smytheton, one of the Tavistock's chief patrons, Bertrand turned to Suzanne, his posture still easy but his gaze gone serious. "I haven't been able to find a trace of Germont. He's vanished with the skill of a more seasoned agent than he appeared to be."

"Do you think he could have met with foul play?" Suzanne remembered the fear and urgency in Louis Germont's fever-wracked voice.

"Only if whoever attacked him covered their tracks exceedingly well."

Suzanne bit back a cry of frustration. A visit today to Sancho had merely given her a vague description of an anonymous-sounding man, fairly obviously in disguise, who had sought Sancho out with news of the Phoenix plot.

Bertrand took a sip of champagne and gave a smile intended for the benefit of anyone observing him. "I did talk to someone who knew him in France. Apparently Germont's mother was the daughter of a minor French aristocrat who married into the bourgeoisie. My contact couldn't remember the family name, but he thought Germont had an uncle or aunt who might have escaped France during the Terror and settled in Austria or possibly England."

"He didn't mention them to you?"

"No, but there's obviously a great deal he didn't mention to me."

"So he could have sought refuge with his family in Britain."

"Potentially, though it sounds as though he hadn't been in contact with them for years. I'll make inquiries in the émigré community."

Suzanne drew a breath. "If only we'd—"

Bertrand gripped her wrist. "I know. But it does no good to refine upon it. And whatever's driving Germont, he made his own choice to leave."

14

"Mrs. Rannoch."

Bertrand had moved off, and Suzanne found herself smiling into the handsome face of Auguste-Charles-Joseph, Comte de Flahaut. "Monsieur Flahaut. It's been too long."

Except for greetings exchanged in groups at large entertainments, she and Flahaut had not spoken since her ball in April, when Suzanne had given him a letter from Hortense Bonaparte, his former longtime lover. Seven years ago, Suzanne had helped Hortense through the secret birth of her child by Flahaut, who now lived with Flahaut's mother.

Flahaut himself had fought for Napoleon at Waterloo and had sought refuge in England after the Bourbon Restoration. He was making every effort not to let his past intrude on the refuge he had found here, particularly his marriage to the Scottish heiress Margaret Mercer Elphinstone. The fact that he had sought Suzanne out and the concern she saw in his gaze sent a frisson of fear through her.

"A man stopped me yesterday morning when I was walking alone by the Serpentine," he said, his voice pitched for her ears alone. "I could scarcely credit—"

"Let me guess," Suzanne said, keeping her voice level. "It was something about mythical birds that rise from the ashes."

Fear shot into his gaze, the gaze of a man who had faced countless battles. "Oh, God. Are you—"

"I've only heard rumors. No one's even approached me. And I'm certainly not involved."

Some of the tension left Flahaut's shoulders. "I couldn't. My life is here now." His gaze shot across the salon to his wife, standing with Emily Cowper and Rupert Caruthers. "Even a whisper of involvement—"

"I know," Suzanne said.

"And yet, if there were a chance—" Conflicting loyalties tore at his face.

"I know," she said again, in a different tone.

"So much honor lost."

"You fought honorably. You have nothing to reproach yourself with." Suzanne might not believe in honor, but she knew what it meant to Flahaut.

"My life changed that day." Flahaut's hands clenched at his sides, as though involuntarily. "I can't go back."

"We none of us can."

He cast a quick glance round the salon again, looked at his wife for a moment, took in Carfax talking to Malcolm, looked back at Suzanne. "Who? Who is behind it?"

"I don't know," Suzanne said. "Yet. This man who approached you—did he give a name?"

"He said it was Moreau. But I very much doubt he was telling the truth."

"What did he look like?"

Flahaut frowned as though in an effort of memory. "Late thirties or early forties. Brown hair. Middling height. Not heavy but not particularly lean. Brown eyes. Or perhaps gray.

Or even blue. I kept thinking there was something familiar about him, but I couldn't place him."

"The perfect spy."

"You've never been anonymous."

"Perhaps not. But I was always good at blending into a role."

Flahaut shook his head. "Talleyrand would be horrified." Prince Talleyrand, who had been Flahaut's mother's lover and was Flahaut's true father, had helped Flahaut escape to England after Waterloo. "Unless—" Flahaut broke off, unvoiced questions racing through his eyes.

"No," Suzanne said. "Talleyrand wouldn't."

"Can you really be sure of that?"

Suzanne drew a breath that was not as even as she would have liked. She thought of Talleyrand, out of power, living in semi-retirement with her friend, Dorothée. Doro's letters made him sound happy. But would a man like Talleyrand ever truly stop scheming? "As sure as I can be of anything when it comes to Talleyrand."

"Precisely." Flahaut watched her a moment. She could swear he was seeing into the past, and then into the possible future. "One way or another, this is bound to involve people we know. If it unravels—It could connect back to us in any case."

That, Suzanne knew, was a very real risk. But she managed the brightest smile she could. "All the more reason to find out whatever we can."

"Malcolm."

The sight of Carfax brought Malcolm up short. "I didn't expect to find you here, sir."

"I may not always have time for the theatre, but I find it agreeable enough. And given the interest my son takes in this theatre, I thought the least I could do is put in an appearance."

"I don't imagine you think much of the play's commentary on government. In fact if it was a contemporary play, I imagine you might have the censor shut it down."

"The censor doesn't work for me, Malcolm. Though I must say the duke in the play seems to have let matters get sadly out of control. And having done so, turning the city over to a man like Angelo is hardly the solution. Still, one must make allowances for Shakespeare." His gaze settled on Malcolm's face. "What have you learned?"

"Was Craven keeping papers for you?"

Carfax's fingers froze adjusting his spectacle wires. "*What have you learned?*" he said again, voice sharper.

"Nothing conclusive. I take it that's a no?"

"What kind of idiot do you take me for? I may make my share of mistakes, but I knew better than to entrust anything of value to a man like Craven."

"And I don't suppose you had Suzanne grabbed at gunpoint last night and the pair of us threatened if we didn't leave off the Whateley & Company investigation?"

Carfax's brows snapped together. "Suzanne's all right?"

"Suzanne's fine. She freed herself with more daring than sense."

Carfax gave a faint smile. "I'd hardly have tasked you with the investigation and then tried to warn you off."

"Not unless you were playing a very deep game indeed." Which sounded entirely like Carfax. "Roth's identified the dead man. A former soldier named Ben Coventry."

Carfax gave a nod, as though his mind was elsewhere. "I don't suppose it really matters much."

"No?" Malcolm asked, remembering Sue Kettering.

"He was just hired for the job. Collateral damage."

"I think I must be growing up," Cordelia said. "I find the intrigue on stage much more interesting than the intrigue in the salon."

Laura smiled at her friend. "I was just saying something of the sort. Though it was good to see James and Hetty." It never failed to amaze her how genuinely kind her brother-in-law was compared to her late husband.

Cordelia scanned the salon. "I don't suppose there's much we can do to further the investigation."

"For once, a lot of the investigation is outside the beau monde," Suzanne said. "Though Malcolm is talking to Carfax. Oh, there's Harry."

Harry Davenport was crossing the drawing room towards them, a man at his side in dress uniform. A tall man with tanned skin, finely sculpted features, and hair that gleamed golden in the candlelight. Laura went still, her blood turned to ice, as she stared at her past approaching through the ranks of well-dressed guests.

"Cordy," Harry said with a grin. "Suzanne. Laura. May I present Lieutenant-Colonel William Cuthbertson? We served together in the Peninsula. Though I don't think he needs presenting to Laura."

Will inclined his head to the three ladies with faultless politeness, but his gaze lingered on Laura.

"Colonel Cuthbertson." Laura gave him her hand with an automatic smile.

"Lady Tarrington." Will pressed her hand to his lips, very correctly, but just a shade longer than was necessary.

She heard the others exchange introductions, though she could scarcely follow the words. A few minutes later the Davenports moved off to speak to Crispin Harleton. Suzanne lingered, her gaze going to Laura. Laura sent her friend a silent assent. She was going to have to talk to Will alone at some point. It wasn't so much that she didn't want to as that it stirred feelings and memories she wasn't sure she was ready to face.

"I could scarcely believe it," Will murmured when Suzanne moved off, his voice in an entirely different key. "Dear God, Jane, if you knew—But I understand you prefer to be called Laura now."

"I answer to both. But I've been Laura so long it seems more natural in some ways."

His gaze moved over her face as though seeking something he'd lost. She'd got used to people looking at her that way—her father, her stepmother, other friends and acquaintances. But only her father had come as close to scraping beneath her defenses as Will did. "I knew men with head injuries in the war," he said. "A damnable thing. Thank God your memory came back."

She suppressed an inwards grimace, as she always did over her cover story of amnesia. Though it seemed to be holding up reasonably well. "Being in England helped," she said. It was a lie grounded in truth. Being in Britain and about people she had known had helped her come to terms with who she was. Forced her to, really. Raoul would approve. He said the best cover stories were grounded in truth.

"If you knew how I grieved—" He shook his head. "I don't mean to turn maudlin. My feelings are the last thing you should have to think about."

"Will, no." Remembered tenderness welled to the surface and she pressed his hand. "I'm so sorry for everyone who suffered through my misfortune." That was true too, even if her misfortune was different from the cover story.

His fingers tightened over her own. "I was in Paris when I heard you were alive. I'd have got the news sooner but I was traveling from the south. As soon as I could get leave I came to London."

She jerked inwardly at the declaration. Will had been a romantic, but she wouldn't have thought that level of feeling would have lasted for so many years. He'd been a confidant, a haven from both Trenchard and Jack. And something more. Something born partly of her need for escape, partly perhaps of her desire to prove she could have a relationship separate from her husband and his father.

"I'm honored," she said.

"Can you doubt it?" He lifted her hand to his lips again and held it there a trifle longer this time.

Five years ago she would have laughed at the word "fidelity." Her life had made a mockery of it and so had the two chief men in her life then. But now—

She had a lover. A word that sounded far too transitory for what was between her and Raoul. Though precisely what that was remained undefined. Nights of mutual comfort. Stolen kisses and furtive handclasps. Looks exchanged across crowded rooms where so much could not be said. Letters often in painstaking code. Unexpected moments of kinship, mostly involving the children. She couldn't be certain he'd be back. He'd warned her of as much. How odd that one would feel a commitment when nothing had been formally declared. *I have no right to ask you to feel any obligation,* Raoul had said three months ago. *But I feel one.*

Coming from him, it was perhaps in the nature of a declaration. She knew what she saw when she looked into his eyes. And what she felt in response. For some reason her fingers tightened. Why now, of all times, should she desperately want to see him? And yet she couldn't deny that it was pleasant for a few moments to be with Will and to recall a time when everything had seemed simpler. Though at the time she'd have laughed bitterly at the idea that her situation could ever be called simple.

"And you have a daughter," Will said.

"Emily. I can't believe we were separated for so long. I'm trying to make up for lost time." This was more delicate ground, because her cover story had her memory gone so that she had been unaware of Emily's existence, whereas in fact she had been keenly aware of Emily's absence for those excruciating four years.

"I'm sure you're a splendid mother."

"That's kind of you, Will. But you always did see me as a much better person than I was."

"I saw you truthfully, which I fear few did. The garrison was filled with fools." He looked down at her for a long moment. "I'm sorry. About Jack. I think you know my opinion of him, and I make no apologies for it. But I wouldn't have wished that on any man. And I know you enough to know you mourned him."

That was true, in an odd way. Difficult, now, to sort out her feelings for Jack Tarrington, save that they were a mixture of guilt, frustration, and occasional flashes of nostalgia for something that had never really been possible between them. "Thank you," she managed. "Jack and I scarcely had a comfortable marriage, but he deserved better."

"And Trenchard. I know you were fond of him."

It was fortunate she wasn't holding a glass of champagne because she undoubtedly would have choked or dropped her glass. The thought of what sweet, honorable Will would think if he knew of her love affair with her husband's father might have been comical if it hadn't gone straight to the heart of all the things about her she knew were unforgivable.

"Trenchard's death was tragic," she said. That too was true, though the tragedy was more Louisa Craven's.

Will hesitated, as though not sure whether or not he would speak. "You—saw him before he died?"

Will would have heard, of course. Her discovery of the dying duke and her arrest for his murder were too salacious not to have been reported, despite all Malcolm and Suzanne's excellent efforts.

"I had just recovered my memory," she said. "I went to see Trenchard and found him just after he was shot. He was too far gone for speech. I'm not even sure he recognized me."

It was the story the Rannochs had devised, and given the facts that were public, it worked remarkably well, though it made her look a bit too passive for her taste, and she feared it wouldn't stand up to close scrutiny. Fortunately, most of the people she knew capable of that sort of scrutiny already knew the truth.

"You've been through so much. I feel a fool that I was wallowing in my own grief when you were desperately in need of a friend."

"You couldn't have known. I'm glad to see you came through Waterloo well."

"To think that you were in Paris when I was in the Netherlands." He shook his head. "I can scarcely credit that you were a governess."

Laura smiled, seeing the woman she had been in India. "You don't think I'd have the wit for it? Or the patience?"

"No, of course not. But you were hardly—"

"Until I became Lady Tarrington, it wouldn't seem such a surprising fate. My stepmother was a governess."

"Who married her charge's father."

"And I in turn married far above me."

Will shook his head. "You never cared for such things."

"I don't. Neither do the Rannochs, fortunately, which is part of why we get on so well together. And I learned that I quite like children. Good preparation for being a mother."

"Amazing that you're so sanguine."

"Difficult to be anything else and hold on to one's sanity."

"Yes." He regarded her for a moment, unvoiced questions shooting through his gaze.

She felt something about her own concerns for him was called for. "I was glad to hear from Harry Davenport that you were well."

"You know him well?"

"He and Lady Cordelia are close friends of the Rannochs."

Will shook his head. "A brave man, Davenport. And a brilliant one. He saved my life once on a reconnaissance mission when I was in over my head. He used to swear off marriage with the bitterness of one who has been truly burned. But it seems his attitude has changed." His gaze moved across the room to where the Davenports stood with Crispin and Simon. Harry had his arm round Cordelia's waist and she was leaning in to him companionably, her head tilting against his shoulder.

"I gather Waterloo changed a lot for them," Laura said. "They're a marvel. As are the Rannochs."

"At the time Davenport was advising any who'd listen never to marry, I was inclined to take his advice. Though for very different reasons."

She felt herself color. When was the last time she'd felt a telltale blush? "Difficult to think of the future in the midst of a war."

"Especially when the future seems a bleak wasteland. But a number of things have changed."

A frisson shot through her. Was she horribly shallow to warm so to admiration? But it was more than that. How could it not mean something to know someone cared? At the same time, his words and her response showed her the dangers for both of them.

15

"Whateley." Malcolm found Eustace standing alone in the grand salon. "I'm glad to see you here."

"Rannoch. It's too much of an occasion for Cecilia to stay away." Eustace nodded towards his wife, in animated conversation with three other women. "Especially now la Caret is Lady Harleton. I wonder how she finds it to have married into the beau monde?"

"I'm sure you could have an interesting conversation with Lady Harleton about the challenges."

Eustace gave a dry smile. "I think there are more differences than similarities. She doesn't have a fortune that I've heard of, Harleton's pockets aren't to let, and he appears to be, in the common parlance, head over ears in love with her. None of which applies to my marriage to Cecilia." His gaze flickered over Malcolm's face. "Have you learned anything?"

"Several things. Nothing conclusive. But you neglected to tell me how dangerous the goods you were transporting were."

Eustace's brows drew together. "Tea and iron?"

"And guns."

Tension shot through Eustace's shoulders beneath the well-tailored fabric of his coat. "Who the devil says so?"

"A man named Ben Coventry who was doing reconnaissance before he broke into the warehouse and lost his life."

"And you're taking the secondhand word of a thief?"

"Given that I see no particular reason why he should have made this up."

Eustace cast a quick glance round and turned back to Malcolm. "I should have realized you'd work it out. To own the truth, I more than half thought you already knew."

"What on earth made you think I knew you were transporting guns?"

Eustace drew a breath. "It was part of Craven's plan when he brought me the idea for the company. Oh, he made a case that it could be a profitable business venture. But the idea was that it would be a way to transport information and certain goods secretly."

Malcolm stared at Eustace, the pieces falling into place even as he cursed himself for a fool.

Eustace returned his gaze steadily. "You see why I thought you knew. Given that you and Craven both worked for someone who would have need of those services—"

Malcolm found Carfax across the room, moving away from a conversation with Lord Liverpool and the Duke of Wellington. Malcolm touched his spymaster on the arm. "Anteroom across the passage, sir," he said in a low voice. "Unless you want to me make a scene here."

"My dear Malcolm." The gaze Carfax lifted to his face was, if anything, amused. "You had merely to ask."

Malcolm closed the anteroom door with a quiet click, though all his instincts were to slam it. "You didn't think it was relevant information that the break-in occurred at the warehouse of a company you started?"

"Nonsense." Carfax set his champagne glass down on a marble-topped table. "My name isn't on any of the paperwork."

Malcolm sent his spymaster a withering look.

"Yes. All right." Carfax tugged at one of his shirtcuffs. "I may have suggested to Craven that it would be convenient. To own the truth, I don't know why I didn't think of it earlier. All the times we had to transport information or people or goods in secret. The times we've had to trust ourselves to smugglers or make use of the navy—and I'm not sure which is worse."

"Were you shipping guns?"

Carfax picked up his glass and swallowed the last of the champagne. "There are times we want to get weapons into certain people's hands unofficially."

"Who were the guns Coventry saw intended for?"

"You can't seriously expect me to answer that."

"Sir—"

Carfax clunked the glass down. "You can't be shocked, Malcolm."

"That you had Craven set up such a company for you? No. That you were shipping weapons? No. That you didn't tell me when I was investigating a murder in the company's warehouse—"

"I knew I didn't have anything to do with the break-in or the murder. It would only have muddied the waters for you."

It was almost the verbatim answer Wellington had given Malcolm when the duke had withheld information during the investigation in Paris three years ago into Antoine Rivère's death. "Damn it, sir. You know one can never tell what information will be relevant."

"And you don't trust that I didn't have anything to do with the break-in."

"That too."

Carfax folded his arms over his chest. "Why would I break into the warehouse? I could simply ask Eustace if I wanted anything there."

"Perhaps Eustace had something he didn't want to give you. Perhaps you thought Craven had hidden something in the warehouse Eustace didn't know about."

"What, for God's sake?"

"I don't know. Yet."

Suzanne stared at her husband. Malcolm hadn't had a chance to tell his wife about Carfax and Whateley & Company until the play was over. Almost as soon as the bows were done, he had pulled her out of their box and into an antechamber at the Tavistock. They had a few minutes to talk while they waited for their friends to assemble for Crispin's post-performance supper party in Manon's honor at Rules restaurant nearby. As usual Suzanne didn't waste time on expressing shock. "I don't know why we didn't see it," she said.

"Nor do I, now we've figured it out."

"It's damnably clever. I don't know why—"

"O'Roarke didn't try it?" Malcolm asked. "He would have had a harder time setting up a shipping company."

"True. But in Paris—Of course, for all I know, he did do something of the sort and never told me."

Malcolm gave a faint smile. There was a lot he was still coming to know about his father, but he knew just how deeply O'Roarke trusted Suzanne. Better perhaps than Suzanne recognized that trust herself. "I think you'd know."

She shook her head. "He tells me a lot, but not everything."

"Compared to Carfax and me—" Malcolm shook his head.

"Carfax has a point," Suzanne said. "It doesn't prove he had anything to do with the break-in."

"No, but it makes it far more likely whatever the thieves were after has something to do with Carfax. In fact the likeliest explanation is that the thieves were hired by someone seeking information to use against Carfax."

Suzanne met her husband's gaze. "Wellington?"

Malcolm frowned, seeing Wellington and Carfax together in the salon with Liverpool. "Carfax and Wellington have always been allies, but far from in lockstep."

"If Wellington disagreed with something Carfax was doing, especially if it involved shipping weapons—"

"Quite. So Wellington could be the one who ordered Fitzroy to orchestrate the break-in. But not because of a love affair."

"And Fitzroy might not have told you because he knows you're loyal to Carfax."

Malcolm gave a short laugh.

"At the very least, Fitzroy would know you might be conflicted when it came to choosing between Carfax and Wellington, darling."

"Or not loyal to either of them." And that was without Fitzroy's knowing the truth about Suzanne. Malcolm scraped a hand over his hair. "You're right. I need to talk to Fitzroy again."

"If Carfax suspects Wellington, he has to wonder about your loyalties as well."

"Carfax always wonders about my loyalties."

"He knows you're you, darling."

"He doesn't know everything about me."

At least, Malcolm profoundly hoped his spymaster didn't.

16

The glittering mirror in the private room at Rules caught Manon's dazzling smile, brighter than the profusion of wax tapers. The soft gold walls, the dark paneling touched with gilt, and the red upholstery were the perfect foil for her golden hair and gown of white net over peach satin. She was the effortless center of attention, but somehow as the guests milled about, sipping champagne and waiting for everyone to arrive from the theatre, she contrived to stand beside Suzanne. "I saw Jennifer this afternoon."

Jennifer Mansfield was the Tavistock's other leading actress. Like Manon, she was French, though she had changed her name upon coming to England. Like Manon, she had become the mistress of an English aristocrat, in Jennifer's case Sir Horace Smytheton, a patron of the Tavistock. And like Manon, Jennifer had once been a French agent.

"I waved to her and Sir Horace across the theatre," Suzanne said. "But they seemed to leave early."

"Jennifer said they might," Manon replied with a smile. "She confesses to being unusually tired these days. It seems I'm not the only actress at the Tavistock who is expecting."

Jennifer was a decade Manon's senior, but it should not be so surprising. Suzanne found herself smiling. "I hope she's pleased. I'm quite sure Sir Horace is."

"Prodigiously, I gather. Both of them, though Jennifer is quieter about it." Manon smiled at her daughters, standing on either side of Crispin, looking very grown up in white muslin dresses sashed in peach. "It's also prompted them to confess that they've actually been married these eight years and more."

"Good God. Since before their first child was born? Why on earth keep it a secret?"

"Jennifer said she was the one who insisted on it. She didn't want there to be any question about her continuing her career. She said they knew and they had papers to prove their daughter legitimate should it be it be important." Manon cast a glance about. "I think she also feared Sir Horace being tainted if her past ever came to light. But now he knows the truth, and they have Crispin's and my example of an actress continuing her career despite marrying into the beau monde. For which she thanked me."

"I'm glad. For both of them."

"So am I. But there's more. Jennifer received a visit yesterday. From a young man talking of Phoenixes."

Suzanne sucked in her breath. "Did she describe him?"

"French. Midtwenties. Fair hair. Blue eyes. Obviously recovering from a recent wound to the chest, though he did his best to hide it."

"Louis Germont."

"So it seems. Jennifer, needless to say, wanted even less to do with the plot than I did."

"This confirms that Germont is working with whoever is behind the plot, and his warning to me was a set-up." Suzanne fingered the stem of her glass. Jennifer had been an agent in the service of the Revolutionary and Directoire governments, but she had fled France before Napoleon Bonaparte had fully risen to power. She could scarcely be called a Bonapartist. "Their reach is deep," she said.

"My thoughts precisely," Manon said. She looked across the room and met her husband's gaze. The smile she gave was not the dazzling one of Manon Caret, leading lady, but the private one of a wife. She turned back to Suzanne and for a moment her gaze was that of a hardened agent. "And given how many people they've talked to who haven't agreed to be part of the plot, I can only wonder how many others have actually been drawn in."

Simon closed the door of the Rannochs' barouche after handing Suzanne and Laura into the carriage and gave a wave as the carriage set off down Maiden Lane. He turned to David, standing beside him on the pavement. All the guests at Crispin's supper party had now departed. The night was clear, a freshness in the air after the recent rain. He and Simon usually walked home on evenings such as this, though it was closer to the Albany than to Brook Street.

"We could walk together as far as the Albany," Simon suggested. It would give them time alone together, rare these days.

David twitched his cuff smooth. "Come back to Brook Street."

Simon stared at his lover. "Who are you, and what have you done with David?"

David gave an abashed grin. "At least for a drink."

"We've been drinking for the past two hours."

"Not alone." David glanced up and down the street. A hackney clattered by and a trio of young men emerged from a coffeehouse across the street, but even Covent Garden was beginning to settle down for the night. "I have a key. I told the servants not to wait up. Unless Bridget couldn't get Jamie to sleep—in which case, we will certainly need you—the house should be quiet."

"And then I can climb out a window some time before dawn?" Actually, Simon thought, that wasn't a bad idea. "I've always seen myself as more of a Mercutio than a Romeo."

"If you were Romeo, Juliet might have a hard time getting a word in edgewise." David took a step along the pavement. "We'll sort it out."

Simon fell into step beside his lover. Not quite touching but within touching distance. He felt a crazy desire to laugh. The light of the street lamps seemed to glitter particularly bright. The blue-black sheen on the cobblestones held mystery and promise. Danger could quicken the blood. Danger and time alone with the man he loved.

They talked about the performance, about the crowd's response, about Crispin's obvious pride in his wife.

"Though I can't say which he was most pleased by," David said. "The performance his wife gave or the child she's carrying."

"Oh, that's easy." Simon grinned. "Crispin's very supportive of Manon's career and he has a genuine appreciation of her talent. But he's in transports about the baby. Which is as it should be. Wouldn't be fair to the child otherwise."

"He loves Roxane and Clarisse like they're his own," David said. "You'd never guess they weren't, seeing him with them."

"No. But this time they're starting together from the first."

"Like—"

Simon shot a look at his lover. "Like we are?"

David flushed. "I know you never asked for this."

"Nor did you, if it comes to that. It doesn't mean I'm not enjoying it."

David's eyes widened.

"Is that so surprising?" Simon asked. "You know I've always liked children. It's surprisingly agreeable not to have to hand them back after an hour or so."

David continued to watch him. "I never thought—"

"Rather nice after ten years I can still surprise you."

They had reached the Brook Street house. David studied Simon for a moment in the muted glow spilling through the fanlight over the door. Then he gave a smile, faint but of the sort that shot straight through to Simon's heart. Without further speech, David, turned, climbed the steps, and unlocked the gleaming front door.

A single lamp glowed on the console table in the entrance hall, casting shadows over the marble-tiled floor, the mahogany-railed staircase, the velvet benches, the gilt-edged mirror. The air was thick and still, holding only a faint whiff of the recently extinguished candles in the wall sconces.

David pushed the heavy door to. Odd, considering they'd shared a home for a third of their lives, to feel awkward walking into his house with him. Or, if not his house, the house where he lived. And Simon didn't. "Bridget appears to have got Jamie to sleep," Simon said, and then wondered if he'd spoken too loudly.

"Yes." David pocketed the keys.

"If this goes on, you'll hardly need me at all." Simon kept his voice light.

"Damn it, Simon, you know—" David grabbed him, pushed him against the door, and kissed him.

Simon's arms closed round his lover. Family pressures, social realities, competing loyalties fled away. "Just in case," he said against David's cheek a few moments later, "let's—"

He broke off and went still. A sound. From within the house. The sound made by a footfall on a squeaking floorboard.

One of the servants? One of the children who had wakened? In an instant, David was out of Simon's arms. He snatched up the lamp from the console table and moved to the stairs. Simon followed. After all, he could simply have come back with David to have a last drink.

Silence hung over the house again. Odd. If one of the servants or children were awake, why should they go still? Then Simon sensed, more than heard or saw, a rush of movement. He raced up the stairs past David to see a shadowy figure running up the next flight to the second floor. Lamplight bounced behind him as David followed. The shadowy figure rounded the landing on the second floor and made for the third floor. The nursery.

Propelled by an energy he didn't know he could possess, Simon launched himself in a flying tackle and caught a leg and a kid shoe at the third-floor landing. He and the intruder both crashed to the floor.

A foot caught Simon in the eye. David raced past him, but the intruder was already at the end of the passage. Something whizzed through the air. David staggered and let out a cry. Wind whistled through the passage from an open window. Against the starlit sky, Simon saw the intruder drop to the ground.

Behind the closed nursery door, Jamie began to scream.

"Sound asleep, all three of them." Blanca smiled at Suzanne, Malcolm, and Laura across the Berkeley Square library. "It only took three stories."

"And two songs." Miles Addison sat on the settee beside his wife, his arm round her shoulders. Laura smiled as she settled back against the velvet sofa cushions. A year and a half ago, when she first joined the Rannoch household, Addison would not have dreamed of showing his (quite obvious) affection for Blanca in front of their employers, and if he'd spent an evening helping in the nursery he wouldn't have been so open about it. Laura wasn't the only one whose role in the household had changed in recent months.

"Jessica likes Miles to sing to her." Blanca grinned up at her husband. "She has good taste."

Malcolm got to his feet and moved to the drinks trolley. "Stay for a drink?"

Blanca shook her head and stifled a yawn. "The little one isn't even born yet and he or she makes me sleepy."

"It should get easier soon," Laura told her. "I was amazed at how much energy I had in the middle months." Odd now to be able to look back on her pregnancy with equanimity, even flashes of happiness. It made all the difference that the result of that pregnancy was tucked safely in bed upstairs.

"Blanca with more energy," Addison murmured with a grin. "Difficult to imagine."

Blanca pulled a face at him. "You can stay."

"I wouldn't dream of it," Addison said, tightening his arm round her. "Another time."

"I'd give a lot to hear Addison singing to children," Malcolm said softly, as the door closed behind the couple.

"By the time the baby's born, I expect you will," Suzanne said. "Amazing how people can change. Speaking of which," she added, turning to Laura, "I'm so glad you came with us. I keep saying that, don't I?"

Laura smiled as she unwound the silver gauze folds of her shawl. She could still hear the buzz of conversation round the table at Rules and feel the pleasant afterglow of the champagne. "It wasn't nearly the ordeal I feared. And the play and supper were heaven. Though I feel as though I'm going to have to immerse myself in your quartos and folios to keep up. Did you both grow up on Shakespeare?"

"Just about." Suzanne undid the ties on her evening cloak. "My parents were both actors." She shook her head. "Odd to be able to say that so openly."

"And I had my grandfather and O'Roarke." Malcolm put a glass of whisky in Laura's hand. "You're being modest, Laura. At Christmas, you knew the source of the quote O'Roarke and I were arguing about. And you more than held your own tonight."

"I've always liked Shakespeare. We put on a lot of amateur theatricals in India." She could hear Raoul's voice in the Berkeley Square garden three months ago, just before he left for Spain. *But shall I live in hope?* And her own, capping his quotation, *All men, I hope, live so.* Richard III and Anne Neville were not perhaps the most auspicious couple to have been quoting, but somehow it had felt right. She hesitated a moment, fingers curled round the glass Malcolm had given her. Aware something more was required but not sure how to address it. "It was nice to see Will Cuthbertson. Though the time I knew him seems like a different world."

Malcolm gave a glass to Suzanne. "It can be complicated, seeing someone from one's past. Even a friend."

Laura took a sip of whisky. "I'm not the woman Will knew. Of course, the woman Will thought he knew was much nicer than the actual Jane Tarrington."

Suzanne met her gaze for a moment in understanding. Was that the way her friend felt about herself? Laura wondered.

"We seemed to get by with the cover story, though," Laura said. "And Will has a keen understanding."

Malcolm picked up the glass he'd poured for himself and dropped down on the sofa beside Suzanne. "Half the key to making a cover story work is repeating it with absolute conviction. You have formidable skills to pull that off."

Laura stretched out her feet in their satin evening slippers. "God, it's a relief not to have to pretend. I don't know how you did it so long, Suzanne—not having any moments you could be yourself." She bit her lip. Even among the three of them it was hard sometimes to know what they could and couldn't say.

"She's a marvel," Malcolm said in an easy voice. "But then, you did the same for four years."

Laura shuddered. "Governesses don't tend to have confidants in any case. I suppose that made it seem more natural."

"I at least had Blanca to confide in," Suzanne said.

"And O'Roarke sometimes," Malcolm added in the same easy voice.

Raoul's name hung oddly the air. "Wherever he is, I hope he has someone he can talk to," Laura said.

She thought of the letter she had sent off to him, the letter Suzanne had sent. She wouldn't have wished whatever trouble had caused Suzanne to send for him, but she couldn't deny the rush of delight she felt at the prospect of seeing him. She had no doubt he would try to return when he received the letters. If he received the letters. If he was safe.

"Raoul's been taking care of himself for a long time," Suzanne said. "If—"

A rap fell on the door. "Forgive me." Valentin entered the room. He'd waited up for them, thanks to the recent attack, but Malcolm and Suzanne had told him to go to bed when they returned home. "But Lord Worsley's footman just brought a message. Someone broke into the Brook Street house."

Simon was sitting in a wing-back chair in the Brook Street library with two-year-old Jamie draped over his shoulder and Amy, six and a half, sitting on his knee. David sat on the sofa across from them, Teddy and eight-year-old George on either side of him. They looked like a family, Malcolm thought, as the footman showed Suzanne and him into the room. Perhaps one good development in the midst of all this.

Simon, David, and the four children looked up as Malcolm and Suzanne stepped into the room.

"Uncle Malcolm," George said as the footman closed the doors. He had a mop of fair hair and inquisitive blue eyes. "Aunt Suzanne. Are you going to find the people who broke into our house?"

"Are they going to come back and murder us?" Amy asked. Her eyes were wide in her pale, freckled face, but she sounded more curious than frightened.

"No one is going to murder anyone." David pushed himself to his feet. "Thank you for coming. The intruder's gone—and not coming back"—he glanced at the children with a smile both firm and reassuring—"but I thought you should look at the house as soon as possible."

"'Truder." Jamie turned his head from Simon's shoulder.

"Excellent, old chap." Simon kissed the little boy's hair. "We got a new word out of this."

Amy twisted one of her long fair plaits round her finger. "The person jumped out of the window by the nursery. Maybe they wanted to kidnap us."

David turned to smile at his niece. "No one would dare kidnap you, Amy. They'd know they'd have me to deal with. And Uncle Simon."

Amy actually giggled, snuggling against Simon.

The library door opened again, and the footman showed Jeremy Roth into the room. "I came as soon as I got your message," he said to David, then surveyed the children. "I hear you were very brave."

"Uncle Simon was brave," Teddy said. "He tackled the intruder."

"Good work that," Roth said to Simon.

Simon smoothed Jamie's hair. "But unfortunately I wasn't quite quick enough."

"If we'd woken up sooner we could have helped," George said.

"And I have no doubt you would have," Simon said. "But in some ways perhaps it's as well the man got out the window. I'm not sure we have enough rope in the house to have tied him up."

Amy frowned in consideration. "We would have used the window cords."

"You have the makings of an investigator, Miss Craven," Roth told her. "But, with any luck, the intruder left behind some evidence for us to discover."

"I'll show you where it happened," David said. He turned to the children. "Keep an eye on Uncle Simon for me."

Amy and George grinned. Teddy was frowning at the toes of his slippers, but even he gave a fleeting smile. Jamie swiveled round in Simon's lap and waved at Malcolm and Suzanne.

"They're taking it well, all things considered," David said, when he, Malcolm, Suzanne, and Roth were in the ground floor hall. "Unfortunately they woke up to the sounds of us trying to tackle the intruder. I think he just ran up to the nursery level trying to escape, but it's still concerning."

"A parent's nightmare," Roth said. "Did—"

He broke off as the library door eased open and Teddy slipped out. "Uncle David. I told Uncle Simon I had to talk to you. He said it was all right." His gaze shot from David to Malcolm to Suzanne to Roth and then back to David. "Is it my fault?"

"Your fault?" David moved towards the boy. "Why on earth should it be your fault, Teddy?"

"The man who broke into the house. Is it because I went into the warehouse?"

"Teddy, no." David put his hands on his nephew's shoulders. "Your going to Whateley & Company has nothing to do with this."

Teddy released his breath but watched David with steady eyes. "But someone breaking into our house might have to do with someone breaking into the warehouse, mightn't it?"

"It might," Malcolm said. "But not because of anything you did. You just happened to be in the wrong place at the wrong time."

Teddy gave a slow nod. "Is it because of my father? I mean, it was his warehouse, his and Uncle Eustace's, and this was his and Mama's house."

"It seems likely," Roth said. "But we can't be sure of anything."

Teddy nodded again. "Thank you. Thank you for telling me. For not lying and saying it's all in my head."

David lifted a hand and ruffled Teddy's hair. "We'll try very hard never to lie to you, Teddy. Do you think you can help Uncle Simon with your brothers and sister?"

Teddy straightened his shoulders and nodded.

"You're good at this," Roth said to David when Teddy had gone back into the library. "Took me years to master the right tone with my sons. Assuming I have mastered it."

David shook his head. "Most of the time I feel hopelessly out of my depth."

Malcolm clapped him on the shoulder. "Welcome to parenthood."

David gave a wry smile.

"Is anything missing?" Suzanne asked.

"Not as far as we can tell. It was an efficient search, most things put back as they were. But it looks as though he started in the study." David's gaze moved from Suzanne to Malcolm to Roth. "Teddy's right. It seems someone is looking for something of Craven's. So whatever was hidden in the warehouse wasn't what they really wanted? Or they're after something else?"

"Difficult to say," Roth said. "How carefully did you go through the house when you moved in?"

"Depends on what you mean by 'carefully,'" David said. "I went through all Craven's papers and Louisa's. The servants packed up all their clothes. But I didn't pry off the molding or tap on the mantel looking for hiding places."

"No reason for you to do so," Malcolm said.

"Whoever the intruder was," Suzanne said, "either he was singularly lucky in his timing or he knew you enough to know you'd be at Simon's play and out late tonight."

David nodded. "Anyone who made a few inquiries about me could surmise I'd be at Simon's opening, perhaps that I was likely to go out afterwards. But it would take inside knowledge to know I'd told the servants not to wait up. Do you think—"

Roth touched his arm. "Don't start suspecting your staff yet. If the intruder did know, it's possible one of them let something slip inadvertently. But we can make a few inquiries."

David nodded. "I could well have come home alone." He drew a breath.

Malcolm could guess what it had meant for Simon to come home with David, what a step it had been for them, what a night together would have meant to them. "Just as well Simon was here," Malcolm said. "Though it wasn't the night either of you planned on."

David led them up the stairs to the first floor. "We first saw the intruder up here. He made for the stairs. I think because he realized he'd been discovered."

"Did you get a good look at him?" Roth asked.

David shook his head. "Slight. Not too tall. But it was too dark to see more than that."

Malcolm, Suzanne, and Roth examined the floor and the stairs in the light of lamps they carried. No traces of mud, no convenient threads or hairs. They followed the intruder's path up to the second floor and then to the third floor and the nursery. "Simon tackled him near the head of the stairs," David said. "He broke free and threw a paperweight at me. He must have snatched it up on his search. Then he went out that window."

"It looks as though there's some blood on the carpet," Malcolm said. "He may have bloodied his nose when he fell." Which was interesting but wouldn't help them trace the man.

They moved to the window at the end of the passage where the intruder had escaped. Malcolm eased the sash up and was rewarded by a dark hair, surprisingly long, caught against the window ledge. He reached lower, scraped a few black threads from the stone.

"A dark-haired man in a dark coat," he said. "Hardly much help in identification."

Suzanne was kneeling on the floor, a corner of the carpet turned back. She lifted a hand, holding a tangle of gold and red. "A dark-haired man who dropped a carnelian bracelet," she said.

17

Laura unfastened her blue topaz earrings and set them in their satin-lined box. Her fingers lingered for a moment on the blue velvet of the lid. Raoul had sent the earrings before the ball Suzanne had given in April, the first major social event Laura had attended since resuming her position as Jane Tarrington. They were perfectly matched to the gown she'd worn that night. Had Suzanne told him somehow? Did he have some other source of information? Had he simply guessed based on her eye color?

Raoul wouldn't have known when he sent them that events would bring him to London and to Berkeley Square the night of the ball. Laura closed her eyes for a moment, remembering his arms round her that night when they'd finally had a moment alone, and the sudden shock of his kiss. Still later that night, lying in his arms. They'd had ten days together. A picnic at Richmond. Mornings in the park with the children. Evenings building block towers on the library hearthrug and playing chess. A night at the theatre. A dinner party with friends at which they'd both been at scrupulous pains to avoid looking like a couple. Amazing how much they'd been able to forge in those few days. Whatever she'd had with Will, it seemed pallid in comparison.

She unclasped her pearls and laid them in her jewel case. Seeing Will had been a reminder that there were things in her old life she wasn't sorry to remember. But pleasant as it was to know he still cared, it would be much simpler if he didn't. She was going to have to—

A soft scrape and thud sounded behind her. Laura spun round to see Raoul O'Roarke sitting on her windowsill, one booted foot tucked under him, the other swinging against the floorboards.

For a moment she thought her imagination had conjured him. Then he sprang down from the window ledge. "Sorry. I thought it was a bit late to go round to the front door, and I didn't want to wait."

Air rushed through her lungs. Whenever she saw him and knew he was safe, at least for the moment, she felt she could breathe again. She could never say as much to him, of course. She studied the familiar, mocking gray eyes, the quizzical mouth, the disordered dark hair that fell over his forehead. "And you have a weakness for dramatic entrances."

Raoul stretched his arms. His back, she knew, had a tendency to ache. "That sounds a bit schoolboyish for a hardened spy."

Laura folded her arms across her chest. "If the shoe fits."

He grinned, looking even more like a schoolboy. Then he unclasped his cloak and tossed it over a chair back, and moved towards her, his face gone serious.

"You got my message?" she asked.

"And Mélanie's. I don't suppose she's told you what it is?"

"No. And I don't think she's told Malcolm either. She thinks she's protecting him."

Raoul grimaced.

"It's dangerous," Laura said. "But I don't think she'd do it without good cause."

"Nor do I." Concern darkened his eyes. "I'll talk to her in the morning." His gaze shot to her face. "Laura—"

"It's all right. I've been enough of a spy to understand what you can't tell me."

His gaze shifted over her face. "It's not—"

"We agreed from the first we wouldn't make demands on each other. Not that I'd ever demand secrets as proof of intimacy."

"My God," he said. "Have I told you you're remarkable, Laura?"

She let her face relax into a smile. "One never gets tired of hearing it." She put out a hand to touch his arm. Even now, he almost always left it to her to make the first move, but at her touch, he seized her hand and pulled her into his arms. His kiss was swift and unexpectedly urgent. She wrapped her arms round him and let her head fall against his shoulder for a moment. Warmth. The smell of sandalwood. When in God's name had being in his arms come to feel like home?

"You got here quickly," she said, aware that her own voice sounded husky.

"I was already on my way. Both messages got to me at Dover."

She lifted her head and drew back to look at him. "You had other business in London?"

"You could say that," he said with an odd smile.

"What?" she asked, and then wondered if that was pushing past boundaries that should remain in place.

He lifted a hand and pushed her hair behind her ear. "I'm looking at it."

Her breath caught. He slid his fingers behind her neck and stroked his thumb against her cheek. "How are you, Laura?"

Much better now that you're here seemed too trite for them, so instead she said, "Blessedly unmired in intrigue, except the ones I'm assisting the Rannochs with. They're in the midst of an investigation now as it happens. There was a break-in at the warehouse of a company Lord Craven had invested in."

Raoul's brows drew together.

"Yes. It's concerning," she said. "They haven't figured out what the thieves were after yet. But one of the thieves was killed and left in the warehouse. And then tonight someone broke into the Craven house in Brook Street where David is living with the children. Malcolm and Suzanne are there now."

Raoul cast a quick glance at the door. "Do you know—"

"I was there when they got the message. The footman said David and the children were unharmed. Apparently Simon is there too. I more than half wanted to go with them, but there wasn't much I could add to what they could do themselves, and it made more sense to stay here in case any of the children wakes."

Raoul pushed a strand of hair behind her ear. "That's my Laura. Sense over impulse."

"I've been plenty impulsive in the past. On more than one occasion involving you."

"Thank God for it." He pressed a kiss against her forehead.

"If you want to go after them—"

"I couldn't add much either. And I'd be at a loss to explain how I knew of the situation. Besides, I'm singularly loath to leave my present circumstances. You haven't finished telling me how you go on. Is Emily over her chill?"

"Oh, yes, it was just a cold. Colin and Jessica didn't get it this time, thankfully. You didn't come back—"

"Not entirely. I missed you both."

When he looked at her like that, her wits had a way of scattering. "I've written another article, I've dined with my father and Sarah, I've been to a ball at the Davenports'. There's less talk when I go out than there used to be. I'm—glad you're here."

"So am I."

Their kiss lasted longer this time. In fact, by the time it ended he had lifted her in his arms and they were halfway to the bed. Delight washed over her.

Later, his fingers twined in her hair, he said, "I liked your article about women's education."

Laura lifted her head from his shoulder to look down at him. "You had time to read it?"

"You know how much of the business of being an agent is sitting about."

"Lady Grantham actually told me she was going to take it into account in finding a new governess for her daughters. As you're always saying, one takes victories where one finds them."

"A far from insignificant victory from the perspective of Lady Grantham's daughters."

She shifted and rested her head on his chest. They'd been in a bit of a hurry, and he was still wearing his shirt. She slid her hands under the linen. Her fingers brushed the puckered edge of a healing wound that hadn't been there the last time she'd lain in his arms. She lifted her head again and looked at him in inquiry.

"I was meeting with an agent in a tavern. We got caught up in a brawl. Minor collateral damage."

The wound wasn't long but it was dangerously close to his lung. She had a keen memory of gripping his shoulders, pulling him against her. "You should have said something. I'd have—"

"Its all right, Laura." His lips twitched. "You were very gentle with me."

"Wretch. It must still pain you."

"In truth, with you in my arms it's the last thing on my mind."

She studied his familiar gray eyes, thinking of the things they saw that were only on the edges of her world. "Are you sure someone wasn't using the brawl to try to kill you?"

He folded his arms behind his head. "One can never be sure. It can be fatal to let one's guard down. But my work now is less dangerous than it was during the war."

She rested her arms on his chest—carefully avoiding the wound—and looked into his face in the flickering candlelight. Impossible to imagine a world without his vivid presence. Yet she lived with the possibility every day. "Given what I know about your work during the war, I hardly find that reassuring."

He reached for one of her hands and pulled it against his lips. "Life's a risk." She saw him hesitate, saw him wonder, per-haps, how much to put into words. "I'll own to feeling more apprehension than I have in the past."

"Because you're more aware of the risks?"

"Because of what I have to come back to."

Her breath caught in her throat. She put her free hand against his face. "I'll say this for the separations. They make for lovely reunions."

His mouth twisted. "You deserve better, Laura."

"For two hardened spies, you and Mélanie have a distinct tendency to underrate yourselves."

"In my case I'd call it realism."

"And in Mélanie's?"

"Mélanie's always tended to be a prey to guilt."

"While you're a clear-eyed realist?"

"I can see what you deserve."

"I've never asked for more."

"That doesn't change it."

Laura laced her fingers through his own. "It means a lot having a future that's more than necessity. You gave me that. You and Emily."

She wasn't sure if it was wise to link him with Emily like that, but he smiled. "My dear—thank you. It's a great honor to be bracketed with Emily."

Laura let her head fall down against his chest. The sound of his heartbeat was strong and reassuring beneath her ear. Whatever was to come, for him, between them, right now he was here, alive and vibrant and in her arms. "They've seemed better," she said. "So far as I can tell. They laugh more. And there are fewer of those unexpected silences. And she's been helping him with his speeches. She wasn't for a while."

"A good sign."

"I thought so. I think if anything they talk about politics more. And she challenges him more. Of course, it's all inference. I don't think a detached observer would notice anything was wrong."

"You're one of the most astute observers I know."

"And I got in the habit of observing them when I was reporting to Trenchard."

Raoul's hand stilled on her hair.

Laura lifted her head. "You aren't the only one to question your past actions."

Raoul's eyes had darkened the way they still did at mention of Trenchard. "One of my great regrets is that I never got to call the duke to account."

"That wouldn't have helped anything."

"But it would have been highly satisfying."

Malcolm pushed the door of his and Suzanne's bedchamber to. "I suppose it's just possible a man dropped the bracelet."

"It could have been a gift for a mistress." Suzanne undid the ties on her cloak and dropped it on the dressing table bench. "Or perhaps his mistress or wife put it in his pocket and it fell out. I've done that with you when a clasp is loose."

Malcolm pulled the gold-and-carnelian bracelet from his pocket. Roth had suggested they keep it for now. "The clasp appears fine. It's also possible the intruder sometimes dressed as a woman. Or perhaps more accurately sometimes became a woman."

"And forgot to remove the bracelet when changing clothes?" Suzanne struck a flint and lit the tapers on her dressing table.

"Again possible. But not likely. The likeliest explanation, especially given the long hair I found and David's description of the intruder as slight, is that the intruder was a woman in all guises."

"Who still would have had to leave the bracelet on when donning clothing for the break-in," Suzanne said. "But I've been known to do that when making a quick change."

"Which doesn't get us any closer to knowing who broke in." Malcolm held the bracelet up to the light of the lamp on the table by the door for a moment, watching the play of light on the carnelians, then set it down. "Or to what they thought Craven possessed that they risked two break-ins to recover."

Suzanne dropped down on her dressing table bench. "That bracelet could support Sue Kettering and her child for a year. I doubt it belonged to a confederate of Ben Coventry's."

"So do I." Malcolm prowled across the room. "And we know Fitzroy engaged Ennis to hire Coventry. Whatever Fitzroy's motives, it's difficult for me to see him hiring a woman for such a mission."

"He is the protective sort," Suzanne agreed. "Though he's seen what I can do. That is"—she swallowed—"some of what I can do. If he found the right person—"

"A female agent living in London who wears expensive jewels? I suppose Ennis might have found someone—he was in military intelligence. Or perhaps whoever broke into Brook Street tonight is the person who killed Coventry. Or the person who hired that person."

Suzanne rubbed her forehead. "I could see a mistress of Craven's searching for letters she'd written him. But if it's a love affair, it's more difficult to see Fitzroy wanting the papers."

"Unless it's a love affair of Wellington's." Malcolm's voice turned grim.

"And the woman who broke into Brook Street tonight was Wellington's mistress?" Suzanne frowned. "Darling, the break-in tonight was the work of a professional."

"A point." Malcolm shrugged out of his coat and stared at the black superfine. "You aside, there aren't many society beauties who could have pulled that off. It looks far more like the work of—"

"An agent."

Malcolm laid his coat over the tapestry chair back. "It's possible Wellington had a mistress who was an agent. Especially if he met her on the Continent. Given that Craven was an agent for Carfax, it's possible this same woman was also

Craven's mistress. But it's far more likely the papers and her motive for seeking them are political." His fingers whitened for a moment against the black fabric of his coat.

"Malcolm." Suzanne's fingers stilled, unfastening the garnet pendant he'd given her six weeks ago. "There are all sorts of people in London who are or have been agents. Most of them don't know about me."

"No." He started on his waistcoat buttons.

"It still seems likeliest the thief, or thieves, was after papers having to do with Carfax's use of Whateley & Company. And that this woman was either hired by Ennis and Fitzroy or was after the same papers on behalf of someone else." Suzanne glanced at the bracelet again. "She doesn't sound like anyone you worked with?"

"Most of the people I worked with were Spanish or Portuguese and are still on the Peninsula. I'll talk to Harry tomorrow. He may have an idea."

Suzanne turned on her dressing table bench to face the looking glass. There was little more to be learned tonight, and Malcolm had a tendency to brood when he thought the spy game might be touching too close to her. "At the least, this quite distracted me from any worries about Laura encountering Colonel Cuthbertson."

"Laura was bound to run into someone she knew in India." Malcolm was frowning, but he accepted the subject change. "Best perhaps to have got past that, and with someone like Cuthbertson. Harry says he's a good man, which is high praise from Harry."

Suzanne pulled one of her aquamarine earrings from her ear. "I think he and Laura were quite close in India."

"I hope so. I'd like to think she had men in her life other than Trenchard and Jack."

"You only had to see the way he looked at her crossing the salon at the Tavistock to know he's still fond of her." Suzanne unfastened her second earring. "And from the way she looked talking with him, I'd say she's still fond of him."

"I don't have to point out to you, of all people, that one can continue to care for a former lover, do I?"

Suzanne met her husband's gaze in the dressing table looking glass. They didn't talk about Raoul a great deal, but they did manage now to discuss him on occasion. Malcolm's forbearance, in this, as in so many other things, was remarkable. But something always tightened within her chest at such moments, as though she was waiting for him to snap. "Of course not," she said. "I suppose I'm just afraid that in Laura's case"—she laid a bit more emphasis on "Laura's case" than was perhaps required—"it might be something more."

"I suppose it could." Malcolm tossed his waistcoat after the coat. "Laura's her own person, with the right to make her own decisions. And close as we've all become, it would be folly to think we know what goes on in her head." He started on his shirt cuffs. "But for what it's worth, I don't think it likely."

Suzanne tugged two of Blanca's carefully arranged pins from her hair. "I just don't want him to be hurt."

This time it was Malcolm's gaze that locked on her own in the looking glass. It held understanding and a concern that echoed her own. No need, his gaze told her, to ask whom she meant by "him." "Nor do I."

She drew a sharp breath.

Malcolm continued to unfasten his shirt cuffs, with perhaps a bit more concentration than the act required. "In all the years I've known O'Roarke, I don't think I've ever seen him as happy as he was on his last visit. And yes, his happiness does matter to me."

Malcolm dragged his shirt over his head. Suzanne sat still, stunned by the admission her husband had just made. As usual, Malcolm managed to make his most important declarations at the most trivial moments, wrapped up in the minutia of everyday life.

Malcolm tossed his shirt after his coat and waistcoat. "You, on the other hand, could be pardoned for having somewhat conflicted feelings."

Suzanne looked at her husband, bare-chested, his hair disordered and falling over his forehead. Vulnerable in ways that went far beyond the physical. His gaze demanded nothing but said he would listen to whatever she wanted to confide. Would he have let his guard down, she wondered, if he hadn't wanted to give her the chance to talk? How very like the generous, maddening, remarkable man she had married.

She turned round on the dressing table bench, meeting his gaze without the filter of the looking glass. "I wasn't sure how I'd feel," she said. "If he ever—But I'm happy, truly. Of course, I've had a twinge now and then. Sort of for old times' sake. But mostly I'm just glad that Raoul can—that they both can—let themselves be happy. And relieved—"

"That it doesn't really change anything between you and O'Roarke?"

Suzanne swallowed. Trust Malcolm to put into words something she hadn't fully articulated to herself yet. She hesitated, but she owed him honesty for honesty.

"I'm glad," he said. Her surprise must have shown on her face, for he smiled. "I don't want you to lose what you have with O'Roarke. I may not fully understand what he means to you, but I have enough of a sense of it to know how important he is to your happiness."

"He's not—" She spoke quickly, because it seemed vitally important Malcolm not misunderstand.

"He is, Mel."

"You have a right to be angry, Malcolm. Sometimes I wish—"

"That I'd what? Rant? Forbid O'Roarke the house? Plant him a facer?" Malcolm crossed to the dressing table bench and dropped down beside her. "I'm not jealous. Not in that way. Mostly not in that way."

She scanned his face, seeking clues. She felt as though they were stepping on glass. At some point they were going to have to talk about this, but saying the wrong thing could be worse than not talking about it at all. "Malcolm, I know there must be times—"

He took her hand and looked down at their linked fingers. "I'm not worried about whose bed you're in. You're in mine"—he smiled—"to my constant amazement—and you seem happy there. You could have left in the past if you'd wanted to. But—you and O'Roarke shared a cause. You were partners."

"We deceived you."

"There is that. But I think I've got past raging at myself for being a fool. But—I think O'Roarke sees a part of you I don't. He sees you in a way I never will."

"Darling—" Instead of stepping round glass, she now felt as if the glass was bottled up in her throat. She couldn't deny it. If Malcolm ever did see her completely, she still wasn't sure he'd like her very much. "That's nothing beside what you and I share. The children. The speeches and articles we've written together. The cases we've investigated. The home we've made."

"You've made." He gave another quick smile. "He's your past, and in a way the only family you have left. Having dragged you into this life, I'd be a selfish brute if I wanted to deny you that."

She shook her head. "You didn't drag me into anything, Malcolm. Raoul and I—"

"Brilliant as you are, you and O'Roarke couldn't have done anything if I hadn't asked you to marry me."

"That's—"

"Perhaps not the whole truth, but a piece of it." He lifted a hand to push her loosened hair behind her ear. "There are things I shared with David growing up that I'll never share with anyone else." His gaze was steady on her face, but she sensed he was choosing his words with the care of one moving round mines and mantraps. It was always that way on the rare occasions Malcolm talked about his feelings. As though he feared that a wrong step would lay an emotional demand he had no right to make. "That will always be between us. It doesn't lessen what I share with you or what David shares with Simon. But it's an unshakable bond. I think it's much the same for you and O'Roarke, for all there was never anything romantic between David and me." He gave a faint smile. "Despite the rumors."

She nodded, afraid to speak. "It's very like that, dearest. But I wasn't sure you'd ever understand."

"I'm trying. And if O'Roarke's forming a romantic attachment doesn't affect what's between the two of you—Well, you can't blame me for being pleased at the corollary, can you?"

She turned her head, pressing her cheek against his hand. "Darling—" Her voice was thick.

"There's still a lot to sort out," he said. "But I'm managing some of it. Including the fact that I'd just as soon O'Roarke not disappear from our lives either." His slid his hand down so he could wrap his arm about her.

Suzanne leaned against the comforting warmth of his shoulder. "Laura cares for him. And he's got her through a hell I can scarcely contemplate. But I can't tell—"

Malcolm's fingers stirred against her collarbone, above the black satin that edged the neck of her gown. "Nor can I. I think it rather comes down to what Laura decides she wants as she comes back to herself. And if O'Roarke can give it to her."

Suzanne lifted her head from her husband's shoulder to look at him.

"He doesn't give of himself easily," Malcolm said. "I know a bit about that. One might say I inherited it from him. You know better than any how difficult that can be to live with."

"You're not nearly as difficult to live with as you claim, dearest. And you put your family first. Raoul's never going to stop tilting at dangerous windmills." She shivered, because she was keenly aware these days of just how dangerous those windmills were.

Malcolm tightened his arm round her. "You don't find it a bit ironic that we're trying to arrange O'Roarke's life for him, given his tendency to try to do the same to us?"

"No. Well, perhaps a bit. But one could say we're balancing the scales. Or returning the favor. He's not remotely as well able to take care of himself as he thinks."

18

Laura walked into the breakfast parlor with Emily, who had come bounding into her room in the early hours of the morning. Fortunately, some time before that, Raoul had kissed her and slipped from the bed and then back out the window. He'd been asleep—she'd woken once to feel the even stir of his breath and to see his face relaxed as it so seldom was—but he had an uncanny knack for waking at just the right moment.

Jessica was in Suzanne's lap, displaying her dexterity at eating cut melon with a fork. Colin was finishing a bowl of porridge and peppering his parents with questions about the Julio-Claudian emperors stirred by a talk with Uncle Harry.

Emily released Laura's hand and ran over to Colin. Laura bent to pet Berowne, who was lapping a saucer of milk on the floor, and went to pour herself a cup of coffee, feeling as though the events of the previous night were somehow branded on her forehead. Given how long she had effectively been a spy in the Rannoch household, it was ironic that now so many secrets were in the open she was acutely aware of dissembling in front of Suzanne and Malcolm.

Malcolm and Suzanne greeted her with careless smiles that gave no indication that either of them had any notion of her late-night visitor. But then they were experts at dissembling too.

"But what did Caligula do that was so awful?" Colin asked. "Uncle Harry usually explains things, but he wouldn't really explain that."

"It's like he put a spell on people," Emily said.

Malcolm and Suzanne exchanged glances over the children's heads. "Caligula wasn't a very good ruler," Malcolm said. "At least according to many sources." Malcolm Rannoch was scrupulously fair-minded and an excellent scholar.

"You mean he passed Corn Laws and suspended Habeas Corpus?" Colin asked.

"Something like that," Malcolm said.

Colin frowned. "It has to be more than that or you'd tell me more."

Laura dropped down at the table and reached for a piece of toast, just as the door opened and the man she had spent the night with walked into the room.

"Uncle Raoul." Caligula forgot, Colin sprang to his feet, closely followed by Emily and Jessica. Raoul was lost in a tangle of childish arms and legs as all three children hurled themselves at him.

Laura saw relief flash into Suzanne's eyes. More surprisingly, she saw the same relief cross Malcolm's face. Malcolm might not know about the messages his wife and Laura had sent to Raoul, but they were all relieved to see him unhurt.

"O'Roarke." Malcolm gave a quick smile. "I was wondering when you'd put in an appearance."

Raoul scooped up Jessica and moved to the table with Colin and Emily on either side of him. "Forgive me for not writing in advance. I was able to get away unexpectedly."

"If you sent advance notice, we'd all be sure something was wrong." Suzanne poured a cup of coffee and set it in front of the chair Raoul had moved to.

"I'm sorry I missed your birthday, Colin," Raoul said. "But I've some presents in my bags."

Colin grinned. In point of fact, Laura suspected Raoul had deliberately avoided arriving for Colin's birthday for fear of intruding. "We didn't think you'd be able to get back from Spain again so soon," she said, realizing something was required from her if Suzanne and Malcolm weren't to guess that she'd already seen Raoul. Oh, devil take it, they'd probably guess anyway. Not that it really mattered. It wasn't as though they weren't both well aware of her relationship with Raoul.

"I was still in France, as it happens." Raoul sat down, Jessica in his lap, and pulled Emily up onto his other knee. "I had business that pulled me back to London."

That was a private message, for all he wasn't looking at her, and very agreeable even if not precisely prudent.

"Can you make us another boat?" Colin scrambled onto the chair next to Raoul.

"Can we go to the park?" Emily asked.

"I can certainly make another boat," Raoul said, taking a sip of coffee before Jessica could reach for the cup. "And the park sounds like an excellent idea, if your parents agree."

Laura had no doubt that he genuinely wanted to spend time with the children. But she also understood the spy game enough to know it would provide the perfect cover for him to talk to Suzanne.

Malcolm swallowed the last of his coffee and pushed himself to his feet. "I need to see Harry. We're in the midst of an investigation, as it happens, O'Roarke. Suzette and Laura can catch you up on the details. It would be good to have your perspective. We're going to a ball at the Lydgates' tonight. I'm sure they'd want you to join us." He bent to kiss Suzanne. "If not before, I'll see you all at dinner."

Suzanne released her breath, gaze on Colin and Emily scrambling up a tree and Jessica reaching up to grasp a branch from Laura's arms. "Thank you," she said, keenly aware of Raoul standing beside her.

"Of course. You couldn't have thought I wouldn't come."

"I wasn't sure you'd be able to. At least, not so soon." Colin was pulling Jessica up to sit on a branch. Laura steadied her.

"I was already on my way to London, as it happens. England has an unusual pull on me these days."

Suzanne shot a look at her former lover. "I'm glad. Laura's missed you."

Raoul's gaze lingered on Laura. "I've missed her."

After seeing the careful casualness of Raoul's and Laura's greetings to each other in the breakfast parlor this morning, Suzanne was quite sure Raoul had slipped into Laura's room during the night. She had no desire to dwell on the details, but she was rather glad he could act on emotional impulse.

"Not that she'd say so," Suzanne added. "She's very like you in a number of ways."

"She's getting out more. That's good."

"I think she's remembering there are things she liked about society. I don't think she'll ever go back to the girl she was."

"It's good for her to live a less confined life."

"You mean so she can meet a sadly conventional man and marry him?"

"I don't think Laura would look twice at a sadly conventional man. But"—he stared down at his hands—"she deserves a lot more than I can offer her."

Suzanne put a hand on his shoulder. "Malcolm deserves better than me. But we're what they've got. And what seems to make them happy."

Raoul gave a wry smile.

Suzanne gripped her hands together. "I didn't tell her. I haven't told Malcolm."

"So I gathered."

"And you think I'm a fool."

"I assume you have your reasons." He glanced at Laura and children, lifted his hand to return a wave from Emily, then looked back at Suzanne. "What is it, *querida?*"

She drew a breath. Suddenly she wasn't sure she wanted the answer. "Is there a plan to get Bonaparte off St. Helena?"

Raoul stared at her with naked shock. At least, seemingly naked shock. With him one could never be sure.

"Damn it, I know." The impossibility tore at her chest, a knife twisting in an old wound. "You probably wouldn't tell me even if there were. I'm not sure I want to know. But—"

"What have you heard?" Raoul asked in a level voice.

"It was a man who called himself Louis Germont, who Bertrand just got out of Paris. Germont was wounded, and I tended him two nights ago at Marthe's house. He was feverish, but he definitely mentioned the Phoenix. You know what that's always meant."

"What did he say about it?" Raoul's gaze was level, his voice tense.

"Just that he had to warn someone. And then he slipped out of Marthe's house in the middle of the night." She swallowed a bite of frustration. "I should have—"

"No sense refining upon that now. Have you—"

"Sancho was approached about the plot, and he went to Manon. Flahaut was approached as well."

She saw the flinch in Raoul's eyes. Flahaut wasn't a trained agent. And his high-profile position and connection to the Bonaparte family left him very exposed.

"None of them are involved in the plot," she said. "At least, not that they admitted to me. And then last night Manon told me Jennifer Mansfield was approached, but by a man who sounds like Germont. Which means his warning to me was probably an effort to embroil me in the plot."

"And you were afraid Malcolm—"

"I couldn't put him in that situation. I couldn't ask him to keep secrets that were treason. And I couldn't—"

"Yes?" Raoul said.

Suzanne swallowed. A gust of wind off the Serpentine cut more sharply than one would expect in June. The ribbons on her bonnet seemed to bite into her skin. "God help me, I'm not sure I want Bonaparte to escape. But I'm not sure I don't want it either."

"There's no denying it would turn our lives upside down," Raoul said. "There's also no denying there are some things in France now it would be good to turn upside down." He regarded Suzanne for a moment. His gaze was steady, but his eyes were the gray of turbulent seas. "I know of no such plot. I have no idea if you'll believe me. I don't know that I would, in your shoes."

Suzanne released her breath. Her chest ached with what might have been relief. "I believe you. Which may mean I've gone dangerously soft."

Raoul's mouth lifted with familiar irony. "That doesn't mean there isn't a plot. Things are more diffuse these days."

"You still have your ear to the ground."

Raoul glanced ahead at Laura and the children. They had moved to the water's edge, and Laura was passing out bread to throw to the ducks." "It could be a trap."

"To draw us in?"

"Or other Bonapartist agents. That would fit with this Germont's approach to you." He waved again and Jessica waved back with enthusiasm. She was dancing on the balls of her feet while Laura crouched down behind her, holding her steady. "Whatever it is, Malcolm is likely to learn the truth."

Suzanne's fingers clenched on the jaconet of her skirt. "You think I should tell him."

"I think it's your decision, and a difficult one."

"I'd be putting him in an appalling dilemma. I can't ask him to protect my friends at the cost of his country."

"You don't know that your friends are involved."

Jessica was leaning out over the water, bread in her hand, Laura's arm securely round her. "I'm going to tell him." Until she said the words, Suzanne hadn't been quite sure that was her decision. "Before I did, I needed to be sure—that you weren't involved."

"That's more consideration than I deserve, *querida*."

"I couldn't do that to you. But more important, I couldn't put Malcolm in a situation where he felt he had to betray you."

Raoul was silent for a moment. His gaze moved over the water, though she was keenly aware of its pressure. The wind carried back an excited cry from Jessica.

"Putting personal considerations ahead of larger loyalties," Suzanne said. "Malcolm should appreciate that I'm starting to think like him."

Raoul's breath grated through the air. "If there is a plot—"

"Do you want there to be?"

She saw the tug of competing loyalties in his gaze. "I want what's best for France. And I want you as far away from it as possible."

She gave a quick smile, scrabbling for her defenses. "Nothing to be done until we know more."

"No," he agreed. "I'll make some inquiries. I have a few sources you don't."

"And they may be more likely to admit knowledge of a plot to you than to the wife of a British agent."

"Possibly. As you say, we need to learn more before we can speculate." He drew a breath, as though warding off what the future might hold. "Speaking of speculating, tell me about this investigation."

"Didn't Laura tell you about it last night?"

He shot a look at her.

"Sorry," Suzanne said. "I'm still rather proud when I can see past your deceptions."

His mouth twisted in a smile that was faint but less dry than usual. "I always knew we hadn't a prayer of deceiving you and Malcolm. Especially after last April."

"But you still felt obliged to climb in the window? And then back out again—or did you go out the door?"

"The window. You have an excellent and very trustworthy staff, but I was trying to preserve Laura's reputation."

"You're a remarkably thoughtful man, Raoul."

"Don't talk twaddle, *querida*. Do you want to tell me about the investigation? You needn't, if you'd rather not."

"No, I'd welcome your perspective." She outlined the Whateley & Company investigation as concisely as she could. Raoul listened in focused silence.

"Clever of Carfax," he said when she had done. "Something like Whateley & Company would have been extremely useful during the war."

"But you never had anything like it?"

"Do you imagine I could have kept it from you?" Raoul frowned. "Unless Ennis is lying about only engaging Coventry, Coventry must have been killed by someone hired by someone else."

"Presumably the same person who broke into Brook Street last night. The carnelian bracelet doesn't put you in mind of any agents you knew in the Peninsula, does it?"

"No, but I can hardly claim an intimate acquaintance with the jewelry of every agent I worked with. Or worked against."

"Simon tackled the intruder outside the nursery." Suzanne's gaze moved ahead to Laura and the children. "Probably coincidence that the thief was escaping that way. But somehow that, on top of the threats by the men two nights ago—"

"You're doing everything you can to protect the children. As you always have." Raoul's voice was steady, but his gaze had gone to the children as well. Emily was kneeling on a rock outcropping to toss bread to the ducks and appeared to be having a conversation with them. Colin was holding her hand, part in comradeship, Suzanne thought, part to steady her. A few feet away, Jessica had snatched up a leaf and was holding it out to Laura.

"You don't ever forget," Raoul said, "no matter how far you are away from them."

"No," Suzanne said.

19

Harry stared down at the bracelet, glittering in a patch of morning sunlight on his desktop. "You're sure the intruder dropped this?"

"As sure as can be," Malcolm said. "It was by the window the intruder escaped out of. David and Simon didn't recognize it, and it was on the passage floor outside the nursery, where it's unlikely a guest would have dropped it."

"No." Harry's gaze continued trained on the bracelet, neutral in a way it only was when he was holding his feelings in check. In a way he rarely did with Malcolm these days. "I don't suppose she would have been a guest there."

"Harry?" Malcolm asked. "You recognize the bracelet?"

"Oh, yes." Harry looked up and met Malcolm's gaze, though his own was still armored. "I bought it."

Malcolm stared at his friend. It seemed highly unlikely the bracelet was Cordelia's, for any number of reasons. "Harry—"

Harry touched one of the carnelians. "I think your intruder is a woman named Maria Monreal. I know her. Or, at least I knew her. In the Peninsula. She's a Spanish noblewoman whose husband died fighting with the guerrilleros. At least that's the story she told when she offered her services to British intelligence."

"And you worked with her." Malcolm had worked with Harry in the Peninsula on more than one occasion, but there was much about his friend's work in military intelligence that he did not know.

"On a few missions. On one of which I gave her the brace-let. Presented it to her ostentatiously in a crowd in a tavern, as it happens. She was posing as my mistress and it needed to look believable."

That sounded more like Harry than the more conventional explanation when a man gave a woman a piece of jewelry. And yet—"Did you have any idea she was in London?" Malcolm asked.

Harry nodded. "She settled here after the war. I saw her once. When she needed assistance."

Which was more noteworthy, because since Harry had been back in London, he and Cordelia had been reconciled. "Do you think she'll tell you the truth about the Brook Street break-in?" Malcolm asked.

"I don't know. But I probably stand a better chance of getting the truth from her than you do. I'll just have to explain it to Cordy."

Malcolm studied his friend. Close as they were, neither pressed the other for confidences. Quite the reverse. Their friendship in some ways was built on their mutual understanding of the other's secrets. And yet they did confide in each other. More perhaps than in other friends. Despite the fact that he'd known Harry for much of the time Harry and Cordelia had been apart, Malcolm had never known Harry to so much as look at another woman.

Davenport's gaze was steady, though a touch of color stained his cheeks. "Not that I had as varied a career as Cordy in the years we were apart. But Maria was one of my few—transgressions, or whatever one chooses to call it."

Malcolm swallowed. Odd how one could know someone so well and yet still feel awkward round certain topics. "You know how fond I am of Cordy, but I imagine she'd be the first to agree that anything you did in the time the two of you were apart hardly counts as part of your marriage. Not the marriage you have now."

"Perhaps. Perhaps what I'm really afraid of is how little it may matter to her." Harry gave a twisted smile. "Always difficult to be rational about these things. Even when one prides oneself on one's rationality."

And always difficult to know how to talk about them, even to a friend with whom one shared so much. "I think you're wise to honest about it."

"Is that what you do with Suzanne?" Harry's color deepened. "Not that—"

"I have past indiscretions to confess to? True enough. None since my marriage."

"That," said Harry, "is blatantly obvious."

Malcolm cast a sidelong glance at his friend. "I don't know whether that's a compliment or an aspersion, Davenport."

"My dear fellow, what do you think?"

Malcolm grinned and felt some of the tension drain from his shoulders. "But that doesn't mean there aren't things I have to confess to Suzanne." Memories shot through his mind. The night he'd proposed on a balcony overlooking the River Tagus in Lisbon, what he'd told Suzanne, and what he hadn't. Staring at her in Vienna over the murdered body of Tatiana Kirsanova, knowing Suzanne believed Tatiana to be his mistress, unable to say Tania was in fact his sister. Handing papers over to Wellington that would expose a French spy ring, the guilt rank in his throat, a guilt he hadn't shared with her for over a year, though he hadn't yet known she was a French agent herself.

"And you're honest about it." Harry's tone made it not quite a question.

"Yes. Most of the time." Malcolm gave an abashed smile that he hoped covered the multitude of issues between him and Suzanne that he was keeping from Harry.

"Impossible to manage honesty all the time, isn't it?" Harry stared across his study at a pastel drawing Livia had done of her stuffed cat. "I suppose—I never thought to have what I have with Cordy. Sometimes I even forget how precariously balanced it is. But I never forget for long."

"And you fear this could upset that balance?"

Harry nodded.

"I can see that. Speaking as one who's all too aware of the fragility of any relationship. But surely it's better if she learns it from you."

"I think so." Harry drew a rough breath that trembled with the fragility of hope. "I hope so."

Cordelia looked up from the table in the nursery where she and Livia sat together over a slate and a book. Her husband stood in the doorway, watching them with that smile she sometimes saw in his eyes when he looked at her and the children but didn't realize they were watching. She looked up and smiled at him. An answering smile crossed his face. Along with a concern she hadn't noticed before.

"Malcolm was just here," he said. "I need to go out for a bit."

"Of course." Not surprising, given that they were in the midst of an investigation. But something in Harry's gaze made

Cordelia kiss Livia's hair and say, "See how far you can read ahead, darling. I need to talk to Daddy for a minute." She glanced towards the hearthrug, where Drusilla sat playing with blocks, then moved to the doorway and took her husband's hand. "Is everything all right?"

Harry cast a glance at their daughters, then drew her into the passage. "Someone broke into the Craven house in Brook Street last night. David and Simon and the children are fine," he added quickly, in response to the concern that must have showed in her eyes. "Malcolm and Suzanne went there last night. They found a bracelet the intruder apparently dropped. It seems to belong to a woman I knew in the Peninsula. Maria Monreal. She worked as an agent for the British and then settled in London."

"My God." Cordelia leaned against the doorjamb and looked up at her husband. "It seems we can't turn round without fairly tripping over someone one of us knew. Though given the number of former agents who've sought refuge in England, I suppose it isn't as surprising as it seems at first blush."

"Perhaps not." Harry's gaze was fixed closely on a patch of light from the nursery windows spilling onto the passage carpet, as though it presented an unusual conundrum. "So I've told Malcolm I'll talk to her. She may speak more freely to me."

"That makes sense." Cordelia glanced into the nursery at a cry from Drusilla, ascertained that it was a crow of delight, and looked back at Harry. "I know you've been itching to get involved."

"Perhaps. And yes, it does make sense." Harry shifted his weight from one foot to the other. "But it does rather put us in the position we were in in Paris when the investigation involved Edmond Talleyrand and Gui."

It was a moment before she understood. Her hands closed on the doorjamb, so hard a splinter went into her palm. Damn. She'd always known Harry hadn't been celibate in the time they'd been apart. Once or twice he'd come out and admitted it. But she'd never had a name. Let alone the name of someone he knew well enough to have a relationship he could put to use in the course of an investigation.

Which, of course, was no more than she'd done with Edmond Talleyrand and Gui Laclos. She'd even admitted to caring for Gui. She should be relieved Harry had found consolation. It should help balance the scales a bit. She had no right to be jealous. Which made it all the worse that she was.

She met Harry's gaze with a determined smile. "I don't see why that should be a problem. It's long past my turn to be forbearing."

Harry watched her for a moment with the gaze she couldn't read easily but which always seemed to see so much. "Speaking from personal experience, knowing one should understand isn't the same as understanding."

"So you're saying it was more difficult for you when I had to talk to Edmond and Gui than you admitted at the time?" she asked.

Harry leaned against the doorjamb opposite her. "No comment."

The light in the passage was shadowy, but it caught other scars in his gaze. Old wounds, wounds she had perhaps reopened without thinking in the course of their investigations in Paris and London. "I wouldn't have talked to them if you'd told me it disturbed you in the least."

"Which is precisely why I didn't say anything."

"Well, then." What they had almost lost, what they had and how precious it was, hung between them. "You can't think

I won't rise to the challenge." She glanced into the nursery again. Livia's head was bent over her book. Drusilla was on her stomach, lining the smaller of her dolls up in front of her block tower. Cordelia turned back to Harry, angling herself to pitch her voice away from the nursery. "Tell me about her. Not those details, but—You know what I mean. I'd rather understand."

"I met her on a mission," Harry said. "Well, pretty much everything I did in the Peninsula involved a mission one way or another. Liaising with a group of guerrilleros in this case. They were delayed and Maria and I were stuck together in a Spanish village for a fortnight."

"Boredom." Cordelia managed a smile. "Odd how it can be an aphrodisiac."

"I suppose so, in a way. It wasn't—It was a diversion." Harry dragged the toe of one of his boots over the carpet. "But I suppose you could say we were friends, after a fashion." He looked up at her with a crooked smile. "At the time, it never occurred to me that it would ever bother you."

She bit her lip. For some reason that cut through her even more. "I think it would have, even then. Though I wouldn't have admitted it." What had she been doing when Harry formed a liaison with this woman? Playing cards at a house party, sipping champagne by the Thames, waltzing in the heat of an overcrowded ballroom? Whose bed had she been sharing? "Did you see her again after that?"

"Once or twice on missions."

Cordelia's throat tightened. He didn't say whether or not he'd slept with her again, but in a sense it didn't matter. In the years since she and Harry had reconciled and she had met the Rannochs, Cordelia had seen just how much agents could share on missions, and how strong were the bonds that could form. Those bonds in some ways seemed more of a threat than physical intimacy. She knew full well how cheap one could hold that. "And in London?"

"In public a few times. Once when she needed my assistance." He hesitated. "I'd have told you, but—"

"You were helping a fellow agent. Telling me could have jeopardized the mission."

"Cordelia—" Harry put out a hand in the shadows, then let it fall to his side. "You told me in Brussels that you wouldn't share anyone else's bed in the future. It occurs to me that I didn't say the same. But—"

"You didn't need to make promises, Harry." Her throat had gone thick. "I know you. Once our vows were real again you wouldn't betray them."

He gave a twisted smile. "You sound very certain."

"I am." Probably a deal more certain than he was about her, she realized. With good cause.

Harry's gaze lingered on her face. His eyes were dark, yet strangely open. "Even in the Peninsula. It couldn't ever have become more than a diversion."

"You were in the middle of a war."

"I was still besotted with my wife."

For the first time, Cordelia wondered about the life Harry might have had if they hadn't met, if she hadn't danced with him that night at Devonshire House, if he hadn't tumbled so desperately and inexplicably into love with her, if she hadn't accepted his proposal. Who might he have met and loved if he hadn't been wasting his heart on a woman who didn't deserve him? "You wasted a lot of time on me."

His smile deepened. "I wouldn't say it was wasted."

"No?"

"You're here with me now."

Cordelia went to her husband's side and put her arms round him, feeling the warmth of his skin through the layers of shirt and waistcoat and coat. "I don't deserve you, Harry." She pressed her lips to his jaw. "Perhaps that makes me anxious more than anything."

He pulled her out of view of the nursery and kissed her with unexpected fierceness. "My dear girl. If you think you have anything to fear, you don't know me at all."

Cordelia returned his embrace. And yet this Maria Monreal meant enough to Harry for him to call her a friend. Harry had few friends, and he didn't take any of them lightly.

Malcolm pushed shut the door of Fitzroy's study. "Did Wellington have you investigating Whateley & Company?"

Fitzroy pushed himself to his feet. "Malcolm, I told you—"

"That was before I knew Carfax is running Whateley & Company as his own private service to smuggle information."

The start of surprise in Fitzroy's gaze seemed genuine. But while his friend wasn't an agent, he was experienced enough to know something of deception.

"Let me tell you what I think happened," Malcolm said. "You can nod or let me try to read it in your face. Wellington got wind of what Carfax was doing. Perhaps of a specific mission he disagreed with. Carfax has been known to make some unsavory alliances. He asked you to investigate. Somehow you or Wellington learned enough to determine there were likely papers in the warehouse you wanted to get a look at. You needed someone to break in. Someone who couldn't easily be traced back to you. Someone who wouldn't ask questions, as Davenport or I would have done. So you went to your friend,

Ennis, who engaged his friend, Coventry. You didn't realize someone else was after the papers or that Coventry might end up dead—"

"Malcolm, no." Fitzroy's voice cut across the room with sudden force.

"No, what?" Malcolm asked.

Fitzroy scraped a hand through his hair. "I suppose I should be relieved even you can be wrong. But I can't bear to see you putting together false theories. Especially involving the duke." He regarded Malcolm for a moment. "Is that why you said all that? To get me to talk?"

"No." Malcolm leaned against the table, hands braced behind him. "I really thought I was on the right track. But I'm glad my theory was at least good for something. Go on."

Fitzroy drew a rough breath and took a turn about the room. "You know—You *know*, Malcolm, how much I trust you. I've trusted you with my life. I'd willingly do so again. I'd trust you with Harriet and our children without a second thought. No man more so. But there's such a thing as a confidence. When a friend, someone one trusts, asks one to do a thing and keep it in confidence, one doesn't ask questions. And one respects the confidence."

Malcolm met his friend's gaze. Unusual to see such torment on Fitzroy's usually equable face. "Someone asked you to find someone to break into Whateley & Company and asked you to keep it in confidence?"

Fitzroy drew a breath. "If that were the case, I could hardly tell you without breaking the confidence."

"Who?"

"And I certainly couldn't answer that."

"Fitzroy, a man is dead."

"And nothing I tell you can change that." Fitzroy's sunny face could take on an unusually stubborn set.

"And someone broke into the Craven house in Brook Street last night. The intruder got out the window, but only after Simon tackled them only feet away from the nursery."

"Good God." The shock in Fitzroy's gaze again appeared genuine. "Are David and Simon and the children all right?"

"Yes, though they had a scare." Malcolm fixed his friend with a hard stare. "Ennis came to see you yesterday. It wasn't to orchestrate this?"

"Malcolm"—Fitzroy's voice shook with what seemed like outrage—"do you really think I'd have anything to do with breaking into the home of a friend? Where children were sleeping? Who have already been through far too much?"

Malcolm continued to hold Fitzroy's gaze for a long moment. One could never be certain of anything. But he was strongly inclined to believe Fitzroy was telling the truth in this at least.

Which only made the situation more complicated.

20

Cordelia and her daughters were waiting in Berkeley Square when Suzanne, Laura, and Raoul returned with the children. That wasn't surprising. Livia did lessons with Colin and Emily most afternoons. But the concern Suzanne caught at the back of her friend's gaze was another matter. She waited until Laura had taken the three older children up to the nursery, and Raoul had left to "call on friends" (or, in other words, to make inquiries about the Phoenix plot). At last, when she and Cordelia were settled in the small salon with a tea tray and Jessica and Drusilla playing on the carpet at their feet, Suzanne said, "Cordy? Is something wrong?"

"No. That is—" Cordelia set down her teacup and drew a breath. "Harry recognized the bracelet dropped by the woman who broke into the Brook Street house last night. He's questioning her. She's someone he worked with in the Peninsula."

"Thank goodness, we weren't sure we'd—" Suzanne stared at her friend, taking in the taut confusion in Cordelia's gaze. "Oh, dearest. I'm sorry. It can't be easy."

"I'm being silly." Cordelia cast a quick glance at Drusilla and Jessica, pulling a collection of dolls out of a wicker basket, then looked back at Suzanne. "I knew he wouldn't have been celibate the entire time we were apart. He admitted as much to me. I confess I felt a small twinge, but I told myself I had no right to feel it and didn't let myself dwell on the possibilities. Well, not much at any rate." She took another sip of tea. "It's different somehow. Having a name. Not to mention knowing he's talking to her." She stared into her cup.

Not for the first time, Suzanne wondered about Malcolm's past. Except for Tatiana Kirsanova, who had proved to be his sister, and a few eligible debutantes she knew had aspired to marry him, she'd never heard rumors about him and another woman. But he'd been five-and-twenty when they met and far from inexperienced. He was no rake. Which meant any past relationships were likely to have been longer term. She couldn't imagine Malcolm making love to a woman without being emotionally invested. Which in itself was unsettling.

She couldn't ask Malcolm, of course. Especially not now, when she had burdened him with so much else. When he was so scrupulously careful to leave her own past in the past.

"Cordy," she said, "Harry wouldn't—"

"No, of course not." Cordelia gave a quick smile, a bit too bright. "That is, I very much doubt it, and if I have any qualms it's no more than I deserve. Harry as much as said he never really forgot me. But it can't help but remind me that Harry might have had an entirely different life if he hadn't wasted time on me."

"I doubt Harry considers it wasted."

Cordelia set down her cup, hard enough to spatter tea in the saucer, and hugged her arms about herself. "Sometimes I wonder what Harry sees in me."

"Cordy, you can't be serious."

Drusilla and Jessica were tugging a doll between them. "Share," Cordelia said.

Suzanne got up to put another doll in Jessica's hand. When she returned to the sofa, Cordelia had pulled the cherry-colored gauze of her scarf close about her. "When we first met, Harry was dazzled by me. I think he imagined me as all sorts of things I'm not and never will be. He understands me now. So much better than he did at first. But I still think he thinks I'm a better person than I am."

It was so like the thoughts Suzanne sometimes had about Malcolm that the breath stopped in her throat. She realized she was clenching her pearl bracelet tight enough to snap it and forced herself to loose her fingers. "Perhaps you're the one who's too hard on yourself, Cordy."

Cordelia shrugged.

Drusilla pulled a white horse from the basket and held it out to Jessica. "I shared, Mummy."

Cordelia smiled at her daughter. "Excellent, darling." She looked at Suzanne. "It's funny. We want our children to learn to share. But it's damnably hard to share's one's spouse."

"There's sharing, and sharing," Suzanne said. "I don't think Harry would much welcome your wanting to share him. But—"

"I should trust him?"

"That, too. But when it comes to sharing, perhaps sharing your feelings with him wouldn't hurt."

Cordelia regarded her for a moment. "Is that what you do with Malcolm?"

Suzanne swallowed. Hard. "When I'm brave enough."

Malcolm found Carfax in the Morning Room at White's talking to the Duke of Wellington. Probably coincidence that two men connected to the Whateley & Company investigation happened to be in conversation, but Malcolm was wary of coincidence. Though still British ambassador to France, Wellington was in London for the upcoming Waterloo anniversary. Last night at the Tavistock Wellington had been talking to Carfax as well, along with Lord Liverpoool, the prime minister. Of course, that might indicate the duke was considering a government position when he gave up the ambassadorship. A post in the government would mark him as a Tory, but given the views Malcolm had heard Wellington espouse, that should hardly come as a surprise.

"Malcolm." Wellington greeted him with an easy smile that gave no hint that he knew anything of Malcolm's questions to Fitzroy. But while Wellington was blunt-spoken and impatient of pretense, Malcolm had also seen the duke be more than capable of deception when the situation required it. "I assume you're braving White's to meet with one of us. Carfax, at a guess? I heard a rumor you're in the midst of another investigation, though I couldn't quite make sense of what it's about."

Malcolm met the duke's gaze. "I'm still endeavoring to do so myself, sir."

Wellington gave a grunt of acknowledgement. "You'll work it out. Or Suzanne will. Caught a glimpse of her in the salon at the Tavistock last night. Along with the lovely Lady Tarrington. Glad she's going about. I remember her as a girl when I was in India, long before she married. Thought it a sad waste when I heard she'd married Jack Tarrington, truth to tell."

"No argument from me there," Malcolm said.

Wellington's eyes glinted in acknowledgement. "Cuthbertson looked quite taken with her last night."

"I believe he also knew her in India."

Wellington nodded again. "Good man, Cuthbertson. Solid." From the duke, that was high praise. He nodded to Carfax and moved off.

Carfax regarded Malcolm. "I suppose you're here about the break-in in Brook Street."

"Do you know everything that happens in London, sir?" Malcolm asked. Though in fact, his suspicions would have been roused if Carfax had claimed not to know.

"No, but I make it my business to know when it's in the homes of my children."

"You may not have trusted Craven with information, but someone thinks he possessed something worth recovering."

"Don't think I haven't been pondering that."

"Sir." Malcolm took a step forwards. "You have to stop pretending your business at Whateley & Company is unconnected to the break-in."

"Craven wasn't actively involved in Whateley & Company and yet the thieves went to Brook Street rather than to Eustace Whateley's home when they didn't find what they wanted. For that matter, if they were after something connected to something I was involved in, you'd think they'd have ransacked Carfax House."

"Even trained agents would hesitate to ransack Carfax House if they had a care for their lives." Yet Malcolm had to admit Carfax had a point. Still—Loyalties tugged in Malcolm's mind. Suzanne's words the night before echoed in his head. "Is there any chance Wellington was on to what you were doing with Whateley & Company?"

Carfax's brows snapped together. "What do you know?"

"Two can play at withholding information unless it's necessary, sir."

"I have no reason to think the duke knows anything about Whateley & Company."

"But if he did, he might not be happy about some of the uses you've put it to."

"One can hardly call Wellington effusive, but he's always been grateful for the information I've acquired for him."

"And he prefers not to ask questions about where the information comes from."

"Most people prefer not to ask questions when it comes to intelligence. But Wellington isn't squeamish."

Malcolm folded his arms across his chest. "Who were the guns that the thief saw at Whateley & Company intended for?"

Carfax hesitated. "Rebels in Naples."

"Why would you want to help rebels in Naples?"

"Because they had information about the Elsinore League." Carfax adjusted his spectacles. "I wouldn't say that to many people. But you, of all people, should appreciate why such information would be valuable."

It was a greater admission than Malcolm would have expected the earl to have made. And Carfax might well have made it precisely to disarm Malcolm.

"Wellington doesn't, as far as I know, know a great deal about the Elsinore League," Carfax continued. "But if he did, I think he'd agree with me."

That might well be true. And if Fitzroy was to be believed, he hadn't been acting for Wellington in any case. "It continues to look as though two people broke into Whateley & Company," Malcolm said. "The man Coventry and someone else who killed him. The intruder who broke into Brook Street appears to have been working for the second person as well."

"I understand you found a bracelet the intruder dropped," Carfax said.

Malcolm hesitated. But he wanted to see Carfax's response. "Harry thinks it belongs to a woman named Maria Monreal who was an agent in the Peninsula. Have you heard of her?"

Carfax's brows rose. "Interesting." He pushed his spectacles up on his nose. "Yes. You could say she was one of my agents, though I only met her once or twice. She was very capable. I saw her a few times more after she settled in London. I assumed she was retired. But it's difficult to leave the game, as you know. I suppose it's not entirely surprising someone hired her."

"You didn't hire her yourself?"

"To search the house where my son and grandchildren live?"

"They weren't hurt. If she'd succeeded, they might not even have known. And you might not have wanted to tell David about whatever it was you were after."

"Possibly. Assuming I really was after something."

Carfax sounded convincing. He might even have been telling the truth.

Harry had called once before at the neat house in Half Moon Street that was now Maria Monreal's abode. She'd wanted to get a message to a former contact in Spain and Harry had helped trace him. A former lover, he'd assumed, though he hadn't asked, just as he hadn't asked how she paid for this elegant house, small but exquisitely proportioned. The sort of house in which well-to-do widows lived. Or in which gentlemen set up their mistresses. But of course he hadn't asked about that either. There were a lot of things he'd never asked Maria. Even when they were at their most intimate, their relationship could hardly have been called—intimate.

Harry rang the bell at the glossy green-painted door. A maid answered, a bright-eyed young woman with coppery curls and a Yorkshire accent. She hadn't been there the last time he'd seen Maria. He gave her his card, fully prepared to hear Maria was not at home, but a few moments later the maid returned to say her mistress would receive him.

She conducted him up the stairs to a sunny parlor hung with pale green silk. Maria came forwards as the maid showed him in. He'd have known the sharp, proud bones of her face anywhere, yet in some ways she couldn't have looked more different. The hair that had been twisted into a loose knot or left tumbling over her shoulders in Spain was arranged in an intricate twist with ringlets spilling about her face, not natural curls but the sort it took Cordy or her maid a meticulous effort with the curling tongs to create. In the Peninsula she'd worn plain gowns of wool or cotton. Or sometimes breeches and a shirt. The few times he'd seen her in a more elaborate gown, it had usually been spattered with dust. Now she was in diaphanous muslin, embroidered and flounced and edged with pale green cording. Harry knew enough to recognize the elegant lines of a Parisian dressmaker.

But then he probably looked different as well. Civilian clothes. More scars, though most of those were hidden.

"It's good to see you," she said with a faint, familiar smile as the maid closed the door.

"You as well," Harry said, and then wondered if he'd betrayed Cordy by uttering the very words.

"I've wanted to talk to you many times," she said. "But it didn't precisely seem appropriate to call. I don't expect your wife knows about me." Her tone held just the faintest of questions.

"She didn't," Harry said. "She does now."

"I see." Those words too held a further question, and a sense that she wouldn't as yet push for more information. She dropped down on the sofa, one arm extended along its back, her flowered silk shawl trailing off her shoulder. "We didn't have much chance to talk the last time I saw you. I gather you've left the army?"

"Not precisely a sacrifice."

"And you're settled in London full time now?"

Harry moved to the chair opposite her and dropped into it. To treat the interview as too formal seemed to dignify too much the idea that there was a need for formality. "With my wife and daughters."

Her brows rose. "I forgot you had a second."

"Almost two years ago now."

Maria tilted her head back and regarded him for a long moment. He'd seen the same look in her eyes when she evaluated how to approach enemy terrain. "I remember you swearing you'd never so much as meet your wife again."

Harry could hear his voice, could see himself, so determined, so absolute. So defiantly sure he saw the world for what it was. So alone. "A lot of things have changed."

"You forgave her?" Maria's voice hovered somewhere between disbelief and scorn.

Harry saw his wife, pulling him into a desperate embrace at the Duchess of Richmond's ball, sitting beside his sickbed after Waterloo, smiling at him across their library with ink on her nose. "I'd say more we both decided to put the past behind us."

Maria shook her head, stirring the ringlets about her face. "You're either a fool or an incurable romantic, Harry."

"I'm certainly a fool. On occasion others have accused me of being a romantic. Not that I'd ever admit to it."

Maria adjusted her shawl. It slithered back off her shoulders. "I hope she realizes how fortunate she is."

"I don't know. I do know that every day I find I can scarcely believe my own good fortune."

Maria regarded him for a moment, her gaze now level and direct, the gaze of a comrade at arms. "I'm not surprised you're still in love with her. It was always plain to me that would never change. I am surprised you're apparently still existing in this state of newfound bliss. Especially after three years."

He saw the nursery before he'd left, Livia bent over her book, Drusilla arranging her dolls in a house of blocks, a glass of milk spilled, Cordelia blowing him a kiss from the floor where she was looking for a lost doll shoe, seemingly torn between frustration and laughter. "I wouldn't call it bliss. Everyday reality, which is much more agreeable."

"*Dios*, you're far gone."

"Perhaps. Perhaps it's a delusion I'll wake from." He kept his voice light, because he feared Maria might be closer to the truth than he'd ever want to admit. "But meanwhile, I'm happy in a way I'd once have sworn only fools or madmen could be."

Maria tilted her head to once side. "I worry about you, my dear. Do you really think she'll be faithful this time?"

Unbidden fear shot through him. Which it shouldn't, because he'd known Cordelia's being unfaithful was a possibility from the moment they reconciled. "I don't know," he said. "I think she means to be now. And that counts for a lot."

"My dear. You sell yourself short."

"No. I know what we have." He hesitated, then added something he'd only admitted to Malcolm. "If she were unfaithful again, I think I'd prefer not to know."

"Good God, Harry." Maria's gaze moved over him as though looking for injuries. "What happened to the hard-headed realist who was my lover? Are you so determined to be blind?"

"I'm so aware of what I have. And determined to preserve it."

"Even at the risk of living a lie?"

Harry could hear the scorn with which he'd have greeted such a pronouncement in past years. The same scorn he heard in Maria's voice. But now—"What Cordy and I have isn't a lie," he said. "Whatever else happens."

"Well." Maria's dry tone made the single word both a comment and a question. "All I can do is wish you very happy." She pushed herself to her feet and crossed the room to a table that held a set of decanters. "But I don't think you came here just to reminisce about old times. You may not be an agent officially any more, but you haven't left the game."

"Not entirely." Harry settled back in his chair in the sort of pose that invited confidences. "My friend David Worsley's house in Brook Street was broken into last night."

"I'm sorry to hear it." Maria lifted a decanter, cocked a brow at Harry, and poured two glasses.

"He's raising his late sister's children. He's living with them in the house that belonged to his sister and her husband. Lord and Lady Craven."

He couldn't read the smallest jerk in Maria's hand as she poured the brandy. But was she holding her hand just a bit too carefully steady? "Should the name mean something to me?"

"I assume so. Given that I found this in the house." Harry reached inside his coat and pulled out the bracelet.

Maria watched him for a moment, her face a mask. Then she gave a rueful smile. "Devil take it. I knew you were a friend of Worsley's. What possessed me to wear jewelry you would recognize?"

"I don't imagine you were planning to lose it."

"No. There is that."

"What were you doing in the house, Maria?"

Maria picked up one of the glasses and tossed down half the contents, then crossed to Harry and put the other glass in his hand. "I did know Lord Craven. He didn't have anything like your understanding. Or your wit. Or your skill in other ways. But he amused me for a while."

"Good God, Maria," Harry was startled into saying.

She raised a brow. "We all take our pleasures where we find them. Craven was Carfax's son-in-law and one of his agents. I expect you know that. He called on me because Carfax wanted information about some people I had known in Spain. One thing led to another. My society is more confined since I've come to England. And he was clever enough to be amusing at times. I even went so far as to write him a letter that was rather indiscreet. I've managed to establish a quite comfortable life here in England. You aren't the only one who values what you've built since the war."

"You're saying you broke into the Brook Street house to steal the letter back?"

"Is that so surprising?" Maria dropped back down on the sofa. "Your own wife's history must have taught you what scandal can do to a woman."

"Craven's been dead over three months."

"And now Lord Worsley is living in the house. I have no notion where Craven hid the letter."

"If that alarmed you, surely you'd have worried when David moved into the house."

Maria twitched the folds of her shawl closer about her. "I've been engaged in a rather agreeable flirtation with Reggie Sanderson. A former major in the 95th. I knew him a bit in Spain and we met up again in London. Lately it's turned more serious. And it occurred to me—Well, if you can sing the praises of marriage, can you blame me for contemplating it?"

Harry folded his arms across his chest and regarded her. "You're saying you're considering marriage to Sanderson and that suddenly made you worried about this indiscreet letter to Craven?"

She reached for her glass and took a sip of brandy. "I assume in your besotted state you understand the advantages of marriage, and there are rather more advantages for a woman than a man. Reggie has many things to recommend him, but he doesn't quite have your flexible thinking. I think that letter might give him pause."

"David would hardly show it to him."

"There's no telling what might happen if it fell into the wrong hands."

"Did you find it?"

"No. Though I was interrupted before I could search the whole house, as you must know. It seemed prudent to beat a retreat."

Harry leaned back in his chair and considered his former lover. Their affair had been brief. But one learned a lot about an agent working with them. And whatever mistakes he'd made in his marriage, he wouldn't have survived as a spy if he hadn't learned to read people. "It's a good story, Maria. There may even be truth in it. But not the whole truth. I could always tell when you were lying."

"You're jumping at shadows, Harry."

"I think not."

"My dear." She set her glass down with care, barely sloshing the brandy. "If I was lying, do you imagine there's a chance I'd tell you the truth?"

21

"Raoul!" Lisette Varon ran down the passage and seized his hands. She wore a blue sprigged muslin dress and her thick fair hair was caught back with a blue ribbon. A far cry from the male attire she'd worn when he and Bertrand helped her escape France a month and half ago. Or the evening gown of Suzanne's she'd dressed in to elude pursuit when they'd sought refuge at the Berkeley Square house in the midst of a ball.

Now she looked much like the girl of two-and-twenty she in fact was, but when she drew back after giving him an exuberant hug, she looked at him with the keen gaze of one of his best agents. She scanned his face, seeking clues, but merely said, "It's so good to see you. Come into the sitting room."

"You look well," he said, as she poured coffee.

"It's good to be with my mother and sister again. In some ways it's been easier than I thought. In others—" She glanced out the window, as though the heavy gray of the sky in and of itself told the story of what was difficult about living in London.

"It's an insular country," O'Roarke said. "Not easy for outsiders. But the British can be surprisingly kind when one gets to know them. They've embraced outsiders more through history than many of them would care to admit. I'll own to having grown more comfortable in England than I'd ever have thought possible."

"In truth, many people have been kind. And Maman and Ninette seem more at home than I'd have thought possible. I daresay I shall as well. In truth, I think the hardest part is not having a mission. A huge part of my mind feels empty."

He touched her hand. "I know the feeling. Though I confess at times I've longed for it."

She handed him a cup of coffee. "Something serious must have happened to bring you back to London so quickly. Unless—" A question she couldn't quite put into words flickered in her gaze.

Raoul froze, the coffee cup halfway to his lips. "Damnation. I should have realized. You're much too acute."

Lisette colored, reminding him of how young she was. And in some ways quite inexperienced. "I don't know anything for a certainty—But I'm not blind. I saw you looking at her."

He took a sip of coffee. "Which says a great deal for your skills and that mine must be slipping."

"Or that you felt safe in front of those you were with. Besides, you said you trusted her. And that you'd tell her what happened in any case. From you, that's better than a declaration."

He thought back to that night, the myriad tensions, the sheer, intoxicating relief of seeing Laura again. Was he slipping?

"I'm glad," she said. "You deserve some happiness."

"I don't deserve anything of the sort, but I've found more of it than I ever expected." He blew on his coffee, dispelling the steam. "In truth, I came back for two reasons. I was on my way for reasons that are far more personal than I would admit to any but my closest friends"—he gave a faint smile—"I do have a reputation to maintain. But when I got to Dover I found a message from Suzanne."

Lisette's gaze flickered over his face, wide and questioning. Raoul took another sip of coffee, relief warring with dread. Relief because Lisette betrayed no knowledge of the Phoenix plot. And dread because he didn't want to tell her.

"Has anyone from the old life been to see you recently?" he asked.

"Suzanne," she said without hesitation. "She brought her children, they're charming. Bertrand. Manon Caret. Suzanne brought her and she engaged my mother to repair her costumes. She brought another actress, Jennifer Mansfield, who I think also may once have been an agent—"

"Long ago. No one who's come to England more recently has sought you out?"

"Should someone have?" Lisette sat back and regarded him. "Raoul, why did Suzanne send for you?"

"My dear—Have you ever heard the words 'Phoenix plot'?"

"It was a code name for plans to get Bonaparte off St. Helena. Highly theoretical plans, but—*Mon Dieu.*"

"We don't know anything for a certainty," Raoul said. "But someone's been visiting former agents, trying to get them involved in the plot. And the man who warned Suzanne about it slipped away in the night with a raging fever before he could explain more, and then turned up again trying to recruit agents to assist with the plot. I don't suppose you ever met a Louis Germont?"

Lisette clunked her cup back in its saucer. "Germont? He's the man who talked to Suzanne? I saw him."

"In Paris, before you left?"

"No, in London, yesterday. In Les Trois Amis. It's—"

"A coffeehouse frequented by émigrés. I know it well."

"I go there when I'm homesick. I was with Ninette. I looked over and saw a fair-haired man who looked familiar. At first all I could see was his hair and a bit of his profile. I didn't think much of it, because one is always seeing familiar-looking people at Les Trois Amis, but I was trying to place him while Ninette and I sipped our coffee. He was with another man, a bit older, brown haired, nondescript. Then Germont turned to the side and I recognized him."

"Did you speak to him?"

"No. I grabbed my sister's hand and got her out of the coffeehouse as quickly as possible."

Raoul watched her. Lisette wasn't given to fancies. "Bertrand helped Germont flee Paris. The story was that Germont was a clerk in the foreign ministry. Was that not the case?"

"No, he was. And he'd passed information to the Bonapartists. That's true as well. I could see why Bertrand would have helped him. Why perhaps he'd really needed to flee France."

"But?"

"Germont tried to steal letters I was carrying for Queen Hortense. That was when I learned about his other master." She looked into Raoul's gaze. "He's an agent for Fouché."

"We seem to have identified the bracelet's owner." Malcolm dropped into a chair across from Jeremy Roth in the Brown Bear Tavern.

Roth pushed aside the notebook in which he'd been writing and signaled to a waiter to bring Malcolm a pint. The

Brown Bear, which adjoined the Bow Street Public Office, was frequently used by runners to conduct business. Laura had been detained in one of the rooms upstairs when she was first taken into custody after the Duke of Trenchard's murder.

Malcolm told Roth about Maria Monreal. He omitted the full details of Harry's past association with her, but he suspected Roth read between the lines.

"A fortunate break that we found her. And God knows we could use a break in this case." Roth leaned back in his chair. "Does she know Worsley or anyone connected to him? I've been interviewing the Brook Street staff to see if anyone was approached about the household's arrangements for the evening, but none of them reports talking to anyone. So, unless they're lying—and I could detect no evidence of that—we don't know how this Maria Monreal knew Worsley would be back late and had told the staff not to wait up."

"I haven't seen David since I learned her name, but I doubt he knows her. But Carfax does." Malcolm took a sip from the pint the waiter had brought him. Last night, after their search of the Brook Street house, he and Suzanne had updated Roth on Carfax's use of Whateley & Company as his private system to transport goods and information. Now he told Roth about his interview with Carfax that morning.

Roth turned his tankard in his hand. "Would Carfax have known Worsley's plans for evening?"

"He'd certainly have known David would be at the performance at the Tavistock and very likely that he was going to the supper party afterwards. He might have known from the past, or been able to guess, that David would tell the servants not to wait up." He might even have been able to guess that David would bring Simon home with him, though that was too great a confidence to share, even with Roth.

"You think we're caught in a private battle between Carfax and Wellington?" Roth asked.

"I did," Malcolm said. "But Fitzroy is convincing when he denies it. I think it would be particularly difficult for Fitzroy to lie when it comes to the duke."

"He always struck me as one who'd have a difficult time lying in general." Roth gave a twisted smile. "Speaking from an enlisted man's perspective."

"A good perspective."

"But distant when it comes to officers. As distant as a Bow Street runner is from the denizens of Mayfair, though I seem to get caught up in their affairs surprisingly often." Roth took a sip from his tankard. "I remember hearing Somerset had lost his arm. Hard to believe it's three years since Waterloo tomorrow. In some ways it seems like yesterday. In others as though it were another world."

Malcolm nodded. Another world in which his wife had still been actively spying for the French. How different might their lives be now if Bonaparte's forces had been victorious that day? Would it have been easier for her to stop spying? Or harder?

"Whom besides the duke would Fitzroy Somerset do such a favor for without question?" Roth asked.

Malcolm had been asking himself the same question since his interview with Fitzroy the previous day. "I don't know. But I'd hazard a guess it's another soldier."

Suzanne leaned back on one of the black metal benches in the Berkeley Square garden. Colin, Emily, and Livia were playing tag, while Jessica and Drusilla attempted to join in, and Berowne alternately chased the children and rolled over on his back. Cordelia and Laura sat beside her. Cordy, she knew, was loath to go home while Harry was out interviewing Maria Monreal, and Laura, she suspected, had her own anxieties about what Raoul was doing. Malcolm could be back at any moment, or not until dinner. And Suzanne was less anxious about what he was doing than about what she was going to say to him when he returned. It was one thing to make up her mind that she had to tell him about the Phoenix plot, and another to actually tell him and face his response.

"I'm glad Raoul's back," Cordelia said. "You must be relieved, Laura."

Laura gave a dry smile. "I suppose now I have to stop pretending with you as well."

"Not if you don't wish to," Cordelia said. "I'm quite adept at feigning blindness."

Laura's smile deepened. "In truth, it's rather a relief not to have to pretend with friends."

"I'm fortunate that Harry was mostly done living a life of danger when we reconciled," Cordelia said. "Not that it stops me from worrying." She spread her fingers over the cherry-spotted muslin of her skirt. "Given that, it seems petty of me to be concerned that he's presently interviewing his former mistress."

In an odd way, the comment was an offer of friendship, and Laura's gaze said she took it that way. "On the contrary. That sounds beastly. Though knowing Harry, I wouldn't say you have any cause to worry."

"No, of course not." Cordelia pleated a fold of the sheer fabric between her fingers. "But it's hard to—"

"Let go of the past?" Laura glanced at her daughter, hiding behind one of the plane trees. Tag seemed to have given way to hide and seek. "Don't I know it. But I think that's just what one has to do if one wants to move forwards."

Suzanne wondered if Laura was thinking of her own past or of Raoul's. Which included Suzanne herself. She put up a hand to tighten the ribbons on her Leghorn hat, just as a familiar lean figure appeared approaching the square. Suzanne lifted a hand to wave. The warmth she always felt at the sight of her husband washed through her; at the same time she tensed at what she had to tell him.

Colin, Emily, and Livia ran to the square railing to wave to Malcolm. He stopped to talk to them, ruffled Jessica's and Drusilla's hair, picked up Berowne, and walked over to the three women with the cat draped over his shoulder. "Your afternoon looks much more agreeable than mine. I've been to see Fitzroy and Carfax. Fitzroy claims to have engaged Ennis at the request of a friend for whom he was acting in confidence."

"Do you believe him?" Suzanne asked.

I'm inclined to do so." He perched on the arm of the bench. "He also emphatically denies hiring the person who broke into Brook Street. In which case, there are definitely two different people looking for whatever Craven had."

"And Maria Monreal was working for the person who had Coventry killed," Cordelia said.

"It looks that way. Though it doesn't mean she killed Coventry. Someone else working for the same person could have broken into Whateley & Company. In any case, Harry's well able to take care of himself."

"Of course," Cordelia said.

Malcolm touched her arm. "Carfax admits Maria Monreal worked for him during the war, but he denies any knowledge of the break-in. Which is just what he'd do if he was behind it."

"Do you think he was?" Laura asked.

"No, but I don't discount it as a possibility." Malcolm pulled Berowne from his shoulder into his lap.

"Perhaps Harry will learn something from Maria Monreal," Cordelia said.

Malcolm met her gaze for a moment. "I hope so."

The children fell on their parents demanding refreshment, which necessitated a return to the house. Once they were all settled in the day nursery with lemonade and biscuits, it was a simple enough matter for Suzanne to say she needed to speak with Malcolm. After a few sips of lemonade, they went a few doors down to their bedchamber.

"Cordy's a bit concerned," she said. "And aware she has no right to be."

Malcolm shook his head. "She has to know Harry has eyes for no one but her."

"Sometimes it's difficult to see that oneself. But I think it's more that she's realized Harry could have had a life without her."

Malcolm dug a shoulder into one of the bedposts and regarded her. "I'm quite sure Harry couldn't imagine life without Cordy. Because that's precisely how I feel about you."

Suzanne's chest constricted. "You always know just what to say."

"Hardly, but after five and a half years of marriage I have learned a bit." He watched her for a moment. "What's wrong, sweetheart?"

Suzanne drew a breath. Always best to say these things straight out. She dropped down on her dressing table bench. "The night of the Whateley & Company break-in. I told you I left the Grandisons' because Bertrand summoned me to Marthe's to tend an injured émigré."

Malcolm regarded her with a steady gaze. "You said he'd been wounded. With everything that's happened, I forgot to ask you how he got on."

"As it happens, we don't know. He ran from Marthe's in the night."

"Odd." Malcolm's brows drew together, but he was silent, waiting for her to go on.

"It makes a sort of sense when one knows the whole story. He babbled to me while I was tending him. After Bertrand and Marthe left the room." She locked her hands together. "Have you heard of the Phoenix plot?"

His gaze narrowed but held no flash of recognition. "No, but it sounds like a code name. For resurrecting something? Or someone?"

She managed a faint smile. "What it is to have an agent husband with a good classical education. Yes." Her fingers tightened. When crossing a precipice, ultimately one had to leap. "It's a code name for a plot to free Napoleon."

She saw the realization settle in his eyes but he held himself perfectly still. "You wanted to talk to O'Roarke before you told me," he said.

She swallowed, her throat raw. This was another of the moments that could push their relationship forwards or send it crashing to bits. But there was nothing to be gained from avoiding the truth. "Yes."

Malcolm nodded, his gaze steady as still water. "You sent for him?"

"Yes, though apparently he was already on the way home to see Laura."

He gave a faint smile, though his gaze remained serious. "I understand."

"Do you?"

"In this instance, you couldn't think like my wife."

"I am your wife, Malcolm."

"But you're not just my wife, as I constantly try to remind myself. You have other loyalties. In this case, you had to think as an agent first. If I suspected Carfax was trying to break up a Bonapartist plot, I wouldn't tell you. At least not before I'd investigated and knew what we were really facing."

She released her breath. "Darling—you never cease to amaze me."

"I could say the same for you. Also, I assume you wanted to make sure O'Roarke wasn't involved."

She drew another parched breath. "He says he isn't. I believe him. Which may mean I'm going soft."

Malcolm gave a twisted smile. "I'd never expect you to turn on him, sweetheart. And I appreciate your not putting me in a situation where I had to betray him or decide to let the plot go undiscovered."

This time the breath she drew had a touch of wonder.

"I can't claim to fathom my feelings when it comes to O'Roarke," Malcolm continued. "But you and Laura aren't the only ones who worry about his safety in Spain. It was a distinct relief to see him walk into our breakfast parlor this morning. The thought of him embroiled in a plot—"

"I know." She gripped her elbows.

"Does he have any idea who's behind it?"

"He says not. He's out making inquiries now. I think he'll tell us what he learns. At least, as much as he can."

Malcolm gave a twisted smile, then stepped forwards and drew her to her feet and into his arms. "It usually comes down to that, doesn't it?" he said into her hair.

22

Harry climbed the steps of the Berkeley Square house. He knew instinctively that Cordelia would have stayed there after Livia's lessons. He told himself that what he had to report could only reassure her. But he knew from personal experience that it wasn't the facts that would worry her. It was the unvoiced thoughts and feelings that underlay those facts. What actors filled in in a script. What a composer added to a libretto.

Impossible to define. More powerful sometimes than words, and certainly more elusive. How often had he looked at Cordy, seeking clues about some man she had danced with, spoken with, shared a glass of champagne with? Far more often than he would admit to anyone, even Malcolm. It was a reflexive reaction. Even now. Even with everything they had built.

"They're in the library, Mr. Davenport," Valentin said, accepting Harry's hat as he admitted him to the house.

"They" turned out to be everyone. Colin's wooden castle gleamed white and silver in a patch of sunlight. Malcolm was on his knees, helping Colin, Livia, and Emily sort through the knights and ladies. Drusilla and Jessica were galloping wooden horses round the outer battlements. Berowne dozed by the window. Cordy, Suzanne, and Laura sat on the sofa with a tea tray and a plate of almond cakes before them.

"Uncle Harry." Colin looked round over his shoulder. "We're picking the knights of the Round Table."

"And the ladies." Livia held up a fair-haired lady in white. "She'd make a good Guenevere. I don't think we need Lancelot. They'd be happier without him."

"Excellent point," Malcolm said without a blink. He pushed himself to his feet. "We've made a good start. I'll leave you to sort out the details. I need to speak to Uncle Harry."

"I'll help." Laura took Malcolm's place on the carpet. "I've always quite liked Arthur and his knights. And ladies. We need a Nimue."

Suzanne poured Harry a cup of tea, and they and Cordelia and Malcolm moved to the far end of the room. Harry dropped down on a settee beside his wife and shot a smile at her. Cordelia smiled back. In the light from the windows, her eyes were wide and bright. His mind slid back to the girl she'd been when they married. Not the brittle sophisticate she'd usually seemed, but the young woman beneath, whom he had only caught occasional glimpses of, but who had sometimes seemed as lonely and uncertain as he was himself. "Maria says she was Craven's mistress," he said. "And that she broke into the Brook Street house to steal an indiscreet letter."

"A good story," Malcolm said. "But we've heard a lot of good stories lately."

"That's what I thought. What I told Maria. She said if there was more, did I really think she'd tell me?"

Cordelia wrinkled her nose. "I was going to say it's difficult for me to imagine a woman with the wit to be involved with you sparing Craven a second glance. Although perhaps my own example doesn't precisely support that." She smiled brightly into his eyes, one of her defying-the-past smiles.

Harry took her hand and raised it to his lips. "Maria claims they met because Carfax sent him to her for information. That she was bored and lonely and didn't have a lot of options."

"There's no denying a shared mission can draw people together," Suzanne said. "And it can lend a person glamour. Still—"

"As an explanation it's a trifle obvious," Malcolm said.

"She also claims to know nothing about the Whateley & Company break-in," Harry said. "Which would mean we have two, or possibly three, separate people or groups looking for something of value that Craven had."

"Fitzroy claimed quite convincingly not to have been behind the Brook Street break-in," Malcolm said. "Which would mean we're almost certainly talking about at least two separate people. But whoever asked Fitzroy to engage Ennis, I can't imagine they were after love letters Maria Monreal wrote to Craven, so that would not just be two separate people, but two separate documents. Which does stretch credibility."

"So Maria is most likely lying," Harry said. "Hardly a surprise. I can see through her enough to be fairly sure of that. But not of what she's lying about."

"That's rather a relief," Cordelia said.

"Do you have any idea whom she might be working for?" Malcolm asked.

Harry considered a moment, sifting through what he knew of Maria. "She never seemed to have particular loyalties beyond disliking the French. Mostly, she seemed to enjoy the espionage game. I can't see her being happy in retirement. So she might have let just about anyone engage her services."

"Including Carfax." Malcolm drummed his fingers on the arm of his chair. "Whom we already know she knows. If

Carfax got wind someone else was looking for something Craven had hidden, he might have tried to retrieve it first. When his people failed to find it at Whateley & Company, he could have sent an agent to search the Brook Street house."

"You're suggesting Maria killed Coventry?" Harry kept his voice as even as he could.

"Do you think she's capable of it?"

Harry willed himself to dispassionate consideration, keenly aware of Cordelia's gaze on him. "Of killing? Oh, yes, in the right circumstances. But simply because someone surprised her—I'm not sure."

"If she was recognized, her life here could have unraveled," Suzanne pointed out.

"True." Harry frowned, seeing Maria sitting across from him today on her sofa, shawl slipping off her shoulders, and then remembering her lying in his arms, her dark hair spilling over his chest. That shouldn't change anything. And yet— "Perhaps it's that I don't want to see it," he said.

"It's difficult," Cordelia said in a quiet voice. "Thinking someone one's been intimate with could be capable of murder."

Harry's gaze shot to his wife's face, the ghost of George Chase between them.

"Carfax could have engaged two different people for the two break-ins," Malcolm said.

"If Carfax is behind it," Suzanne said.

Malcolm's gaze jerked to his wife's face.

"I'm the last person to defend Carfax," Suzanne said. "But we don't have any proof."

"Rational as always, Suzette. But nor do we have it against anyone else."

Carfax leaned back in the chair at the desk in his study. "The children seem to have settled down well from last night."

David smiled, remembering the trouble he and Simon had had getting them back to sleep. He had brought the four children round to see his parents and his youngest sister, Lucinda, this afternoon. Isobel had stopped by briefly, then left to prepare for her ball. Though not before George had blurted out the news of the news of the break-in, and David had been obliged to explain, downplaying the dangers for Isobel's sake as much as the children's. Carfax had spent half an hour in the drawing room with his grandchildren, seeming a bit awkward but genuinely interested. Then he had taken David down to the study to talk, leaving the children with Lady Carfax and Lucinda. "They saw it as an adventure more than anything," David said. "Amy and George were convinced it was pirates after some undefined treasure."

"It's good they can laugh." Carfax's brows drew together. "These taunts that caused Teddy to run away from Harrow. Someone claimed George was a bastard?"

David had had the same instinctive reaction when he first heard the story, but time had tempered his response. And he didn't want Carfax making a big to-do about Teddy's adventure for any number of reasons. "I'm not entirely sure what was said. There was some sort of smear on Louisa's honor, but it's the sort of insult boys hurl at each other all the time, particularly those lacking in imagination. It doesn't necessarily mean more than that."

Carfax leaned forwards in his chair, arms on his desktop, fingers tented beneath his chin. "Still. In the circumstances, it's concerning. I'll make some inquiries."

David's alarm must have shown in his face, for his father gave a dry smile and added, "Discreetly, of course."

David willed himself to relax back in his chair. "The whole incident was unfortunate, but in some ways I think it's good to have Teddy home. It's easier for me to gauge what he's going through, and it's certainly good for the younger ones."

Carfax nodded. "In truth, I wouldn't have thought to see them as happy as they appear to be now. You're doing well with them."

Praise from his father always made David brace himself. He looked at Carfax, wondering what was coming next.

Carfax gave a dry smile. "It's a simple statement of fact. I had doubts about your taking the children at the time, but now I see it was far and away the best solution. The whole family has cause to be grateful to you. As I'm sure Louisa would be." He coughed.

"Sir." Something in Carfax's expression took David down a path he had never intended to follow. "I don't pretend to understand what happened to Louisa. But whatever choices she made, whatever drove those choices—it can't possibly be owed to anything you or my mother did or didn't do. You've both always been the best of parents."

Something wavered in Carfax's gaze, like a curtain moving in the wind. For an instant, David thought he was catching a glimpse of a side of his father Carfax almost never revealed. A glimpse too fleeting to grasp hold of. "Thank you, David." When Carfax spoke, his voice was dry and brittle as leaves about to disintegrate. "But now that you are to all intents and purposes a parent yourself, I'm sure you'll appreciate that one can't help but wonder." He coughed again. "It's an inestimable comfort to know her children are in good hands."

"Thank you." David coughed himself. He couldn't remember when he had felt so in charity with his father. At the same time, in a raft of difficult conversations, he couldn't remember when he had felt so unsure of what to say to Carfax.

"Have you decided what you'll do, come the new term?" Carfax asked, in a voice of almost forced normalcy.

"Not yet." David was not yet ready to face that particular battle with his father.

"Can't let time waste," Carfax said, "Perhaps another school—"

"Yes. We're—I'm"—damn, the very word change was an insult to Simon—"considering it."

Carfax's gaze flickered over his face, but he merely inclined his head.

David pushed himself to his feet. Carfax settled back in his chair, but as David moved to the door, Carfax said, "David."

David turned back, one hand on the door handle. He met his father's gaze and couldn't be sure if Carfax had decided at the last minute to detain him or if the timing was one of his father's carefully orchestrated ploys. Malcolm could sometimes read Carfax. David had long since given up even trying to do so. "Yes?"

Carfax regarded him for a long, controlled moment. "It's time you were married."

Hell and the devil. The talk had been going entirely too well. David released the door handle. "Sir—"

"It's one reason I was concerned about your taking on Louisa's children," Carfax said. "I was afraid it would be a distraction, an excuse to avoid getting on with your own life. But seeing how natural you are with them—far more so than I ever was myself, I confess—I can only hope it's made you realize how much is to be gained from having your own household."

David moved back to his chair. "I have my own household."

Carfax tugged a sheet of paper straight in a pile on his desktop. "Any woman worth her salt will understand your commitment to the children. Will honor your commitment to them and take them on as her own. Not easy, but you wouldn't want a woman without backbone—"

"Damn it, Father." David drew a breath.

"I've tried to wait for you to come to your senses on your own. You've always had a good sense of your responsibilities. I was sure that would triumph in the end. I can be patient. But not indefinitely. This family has been through enough. The succession must be secured."

David dropped back into the chair, his hand rigid on the back as he lowered himself into it. "It is secure. Cousin Michael has two sons. His younger brother has three."

"Oh, for God's sake. That's not the same and you know it."

"You inherited from Uncle John—"

"Not through any choice of his. John married, he had a son—" Carfax drew a breath at the mention of his nephew's untimely death. "No one can foresee how every eventuality will play out."

"Precisely. The Carfax lands will do well enough in the hands of Michael's sons." It was the first time David had said as much to his father. He'd barely articulated it to himself.

"Michael's a decent enough man, but he's a country gentleman. He wasn't bred for this stage."

"I'll make sure his sons are." Until he'd taken in Louisa's children, David hadn't realized that was a role he could play.

"It's not the same. A few holiday weeks can't equal the training of a lifetime." Carfax leaned back in his chair, hands taut on the chair arms. "God knows we don't agree about everything, David. You have a right to be your own man. But the country needs men like us. Malcolm doesn't understand that, but I think you do."

David's hands locked as he imagined what Simon would say to that, what Malcolm would. It went against everything they believed in, everything he believed in. And yet he couldn't deny that a part of him felt the tug of the image his father evoked. He saw the ranks of ancestors in the portrait gallery at Carfax Court, men who had shepherded the trust that would one day be his to pass along to the next generation.

"I don't dislike Tanner, you know," Carfax said in a quiet voice.

David felt himself jerk. His father rarely mentioned Simon at all and had never come close to alluding to David's relationship with Simon.

Carfax gave a wry smile of acknowledgment. "Oh, I may deplore his politics, but I don't deny his wit or the keenness of his understanding. I don't share your proclivities, but I can understand the attraction."

"Sir—" David could barely get the word out.

"Yes, I know. I wouldn't have wanted to discuss any of my love affairs with my father either. What I'm trying to say is that taking a wife doesn't necessarily have to end your relationship with Tanner. You know as well as I do that most married men in Mayfair have at least one lover."

"You don't." David was quite certain of that. Every thought revolted from the idea of prying into his parents' love life, but one of the many contradictory things about Carfax was his devotion to his wife, and David had never seen his father so much as flirt with another woman.

"No." Carfax adjusted his spectacles. "I'm very happy with your mother. We've been fortunate. But I'm not saying you have to have the same sort of marriage."

"You're giving me permission to have a marriage that's a lie."

"Marriage is about establishing a foundation for future generations. Do that and you and your wife can both have the lives you choose."

"Simon would never stand for being part of such an arrangement."

"No?" Carfax gave a faint smile. "I think you underestimate him."

"On the contrary. I know how honorable a man he is. He wouldn't be part of a lie."

"Yes, he has ideals. I'm sure that's part of the attraction. But ideals are one thing in theory and quite another when put to the test. I've seen the way he looks at you. Whatever he may say, I don't think he'd stay away."

David flushed. "*Father*—"

"For God's sake, David." Carfax slammed his hands down on the desk, sending a stack of papers fluttering to the floor. "I'm telling you you don't have to give up the man you claim to love. I'm telling you there are ways to have the life you want and still do your duty by your heritage. I've been patient. I thought your sense of duty would bring you to that realization on your own. But my patience has come to an end. I want to see the line secure. What happened to Louisa shows us how fragile life can be—"

"Don't, Father." David gripped the arms of his chair. "Don't turn Louisa's tragedy into a bargaining chip. That demeans both of us."

"I'll do what I need to do to protect my family."

From Carfax, those words were bone-chilling. "You wouldn't—"

"Take a leaf from Dewhurst's book? No, for any number of reasons. But poorly as I think of Dewhurst, I can understand what drove him."

David pushed himself to his feet. "Give it up, Father. It's over."

"My dear David. It's nothing of the sort."

23

Raoul looked up at the Berkeley Square house as he stepped into the square from Bruton Street. The fanlight over the door. The gray stone walls. The cream work on the ground floor. The greenery spilling through the wrought metal railing on the first floor. The pediments over the windows. The house he'd visited through the years, at a ball, at a reception. For a stolen meeting with Arabella. Arabella's house. Alistair Rannoch's house. Malcolm and Mélanie's house. And now, amazingly, perhaps the closest thing he had to a home.

He climbed the steps and rang the bell. Valentin admitted him with the sort of easy smile he gave to the family. As Raoul relinquished his hat, Laura came out the double doors of the library. "Suzanne and Malcolm are reading to the children." She gave Raoul a quick smile that froze midway with unwonted awkwardness. "Do you want to—?"

"Quite." He followed her back into the library. In the cheerful chaos of the household, it was rare for them to have a moment alone together, except in her bedchamber at night. Though they'd enjoyed a stolen kiss in the library before he left for Spain the first time. He pushed aside the memory. Time to dwell on such things later. He needed to tell her about the reasons Mélanie had asked him to come to London, and in her bedchamber he was all too likely to get distracted.

Laura gestured towards the decanters. "Do you—?"

He hesitated a moment. "Thank you."

She poured two glasses of whisky. The late afternoon light from the windows glittered off the decanter and gilded her hair. For a moment, it was so easy to imagine they were in their own home, sharing a drink, their child safe upstairs, enjoying time alone together with no need for subterfuge. The thought made him dizzy.

"Malcolm finally convinced me I should feel free to help myself," she said. "Actually, he tried when I was still their governess, though I could never quite bring myself to do so." She crossed back to him and held out one of the glasses. "I think Suzanne told Malcolm about whatever made her ask you to come to London. This afternoon."

Relief shot through him like a draught of whisky. "I'm glad." He took the glass she was holding out and touched it to her own. "Now I need to tell you."

Laura looked into his gaze, her own steady. "You don't need to tell me anything."

"Yes, I do." He took her hand and drew her over to the window seat. Laura said nothing but sat watching him, the sunlight spilling over her face.

He laced his fingers through her own, and told her about the Phoenix plot.

She listened in silence, the widening of her blue eyes her only reaction. "I can see why Suzanne didn't tell Malcolm," she said when he had done.

"Yes." Images from the past shot through Raoul's mind. "I can only hope Malcolm does."

Laura squeezed his hand. "She's right, you know. It would put an intolerable burden on Malcolm for him to feel he had to turn you in or conceal the plot."

"Malcolm is an agent. He knows about making hard choices."

"Malcolm is also a son. And learning to think like one."

Raoul's mind shied away from the images her words conjured. There were some things he'd told himself were out of reach for so long he wouldn't let himself imagine them. "Don't start thinking in fairy-tale terms, Laura. You're more sensible than that."

"I'm a good observer, as you've often said." She took a sip of whisky, her gaze lingering on his face. "You didn't have to tell me any of this."

"No? If I owe you nothing else, I owe you as much honesty as we can muster between us." He tightened his fingers round her own. "Do you believe I'm not involved in a plot to restore Bonaparte?"

"If I say yes, will you accuse me of thinking in fairy-tale terms again?"

He grinned. "Perhaps, but I'm relieved to hear it."

She released her breath, leaning in to him, a loose strand of her hair brushing his shoulder. "Did you learn anything from your inquiries today?"

"An anonymous-sounding man—or possibly more than one anonymous-sounding man—has visited several people, with vague mentions of this plot. No one admits to taking the bait." He drew a breath. "But it seems Fouché may be involved."

He hadn't talked to her much about the former French minister of police, but he saw the instinctive fear in her eyes. "You think he's running the plot?"

"It seems likely. I'm less sure of his reasons." He stared down at their clasped hands. How long was it since he'd been able to sit like this, simply holding someone's hand? He'd crossed lines in the past months that he'd always avoided crossing, that a good agent crossed at his or her peril. There were things it was better to leave unvoiced, even in the privacy of one's own mind. And yet he found himself saying, "You know how I fought to keep Bonaparte in power, whatever my quarrels with him. You know what I think of the situation in France now. Yet when Mélanie told me about this supposed plot, my first reaction was dread."

"Because you thought it would fail?" Laura's gaze was steady on his face.

"There is that. But mostly because if there is a plot I'd feel impelled to play a role, one way or another. And I don't want to be pulled back into that maelstrom. Because, unlike at the end of Waterloo, unlike for most of the war, I have something to lose."

Laura drew back, her gaze wide and still. Her understanding confirmed the dangerous waters they'd moved into and also what he had gained from speaking. "It's hard to live a life without ties," she said. Her voice was level but slightly husky. "You taught me that."

"I'm immeasurably glad if I did."

Laura regarded him in that way that had the damnable ability to slip past his defenses. "You're missed. But you know I can look after myself, whatever comes."

"That, I'm well aware of." Though it hadn't stopped him, months since, from arranging for certain contingencies.

"One needs to snatch happiness where one can. You taught me that as well."

"A good lesson." But it didn't stop him from wanting more. Which perhaps was the most dangerous thing of all. Because what he wanted wasn't what was best for her. He needed to take his own advice and find joy in the moment. He set down his glass and reached for her. He felt the jolt of response that ran through her, let himself savor the warmth of her breath and the glow in her eyes before she melted into his kiss.

There was a lot to be said for living in the moment.

"You think Fouché is behind the Phoenix plot?" Malcolm dropped his arm round Mélanie's shoulders, his habitual reaction when news cut too close to the tangle of her past. Raoul was conscious of a keen wish that he could do the same with Laura, but she was sitting in one of the Queen Anne chairs while he was in the other, several feet of library carpet between them. For the first time he wondered if Malcolm reached for Mélanie as much to reassure himself as to protect her.

"It seems likely," Raoul said, surprised by the coolness he could muster in his own voice. "Fouché's in exile, but he's been in exile before, and it's never stopped him from plotting. Quite the reverse, in fact."

"And he thinks restoring Bonaparte will also restore him to power?" Malcolm asked.

"He might." Raoul gripped the carved arms of his chair, remembering his confrontation with the former minister of police in Paris three years ago. Fouché had been threatening to unmask Mélanie then. "If he could pull it off, Bonaparte would certainly be grateful, whatever he thinks of Fouché. But the key words are 'if he could pull it off.' It's possible Fouché's desperate enough he thinks it's worth the gamble. But it's also possible he thinks that if he can ferret out Bonapartists willing to engage in a treasonous plot, and give the French cause to ask the British to arrest them or send them back to France, he'll worm his way back into the good graces of the Ultra Royalists."

Mélanie drew a rough breath. "That sounds like Fouché."

"Quite." The acanthus leaves carved on the chair arms were probably imprinted on his palms. "Going back to the Revolution, his loyalties have shifted with where he thought the greatest advantage lay. And using a dummy plot to ferret out spies would be much easier than actually helping Bonaparte escape."

"So this man Suzanne helped, whom Bertrand got out of Paris—he's part of the plot?" Laura asked.

"He's most likely working for Fouché, given that he has in the past," Raoul said. "If the plot's a fake, he was probably sent to England to fan the fires."

"We know he tried to recruit Jennifer Mansfield to take part in the plot. So his seemingly feverish ravings were intended to entrap me," Mélanie said. Her fingers locked together in her lap. She hated to be outwitted.

"Apparently his wounds were real enough," Raoul said. "You probably saved his life."

"I don't wish anyone dead," Mélanie said, "but it looks as though I put others at risk in saving him."

Malcolm met Raoul's gaze. "Fouché knows about Suzanne."

Raoul saw again the cold terror that had filled Mélanie's eyes after Fouché had attempted to blackmail her three years ago, felt again the rage that had swept through him, remembered his chess game with the minister of police. He could see the same memories shoot through Mélanie's eyes.

"If Fouché wanted my assistance with a plot to free Bonaparte, he could have tried to blackmail me again,"

Mélanie said. "He'd have no way of knowing Malcolm knows the truth. And even if he did, he could threaten to expose me to the world in general."

Laura frowned, as though putting together the pieces. "But if the plot is actually an attempt to entrap former Bonapartist agents—"

"He might well have sent one of his people to confide in me in the guise of a man trying to stop the plot," Mélanie finished for her in a flat voice. "If we're right, it is interesting he didn't send someone to try to draw me into the plot directly."

Malcolm turned his head to look at his wife, his gaze that of a fellow spy, and yet at the same time, oddly tender. "He may have realized you probably wouldn't have been drawn into a plot," he said. "But he knew he could play on your loyalty to your comrades. And your compassion."

"Stop making me sound like a ministering angel, darling."

"Perish the thought. But you're also not as hardened as you let on."

"And this way you knew about the plot," Laura said. "He could watch for what you did next. See if by any chance you took the bait."

Raoul smiled at his lover. "You have remarkable insights into Fouché for someone who never dealt with him, sweetheart," he said. Only belatedly did he realize he'd called her sweetheart. But there was really no sense in even pretending to pretend in front of Mélanie and Malcolm anymore.

"It's the sort of thing Trenchard would have done," Laura said. "Fouché sounds all too like him."

Raoul felt his mouth tighten. "An apt comparison." He got up and moved to perch on the arm of her chair, his hand on her shoulder. Laura looked up with faint surprise, then leaned in to him.

Malcolm was frowning at the carved arm of the settee. "This settles it. I can't go to Carfax."

Mélanie cast a quick look up at him. "Darling—"

"Think, Mel. If we're right, we'd be playing right into Fouché's hand. Carfax would want former Bonapartists discredited every bit as much as the Comte d'Artois. And obviously there's no real risk of a plot to free Bonaparte."

Mélanie looked steadily into her husband's eyes. "And if we're wrong?"

Malcolm drew a measured breath. The sort, Raoul knew from experience, that took an intense effort. "That's why we have to investigate to learn the truth."

"We?" Mélanie continued to watch him.

Malcolm gave a sudden grin. "When investigating a possible plot to free Bonaparte, who better to turn to for help than two of Bonaparte's best spies?"

"We were never Bonaparte's," Mélanie said, "but I'll take it as a compliment."

24

Laura wondered if she should release Raoul's arm. But Suzanne was still holding Malcolm's, so perhaps moving away would look more ostentatious. Somehow standing in a crowd, her gloved fingers curved round the black superfine of his sleeve, seemed more intimate, in a way, than the nights they'd spent together.

Laura smoothed a hand over the folds of her skirt. She had a new gown, seafoam silk and ivory gauze with slashed sleeves edged in pearls. It was cut in what was called "the Spanish style" which had amused her greatly, though she doubted Raoul was even vaguely aware of the term. She had, however, caught the glow in his eyes when she came downstairs in the gown. Perhaps it was shallow, but there was no denying clothes could lend one much needed confidence. "Out two nights in a row," she said. "I don't know what I'm turning into."

Raoul cast a glance round the crowded room, gaze lingering on the delicate white-and-gold paneling, the tall French windows, the coffered ceiling. "I don't think I've been here before. It's a beautiful house."

"Like the Berkeley Square house, it looks more like a family home when they aren't entertaining," Suzanne said. "I still remember how kind Bel and Oliver were when Malcolm first brought Colin and me here. It's good there's one Mallinson daughter with a happy marriage."

"They were always kind to me," Laura said. "Even when I was a governess they treated me"—she smiled, not trying to keep the irony from the smile—"like a person."

"It doesn't hurt that I've never seen anyone coax Rose out of her tantrums as well as you do," Malcolm said.

"I saw the small heads peeping over the stair rail when we came in," Raoul said. "You're obviously a favorite."

"I'm a good storyteller," Laura said. "It goes a long way with children." She cast a glance about the room. The candles in the gilt sconces warmed the air and glittered in the tall mirrors hung on all sides. Just in the throng near them, she spotted a royal duke, three patronesses of Almack's, and the Duke of Wellington. "I confess spending the evening in the nursery doesn't seem a bad option now."

"Thank goodness we found you," Cordelia said as she and Harry came up beside them. "It's so crowded one can scarcely see who's in the room, and my gown's been trodden on three times. So Isobel can be sure her party will be deemed a great success."

The words were light, but the way Cordelia was holding her husband's arm and leaning in to him said a great deal about how she felt in the wake of Harry's visit to Maria Monreal. Cordelia met Laura's gaze and gave a faint smile that confirmed her thoughts. And also, Laura realized, said a great deal about how well she'd come to know Cordelia.

"No sign of the Whateleys," Harry said, "though I imagine they've been invited. And Fitzroy and Harriet are here." He met Malcolm's gaze for a moment.

"I doubt I'd get very far talking to him again," Malcolm said. "Not without more information."

"There you are." Isobel Lydgate materialized out of the crowd, elegant if a bit pale in white British net over pale lilac satin. She cast a quick glance round and lowered her voice, though it was scarcely necessary with the buzz of conversation bouncing off the gilded ceiling. "I stopped by Carfax House this afternoon. David had brought the children to see my parents. He told me about the break-in last night. God in heaven—"

"It's concerning," Suzanne said. "But everyone's all right. Whatever the thief's intention, I don't think she meant harm to any of them."

"It was a woman?" Isobel asked in disbelief.

"It seems to have been." Malcolm squeezed her hand. "The children are well protected and Suzette's right. The thief didn't mean them harm. Don't let it spoil tonight, Bel."

Isobel's tight face relaxed into a smile. "Dear Malcolm. You could reassure anyone. Though what really stops me from worrying is that all of you are managing the investigation." Her smile encompassed the whole group, including Laura.

"We'll try not to let you down," Malcolm said, lightly, but Laura caught an undertone of seriousness.

"You couldn't if you tried," Isobel said, then drew a quick breath. Laura wondered if she was remembering the end of the investigation in Trenchard's and Craven's deaths. With the aplomb of an experienced hostess, Isobel forced another smile to her lips. "On a more mundane note, I'm on my way up to say goodnight to the children, and I promised I'd bring Laura and Suzanne up with me. And you, Cordy, if I could find you. Ellie keeps asking about your gown. She says the one you wore last time you were here was her favorite ever. I imagine tonight she'll think you're a fairy princess." Isobel ran an appreciative gaze over Cordelia's silver-embroidered gauze gown and diamond circlet and then smiled at the men. "I promise I'll return them for dancing in a quarter hour."

"Malcolm is longing to find somewhere to talk politics," Suzanne said with a laugh. "Can we take the children some ices?"

Cordelia laughed as well, but as she followed the other three women into the passage, Laura wondered if her sharp-eyed friends had noticed the strain behind Isobel Lydgate's steady blue gaze.

Malcolm took up a position on the edge of the dance floor, scanning the crowd for Eustace Whateley or anyone else it might be good to talk to. He caught a glimpse of his wife across the room with Bertrand, the softly pleated stuff of her gown swirling round her like mist on a dark night. Harry and O'Roarke were dancing with Cordelia and Laura, but when the ladies returned to the ballroom, Suzanne had met Malcolm's gaze with a look that said she intended to circulate. They needed to put their time to use. Time enough for dancing later.

"Malcolm."

Even before Malcolm turned his head, he recognized the familiar, incisive tones of the Duke of Wellington. "What are you doing not dancing with your wife?" Wellington inquired.

"This is Mayfair, sir. Surely I needn't remind you husbands and wives aren't expected to spend the evening dancing together?"

"Since when have you been one to do the expected? Any more than your friend Davenport." Wellington jerked his head towards Harry and Cordelia. Then his gaze moved round the ballroom. "Sensible girl, Isobel. Always does things well. Good to see the family getting on with their lives." He cast a glance at Malcolm. "You've been to see Fitzroy twice."

"You don't miss much, do you, sir?"

"Hope not. Part of your investigation?"

"Fitzroy's a friend. I often go to see him."

"And you're not denying it's part of the investigation, which means it is. Is Fitzroy in trouble?"

For a moment Malcolm could hear the crack of the cannon shot that had taken Fitzroy's arm, a handsbreadth away from Wellington and Malcolm himself, feel the weight of Fitzroy falling against him, hear the sharpness in Wellington's voice. "You know Fitzroy, sir. Can you imagine him doing anything to get himself in trouble?"

"Hmph." Wellington's gaze continued to skim the ballroom. "Only if he thought that was the only honorable way to proceed. Good God, is that Raoul O'Roarke dancing with Lady Tarrington? Thought he was in Spain."

"He's visiting London, like you, sir. He only just arrived." Malcolm hesitated a moment, but there was no reason for Wellington not to know, and it would look odd for Malcolm not to mention it. "O'Roarke is staying with us while he's in London, as it happens."

Wellington frowned, then nodded. "Forgot he was a friend of your family." His gaze continued on Laura and O'Roarke as they circled the floor. O'Roarke was holding her at a very correct distance, but even from the edge of the dance floor the glow in his eyes was unmistakable. "Looks as though Lady Tarrington is a friend of O'Roarke's as well."

"Yes," Malcolm said with an easy smile. "They've got to know each other through the years at our house. O'Roarke is a favorite honorary uncle with our children and Lady

Tarrington's daughter." Always good when one could work in the unvarnished truth in the midst of deception.

Wellington's brows drew together. Malcolm remembered the duke's noting William Cuthbertson's interest in Laura at the Tavistock the previous night. "O'Roarke's no Jack Tarrington, but he offers his own risks. Back in '98 I'd have called him one of our greatest enemies, but I can't deny he was useful in the Peninsula. I suppose he's stirring things up in Spain now."

"I'm quite sure he's in sympathy with the Liberals," Malcolm said. There again he could speak the truth.

Wellington gave a brusque nod. "Suppose it was too much to expect he'd remain an ally. Still, if he's staying with you, you should bring him along to the Waterloo dinner tomorrow. He was certainly part of our victory."

Malcolm bit back an ironic laugh and kept his gaze steady. "Thank you, sir. I'm sure he'll be honored."

Wellington waved a hand. "Good to remember the war made strange bedfellows."

⚜

"Thank God for parties." Bertrand materialized out of the crowd at Suzanne's side shortly after she returned from her trip to the nursery. "We'd have the devil of a time sharing information otherwise."

"You have information?" Suzanne asked.

"Not as much as I'd like." Bertrand retrieved two glasses of champagne from a passing waiter and gave one to her. Of one accord, they moved to a sofa of gold-spotted blue satin set beneath a gilt-framed mirror in an embrasure in the white-and-gold wall. "Louis Germont's mother was a younger daughter of the Baron de Brillac. Her brother, who had the title at the time of the Revolution, sought refuge in Austria, though it seems there may have been a sister who came to Britain. Someone who might be Germont was spotted at a coffeehouse frequented by émigrés yesterday, but I couldn't get enough information to trace him from there."

Suzanne hesitated, but if she told Bertrand about Lisette's sighting of Germont the whole Phoenix plot would unravel, and with it, a host of revelations. "If anyone can find him, you can," she said.

Bertrand gave a faint smile. "These days, I'm used to responding to pleas for help. It's a long time since I've tried to ferret out information." He took a sip of champagne and considered her in silence for a long moment. It was, Suzanne realized, damnably difficult to tell what he was thinking, for all his easy good humor. Despite his words, he was a master agent among master agents. "I didn't think it through much before I went to France the first time. My family had fled France. I'd grown up in England. The Bonapartists were the enemy."

"They'd killed your brother." Étienne Laclos had gone to France in a mad, desperate plot to assassinate Napoleon and had been caught and executed. Odd that others might now be risking arrest and execution in an equally mad, desperate plot to free Napoleon.

Remembered grief shot through Bertrand's eyes. "Yes. I suppose a part of me wanted to avenge Étienne. But I think chiefly I wanted to be out of Britain." He stared down at his hands, a rare sign of unease. "I wanted to leave Rupert before Rupert was compelled to leave me."

For a moment, Simon and David shot into her memory, in the Brook Street library, the children clustered round them. "Are you so sure he would have?"

Bertrand's brows drew together as though he were seeing into the past. Or perhaps into an alternate future. "At the time I thought so. Rupert takes his responsibilities too seriously not to feel compelled to provide an heir for the earldom. Even looking back now—I never stop being sorry for how Gabrielle got caught up in our sorry story. I know Rupert doesn't either. But there's no denying the cold fact that, in some ways, it makes it easier that Rupert has an heir. Aside from the fact that I can't imagine Stephen not being in our lives."

"It's remarkable." Suzanne recalled the three of them, Rupert, Bertrand, and Gabrielle, kneeling on her drawing room carpet last Christmas with Stephen and Colin and Livia, playing with Colin's new castle. "What you've all managed to make of your lives."

Bertrand's smile was sweet and almost wistful. "I hope so." His fingers tightened round his glass. "In any case, fresh from Oxford, escape seemed the best solution. And it let Rupert and me stay connected. Even let us meet in secret. And then there was—"

"The lure of adventure?" After all, Bertrand, more than any of them, had lived a life of adventure for years.

Bertrand met her gaze and grinned. "Quite. Particularly then, when I had no idea what adventure really meant. It was only after I got to France, after I settled in to my mission, that I fully began to appreciate the rest of it."

"The rest?"

"Betrayal." His mouth curled round the word. "Odd it never occurred to me before that that's what it was. I was set on doing my duty for my adopted Crown and country. Avenging my brother's death. Making my—Rupert proud of me." He gave a faint, self-derisive smile. "It was only when I found myself actually living among the French, dining with them, riding in the Bois de Boulogne, that it occurred to me I was betraying practically everyone I saw every day. The waiters in the cafés where I took my morning coffee and had a glass of wine in the evenings. The porter at my lodgings who complained about his rheumatism and boasted about his grandchildren. The baker I bought bread from most days who had almost saved enough to bring his fiancée from Provence and start a family. Even an idiot like Edmond Talleyrand, who did his awkward best to take me under his wing, though I suspect he was doing so on his uncle's orders and reporting back on my activities. They were all *people*. God, how easy it is to lose sight of that."

"Frighteningly easy. But it sounds as though you didn't lose sight of it at all."

"I did for a time. But it was getting harder and harder for me to swallow the rank taste of it Especially after I met Louise."

Bertrand had acted as a cover for Louise Carnot and her lover to protect them from her jealous husband. "I doubt that which side you fought for matters in the least to Louise," Suzanne said. She could see Bertrand, in Paris after he emerged from hiding, crouched in the garden of Louise's Paris house building a pirate ship out of sheets with her sons and Colin and Stephen while Louise looked on.

"Louise is a generous woman and loyal to her friends. But I was still lying to her. I was lying to everyone, except for the few times Rupert and I met in secret." He swallowed. Suzanne didn't think she'd ever seen such vulnerability in those seemingly open blue eyes. "For all Rupert means to me, sometimes what mattered most about those times was simply being able to tell the truth."

For a moment, Suzanne felt the rush of relief that had always coursed through her when she met Raoul, in a café, a tavern, a garret room. "It means a lot to be able to be one's self."

Bertrand shot a look at her. "Yes. And then I was nearly killed."

"And you learned your own people had betrayed you."

"I learned Rupert's father had."

Suzanne looked at him, fully appreciating for the first time what it must have meant to him, alone in what to all intents and purposes was a foreign country, under deep cover, suddenly no longer able to trust his own people. At least she had had Malcolm. "Lord Dewhurst had made your own people no longer trust you."

Bertrand gave a short laugh. "Branded a traitor when, in fact, I'd been betraying people for the past two years. Just not the people I was accused of betraying."

"One can't be an agent without committing myriad betrayals."

Bertrand met her gaze for a long moment. "I think to be an agent, one has to either believe wholeheartedly in one's cause—or believe in nothing at all save self-preservation and triumphing in the game. Neither of which applied to me. I wouldn't have survived if it weren't for my young friend Inez and her family. In the end, I realized it was the people who mattered. Not taking sides in the game but saving as many as possible from collateral damage."

Suzanne nodded. She suspected Bertrand had not talked this way to many people. "Thank you," she said. "For telling me."

Bertrand gave a quick, flexible smile.

"Why?" Suzanne asked before she could think better of it. "That is, I'm honored and I know we're friends, but—"

"I don't talk this way to all my friends? That's true. But I thought you'd understand." He regarded her for another, silent moment, weighted somehow with both risk and trust. "I didn't choose sides as the Kestrel, but I still heard things. About the Raven, among other things."

Suzanne drew a breath, sharp as glass. And yet, relief shot through her. The relief of being able to talk to someone who was in a unique position to understand. She cast a quick look round, but the buzz of the crowd rendered the embrasure as private as a closed room. "I didn't find betrayal as hard to live with as you did," she said in a steady voice.

"On the contrary." Bertrand's gaze was direct, his defenses down. "I think it very nearly cut you in two. But you believed in what you were doing. I can admire that. I can envy it."

"Are you sure I'm not simply caught up in the love of the game?"

"Not you, though you may enjoy it. Even I enjoyed it at times. Malcolm confessed that even he did."

"Malcolm knows—You've talked to Malcolm about—?"

Bertrand linked his hands round his knees. "Malcolm talked to me. Six months ago. Subtly, trying to sound me out. Establish how much I knew. Without either of us coming right out and saying it, we established that I was the last person to betray either of you. And then he asked for my help."

Suzanne stared at him. "You're the one Malcolm made arrangements with in case we need to leave Britain."

"Arrangements I trust we'll never have to put into effect."

Fear coursed through her in an icy rush. The fear she always felt at the thought of documents in Malcolm's dispatch box that arranged for them to leave Britain. And with that fear came the wonderful, terrible burden of the love that had caused Malcolm to meticulously make plans to abandon everything he knew, should his wife's past compel him to do so. "You let Rupert think you were dead rather than force him to choose between you and his family."

"Yes." Bertrand didn't pretend not to see the parallels she was drawing. "It seemed the right choice at the time."

"And now?"

Bertrand glanced down at his hands and touched the heavy silver ring he wore. It looked like a signet ring, but he hadn't worn it when Suzanne had first met him in France. She suspected Rupert had given it to him. Rupert wore a similar one. "Perhaps I'm a selfish devil. God knows the way things have turned out isn't fair to Gaby—"

"Gaby's happy with Nick Gordon."

"Gaby would have been happier if she could have married Nick Gordon, but, yes. Thank God things have turned out so well for her. Thank God because I love Gaby, and thank God, because it salves Rupert's and my guilt. As for me—guilt or not, I can't imagine my life without him. I can't imagine I was ever mad enough to think that was possible for either of us. I'm grateful every day that he was willing to take me back and that I had the guts to come back." He looked at her for a moment, his gaze at once furtive and oddly open. "I owe part of that to you."

"Me?" Suzanne repeated.

"That day at the inn on the Calais road. Just after my masquerade had broken and Rupert had seen me. After I'd made my speech to Rupert about why I had to disappear and why it wouldn't work between us. You told me you found living with Malcolm in an imperfect world far preferable to being separated from him. At the time, I hadn't put together who you were. Your words still registered, but I couldn't imagine how you could fully understand what it was to fear that simple association with you could destroy the man you loved. It was only on the journey to Britain with the St. Gilles family that I pieced together that you were—"

"The Raven?" Suzanne said. Amazing how easily she put the unspeakable into words with him.

Bertrand nodded. "And so I realized that you knew as much as I did about living with secrets and about your very identity being a risk."

"You're generous, Bertrand. You didn't entrap Rupert. Or lie to him about who you were."

"I lied to him about my very survival. I let him spend four years alone in a harsh world, while I at least had the comfort of knowing how he got on. I've never believed much in convention, but somehow I let myself think Rupert was better off living a conventional life without me than facing the risks we ran together."

Suzanne thought of the life she sometimes pictured for Malcolm, married to a girl from his own world. Someone who understood how to navigate its unwritten rules and unvoiced codes, who might not share his sense of adventure to the degree she did, but who could give him a settled life in a way she'd never be able to, for all her efforts at domesticity. Sometimes, even now, she thought he might have been happier in that life.

Bertrand gripped her hand. "I hope to God we never have to get you to Italy. But I'd take Italy with Rupert over life without him in a heartbeat."

Suzanne swallowed, tasting the embers of fear. "You're a kind man, Bertrand."

"I'm a man who's thrown happiness away and got it back and who knows how important it is to hold on to it." He paused. "When Malcolm came to ask for my help in making arrangements should you need to leave Britain, he didn't seem like a man torn by betrayal. Merely a man desperately concerned for the woman he loves."

"That's Malcolm. If he hated me, he wouldn't even let me see it, let alone anyone else."

"Perhaps not, but I wouldn't have survived if I wasn't more than passably good at reading people. I know what worry looks like. I know what love looks like."

Suzanne drew a breath.

"What?" Bertrand asked.

"I remember Simon saying, back in Paris, that it had been quite obvious to him before you went to France that you and Rupert were madly in love."

Bertrand gave a wry smile. "Simon has his own skills at reading people. Frustrating at times, but also comforting." He paused. "That day Malcolm came to see me. I was concerned for you both. But I was relieved he knew. Relieved it hadn't changed things between you."

"It changed things incalculably," Suzanne said. "But we're still together."

"Malcolm understands betrayal too."

She shook her head. "Malcolm would never do what I did. He's far more like you. I'm more a gameplayer than I care to admit."

"We're all gameplayers to a degree. But I don't think any of us are driven by it."

"Bertrand—" Suzanne drew a breath. Malcolm had trusted Bertrand with their lives. She owed him a trust as great. She put a hand on his own, and told him about the Phoenix plot.

25

Bertrand stared at Suzanne with a still gaze. "I'm honored. I don't imagine it was easy to share that."

"I'm sorry," she said. "That I didn't tell you sooner. And yet, in a way, knowing is a burden."

"You mean whether or not I tell Rupert?" He shook his head. "At this point, I wouldn't put Rupert in that position. Not until we know more."

"You hadn't heard anything?"

He shook his head again. "It sounds as though Germont made a calculated decision to confide in you rather than me. Perhaps to try to entrap you." He touched her hand. "I'm sorrier than I can say that I brought him into your life."

"Whatever the nature of the plot, it would have been in play whether or not you'd brought him to London. He has a confederate who was already here."

Bertrand's mouth tightened. "I'll add him to my inquiries. I can pool my information with O'Roarke." He squeezed Suzanne's hand. "I won't fail your trust."

Despite the situation, she smiled at him. "I never thought you would."

"It's a long time since I've appreciated the advantages of the waltz," Raoul murmured, his hands on Laura's waist as the dance came to an end.

Laura looked up into her lover's eyes. You'd never guess he'd been talking about the risks of a plot by Fouché with hard eyes and suspiciously white-knuckled hands a few hours before. "You've perfected the art of snatching happiness in the moment, haven't you?"

"It's the only way to survive in this business." For a moment she saw a shadow flicker in his gaze. Doubt? Uncertainty? Fear? Then he gave a quick smile and offered her his arm. "Nothing to be done at the moment. And how often do I get a chance to put my arms round you in public?"

Laura curled her fingers round his arm. "I never thought to hear you indulging in trivialities."

"On the contrary," Raoul murmured, leading her off the dance floor. "Putting my arms round you is something I take extremely seriously."

Laura laughed up at him. "And to think—" She broke off at the sight of a familiar figure in a gleaming dress uniform crossing the ballroom towards them, a purposeful look in his eye. Why, why hadn't it occurred to her that Will Cuthbertson might be among the Lydgates' guests?

"Ja—Lady Tarrington." Will gave a very correct bow.

"Colonel Cuthbertson. Do you know Mr. O'Roarke? He's an old friend of the Rannochs'." Laura looked up at Raoul.

She was still holding his arm but conscious now of doing so in a very correct manner. "Colonel Cuthbertson and I were acquainted in India."

"Cuthbertson." Raoul shook Will's hand. "You served with Harry Davenport, didn't you?"

"In the Peninsula. Davenport was on the staff by Waterloo. A good friend. You were in the Peninsula yourself, weren't you?"

"Working with the guerrilleros." Raoul gave his cover story with the ease of an expert agent. "I had the luxury of being safely in Brussels during Waterloo."

Which of course was also a cover story. In fact, Laura realized, watching her former and current lovers, they had both fought at Waterloo. On opposite sides.

"I've heard stories of your bravery on the Peninsula," Will said, in a tone that Laura thought rather unfairly emphasized that Raoul was older than he was. "I was hoping I could persuade Lady Tarrington to grant me the next dance. If you'll excuse us, O'Roarke?"

"Of course," Raoul said. "A relief for her to dance with someone her own age, I should imagine."

Doing it much too brown, Laura thought, but of course she couldn't step on his foot, or shoot him a look, or any of the things she'd have liked to do. There was nothing for it but to release Raoul's arm and take Will's with the most serene smile she could muster.

"A good man, O'Roarke, from what I've heard," Will said. "I suppose he knew the Rannochs in the Peninsula."

"And he knew Malcolm Rannoch's family before that," Laura said, and then sent Raoul a mental apology because somehow that seemed to put him in a different generation. "He's been very kind to me," she added. Somehow, it seemed important to say something of the sort, though she couldn't possibly tell Will the truth.

Will, in fact, was smiling at her as though Raoul was the furthest thing from his mind. "I'm glad to see you again so soon. I had heard you didn't go out often."

Oh, poison. He wouldn't think she was here because of him, would he? "The Lydgates are friends of the Rannochs'. The call of friendship can pull me away from my daughter for a few hours."

"I have no doubt you're a splendid mother."

"That's kind, Will, though I fear I showed little enough promise in India. I do think I'm managing to do at least a passable job, though."

Will shook his head as they took their places for the dance. "You've always been hard on yourself." He smiled down at her. "You've been through a lot. I wish you'd let people take care of you."

"My dear Will. You know me better than that. Being coddled has always driven me mad."

Will watched her for a moment with a rueful smile. "You've been alone for a long time, Laura. You needn't always be."

Laura swallowed as his hand closed round hers. Because the answer to that had far more to do with another person than she could allow Will to imagine. "Will—" She dipped into a curtsy as the dance began. "I wasn't very good at being a wife. No, I know it was partly Jack's fault. But not solely. It's not a road I want to travel again."

He smiled. "I can be patient."

Raoul kept an easy smile on his face as Laura moved off on Cuthbertson's arm. It wouldn't do to look away too soon nor to let his gaze linger too long. He turned, still aware in his peripheral vision of Laura and Cuthbertson taking their places for the dance, and saw Malcolm's aunt, Frances Dacre-Hammond, approaching on the arm of Archibald Davenport, Harry's uncle and a longtime colleague of Raoul's.

"I've seen you dancing more of late than in years," Archie said. "Though it's not surprising, given the incentive."

Raoul gave a smile carefully calibrated to be casual. Archie and Fanny were two of his best and oldest friends, but there were some things he wasn't prepared to share with them. "Lady Tarrington is settling back into society after a difficult time. She's needed the support of friends." He turned his gaze back to Laura, now dancing with Cuthbertson, willing it to disinterest. "She'll soon have plenty of dancing partners her own age."

"Careful, my dear," Frances said. "I'm not that much younger than you, and Lady Tarrington can't be much more than a decade my junior. You should never make comments about a lady's age."

Raoul lifted her hand to his lips. "You're ageless, Fanny."

"Hmph," Fanny said, but her smile was sweet and almost girlish.

"It's good to see you back in England," Archie said. "And I hope recent developments mean you'll be here more often."

Raoul met his friend's gaze. From the days two decades ago when Archie had first given him information of use in the United Irish Uprising, Archie had been one of the closest people Raoul had to a confidant. The instinct to secrecy warred with an odd, unfamiliar instinct to share his happiness. "I have a number of reasons to return to Britain as often as I can."

"Glad to hear it." Archie touched Raoul's arm. "Speaking of dancing with younger women, I'm promised to Cordelia for the next dance. Should go and find her."

Archie moved across the room in search of his nephew's wife. Frances watched him for a moment, a smile playing about her lips. "Odd, I never appreciated Archie properly when I was younger. Of course, I always thought he was in love with my sister, which does rather dim a man's attractions." She smiled at Raoul. "No offense."

"None taken. Though in Archie's case, I don't think you're right. He admired Arabella. They were friends, but they weren't lovers, and I don't think he was in love with her." Archie had pretended to be Arabella's lover as part of the investigation six months ago, but that had been a smoke screen to cover his work with her against the Elsinore League.

"You can't know that," Frances said.

"No. One can never really know what goes on in another's head."

"Or heart." Frances turned back to Raoul. "It's good to see you smiling."

Raoul lifted a brow. "My dear Fanny. I've always been perfectly capable of smiling. It's seen me through some of my darkest moments. To smile any more would risk vulgarity."

"You don't give a damn about vulgarity. Isn't that what you've been so busy fighting for, to have us all considered equal? Perhaps I should have said it's good to see you happy." She glanced round. "This calls for champagne. For once, not because we need it, because we need to celebrate."

Raoul retrieved glasses of champagne from a passing footman. Of one accord he and Frances moved to a settee set against the wall between two potted palms. Frances lifted her glass. "To the future. It's nice to be able to drink to it."

Raoul clinked his glass against her own. They had shared many drinks through the years, glasses of champagne or claret, or more likely, drams of whisky. Usually, as she said, to dull the pain of a crisis. One of Arabella's breakdowns, or later, coping with the gaping hole her death had left in both their lives. Their shared fears for Malcolm, particularly after his mother's death.

Frances smoothed the purple-striped gauze of her skirts over the blue-and-gold satin of the settee. "She's very lovely. More to the point, she has a keen wit and she appears to have a good head on her shoulders. She won't drive you mad the way Arabella did."

Raoul's fingers tightened round the fragile stem of his glass. In the light from the candle sconces above, the cut glass sparkled with all the brilliance of Arabella Rannoch's smile. For a moment her blue eyes danced in his memory, sharp and brilliant as crystal. And just as likely to shatter and draw blood. "I don't suppose there's much sense in my saying I don't know who you're talking about?"

"Only if you want to indulge in verbal fencing."

He took a sip, holding the glass steady in the flickering light. "And to think I've been known to pride myself on my talent at deception."

"I shouldn't think it would be obvious to someone who didn't know you. You were careful not to hang about her too much, and I didn't see you so much as press her hand the entire time I was at Malcolm and Suzanne's dinner last April. In fact, I'd say the way you were careful not to reveal anything gave the most away. Well, that and the expression in your eyes when I caught you looking at her in an unguarded moment. Not to mention the look in your eyes when you were dancing with her tonight."

Raoul settled back in his corner of the settee with a carefully calibrated nonchalance that was probably a waste, given Fanny's powers of perception. "My dear Fanny. You are sounding distinctly like a lending library novel."

"Some lending library novels have remarkably keen insights into human relationships."

He rested his elbow on the settee arm with an assumption of ease. Fanny knew him well. Better than most people. But there were gaps in her knowledge. Such as his having been a French spy and his relationship with Suzanne. "She's a remarkable woman. She's been through a great deal."

"Obviously. I don't for a moment believe that farrago about her lost memory. If that was the best you and Malcolm and Suzanne could come up with, the truth must be extreme indeed." Frances put up a hand. "No, I'm not asking you to confide in me. Goodness knows I can understand secrets. The little girl is adorable. For her sake, not to mention her mother's, I rather hope Jack Tarrington isn't her father. The man was quite appalling. It wasn't the indiscriminate nature of his liaisons I object to, it was his wanton disregard for the trail of destruction he left in his wake." Her brows drew together. "I hope I was never that unfeeling."

"You know perfectly well you weren't, Fanny." Raoul took another sip of champagne, relieved at the change of subject. While Jack wasn't in fact Emily's father, the truth was, if anything, worse, both in terms of the implications and the nature of the man who had fathered her. Fortunately, Raoul was a firm believer that the nature of one's parents didn't form one.

Frances adjusted the folds of her shawl. "I always thought you'd make a good father."

"I'm hardly Emily's father."

"There are different ways of defining these things. You certainly *looked* paternal, when the children came into the drawing room at the dinner last April. You were far less on your guard with the little girl than with her mother."

"Emily's been through her own sort of horror." For a moment, Raoul could smell the cold, sterile air in the school where Laura's daughter had made her home—after leaving the care of a wetnurse, who had tended God knew how many children. Countless children lived in worse conditions. It was part of what drove him in his work. And yet Emily's plight never failed to cut him to the quick. Mélanie's voice sounded in his head. *It's different when it's your own.*

Frances took a sip of champagne. "They're fortunate, both the girl and her mother, to have you."

"On the contrary. Any good fortune in the situation—about which I admit nothing at all—is entirely on my side."

For some reason Frances's smile deepened at that. As though she understood something she wouldn't venture to articulate. Something he couldn't even articulate—perhaps didn't even understand—himself. "I won't tease you further. We're all entitled to our secrets. Speaking of which, do you have any idea what's been going on between my nephew and his wife?"

Raoul nearly choked on a simple breath of candle-warmed air. He took a sip of champagne, pleased his hand was steady. "They seemed well enough when we arrived at the ball an hour since."

"Yes, things are better now. But something happened near Christmas. To own the truth, I was quite concerned for a few weeks. I can't imagine either of them being unfaithful—" She shook her head, her blonde ringlets stirring about her face. "That sounds absurd coming from me. If anyone should be able to imagine infidelity under any circumstances—But I'd swear if any man is incapable of infidelity, it's Malcolm. Suzanne obviously adores him, but I could perhaps imagine her under the right circumstances—or perhaps I should say the wrong ones—"

"It's not infidelity," Raoul said. Stupid. Far better for Fanny to imagine infidelity than to get anywhere close to the truth. But somehow he couldn't bear to have her mind drift that way. Of course whether or not it was infidelity depended on one's definition of the term.

Frances lifted a well-groomed brow.

"I don't know precisely what went on between them," he said. Which was true, leaving aside that he knew more than Frances—he hoped—could possibly guess. "But I think it had to do with Malcolm's work on the Peninsula. It's difficult for an agent to leave the game behind."

"As you would know better than anyone." Frances shook her head. "It was about the same time he learned you were his father."

Raoul's fingers tightened round his glass. He started to take a sip, an automatic defense, but his throat was too raw. Myriad memories choked him. The moment, six months ago, when he'd finally admitted he was Malcolm's father. The vulnerability and surprising openness in Malcolm's gaze. The bleak anger in that same gaze a short time later when Malcolm learned the truth about Mélanie and Raoul and the deception behind his marriage. Malcolm, last April, calmly mentioning he'd had a guest bedchamber made up for Raoul and saying the Berkeley Square house was the closest thing Raoul had to a home in London. Playing pirates with the children by the Thames on a warm spring afternoon at Richmond. Arguing the source of a Shakespeare quote. Malcolm's casual greeting in the breakfast parlor this morning, and other fleeting moments in the past six months when it had almost seemed that something he'd thought would always be out of his reach might be within his grasp.

"He was investigating Alistair's death at the same time," Raoul said. He trusted Frances would put the roughness in his voice down to the fact that he'd always been raw when talking about Malcolm's parentage.

"True," she said, though her gaze told him she didn't think she'd got to the bottom of it. "He faced a number of challenges in that year. And he does tend to withdraw when he faces emotional challenges. I suppose if Suzanne sensed that— I know how challenging it must be for her when he turns inwards, but I'd swear—" She shook her head. "It's all right, I won't tease you to say more. In any case, I'm glad Malcolm knows you're his father."

Raoul managed a sip of champagne, though it caught in his throat. "I don't know that he sees me as his father. But it's good he knows the truth."

Frances's gaze was shrewd and sharp as a blade. "I wasn't just watching you and Laura Tarrington and the child the last time we were all in Berkeley Square. I never thought to see Malcolm so at ease with you. In fact, I rarely see him so at ease with anyone."

"He's a remarkable man." There, at least, he was telling Frances the unvarnished truth. "I'm fortunate to know him. But the revelation of a biological fact three decades old doesn't make someone a parent."

"No. But I think what you shared when he was growing up does. You were a better parent to him than Arabella."

Raoul felt his head jerk up.

Frances regarded him with a steady blue gaze. As keen and shrewd as Arabella's, but warmer. "I loved her too," Frances said. "But she was the devil on people who cared about her. Her children included. You deserve some happiness, my dear. Don't let Laura Tarrington slip away."

The width of the settee suddenly seemed far too confined. "I rather think that's up to Lady Tarrington."

"I hope so. I hope she knows enough not to let you get tripped up by your scruples."

"Fanny, I don't know what's more amusing. Your talking about scruples or the idea that I possess them."

"Just because you trained yourself to keep your feelings about Malcolm to yourself doesn't mean you have to do so with everyone."

"You're too much of a realist for fairy tales, Fanny." Here he felt on firmer ground. "I wasn't made for a domestic life."

"I imagine she realizes that. After living with Jack Tarrington, I doubt that's what she wants."

"It might be precisely what she decides she wants. Given that she's never had it."

Frances's gaze drifted towards the dancers. "That colonel would bore her in a week. If he hasn't already done so over the course of a dance."

Raoul took a sip of champagne. "I think you may be underrating what he can offer her."

"What's that?" Frances sounded genuinely curious.

"Stability. As one who's made a practice of living without it, I confess I can see the attraction."

26

" I 've asked the footmen to throw open the ballroom windows." Isobel Lydgate stopped beside Suzanne near the doorway between the ballroom and adjoining salon. "We were actually worried it was cool before the guests arrived. I've had a report from the kitchen that there was a near disaster with the lobster soufflé for supper, but apparently all is well. And Lucinda found Hugh Carstairs being sick into one of the potted palms, but he's now settled in the library with a pot of coffee. Just a typical Mayfair ball."

Suzanne squeezed her friend's arm. "It's a great success."

Isobel smiled even as her gaze darted about the room. "I'm not sure we have enough scandal for it to become a true *on-dit*." She turned back to Suzanne, her gaze gone serious. "I suppose you're pursuing your investigation even here."

"A ball can be an excellent place to find people one needs to talk to. And to catch them off their guard." Suzanne fingered one of the silver tassels at the waist of her smoke blue gauze gown. Eustace Whateley had sent Malcolm to talk to Oliver, but in some ways Bel was even closer to the man whose papers they seemed to be seeking. "Bel—Craven was your brother-in-law."

Isobel gave a mirthless laugh. "So was Trenchard. I can hardly claim to have known either of them. It sounds very uncharitable, but to you I can admit I didn't want to know either of them."

"I understand. But you saw them. You talked to your sisters. Did Louisa ever say anything about Whateley & Company?"

"Good heavens, no." Isobel gave a quick, rather awkward smile. "I think Louisa was embarrassed by Craven's dabbling in trade, for all other gentlemen do it. I don't think I'd have even known about Whateley & Company if Craven hadn't mentioned it to Oliver."

"Oliver went to see Craven at the warehouse recently."

"Yes, to talk about Louisa's marriage settlement. Oliver told me Malcolm had been to see him about it. But you can't think—"

"Just trying to get a full picture. Someone obviously thinks Craven had something of import."

"Surely that must be to do with—"

"Bel, darling." A woman in spangled yellow crêpe swept by and pressed her cheek to Isobel's. Marianne Fairchild, Suzanne realized. It still sometimes took her a few moments to sort out faces and names of those on the edges of her social circle. If memory served, Marianne was a second or third cousin of Bel's on Lady Carfax's side. "A lovely party. Mrs. Rannoch." Marianne turned to give a careless nod to Suzanne, then looked back at Isobel. "I saw Oliver this afternoon. Outside my dressmaker's, of all things. He was talking to a quite stunning brunette. You're fortunate to trust your husband so well, Bel."

Marianne Fairchild swept off. Bel had gone still, seemingly rooted to the polished floorboards. Suzanne took her friend's arm and steered Bel to a sofa set behind a potted palm. "What a dreadful woman. It's always those who've known us since we were children who seem to be able to hurt us the worst."

"It's all right, Suzanne." Bel gave a shake of her head, gaze focused again. "I'd like to think that I was made of sterner stuff than to be overset by a mention of my husband and his latest mistress."

Suzanne stared at her friend, whom she'd have sworn had one of the happiest marriages in Mayfair. "Dearest—"

Isobel's mouth curled. "Did you really think I escaped the fate of most Mayfair marriages? Of my sisters?"

"But you and Oliver aren't—"

Isobel gave a smile startling in how bitter it was. "No, Oliver isn't Trenchard or Craven. He's much more charming, much more handsome, and a much kinder person. He hasn't got a title or even an old family name. And I'm not Mary or Louisa. I haven't got their beauty or their charm or their knack with clothes. I know people said Louisa lived in Mary's shadow. But I never even tried to compete."

"I don't imagine you wanted to."

"No. Their concerns didn't seem particularly interesting. And I knew I hadn't a prayer of keeping up. I never particularly wanted to. But it did rather leave me at a disadvantage when it came to securing a husband."

Suzanne remembered Isobel and Oliver as she had seen them on her first visit to London four years ago. In the drawing room of this house, Oliver with their son on his shoulders, Isobel with their elder daughter clinging to her skirts. Isobel's and Oliver's shoulders had been a handsbreadth apart, not quite touching. Because they clearly didn't need to. Suzanne wasn't given to jealousy, but envy of what the Lydgates shared had shot through her, a palpable ache. "Darling, I can't imagine you wanting to—"

Isobel raised a brow, suddenly looking like Lord Carfax's daughter. "I was tired of writing out Mama's cards of invitation and seeing her strain to find new eligible bachelors to seat me next to. I wanted my own establishment. I wanted children. Is that so surprising?"

"Of course not. But Oliver—"

"Oliver—" Isobel shook her head. "I could scarcely have failed to notice Oliver, could I? From the time David first brought him down to Carfax Court from Oxford. I may not have tried to play Mary's and Louisa's games, but I wasn't immune to that smile."

"Even I wasn't," Suzanne said. "And I was a married woman in love with my husband when I met him. But I've seen the way he looks at you, Bel."

Isobel shook her head. "You're a romantic, Suzanne."

"I'm not in the least—"

"You love your husband, and you project that onto other people. You've seen Oliver and me settled into marriage. Oliver cares for me. As his partner. The mother of his children. If you could have seen us when we met—Suffice it to say, I had no illusions. Besides, Oliver had eyes for no one but Sylvie de Fancot at that point."

"Sylvie de Fancot?" Suzanne frowned, searching her memory. "Do you mean Lady St. Ives?" She pictured the lovely blonde viscountess, like her a French émigrée who had married into the beau monde. Her husband was in the Life Guards and she had been in Brussels with him before Waterloo.

Isobel gave a dry smile. "She wasn't Lady St. Ives yet. Her parents were friends of my parents. They were at that same house party where I first met Oliver, and I watched Sylvie and him fall madly in love across the dinner table. For years he had eyes for no one else."

Suzanne drew a breath, trying to picture Oliver and Sylvie St. Ives together. She and Sylvie had never been particular friends. Suzanne's instinct was to avoid someone whose background was so close to her own cover story (and who therefore might be able to see through her), but she saw the other woman at a score of entertainments. Surely she must have seen Sylvie and Oliver speak, dance, sit beside each other. How could she have been so blind as not to notice anything?

"The love affair was in the past by the time you met either of them," Isobel said. "And you wouldn't have been looking for signs. You assumed Oliver and I were happy. Which we were, in a way. "

"Dearest—" Suzanne stretched out a hand.

Isobel didn't pull away but neither did she return the clasp of Suzanne's hand. "It was after Sylvie had married St. Ives and I'd been out a few seasons that Oliver began to pay more attention to me. One night he started making love to me in the Carfax House conservatory." For a moment, the wonder and horror of those moments shone in Isobel's face, as though the flesh had been stripped from her bones to reveal the hard reality beneath. "I told him to stop. That I quite liked the idea of marrying him, and I was perfectly prepared to do so. So long as he promised never to pretend to love me again."

Suzanne stared at her friend. One of her first British friends. Who, unlike Cordy and Simon and Laura, she'd thought wholly secure in her marriage and position in the world. "Malcolm never pretended to love me."

"But he does." Isobel's smile was somehow strained but real. "Odd how life works out. I think Malcolm was worried when he heard Oliver and I were betrothed. His letter of felicitations said everything that was kind, but I could read between the lines. And I know you enough now I can own to worrying when I first heard Malcolm, who'd always sworn off marriage, was going to marry a girl we'd never met."

"I can well understand that. And I can well understand I've been blind to much of what was before me. Bel, I'm so sorry—"

Isobel touched her arm and gave a dry smile. Again, Suzanne was put in mind of Carfax more than she ever had been in her acquaintance with Bel. "It's all right, dearest. It's hardly the tragedy it would be if you learned Malcolm had been unfaithful. I went into the marriage expecting Oliver to stray. I gave him permission that night I agreed to be his wife. So long as he never embarrassed me. And for the most part he hasn't. Gossip like tonight stings a bit. Probably more than it should. But I shall be quite all right."

"Dearest—"

Isobel gave a quick, self-deprecating laugh. "It's not the first time I've heard mention of this particular woman. I actually made the mistake of inquiring into her name. Foolish. Much easier to ignore it if I didn't know. I found myself dwelling on things. Like if Malcolm knew her in the Peninsula."

"What made you think that?"

"Because of her name. With that and her coloring, she seems quite obviously Spanish."

Over her concern for her friend, Suzanne felt the scent of a puzzle piece about to lock into place. "What was her name?"

"Maria Monreal."

"You appear to have been enjoying yourself." Malcolm stopped beside Raoul on the edge of the dance floor.

Raoul surveyed his son, a distinct memory in his mind of Malcolm buried in a book in the library during social occasions in his undergraduate days. "I could say the same."

Malcolm gave an unexpected grin. "I don't cut and run as much at entertainments as I once did. Which is part Mel's influence and part the demands of investigating."

"I confess to feeling the impulse to cut and run at a ball more than once in the past. But at times they prove surprisingly diverting. The Lydgates are excellent hosts."

"I confess I've quite come to like dancing with Mel." Malcolm paused for a moment. "You looked very at home on the dance floor yourself."

The feel of Laura in his arms on the dance floor flooded his memory. Odd how dancing with a woman could be so intimate even when one had shared greater intimacies. "I haven't entirely forgot how." He didn't let his gaze linger on Laura but he'd been aware all evening of where she was. She'd danced twice with Cuthbertson, then with Bertrand and then Harry. Now she was standing with Cordelia and Aline Blackwell. As he watched, Cuthbertson brought the three ladies champagne.

"I can't imagine you forgetting a skill at anything, O'Roarke."

"My dear Malcolm. At my age, one is keenly aware one's abilities aren't what they used to be."

"Doing it much too brown, sir." Malcolm's gaze moved over the ballroom. "By the way, I saw Wellington a bit ago. He noticed you at the ball. Said to invite you to his dinner tomorrow."

The anniversary of Waterloo, though Malcolm was tactfully avoiding putting into words the reference to the day that had wrecked so many of Raoul's dreams. "Very good of him," Raoul said.

"He says he appreciates everything you did on the Peninsula," Malcolm said in a steady voice.

Raoul managed a dry smile. "An able man, the duke. It's rather a relief to know that there are things he doesn't see."

"I didn't want to speak for you," Malcolm said, "but we can easily make your excuses. Though it will be an excellent opportunity to gather information."

Raoul raised his brows.

Malcolm gave a smile, faint but real. "Yes, I know. God help me, I can't believe I'm saying that to you, but I am. Besides, we've talked Laura into going. I'm sure she'd welcome your company."

Raoul watched Laura clink her glass against Cuthbertson's. "She might enjoy herself more if she was free to talk to her old friends."

Malcolm was leaning casually against the paneling, but Raoul knew his son's gaze was taking in the same scene. "I don't believe it for a moment. But if that were the case, you can't tell me you don't know how to read a situation and make yourself scarce. You could always take refuge in the library. Wellington has an excellent one."

Raoul flung back his head and laughed despite himself. "Then how can I refuse?" he said.

Malcolm had been speaking with Raoul, but now William Lamb and Rupert had joined them. Suzanne hesitated. The news she had to deliver was better shared in the privacy of their bedchamber. But given that they were in Oliver's house and in the midst of an investigation that the revelations might directly impact, time was of the essence. She joined the men, discussed the forthcoming general election for a few minutes, then asked if they minded terribly if she stole her husband away. Of course, they didn't. Malcolm gave her his arm with a smile and said nothing until she had led him into an ante-room adjoining the smaller drawing room. Then he turned to her with raised brows.

"What do you have to tell me that you thought I couldn't handle hearing in public?"

"Not that. But—" She turned to face him, conscious of a chill, though the brace of candles warmed the air. It must be stepping out of the heat of the crowded drawing room.

"Darling?" Malcolm crossed to her side in two steps and gripped her shoulders. "What is it? You look as though you've seen a ghost."

"Of course not." Unless it was the ghost of her belief in a happy marriage? "I'm just a bit surprised. And sad, I suppose. Dearest—" How to break his faith in two of his closest friends? Malcolm's faith in so many people had been shaken lately. "Bel just told me that Oliver has a mistress."

She waited for surprise to suffuse her husband's face and instead saw a grimace of acknowledgment. "Damnation. How long has she known?"

"Malcolm—" Suzanne took a step back. "Don't tell me you knew—"

"For a certainty? Of course not." Malcolm dug a hand through his hair. "Oliver would hardly confide such a thing in me given how close I've always been to Bel. She was my friend before he was."

"But you aren't surprised." Suzanne continued to stare at her husband. These days she was particularly aware of how reality—one's perception of reality—could shift in an instant, cutting the ground of comfortable certainty away like a sheet of ice.

"That Oliver has a mistress? The possibility has occurred to me, though I'd have hoped not. That Bel knew? Bel's an astute woman. If Oliver has a mistress, it's likely she'd guess. That their marriage is less than idyllic? Most people's are."

He smiled faintly as he said that last, as though to rob it of the sting, and that smile cut straight through to her heart. "Neither of us has—"

"No." He smiled again, straight into her eyes. "But we're certainly not strangers to deception and betrayal."

"You mean I've betrayed and deceived you."

"And I you on occasion, if on a smaller scale. It comes with the territory of being a spy."

She folded her arms over her chest, hugging her gauze shawl round her, as though the fragile fabric could protect her from reality. "Cordy admits she married Harry because she was desperate to escape. Rupert offered for Gaby because Bertrand was gone and he thought he needed a wife. You and I—"

"You married me to spy for the French. I married you because you needed protection. And because I was half in love with you and that gave me an excuse. But you're right. It was hardly a moonlight and roses beginning. Neither was Bel's and Oliver's."

"You weren't here when they became betrothed."

"No. But I'd seen them before I left."

"Bel said she could tell you were worried from your letter of felicitations."

He gave a wry grimace. "I tried to hide it. I hoped they could make it work. But I'd seen how Oliver felt about Sylvie."

"You never told me. That Oliver had been in love with Lady St. Ives." She couldn't remember Oliver and Sylvie together, but she could remember Malcolm introducing her to

Sylvie St. Ives at a reception at Carfax House on their first visit to Britain. He'd seemed to think Suzanne would like meeting someone with a similar background, which might have been true if their backgrounds had indeed been similar.

"It was in the past by the time you met both Oliver and Sylvie," Malcolm said. "But one doesn't get over that sort of love quickly."

The questions about Malcolm's own romantic history that she had struggled with while talking to Cordy that morning came flooding back, but of course she couldn't voice them. "So you thought their marriage was doomed from the start because Oliver was in love with Sylvie?"

"Marriages can work without love. But it's difficult when the love is on one side."

Suzanne frowned. "Because Oliver—"

"Because Bel had obviously been head over heels in love with Oliver for years."

Suzanne saw her friend coolly recounting Oliver's infidelities and the bargain they'd made. And that moment of naked pain in her face when Marianne Fairchild first mentioned Oliver's mistress. "Bel didn't say that. But it makes sense." She studied Malcolm, remembering countless evenings with Bel and Oliver, countless outings with the children. "You never said any of this to me."

"What was there to say? I didn't know anything for a certainty."

"You let me think—"

"You saw them the way you wanted to, sweetheart." He put a hand against her cheek. "Because of the person you are. You believe in happiness."

"That's ridiculous, Malcolm."

"Is it? You were mad enough to believe we could be happy. You were right."

And perhaps to fuel that belief, she'd needed to believe that others could be. And so her skills at reading people had quite deserted her. "I didn't ask you in here just to discuss our friends, Malcolm. Bel confided in me because she was over-set when Marianne Fairchild mentioned seeing Oliver with a beautiful dark-haired woman. Bel said she'd seen Oliver with the woman before. She's even inquired about the woman's name. It's Maria Monreal."

This time she saw shock run through Malcolm, though he scarcely moved a muscle. "Christ. And I thought Eustace was snatching at straws when he told me about Oliver's visit to the warehouse."

"He might have been. But two weeks after that visit, people broke into the Whateley & Company warehouse. And two nights after that, Maria broke into the Craven house."

Malcolm frowned at a pair of blue-and-white Chinese vases on the console table. "What the hell is Oliver up to?"

27

"Malcolm. Haven't seen you all evening."

David's voice stopped Malcolm as he circled the drawing room looking for Oliver, head still pounding from Suzanne's revelations. He stopped, about to ask if David had seen Oliver, when he got a good look into his friend's eyes. "What's happened?"

David passed a hand over his face. "God, is it that obvious?"

"To someone who knows just how you look in a crisis."

David gave a lopsided grin. "I wouldn't call it a crisis. Not like someone breaking into the house with the children in it. Or your investigation. This can—"

Malcolm dug a shoulder into the gilded wall. "Talk."

"I took the children to see Father and Mother and Lucinda today. It went pretty well. Father didn't ring a peal over Teddy, and the children were more at ease than they sometimes are. Though Mother looked a bit pained when Jamie smeared jam tart all over the drawing room carpet. We weren't allowed in the drawing room very much as children, except for half an hour in the afternoon. It makes—"

"David," Malcolm said.

"Father called me into his study. We had a talk about Teddy. Fairly rational for Father. I was feeling quite in charity with him. Then he decided to tell me it was time I married."

"Damn it," Malcolm said.

David shifted his weight from one foot to the other. "It was nothing he hadn't said before."

"But something was different."

David shrugged, gaze focused on a potted palm across the room. "In tone at least. He was more blunt. He actually mentioned Simon directly." David blanched with the horror of one obliged to discuss his romantic life with his parent. "He was so obliging as to suggest he wouldn't object to my continuing my relationship with Simon so long as I produced an heir. And a spare, presumably."

"There are women who probably wouldn't object to such an arrangement."

"Would you?" David turned to face him with sudden intensity. "If you couldn't be married to Suzanne for some reason, would you marry another woman simply to—" He couldn't quite seem to put it into words.

"No," Malcolm said without hesitation. "But I've never felt the obligation to produce an heir."

David's eyes darkened. "As if I would. Or could. As if Simon would ever go along with—I told Father it was impossible. That I never would. I actually for a moment thought, 'Well, at least that's done. Awkward as it was, we can't have this conversation again.'"

"Until?"

The gaze David lifted to him held not anger but worry. "Father said it wasn't over. Of course I know he won't let it go, but I can't but worry about what he may try to get what he wants."

Malcolm shared those worries, but there was no point in dwelling on them with David. "You've always found ways to stand up to your father. And you aren't without friends."

David's answering smile was the smile of their boyhood. "For which I'm inestimably grateful." He scanned Malcolm's face. "You look serious yourself. Are you in the midst of investigating?"

"Only asking a few questions. Have you seen Oliver?"

"Not for the past half hour or so. He and Bel are always running about when they're entertaining." David frowned. "You need to talk to Oliver about the investigation?"

"Possibly. He called on Eustace at the warehouse not long before the break-in." All of which was true, it just didn't explain everything they knew about Oliver's possible connection to the events. And yet—David might have helpful information. "Have you ever heard of a woman named Maria Monreal?"

David shook his head. "No. Is she connected to the investigation?"

"Apparently, though we aren't sure how." Strictly speaking that was true, and Malcolm wasn't yet ready to tell David they knew who had broken into the Brook Street house. "I've just learned Oliver may be acquainted with her."

"He's never mentioned her to me." David stared at Malcolm. "Are you telling me Oliver has a mistress who's involved in the break-in?"

It was blunt speaking for David. As little as they talked about their own personal lives, they were even less likely to discuss those of their friends. "You think Oliver has a mistress?" Malcolm asked.

David drew a sharp breath. "I don't—I don't have any reason to believe so."

"But you wouldn't be surprised?"

David met Malcolm's gaze with an honesty that went back more than half their lives. Difficult to pretend with people who'd known one since childhood. And their knowledge of Oliver went back a decade. "I envy what Bel and Oliver have sometimes. But it's not what you and Suzanne have."

Malcolm bit back a dry laugh. That was certainly true in ways David couldn't begin to understand, if perhaps also in the way he meant.

"I want Bel to be happy." David said in a measured voice. "I had concerns when they married. I didn't hide them from you. But I believe Oliver is a man of honor." David drew a harsh breath. "If he's hurt Bel—"

Malcolm touched his friend's arm. "Whatever's going on, I think Bel is well aware of it."

David's mouth tightened. "Bel doesn't deserve—"

"No," Malcolm agreed.

David glanced away again. "I tried to talk to her once. Before they married. I told her how much I loved them both and that I only wanted her to be happy. All Bel would say is that she knew what she was doing and they were happy."

"Malcolm." Lucinda Mallinson stopped Malcolm as he continued his pursuit of Oliver. "You look as though you're looking for someone. Cousin Eustace?"

"Oliver, actually." Malcolm smiled at David's youngest sister. With the deaths of her sister and two of her brothers-in-law, she had been through far more than most seventeen-year-olds, but she was still refreshingly open and cheerful, especially for a daughter of Lord Carfax.

"He was dancing with Sylvie St. Ives." Lucinda wrinkled her nose. "Very correctly, but I still don't like to see it, for Bel's sake. Even though Bel would tell me not to be silly. I think they went into the card room."

Malcolm found Oliver in the card room, now circulating on his own. Oliver greeted Malcolm with one of his easy smiles. Malcolm would have sworn those smiles were genuine. That Oliver had a mistress was not a shock. A disappointment, perhaps, but not far from the realm of what he imagined. That Oliver's mistress, and perhaps Oliver himself, might be involved in a conspiracy was another matter entirely. He had a clear vision of the four of them—him, Oliver, David, Simon—sitting round a scarred table in the Cup & Rose in Oxford after a rehearsal, debating whether Hotspur or Hal would be more effective in Parliament. He'd sat back in his chair, taken a sip of wine, looked at his friends' faces bathed in the oil lamplight, and for the first time in a long time felt he belonged.

"Never have enough chances to talk to one's friends when one's hosting," Oliver said. "Have you been talking politics?"

"Actually, I've been busy with the investigation." Malcolm turned, his back to the room and directed his voice to Oliver's ears alone. "When we spoke at Brooks's, you neglected to tell me that your mistress had an interest in it."

"My *what?*" One would swear the shock in Oliver's gaze was genuine.

"At least, she broke into the Brook Street house last night which I assume is connected. Couldn't she simply have asked you to retrieve whatever she was looking for?"

Oliver stared at him. He was a good actor. He'd made a very convincing Hotspur and an ardent Orlando. But he wasn't a trained agent. Malcolm could read the shock in his eyes but also a wariness that said he was not as stunned as his expression would lead one to believe. "Malcolm—who the devil are you talking about? And do you mean to say you know who broke into the Brook Street house? I thought—"

"We know. Now. And we know Maria Monreal is your mistress."

Malcolm was prepared for more denials. Instead Oliver spun away. "God, what a farce."

"For what it's worth," Malcolm said, "Bel knows. She's the one who told Suzanne about you and Maria."

"She—" Oliver spun back to him, this time his gaze filled with sick horror.

"Wives tend to notice these things," Malcolm said.

Oliver stared at Malcolm a moment longer, then jerked his head towards the door behind him. Without further speech, he and Malcolm went through the door into an empty antechamber bright with candlelight and a bouquet of blue larkspur.

Oliver strode across the room as though he wished it were an open field, then turned to face Malcolm, gripping a gilded chair back. "I should have realized—I should have known with you investigating it would come to this. I do know Maria. She is not my mistress. She's never been my mistress."

"You didn't tell her David would be out late last night? That he'd tell the staff not to wait up?"

Oliver hesitated. "Maria's not my mistress, but she's a friend. I know what all of you think of me, but I'm not— Whatever I offered Bel, I took my vows seriously."

Oddly, that had the ring of truth. Malcolm folded his arms across his chest and regarded his friend. "Go on."

"We met at an Exhibition at Somerset House. A gentleman was making himself disagreeable to her. Taking advantage of an émigrée and a woman alone. I intervened. Maria was having some legal difficulties. I did my best to help her out. I didn't mention our friendship to anyone because I knew precisely what assumptions people would make."

"And her breaking into Brook Street?"

"I don't know. But—" He drew a breath. "From something she said, I think she may have been entangled with Craven. Perhaps she'd written to him and wanted to retrieve any letters."

"She didn't ask for your help?"

"We're friends, but she'd hardly ask me to break into my brother-in-law's house." Oliver drew a breath. "I may have mentioned the opening at the Tavistock. I think at one point I did say David was considerate of his servants."

"And the warehouse?"

"What about the warehouse?"

"Were you looking for papers for her when you called on Eustace Whateley?"

"Of course not. I was there to talk about Louisa's marriage portion. As I told you. Why would anyone think Craven had hidden love letters in the warehouse?"

Why indeed? It was another reason to doubt the stories Maria Monreal and Oliver were giving. "Oliver, are you asking me to believe two different people broke into the warehouse of Craven's company and Craven's home two nights apart, for two different reasons?"

"I don't know. You're the investigator."

Malcolm stared at his friend, seeing Oliver's open gaze when he confided his love for Sylvie de Fancot, the hesitation in his eyes when he asked Malcolm about Simon and David. "I am. And I can tell you're lying, Oliver."

"I'm not—"

"Damn it, Oliver." For once, Malcolm could scarcely contain the anger in his voice. Anger at far more than Oliver's refusal to talk. Anger at something being smashed that went back over a decade.

Oliver folded his arms across his chest. "You can't pretend you tell me everything. I don't see why you should be so convinced I should confide in you."

"Because we're in the midst of an investigation. That concerns your family."

Oliver glanced away. "You know I wouldn't—"

"You can't possibly know that, Oliver. In an investigation one can never know what piece of information will connect to what other piece."

Oliver spun away, strode the narrow length of the room, then turned back to face Malcolm. "Christ, Malcolm, you always do this. Act as though you know what's right, as though everything's your responsibility, as though you can fix it. I know your capabilities. But you can't fix everything."

"I can't fix anything if I don't know what's going on." Malcolm studied his friend, picking his way through the fog of anger. "Oliver, if you're in trouble—"

"We aren't boys anymore, Malcolm." Oliver sounded winded, as he might after a hard-fought game of tennis. Or a bout with rapiers. "Nothing's as simple as it was at Oxford."

"I don't know that it was simple then."

"But we thought it was. We thought we had the answers."

"Oliver." Malcolm held the gaze of the man he'd trusted for so long. One could never really know another person. But he'd swear he knew something of Oliver's compassion. "A man died in the Whateley & Company break-in."

Oliver's head jerked up. "I know. But that's not—"

He'd fought in the Peninsula and at Waterloo and been wounded in the service of his country. He has a son, a two-year-old. Not so different from our children. A woman I think he loved in his way. He lost the chance to see his son grow up. To try to get the woman he loved out of a brothel. His son lost his father. You may not care about Craven or Eustace, but we owe it to this man to learn the truth."

For a moment, he thought Oliver was about to speak. Then Oliver's gaze closed over. "I can't help you, Malcolm."

"Can't or won't?"

Oliver's mouth twisted, with a bitterness that might have been directed at himself. "Does it matter?"

Malcolm stepped into the ballroom. He had to force his hands not to curl into fists at his sides. His temples throbbed with unvoiced questions and unexpressed anger. He drew a harsh breath. He'd got through the revelation of his wife's betrayal. Of his father's. If he could get through that, he could get through this. He could get through anything.

Oddly, it was the sight of his wife that steadied him. He saw her across the ballroom with Crispin and Manon. The sight of her familiar profile, the pendant he had given her six weeks ago and the pearls he had given her after their wedding gleaming round her throat, steadied him. And he needed steadying. Far more than he would admit to anyone.

Suzanne met his gaze as though aware of his regard. She murmured something to Crispin and Manon and moved across the ballroom towards him. Malcolm met her and took her arm, managing a quick smile. The sort he used to tamp down feelings. "Last I saw, the music room was empty," he murmured.

He glanced round the ballroom again and saw Harry, leaning against the wall. Davenport wasn't alone as he would have been a few years ago but was talking with Rupert and Bertrand. Like Suzanne, he met Malcolm's gaze, excused himself, and fell into step beside Malcolm and Suzanne.

Of one accord, they made their way through the crowd, out into the passage, and to the music room. Malcolm opened the door to find it thankfully still empty, though candles burned on the mantel and the table and beside the pianoforte. Malcolm crossed to the pianoforte and launched into the *Waldstein* Sonata. For cover. But as the anger rippled through his fingers and into the torrent of notes, he knew that wasn't all.

"Darling?" Suzanne leaned across the pianoforte and scanned his face, as she did when she was looking for injuries. "What did Oliver say?"

Malcolm began to pick out a more plaintive Bach sarabande. "He says Maria wasn't his mistress. That they were friends." Malcolm ran his fingers over the keys. "That she was Craven's mistress and may have broken into the Brook Street house to recover letters she'd written to him. But he denies helping her. Or having anything to do with the Whateley & Company break-in."

"And you don't believe him." Harry joined Suzanne at the pianoforte.

Malcolm lifted his hands from the keys and rested his arms on the piano. "Oddly enough, his protestations about not being her lover have the ring of truth. He reminded me—"

"Of the way you sounded when you denied being Tatiana's lover in Vienna?" Suzanne asked.

Malcolm met his wife's gaze in the candlelight. He might now know she'd been spying on him in Vienna, but the pain she had felt over thinking Tatiana Kirsanova had been his mistress had been real. And he'd never forgive himself for causing it. "Yes, actually."

"What he said fits with Maria's story, more or less," Harry said.

"Enough to convince me they planned it together," Malcolm said. His fingers tensed on the polished rosewood of the piano. "I'm quite sure Oliver was lying about not knowing more about either break-in. When I accused him of as much he didn't really try to deny it. Merely told me I couldn't fix everything."

"That sounds rather like the end of my conversation with Maria," Harry said.

Malcolm met his friend's gaze. "Quite."

Suzanne frowned. "What on earth could Oliver and Maria Monreal want that Craven had? Something to do with politics? Craven was a Tory and Oliver is in the Opposition. Could Oliver have made some sort of alliance with Carfax? Is that what he's afraid to admit to you?"

"Difficult to see how," Malcolm said.

"What if Oliver invested secretly in Whateley & Company?" Suzanne said. "Or—"

"Maria had worked for Carfax," Harry said. "Lydgate is his son-in-law. Craven was both his son-in-law and his agent. And Whateley & Company was Carfax's front essentially. Could Carfax have tasked Maria and Lydgate to recover something he thought Craven had, either at Whateley & Company or in Brook Street?"

Malcolm frowned, trying to see his university friend with objective eyes. "Carfax accepted Oliver as his son's friend. I don't think Oliver was the match he wanted for Bel, but at that point Bel had been out a few seasons, and he wasn't going to stand in the way of her marrying. And if she was going to marry a lawyer's son with Radical politics, he at least wanted him to be an M.P., so he made sure Bel's marriage portion was enough to stake Oliver's political career. He might have turned to Oliver for help with family matters, but it's hard for me to imagine him turning to Oliver for something involving his agents. Not to mention the company he was using as a cover for illicit business."

"Suppose Oliver had got wind of what Carfax was doing at Whateley & Company and wanted to learn more?" Suzanne suggested. "If he really had become friends with Maria, he might have turned to her for assistance knowing she'd been an agent."

"Instead of me?" Malcolm said.

"He might have wanted to be sure first. And he knows you worked for Carfax—"

"Suzette, first you thought Fitzroy might think I'd protect Carfax and now you're suggesting Oliver might think I'd do so?"

"I'm suggesting Oliver might wonder if you would, darling. Not that you'd actually do so."

Malcolm frowned at the music stand. "All right. Possibly. But then surely he'd have told me just now."

Harry clapped a hand on Malcolm's shoulder. "It's not easy. Having a friend, especially such an old friend, lie to one."

"I'm an agent," Malcolm said. "You'd think I'd be used to it."

"From fellow agents. Not from someone you've known since university." Harry hesitated. "To you, if not to Cordy, I can confess that Maria's lying to me stings more than a bit. And I'd hardly have said I trusted her as you trusted Lydgate."

Malcolm met his friend's gaze for a moment. Almost, he was afraid that if he said more it would undo him. So he sought refuge in the details of the investigation. "And aside from the question of what Oliver and Maria Monreal might have been after, there's the question of what it could be that this unknown friend of Fitzroy's wanted as well. Unless we have two different groups of people after two different things at Whateley & Company, and that continues to strain credulity." Malcolm ran his fingers down the keys in a glissando. "I'm quite sure Oliver called on Eustace Whateley two weeks ago to do some early reconnaissance at the warehouse. Whether or not Oliver is also the one who broke into the warehouse and killed Coventry remains open to question."

He felt the combined pressure of Harry's and Suzanne's gazes. It was Harry who spoke first. "You don't really believe Lydgate is a killer."

"No," Malcolm said, "God help me. But until tonight, I didn't think he'd lie to me either."

28

Oliver closed the library doors. As was their custom, he and Isobel had repaired to this room after seeing the last of their guests from the house. Malcolm's contained, cold-eyed smile and Suzanne's brilliant, armored one upon leaving lingered in his memory. As did his last, troubling exchange with his father-in-law, who had stayed on with Lady Carfax and Lucinda after most of the guests left. "Congratulations," he said to his wife. "It was a great success."

Isobel gave a tight smile and dropped down on the sofa. "It does seem to have gone rather well. Thank you."

"I did little enough." He held up the decanter, an ornate cut-glass one that had been a wedding present from her parents, and at her nod poured her a glass of brandy as well as one for himself.

"You're so good at circulating. Much better than I am." Isobel tilted her head back and rubbed her neck.

Oliver put a glass of brandy in his wife's hand and moved behind the sofa to rub her shoulders. "Did you have a chance to talk to Malcolm and Suzanne?"

He felt the slightest tremor run through her, but her voice was even. "A bit." She took a sip of brandy. "One never seems to have much chance to talk to one's friends when entertaining. And they're busy with their investigation."

Oliver lifted his hands from his wife's shoulders lest she feel the tension roiling through him. "Bel." He picked up his own brandy and moved round the sofa to face her. "It didn't occur to you to ask me?"

"Ask you?" Isobel looked genuinely puzzled.

"If Maria Monreal is my mistress."

Isobel went still. The perfect, well-bred expression that he had so seldom seen waver, even since she had been his wife—perhaps especially since she had been his wife—cracked open. "Suzanne—"

"Didn't keep your confidence. I imagine she would have done, if Maria weren't tangled in the investigation into the break-ins."

Isobel's pale face went several shades paler. "I didn't realize—"

"No reason you should have done. But that doesn't explain why you didn't ask me."

Isobel took a drink of brandy. "Oliver, you can't seriously imagine I'd ask—" She tightened her grip on her glass. "It's all right. I told you when I agreed to marry you—"

"I know. You as good as gave me permission to be unfaithful in advance. Permission I never asked for."

Bel flushed. "It seemed easier—"

Oliver stood watching her, remembering that night in the Carfax House conservatory. Part of him wanted nothing more than to take her in his arms, but that wouldn't resolve any of this.

Bel drew a breath. "There was no sense in pretending—"

"I didn't have a lot to offer you. I never pretended otherwise. But what I had to offer included fidelity."

The flush drained from his wife's cheeks. "You were in love with someone else."

"Who was married to another man. I've never been Sylvie's lover. I'm not Maria's lover."

"Oliver—" Bel took a drink of brandy and set her glass carefully on the table beside her. "You wanted to stand for Parliament. You needed a wife with money or you wouldn't have been able to do so. There's no sense in either of us pretending otherwise."

Oliver controlled his inwards flinch. "I don't deny it. It doesn't mean I didn't care for you."

Isobel's dry smile somehow slashed right through to his heart. "Would you have married me if I'd been penniless?"

Oliver passed a hand over his face, remembering Bel as he'd first seen her when David brought him down from Oxford to Carfax Court. The house, twice the size of the squire's house in his parents' village, had gleamed white and unattainable against a blue sky. And Bel had sat on the lawn, laughing, a cluster of puppies leaving muddy paw prints on her white muslin dress. He'd liked her at once. Later that night, he'd seen a flash of pain in her eyes at a careless comment from her sister Mary. He'd wanted to protect her. But he couldn't claim it had been romantic love.

Isobel tossed down a swallow of brandy. "I thought not."

"I wasn't going to let myself pine for Sylvie," Oliver said. "But I didn't think I'd love again. Not in that way. But I always cared for you."

"Like a sister."

"Of course not." He dragged a shield-back chair over and sat facing his wife "We can't have such different interpretations of what's been between us all these years. You're the mother of my children. I can't imagine life without you."

Something flared in Isobel's eyes. Then her arms closed over her chest. "If Maria Monreal isn't your mistress, who is she?"

Oliver drew a breath. The air seemed to have grown heavier. "A friend."

"Whom you met in secret."

The story he'd given Malcolm stuck on his tongue. It should be easy enough to give. Unlike Malcolm, Bel might actually believe him. And yet—

Bitterness clogged his throat. Because while he might not have been Maria's lover, he knew full well how much reason he had to feel guilt.

Suzanne looked across the carriage at Malcolm's set profile and at Raoul's contained face beside him, and then glanced at Laura beside her. Malcolm, she suspected, wasn't ready to share his discoveries about Oliver, but there was one development of the evening she needed to confide to all three of them. "I told Bertrand about the Phoenix plot."

Malcolm drew a quick breath. Raoul's eyes narrowed.

"He's looking for Germont," she said. "He might have stumbled across it in any case. Besides—" She clutched the carriage strap, though they had taken the gentlest of turns. "Darling, I learned you trusted Bertrand with the arrangements for us to leave Britain should it prove necessary."

Malcolm released his breath. "I'd have told you. I didn't want to—"

"Burden me." She met his gaze and managed a smile. "I know. And I understand." As much as she could understand any of it. As much as she could bear to contemplate that they might have to leave Britain. "But given that Bertrand knows I'm the Raven, I think we can trust him with this."

Malcolm nodded, though his fingers were tense on the carriage seat. "There are few people I trust so well."

"Nor I," Raoul said. "And his contacts could be useful. I'd been thinking we should consider confiding in him."

"There's something wonderfully reassuring about Bertrand," Laura said. She cast a quick smile at Raoul and then at Malcolm and Suzanne. "Not that there isn't about the rest of you."

For all the chill that ran through her, Suzanne found herself echoing her friend's smile. Odd the four of them sitting like this, enclosed in the intimacy of the carriage, matter-of-factly sharing the details of investigation. At least for this precious moment, they were allies.

"Surely with all of us looking for information, we can learn who is behind the Phoenix plot," Laura said.

"I hope so," Suzanne said.

The question remained, what happened then?

Raoul pulled off his coat and tossed it over a chair back. "Climbing through the window has a certain piquancy, but all things considered it's more agreeable to stroll through the door."

Laura smiled at him. The four of them had received a report on the children from Blanca and Addison and climbed the stairs to the second floor together. Suzanne and Malcolm had gone into their bedchamber and she and Raoul into their separate rooms on either side of the passage. Raoul had waited a few minutes and then rapped lightly at her door. Laura glanced at the door to the night nursery. She'd already peeped in at the children and by now Suzanne and Malcolm should have done so as well. She looked back at Raoul, hesitated a moment, wondering if this might be stepping further than he wanted, then said, "Do you want to—?"

She saw a quick flash in his eyes and at the same time a hesitation. But more that he didn't want to push too far than that he wanted to hold back. At least, that was what she thought. She moved to the door and eased it open. A few moments later, Raoul moved soundlessly to her side. She felt the warmth of his breath over her shoulder.

Jessica's bassinet was empty. Suzanne would have taken her to her cradle in the bedroom. But Emily was curled on her side, facing the door, her red-blonde hair falling over her face, snuggling the stuffed rabbit Raoul had given her before he left for Spain the first time. And Colin was flopped on his back, his stuffed bear Figaro and his new stuffed horse in the curve of his arm, the covers slipping down round his waist. Laura slipped into the room, smoothed the covers over Colin, pressed a kiss to his forehead, then moved to Emily, smoothed her hair back from her face, kissed her as well, patted Berowne who was curled up at the foot of the bed. She deliberately didn't look at Raoul as she did so, not making too much of it, leaving it to him to decide what to do, how far to go.

She looked up to see he had taken a half step into the room. He was standing still, every muscle seemingly held in check, gaze alight with feeling. Laura went to his side and took his hand. They stood together for a moment, in the sort of stillness that hums in the air, then moved back into her bedchamber.

"Thank you," Raoul said when she closed the door, his voice a bit rough.

Laura nodded. "I never get tired of seeing them sleep."

Raoul glanced at the nursery door, hesitated a moment, drew a breath. "Sometimes I'd be at house parties at Dunmkyel. Or the Duke of Strathdon's estate in Ireland. I'd slip up to the nursery when I could . . ."

"And watch Malcolm sleep?"

He nodded, gave a quick smile, looked away, looked back into her eyes.

Odd how the simple sharing of a memory could be at once a statement of trust and a window into someone's soul. She touched the side of his face. "Somehow the simplest things can mean the most."

They stood together again, the lamplight spilling over them, his coat tossed over the chair back, the children asleep just beyond the door. A domestic scene that seemed entirely alien to both of them and yet somehow oddly natural. And yet—

She put her hands on his chest. "Raoul—"

He looked down at her, the smile still in his eyes but more guarded now. "Sweetheart?"

"Will Cuthbertson. I saw him last night at the theatre. For the first time in years. When you came back, it didn't seem—"

He put his hands over hers. "You don't owe me an explanation, Laura."

"Of course I do." She gripped his hands. "Given how I felt just over what I imagined about Lisette Varon—"

He grinned. "Don't ever let Lisette know about that. She'd be mortified. I'm quite sure I'm in the uncle category. Maybe even father. She's a friend. I have a number of friends. So do you."

"Will was more than a friend." She forced herself not to let her gaze move from his face. "The operative word being *was*."

His smile continued easy. "I thought as much."

She managed a smile of her own. "It's difficult having a spy as a lover."

"How he feels, at least, was fairly obvious."

"He was an escape, when I needed one. I don't think I realized how much it meant to him. It was good to see him again, I won't deny it," she added, the words tumbling from her lips even as she wondered if she was talking too fast. "To remember a time that now seems simpler, God help me. But I realized tonight I had to make it clear—I told him I have no desire to be a wife again."

"Of course." Raoul's voice was almost without expression.

"You know what I mean. I couldn't tell him—And it's not a possibility."

"No." His hands were still twined round her own but they felt curiously rigid.

"Will's conventional. He said he wants to protect me, of all things. He'd never understand what you and I have." Not that she understood it herself half the time.

Raoul released her hands, but only to pull her into his arms. His kiss was sweet and urgent, but she had the oddest sense he was trying to commit each moment of it to memory. As though his mind had jumped ahead to goodbye.

She tangled her fingers in his hair and pulled him closer, dragging him back to the present.

Suzanne dropped her shawl and reticule on the dressing table and regarded her husband. He had had himself well in hand by the time they left the music room and had even danced with her again. But now they were alone, the shadows were plain on his face and in the depths of his eyes and the line of his mouth. Bruises to his soul that were just beginning to form as the reality of the night settled over him, like blood pooling beneath the skin. "Harry's right," she said. "This can't but sting."

"More than it should." Malcolm stripped off his coat. "God knows I've faced worse."

Suzanne pulled off one of her gloves. "Perhaps it's the who more than the what. Especially coming so soon after Fitzroy."

He unfastened his waistcoat with precise, mechanical fingers. "Oliver and David and Simon—they were my family in a way for a time. But I should know better than anyone that family aren't always to be relied upon."

"Darling." Suzanne hesitated, holding her second glove by the fingertips. But not saying it wouldn't make it go away. "Harry couldn't know this, but it has to have made you think of me."

Malcolm started on his shirt cuffs. "At least from the moment I learned you lied to me, I knew why and about what."

She dropped her glove on the dressing table in a puddle of ivory silk. "Whatever the truth about Oliver, it can't possibly be as bad."

Malcolm stripped off his neckcloth and threw it on top of the waistcoat. "So if I could survive my wife's duplicity, I should be able to handle whatever Oliver's lying to me about?"

Suzanne controlled an inwards flinch. "I can't imagine anything worse than your wife's duplicity."

"I can. But I trust whatever Oliver's doing isn't so extreme. On the other hand, I doubt his reasons are as good as yours." He dragged his shirt over his head. "Damn it. We've always turned to each other when we were in trouble."

"He may feel he's trying to protect you. There are certainly things you haven't told Oliver."

"A point. But surely he sees—"

Malcolm broke off, right hand curled into a fist. She could see the tension running through his shoulders and in the set of his mouth. Perhaps there was one thing she could do to help. She moved to his side. "Nothing more we can do tonight, darling. It will look better in the morning."

He managed a bleak smile. "Will it?"

"There's always the hope." She slid her arms round him and reached up to pull his head down to her own.

He tensed beneath her touch. His hands went to her shoulders, holding her, but also putting distance between them. "I'm sorry, Mel. I'm afraid I'm not much use to you tonight." He squeezed her shoulders and moved to the bed to pick up his dressing gown.

She watched the precise control in his hands as he wrapped the burgundy silk round him. He'd always avoided any whisper of using her to exorcise his demons. And now she herself was the cause of those demons. When he'd first learned the truth about her, she'd been afraid he'd never make love to her again. But in fact, it hadn't taken so very long. Their wedding anniversary had helped, and the tacit sense they'd both had that if they waited too long it might become unbearably awkward. Relief had flooded through her when she kissed him in a cautious overture, a light kiss that could go either way, and he responded, deepened the kiss, and at last carried her to their bed. Yet at the same time, she'd been afraid. For all his own skills at deception, Malcolm was too honest a lover to act in the bedchamber. It would be understandable if anger had leached through, but that wasn't what she'd feared. It was contempt. Contempt for a woman who'd used her body as a spy and, before that, as a whore.

But she'd underestimated her husband. Malcolm had been more tender than ever. As he tugged gently at the tapes on her gown while his lips moved over her temple, she'd realized he was making love to her differently, but he was making love to the girl she'd been. The girl who had been raped by English soldiers, who'd lived on the streets and found a sort of bleak refuge in a brothel. The girl he hadn't been there to save. She'd wanted to weep.

That was how he'd made love to her since. As though she was something fragile that could be broken. Or that had been broken and was barely mended. Or perhaps, she sometimes thought, because he was afraid of what he'd reveal if he let himself go.

Which sometimes was precisely what she wanted. But if she craved abandon, she had to drag him there with her. As always, Malcolm was quick to give her what he sensed she wanted.

But tonight the problem wasn't what she wanted, it was what he needed. Even if it meant moving across boundaries she usually didn't cross. Even if anger leached through. Even if contempt forced its way between them. They were strong enough now to handle it. Or they should be.

She undid the cord at her waist, unfastened her gauze overdress, tossed it on a chair, and moved towards him, clad only in her silver gray silk slip. "It doesn't matter that you're angry, darling."

He looked up quickly, tying the dressing gown belt. "It's not—"

"It doesn't matter that you're angry at me. I can handle it."

He reached out, perhaps to hold her off, but his hands settled on her arms. "I'm not going to inflict myself on you like this, sweetheart. You deserve better. You can't—"

She pulled him to her again. He went still for a moment, but this time he didn't pull away. His mouth closed over her own. His breath was harsh against her skin, his kiss rough and raw, but not so much with anger as with desperation. He crushed her to him as though he was drowning and she was his last hope of survival, while at the same time he feared to pull her under with him.

He dragged his mouth away from her own. "I'm in no fit state—"

"I won't break, Malcolm." She slid her hands beneath his dressing gown, reminding him of everything she could offer. "We won't break." She fell back on the bed and pulled him down with her, catching his lip between her teeth, tangling her fingers in his hair, melding him to her.

If she couldn't banish his demons, at least she could share them.

29

David splashed brandy into two glasses. Simon had come back from Bel and Oliver's with him, this time as though it were a matter of course. They'd both tensed as they entered the house, but the footman had still been awake and the house encased in quiet. A visit to the nursery showed all four children asleep. Even though David had sent the footman to bed, they'd returned downstairs to the library. What happened later was still open to question. Besides, much as David wanted other things from his lover, he needed to talk to him. "Malcolm seems to think Oliver has a mistress who is involved in the investigation somehow."

Simon stared at David as he accepted a glass of brandy. David wasn't given to personal speculation, even about his family, even with Simon.

"Are you surprised?" David asked.

Simon took a drink of brandy. "That Oliver has a mistress or that she's connected to the investigation?"

David tossed down a long drink of brandy. "Both."

Simon swirled the brandy in his glass. "Difficult to tell about the investigation, as we don't know what the devil is behind it. As to Oliver having a mistress—"

David watched his lover. He had worried about Bel from the moment he learned of her betrothal to Oliver, but he had never discussed it with Simon. It had seemed worse somehow to put it into words. And yet he couldn't believe Simon, of all people, hadn't seen what he had.

"That doesn't surprise you?" David asked.

"I'm not sure." Simon took another drink of brandy.

"Simon." David regarded his lover. "I may not have your insights into people, but it was obvious even to me that their marriage wasn't—"

"That they weren't madly in love? No. Not in that sense. Not both of them."

"You mean Bel was." David grimaced as he moved to the sofa.

"You have plenty of insights into people. And yes, I think she was." Simon dropped down beside David. "But Oliver's always been fond of her. And while he flirts, I'm not sure it goes beyond that."

David's fingers froze on the etched crystal of his own glass. It wasn't like Simon to put a romantic gloss on things. "Why?"

Simon raised a brow. "I may not be a romantic, but I'm not such a cynic as to think infidelity is inevitable. Oliver cares for Bel. More, I'd judge, as the years have gone by. And I think he's all too conscious of what he's gained by marrying her. The Mallinsons aren't an easy family to marry into. In some ways I'm fortunate that I can't."

David frowned. "You think Oliver's faithful to Bel because he thinks he owes her a debt?"

"I think Oliver's very conscious that he owes Bel a debt. Whether or not he's faithful is still open to question. Who is this supposed mistress?"

"Apparently her name's Maria Monreal. I don't know any more." David dug a hand into his hair.

Simon dropped an arm across David's shoulders. "Malcolm isn't going to share everything with you. He can't. Not at this point."

"No. I do realize that. He only shared this because he thought I might have information." David took a swallow of brandy. It was a smooth vintage but it burned his throat. "God, remember the days when the four of us used to tell each other everything?"

"Well, not quite everything." Simon's arm tightened round him. "We never told Malcolm and Oliver about us."

"Not in so many words."

"I think it took Oliver a while to work it out."

David thought back to those years. The four of them with papers and books spread on scarred tables in coffeehouses. Lounging on the floor in one or the other's chambers, sharing their dreams of the future over glasses of red wine. Punting on golden afternoons. Picnics with champagne. And through it all, the sudden silences, the wonder of Simon beside him, the pressure of knowing he couldn't so much as take his hand, even in front of their friends. Simon was right. When one looked back, there'd been more secrets in their charmed Oxford circle than the gloss of memory admitted to. "I wasn't sure—"

"Nor was I," Simon said. "But Oliver didn't fail us then. Perhaps he isn't failing us now."

"I thought you thought Oliver had—"

"Compromised? It was harder for him to enter Parliament than for you or Malcolm. But he's done a lot of good since he's been there. If the Whigs ever get back in power, he might have a prayer of office, which isn't a bad thing. Oh, that's where Jamie's horse got to." Simon set down his glass and knelt on the floor to pick up a wooden horse Jamie had left beneath the sofa table.

David stared at the black-and-red wood of the toy in Simon's hand. "Do you think Malcolm is right?" he asked abruptly.

Simon set the horse on the sofa table. "Malcolm is right about a great many things. What are you thinking of in particular?"

David swirled the brandy in his glass. "Not sending Teddy back to Harrow. Or any other school."

"You know my opinion of the public school system." Simon reached further under the table for a wooden top.

"Yes, but—"

"But what?" Simon sat back on his heels and regarded David. "That was theoretical and this is an actual boy?"

"No. Well, perhaps a bit." David stared into his glass. "It's history. Tradition. The role he'll be expected to play. Unless you manage to foment a revolution, he'll have to manage estates, take his seat in the House of Lords."

"I'm not trying to foment a revolution. Well, not that drastic a one. And I wouldn't have a prayer of success if I tried, whatever your father's fears. And if Teddy's going to take his place in the House of Lords, I'd say all the more reason for him to have a broader view of the world than is to be found in our public schools."

David took a swallow of brandy, feeling the weight of responsibility for the four small people sleeping upstairs.

"Not that you have to take my advice." Simon got to his feet. "It's your decision. To all intents and purposes you're their father now."

David swung towards his lover. "But you're their—"

Simon met his gaze and raised a brow. "Honorary uncle? Not a position with a great deal of authority."

For some reason, fear squeezed David's chest. "Damn it, Simon, you know you'll always be a part of their lives."

"Probably. In what capacity remains less clear."

Simon's blue gaze held challenge, which was not unusual, and, more surprising, an echo of David's own fear. "You don't trust me," David said.

Simon turned and put the top on the sofa table with the care of one settling the most fragile porcelain. "I trust you with my life, David." His voice was rougher than David had ever heard it.

"But you don't trust I won't leave you."

Simon turned back to him. His gaze was unusually free of mockery, which somehow was terrifying. "Can you really tell me that you've never considered taking a wife?"

There it was, the thing that hung between them, that they alluded to but almost never openly discussed. David couldn't have said why putting it into words should make it worse, but somehow it did. An unnamed threat now hung in the air, like a monster from one of the children's storybooks that came to life when one breathed its name.

They'd rarely talked about the future in concrete terms. When they left Oxford, they'd agreed to share lodgings in London without discussing what it meant. At least, not openly. David had always thought Simon's heart had sung at the decision the way his own did. That Simon, like him, had known how significant a decision it was for the future. Fully as significant as a proposal accompanied by all the formality of asking a girl's father for her hand. He could still remember Simon grabbing him and kissing him behind the door the first time they visited the Albany flat and saying, with uncharacteristic seriousness, "You make me very happy." That was probably the closest they'd ever come to wedding vows.

And yet all the pressures of the expectations of the heir to an earldom were still there. "Of course I haven't thought of it," David said.

"No?" The challenge was back in Simon's eyes.

Memories jabbed his mind like shards of glass swirling in his brain. "Only to realize how impossible it would be. For any number of reasons. I know what I owe you, Simon."

"And you know what you owe your name. You're a man who takes his commitments seriously, David. Difficult when those commitments conflict."

"You don't believe in owing anything to a name."

"No, but I understand what it means to you. In a perfect world I don't think there would be peers. But if there have to be, I think you'll make about as good a one as possible."

"That's kind of you."

"I didn't say it to be kind."

David took a swallow of brandy. It couldn't numb the disquiet within him. The tension, not just between the expectations of a future earl and his love for Simon, but between the weight of his heritage and the ideals he passionately believed in, had gnawed at him for years. "I'm not necessarily saying I think it's right that I'll be Earl Carfax. No, hear me out." He put out a hand before Simon could protest. "I'm not saying I'd abolish the House of Lords as quickly as you would, either. To own the truth, I'm still sorting out what I think about all of it."

Simon dropped down on the sofa arm. "Fair enough."

"I wish to the devil I wasn't heir to the earldom, for God knows how many reasons. But given that apparently I will be Earl Carfax, I'll do my best. By my tenants. By those dependent on the estates. To use my voice in the House of Lords well. To steward what's been given me. I'll preserve the estates for the next earl. But that's going to have to be my second cousin Michael or one of his sons. I'm not going to take a wife or father a child. I've known that—well, forever, really. Certainly since I met you."

Simon crossed his legs and linked his hands round his knee. "That's why you waltzed with Lady Clare Townsend twice at Lady Cowper's ball last week? Why you took Georgiana Darby driving the month before?"

"I took Georgiana driving because it's her first season and she's shy and I promised her brother I'd help her get about. I waltzed with Lady Clare once because my mother brought her over to me and it would have been rude not to ask, and again because it would have been equally insulting not to dance with her twice." All of which was true. But David felt himself flush. "You can't seriously think I'm contemplating—"

"No. But your parents continue to put agreeable girls in your way. It's clear what the girls are thinking. I can't imagine it's never crossed your mind as well."

"It would never work."

"So you've thought about it enough to realize it would never work?"

David leaned forwards, his head in his hands. He felt as though he'd run the length of the Serpentine. "I said that at the start. And of course I worry about the girls' expectations. Lady Clare as good as told me—" He bit the words back. It was too much, even to share with Simon.

"What?" Simon asked.

David looked up and tossed down the last of his brandy. "She implied that she knew about us. And that she'd be quite comfortable with our continuing our relationship while she lived as Lady Worsley and had my children."

The conversation, and Lady Clare's complete composure in making her offer, had shocked him, but Simon nodded. "I'm not surprised. She looks a hardheaded young woman, she's been out for a few seasons, and she wants a husband. God knows there are worse compromises made on the marriage mart every day."

"Good God, Simon."

"I'm not saying I advocate it, but I can understand her making the suggestion. Even admire her forthrightness. It's not so very different from what Rupert and Bertrand and Gabrielle have."

"Rupert married Gabrielle when he thought Bertrand was dead. I don't think they'd have any of them willingly entered into such a relationship."

"Nor do I, though it did give Rupert an heir. I suppose if you weren't particular about bloodlines you wouldn't even need to sleep with her. She could find her own equivalent of Gabrielle's Nick Gordon."

David stared at his lover. "You aren't seriously saying you advocate such a scenario."

"No. Merely pointing out your options."

"It's not an option. For one thing, you'd never go along with it. You hate lies."

"I can understand some people's need to live with lies. But I have no intention of being part of such an arrangement. I'm merely trying to make sure you understand your options."

"The option to have a marriage built on lies, without you?"

"With a woman like Lady Clare, you'd at least only be lying to the world round you, not to your wife. And another man might be more willing to go along with it than I am."

David flinched inwardly. He looked at the only person he'd ever been intimate with. "I don't want another man. I want you."

Simon leaned back, one hand resting on the sofa back behind him. "It's a conundrum, isn't it?" His gaze was unwavering. "Whatever you choose, David, that choice has to be yours, not mine."

"It's our life. Together."

"But being the future Earl Carfax is your obligation. Your heritage. Whatever I think of inherited privilege, I'm not going to take that away from you. That's a burden I don't think either of us could live with."

David set his brandy glass on the sofa table. His fingers shook. The oak and satin of the sofa were solid beneath him but he felt as though he stood on shifting waters, cut free of his moorings. "Have you been waiting all these years for me to leave you?"

Simon gave a twisted smile. "Mostly I've tried to enjoy what we have in the moment. But I've always known, even if I didn't consciously admit it, that this was a choice you'd have to face one day. That I'd have to step back and let you make it."

David pushed himself to his feet. Perhaps he'd been wrong about that moment in the Albany being the closest they'd come to wedding vows. He crossed to Simon's side, bent down, and kissed him. "I'm not going anywhere. Now will you stop worrying about things that will never come to pass and help me figure out how to raise our children?"

Suzanne woke with a jerk, every nerve tensed for the sound of sniper fire. Or a crying child. One way and another she could scarcely remember when she had last slept soundly. The dark bars of the canopy frame and the pale silk of the canopy stretched above her. Berkeley Square. Their house. The bed she shared with Malcolm. No sound of footsteps. No crying from Jessica's cradle or the night nursery. But the candle she and Malcolm had left burning still flickered on the night table on his side of the bed. If Malcolm had fallen asleep, he would have extinguished it first. Instead, its glow illumined her husband, sitting up in the bed next to her, the arms that had been embracing her when she fell asleep now wrapped round his knees.

"Darling?" She pushed herself up against the pillows. "What is it?"

"Nothing." His quick smile gleamed in the moonlight. "Just couldn't sleep. Sorry I woke you."

"You didn't wake me. And it's clearly not nothing." She put a hand on his arm and felt the tension running through it. God knows she'd felt tension when he'd made love to her, but afterwards, lying with her head on his chest and his arms encircling her, she'd thought the tension had eased in ways that went beyond physical release.

"Merely playing out scenarios."

"About Oliver?"

"No. You're right, we need more information. About this Phoenix plot of yours."

Suzanne drew a breath. It had been a hellish day. Oliver's lies had come fresh on this new reminder of his wife's betrayal. And his father's. "Hardly mine."

"Figure of speech. But you can't deny it changes things."

"Malcolm." She leaned forwards so she could see the candlelight falling over his face. "It's unsettling. But there's no reason—"

"You can argue about what it would mean if Napoleon Bonaparte escaped St. Helena, but it would certainly change things."

"I think it's far more likely the supposed plot is a trick of Fouché's to curry favor with the Bourbons. Even if there really is a plot, it's highly unlikely it would succeed."

He swung his head round and met her gaze, his own hard. "But if it did?"

The few inches of bedlinen and embroidered silk cover-let between them suddenly seemed an impassable distance. As vast as the gulf between two countries, between two sets of beliefs, between two visions of the world they wanted for their children. They agreed about so much, and yet . . . "After Waterloo, I told Raoul that I wouldn't stop fighting for the things I believed in, but I'd only do so openly, as your wife. That I wouldn't work behind your back. I meant it."

"I have no doubt you did, my darling. But as so often in this damnable business, it's far easier to state a principle than to follow it,"

"Malcolm, I wouldn't—"

"You've gone behind my back a score of times, sweet-heart. When you and O'Roarke rescued Manon and goodness knows how many others. When Fouché tried to blackmail you in Paris. I'm not saying you were wrong to do so. I'd have made the same choices myself."

That day in Brussels, the nineteenth of June, the day after Waterloo, when she told Raoul she would no longer work as his agent, she'd wondered when she would see him again. She'd been sure she would never work with him again. Yet it had only been a few weeks later that she'd been sitting across a café table from him in Paris, insisting she wanted to help him rescue Manon. "It was before you knew the truth about me. It's different now."

"Those choices might be different. We'd be fools to think every possible choice you might face would be."

Suzanne pushed herself up against the pillows. "Darling, what are you saying?"

Malcolm's fingers tightened round his knees. "Mel, what would you do if you really thought Bonaparte could be restored? Or perhaps it's more important to say, if the monarchy could be got rid of?"

For a moment she saw British soldiers encamped in the Bois de Boulogne, thronging the quais and boulevards. The instinctive rage she had felt in Paris in the months after Waterloo shot through her. "I live here. With you. And our children. I'm not going to rush off to be part of a revolution." She swallowed. "Whatever I might want."

A faint smile shot across his face, but his eyes were bleak in a way they had been in the early days of their marriage. "Always honest, my darling. But even if O'Roarke isn't involved, even if Manon isn't. Even if it's a plot of Fouché's to entrap Bonapartists and curry favor, people you know, people you care about, will be caught up in it."

The single candle made a small island of warmth round them, bleeding into shadows. "Malcolm, what are you afraid of?"

His dark gaze gave a glimpse of the scenarios he'd been playing out in his mind. "Of us being on opposite sides."

Outside the circle of candlelight, the dark of the night enclosed them. Alone in their bed in the dark. Nowhere to run. "Darling, we were—"

"On opposite sides for years. Quite. But this time we'd both know. And I'm afraid we could get to a point where neither of us could do what we consider our duty without acting against the other."

"We wouldn't—"

He raised a brow. "We've neither of us changed that much, my darling."

"Malcolm. What would you do if you'd been the one to hear rumors about the Phoenix plot?"

"I've been asking myself the same question." He rested his chin on his knees. "I don't know. I don't think I'd have told you. At least not until I heard more. I wouldn't have wanted to put you in that position."

"You'd have tried to stop it without my finding out?"

A smile like a whisper of December sun twisted his mouth. "I wouldn't have had a prayer of doing so. I don't know if I'd be stupid enough to try." He reached across the coverlet and took her hand. His fingers were cool and blessedly familiar. "If it weren't for the children, I might suggest we consider living apart until we get through this."

"Darling!" Ice shot through her. The spectre of him leaving her had hung over her from the moment she agreed to be his wife. But this was the only time in all the years of their marriage, through revelations she had thought would smash it to bits, that he'd come close to suggesting they separate. "You don't want—"

"Of course I don't want to be apart from you." His fingers tightened over her own. "But it's one way we could get through this. I wouldn't put Colin and Jessica through that, though."

"It's not just that." She looked down at their intertwined fingers. "I don't pretend to have the least idea what we should do. But I do know we can't get through it by running. We have to muddle through it together."

Malcolm lifted her hand to his lips. "That's my Mel. You've always been braver than I am. But then, I'm the man who went to the Continent for the better part of a decade to avoid confronting my demons at home."

"You can't compare this to—"

"No. Of course not."

Had there been just the faintest of pauses before his denial or was her mind playing tricks on her?

As though perhaps he understood, Malcolm leaned back against the pillows and drew her down beside him. "And anything that pulls former Bonapartists out of the shadows, that could involve us, however tangentially, increases the risk—"

"Stop jumping at phantoms, darling." Suzanne settled back against her husband's shoulder. "There's no reason this should lead to my being exposed."

Malcolm's arm tightened round her. His gaze was on the canopy again. "I've stopped trying to keep track of the number of people in London who know about your past. Let alone the number of people in the world in general."

"Most of them with secrets of their own." She shifted back slightly so she could look at him. "There's no sense imagining all the things that could go wrong, dearest. All we can do is focus on getting through it a moment at a time."

He turned his head. Across a few inches of linen, his gaze was sharp and yet unexpectedly open. "Is that what you did for the five years I didn't know?"

"Mostly. When I could. I'd have gone mad otherwise."

He touched her face. "I don't know how you did it."

"It's the same thing we're both doing now."

"We have each other to talk to. And an escape plan." He turned his gaze back to the canopy. "Sometimes I think—"

"Darling, no." She meant to keep her comment light, but her voice came out sharper than she intended. "Running away won't solve anything, even if we do it together."

His fingers moved against her shoulder, but he kept his gaze on the canopy. "We'd be safe."

"We're safe now."

"The safety of those living under a knife blade."

She rolled onto her side and curled into him. "We're agents, darling. We always live under a knife blade."

"And ever since I married you, ever since we had Colin, I've dreamed about escaping an agent's life."

"You really think Carfax would let go you go if we went to Italy?"

"Even Carfax's reach has its limits."

"Yes, but unless we can slip into the realm of the fairies, I'm not sure we can get beyond it."

He grinned. "I'm not that important. If, God forbid, Carfax learned the truth about you, even you wouldn't be that important."

Malcolm was almost a son to Carfax, which made it a deal more complicated. Even if Carfax would let one of his most talented agents go, she wasn't sure he'd do the same for his almost-son. Or that he would forgive that almost-son's wife if he knew how she had betrayed her husband. But Suzanne merely said, "There's a risk to our sanity as well. We'd both go mad."

He grinned. "We'd manage."

She could see them, being painfully polite to each other, stepping gingerly round sensitive subjects. Her own voice, increasingly brittle, his silences growing longer. The strain at the breakfast table. The English papers that would be a constant reminder of what they had lost. How long would it be before he blamed her? How long could love outlast the fact that, if not for her, he wouldn't have had to give up his home, his career, been left isolated, separated, and perhaps estranged from the people he loved?

He turned his face into her hair. "There's something to be said for peace and quiet."

"We'd go mad."

"Or you would?"

"Darling." She pushed herself up on one elbow. "You—"

"Have always wanted a settled life more than you do."

"That's—"

"A fact. I don't think you'd have wanted a settled life at all if it weren't for Colin."

Her denial caught in her throat. It was true. Her greatest qualm about becoming a mother had been that it would drive her from the field of action. In a sense, marriage to Malcolm had been the perfect solution. It had allowed her to continue her work while being with Colin in relative safety. And yet—

"You don't want a settled life either, darling. You just think you should, and it gets all wrapped up in your protective impulses. But you're just as excited as I am when a new adventure drops into our laps."

The candle flame caught his grin. "Well, perhaps not *just* as much. But, all right. Yes. I'm not sure I need it in quite the way you do, though. I understand if you're afraid you won't be able to stand a quiet life with me—"

"It's not that, darling. I'm not the one who'd be haunted by what my spouse had forced me to give up."

Inches away, his gaze moved over her face. She could see the beginnings of stubble on his jaw, even though he'd shaved before they went to the Lydgates' ball, and the faint remnants of a scar that ran into his temple. "Is that what you think?" he demanded. "That I'd blame you?"

"Not consciously. Not deliberately. But how could it not occur to you that if it weren't for your wife, you wouldn't have had to leave Parliament, leave Dunmykel, you wouldn't be cut off from your friends—"

"Have I blamed you? Have I ever blamed you, after those first few days?"

"No." Her throat hurt, as though she'd swallowed acid. "You've kept it all to yourself. You've been a marvel of kindness."

"*Kindness*—"

"I keep waiting for it to all spill over." Even earlier tonight when he'd lost himself in her arms, he'd been angrier at himself than at her.

The candlelight bounced off his eyes. "Waiting for it to, or wanting it to?"

"Why would I—"

"Sweetheart." He touched her cheek with gentle fingers. "It's never going to happen, you know. I'm never going to be as angry at you as you are at yourself."

She gave an impatient shake of her head. "I lived with myself for five and a half years, darling. You know better than anyone how good I am at justifying moral compromise."

"I know just how much of a toll it took on you." He slid his fingers into her hair, smoothing it off her temple. "Don't think I've forgot how thin you got in Brussels before Waterloo."

"Those were rather extraordinary circumstances. Now—"

"Now you aren't spying for the French, you've got all too much leisure to dwell on the past."

She drew a sharp breath. "R—"

"O'Roarke said that's what would happen?" Malcolm asked. His gaze was at once soft and carefully neutral.

For a moment she could see Raoul's taut, exhausted face, in the hot room in Brussels where they'd met, hear his voice, harsh yet with a note of tenderness not unlike that Malcolm's own voice could hold. "After Waterloo. When I told him I was going to stop working for him. He warned me that in a few weeks or months I'd feel an intolerable weight of guilt. That it would be worse when I didn't have the needs of the moment to focus on."

"O'Roarke has always been damnably perceptive."

"I think perhaps you and your father have more finely tuned feelings than I do. I've always been a pragmatist."

He gave no sign that he'd noticed she'd referred to Raoul as his father, though he must have been aware of it. "On the contrary. I think we're both very attuned to what you're feeling."

"You're both inclined to worry about me when you should be focused on the mission." It was something she hadn't fully appreciated about Raoul until recently. He and Malcolm were far more alike than one might think from a casual acquaintance with the two men.

"Well. You're rather important to both of us." Malcolm tucked a strand of hair behind her ear. "I'd miss Britain. I'd miss my friends and family. I'd miss Parliament. God help me, I'd even miss being an agent. Ex-agent. But I could learn to live with the quiet. I grow a bit cold at the thought of what the imagined guilt would do to you though. Not to mention the quiet."

30

The sky was just beginning to lighten when Malcolm woke. He stared at the canopy and the gray light filtering in between the curtains for a few moments, but further sleep was plainly going to elude him. He pressed a kiss to Suzanne's forehead, grateful she still slept, and swung his feet to the floor.

Jessica was sound asleep in her cradle, flopped on her back, a small arm flung over her head. Malcolm smoothed the blanket over her, touched his fingers to her cheek, looked into the nursery where Colin and Emily were both still sound asleep, Berowne at the foot of Emily's bed. Then he went into the dressing room. After years in the field, he was quite proficient at shaving and dressing himself. He rarely rang for Addison in the morning, especially now Addison was a married man. He might not leave the dressing room arrayed quite to his valet's standards, but he was certainly passable. He went out onto the landing and ran lightly down the stairs, intending to seek refuge in the library, for it was early for the breakfast things to be out. But when he reached the ground floor hall he caught a whiff of coffee. The breakfast parlor door was ajar and light spilled out into the shadows.

Malcolm went into the breakfast parlor to find O'Roarke at the table, a coffee cup beside him, the *Morning Chronicle* spread before him, though he didn't appear to be reading it.

"Malcolm." O'Roarke looked up with a quick smile. "Valentin found me in the library when he was opening up the house and insisted on making coffee. Very good of him."

"I couldn't sleep either." Malcolm went to pour himself a cup of coffee. O'Roarke, he suspected, had left Laura's room before the sun was up and had come downstairs rather than attempting to go back to sleep.

O'Roarke sat back in his chair and reached for his own cup. "I'll visit the coffeehouse Lisette mentioned today and see if I can pick up the trail of Louis Germont and the man he's working with. And now that we know Fouché may be involved, there are further inquiries I can make."

Malcolm nodded and took a sip of coffee. Hot. Bitter. Familiar. Not enough to still everything roiling through him, but enough to steady him. "I need to give a report to Carfax. I think I can find a way to ask if he's had news of Fouché without him suspecting anything."

O'Roarke frowned a moment, then nodded. "That should go unnoticed unless Carfax already knows about the plot— and if he does, God help us."

Malcolm dropped down at the table and took another sip of coffee. "Do you really think the plot is a device of Fouché's to curry favor with the Bourbons?"

"I don't know enough to think anything with certainty," O'Roarke said in an even voice. "Based on what we know I'm inclined to think it's the likeliest explanation."

Malcolm turned his cup in his hand. "It fits the facts."

"But you're wary of it," O'Roarke said. It wasn't a question.

"I suppose I'm wary of anything that's easy."

"I hardly think a potential plot of Fouché's that may include Suzanne as a target is easy for any of us."

"No. But given that we know there is a plot of some sort— this explanation keeps us all on the same side."

O'Roarke's gaze stayed steady on Malcolm's face. "Suzanne decided she was on the same side as you a long time ago, Malcolm."

Malcolm set his cup down. "Suzanne decided she wouldn't actively work against me. She decided she'd work with me as long as our interests align. They aren't always going to align. It would be folly to pretend we all can say we'll agree on a course of action when we learn what really is behind this plot."

"No." O'Roarke took a drink of coffee. "It's both redundant and an understatement to say this can't be easy."

Malcolm stared at the steam curling above the cup. "We were bound to face a situation that put us on opposite sides at some point. Even if you're right about Fouché and we escape this time, it's bound to happen again."

Raoul returned his cup to its saucer as though the slightest tremor in his hand might break it. "Suzanne knows what she has to lose, Malcolm."

"It's not that easy." Malcolm's gaze shot to his father. "I don't want her to deny who she is because she's my wife." He could say that to O'Roarke. There was no one else to whom he could voice the fear.

"I can't imagine Suzanne denying who she is."

"Which may put us on opposite sides." Malcolm reached for the coffee pot and refilled both their cups. "No sense in dwelling on it now. All we can do is move forwards with what information we have."

O'Roarke picked up his cup and blew on the steam. "It's a damnable coil. And particularly when you're in the midst of an investigation that touches on Carfax."

Malcolm grimaced. "All too much touches on Carfax. And now it appears Oliver Lydgate is involved as well."

O'Roarke shot a quick look at him. Malcolm drew a breath and found himself updating O'Roarke on the developments involving Whateley & Company. Oddly, just verbalizing the previous night's revelations eased a bit of the strain in his chest.

O'Roarke listened in silence, though his gaze said he was sifting through the information even as he took it in. "It can't be easy about Lydgate. I sometimes wonder what's harder for an agent, living with secrets or living with the fact that most of one's friends have them as well. But your Oxford friends seemed removed from that life."

"I suppose Mama and Aunt Frances wrote to you about us."

"Oh, yes." O'Roarke reached for his coffee. "And I read your pamphlets."

"God. Surely you had more pressing reading matter than undergraduate ramblings."

"On the contrary. They were very cogently argued. Yours in particular—though I admit to a certain bias—and of course Tanner has a brilliant way with words and Worsley can be very persuasive. But Lydgate impressed me as well."

"He's been a good friend. And a good colleague." Malcolm stared into his coffee. "And I don't have the least idea what he's up to."

"You need more data."

"Did you cross paths with Maria Monreal in the Peninsula?"

"Once. I was disguised as a wine merchant and she was disguised as a member of a guerrillero band. Undoubtedly a clever woman."

"Did she see through your disguise?"

"No. At least I flatter myself not."

Malcolm nodded. "We need more data, as you say. Folly to talk ourselves in circles."

O'Roarke leaned back in his chair. "What do you know about Colonel Cuthbertson?"

"Not a great deal. I hadn't met him until the night before last. Davenport served with him in the Peninsula, and he's an old friend of Laura's from India."

"So I realize. He's obviously very fond of her."

Malcolm shot a look at his father. "For God's sake—I don't think you have anything to worry about, O'Roarke."

O'Roarke took a sip of coffee. "Why should I be worried? I want Laura to be happy."

Malcolm watched as O'Roarke again carefully returned his cup to its saucer. "Laura's fond of him. She can remember her past with him. The good parts of her past. I'd swear it isn't more than that."

"My dear Malcolm. I saw the way Cuthbertson was looking at her last night."

"On her side, I meant."

O'Roarke gave a faint smile. "You needn't try to spare my feelings."

"I'm not." Malcolm reached across the table and put a hand on his father's arm. "Look here, O'Roarke, surely I, of all people, don't have to point out to you that a woman may have complicated feelings for a man from her past without betraying her current relationship."

O'Roarke's gaze flashed to his own, one of those rare moments it seemed truly open. "Your forbearance is remarkable, Malcolm. But if you've realized that, I'm inestimably grateful. The situations are scarcely the same, however. Laura doesn't owe me anything."

"When it comes to owing I'd say it's more a matter of personal feelings than legal obligations. It's fairly apparent what Laura feels for you."

O'Roarke gave a wintry smile. "You have a keen understanding, Malcolm. But your own happiness may be coloring your perceptions of those round you."

"And your tendency not to think you deserve happiness may be coloring yours."

"I don't in the least—"

"You and my wife share that. I know a bit about it myself."

Their gazes met. The man who had introduced him to Shakespeare, taught him to fish, helped him write school speeches, come to Harrow for speech day when neither of Malcolm's parents had. It was probably always a shock the first time one spoke to one's parent as another adult about romantic relationships. It was even more of a shock when one had barely begun to accept that the person in question was one's parent. "I appreciate the support," O'Roarke said. "But I've made choices. I hope I'm at least man enough to live with the consequences."

"And leave Laura to live with the consequences?"

"Damn it, you don't think I want Laura to be happy?" O'Roarke drew a breath. "Sorry."

"On the contrary. I think Laura's happiness matters a great deal to you. I just think you have a worrying tendency to think that it doesn't lie with you."

O'Roarke fixed his gaze on the windows. Valentin had looped back the muslin subcurtains, and gray light slanted through the panes. "I don't think Laura herself can say where her happiness lies at present. And that gives me license to— enjoy our time together. Without worrying about what I'm denying her."

"That's rather a bleak outlook."

"I wouldn't call it bleak. I've learned to snatch happiness where I can."

"So you keep looking ahead and expecting the happiness to end? Until you decide she's better off with someone else?" Malcolm paused a moment. "As you did with Mélanie?"

For a moment O'Roarke went as still as if he were encased in ice. "With Mélanie, one can hardly argue I was wrong."

"And with my mother?"

O'Roarke's fingers whitened on the handle of his coffee cup. "I never did end things with your mother, Malcolm. But I didn't do a very good job of making her happy."

The pain in his voice cut through the room.

"Christ, Raoul," Malcolm said. "You can't blame yourself. You knew her demons."

"None better. But one always thinks one should be enough to hold them at bay."

Malcolm found himself staring at the stretch of wall above the sideboard, dappled by the light from the windows. Suzanne had chosen a pale peach for the room. It had been ice blue in his mother's day. He remembered the letter Raoul had sent him after his mother's suicide. An amazingly thoughtful letter. But for the first time, it occurred to him how it must have been for Raoul to receive the news of her death, in another country, with no outwards way to show his grief. "I suspect you did hold them at bay for a long time. Not that I haven't thought the same myself."

"You were a child."

"Not by the time she died. I was old enough to know she needed help and young enough not to have the least idea how to provide it."

"I'm twenty years your senior, Malcolm, and I couldn't answer that." Raoul looked at him for a long moment.

"Nothing. Nothing you could have done would have made a difference."

"Thank you. I'll never quite believe it, any more than you do, but thank you for trying to make me. Laura, however, is no Arabella Rannoch."

Raoul gave a twisted smile. "Fanny said much the same to me last night."

"Aunt Frances—" Malcolm regarded his father for a moment. "I'm rather glad not to be the only one who suffers her emotional insights."

"Yes, it's amazing how a woman five years my junior can make me feel like an undergraduate."

"Laura's sorted out a great deal in the past three months, from what I've seen. And her feelings for you only appear to have grown stronger."

Raoul drew a breath. "I don't expect my own feelings to change. But I'm trying to give her latitude should hers do so."

"And Emily?" Malcolm asked.

Raoul went still for a moment. "Emily sees me as an uncle, as do Colin and Jessica. There's no reason that should change, whatever happens between her mother and me."

Malcolm had an image of Raoul swinging Emily up on his shoulders. "Colin and Jessica love you," he said. Odd how natural that seemed now. "They see you as part of the family. But it's different with Emily. That's been apparent from the moment you and Laura first brought her into our dining room. After Laura, you're the most important adult in her life."

Raoul shook his head. "At that point, I was the only other adult she really knew in her new life. I helped rescue her. It lent a sort of glamour."

"You don't need any help to acquire a sort of glamour, O'Roarke. And that may be part of why you're special to

Emily. But I'd wager the rest is because of what's between you and her mother."

Raoul's brows drew together. "We haven't—"

"I don't mean she could put it into words. I don't mean she's aware of anything that could be considered in the least improper. But I'm quite sure she knows there's something special between you and Laura."

Raoul was watching him with the care of one handling porcelain. "Malcolm—"

"Was I aware of what was between you and my mother? Yes and no. In retrospect, much more yes than no. But I don't think you and Arabella were ever a settled couple in quite the way you and Laura are."

Raoul drew a sharp breath. "Laura and I—"

"Spare me the protestations. I've spent enough time with the two of you to recognize you for a couple." Malcolm leaned forwards, arms on the table. "Speaking from personal experience, relationships being complicated doesn't weaken them. And it's amazing what one can work through."

Raoul met his gaze for a long moment. "You put up with a lot, Malcolm. You'd be pardoned for wishing me at the devil."

"We're all glad to have you back in London."

Raoul hesitated a moment. "It means a great deal to stay in Berkeley Square. And not just because of Laura."

"We enjoy having you here." Malcolm tossed down a swallow of coffee. "Mel's happier when you're about."

Raoul shot a surprised look at him.

"I'm not jealous," Malcolm said. "Not in that way. Mostly not in that way. But she's happier when she can see you. She gave up her whole life to marry me, and I didn't even realize she was doing it and ask her if she really wanted to make that decision. I'd like her to have as much of her old life as possible."

Raoul continued to stare at him, gaze frozen in shock. "Malcolm—"

"What I'm trying to say is that I'm glad you're here. Colin and Jessica should have a chance to know their grandfather." He reached for the coffee pot to refill their cups again. "And I've rather come to like having you about myself."

Raoul drew a breath that seemed to crack in the still air. But before he could speak, the door opened and Valentin came into the room. "This just came for you, Mr. Rannoch," he said, holding out a paper.

Malcolm opened the single stained, unsealed sheet. It had been sent on from the coffeehouse he used to pass messages when he was concealing his real identity. It was from Sue Kettering, Ben Coventry's mistress, and she wanted to see him.

"How have you been?" Malcolm dropped into a chair across the table from Sue at the tavern on the edge of Seven Dials where she'd told him he could find her. "I've thought about you a great deal."

She gave a brief laugh. "I know how to take care of myself. Wouldn't have survived this long if losing someone could destroy me."

"And your boy?"

Sue dragged a hand across her eyes, smearing her eye-blacking. "Jemmy's starting to understand. He doesn't ask when Ben is coming back anymore. But I don't think he quite understands Ben isn't coming back at all."

"It's good if he can hold on to memories of his father."

She gave a quick nod. "I didn't come here for sympathy. I've been trying to think of anything that might help you learn what—learn who did this to Ben. I didn't think this mattered because it was a fortnight before he died. But—One night when we stayed with him, Ben came in late. He looked shaken. He was pale. Paler than I've ever seen him. I said it looked as though he'd seen a ghost. He started to laugh, but then said maybe that wasn't so far off." She hunched her shoulders, pulling her tattered shawl closer about her. "He said one of the worst betrayals he'd seen during the war, in the Peninsula, was committed by one of the most beautiful women he'd ever seen. That it was hard to imagine such beauty existing with such treachery." She lifted her gaze to Malcolm's. "And that he'd seen her in London."

Suzanne was still at her toilette when Malcolm returned to Berkeley Square. Malcolm leaned in the doorway for a moment, watching her finish applying blacking to her eyelashes.

"Darling." Suzanne regarded him in the looking glass, taking in his claret coat and spotted handkerchief. "You've been working."

"Sue Kettering asked me to meet her." Malcolm looked at Jessica, who was sitting on the carpet by the dressing table, pulling lengths of ribbon out of one of the bottom drawers and dangling them for Berowne to bat at. Laura must have taken the older children down to the breakfast parlor. "Mel." Malcolm pushed the door to and advanced into the room. "Is there any chance you crossed paths with Ben Coventry in the Peninsula?"

"No. That is, I don't recall ever hearing his name." Suzanne turned round on the dressing table bench and scanned her husband's face. "Darling? What is it?"

"Sue said a couple of weeks before he died Ben mentioned catching a glimpse of a woman in London. A woman he knew from the Peninsula. One of the most beautiful women he'd ever seen. Who'd committed one of the worst betrayals he'd ever seen."

"And you thought—" Suzanne drew in and released her breath. "Darling, I was hardly the only female agent in the Peninsula who ended up in Britain."

"No, but—"

"And flattered as I am, I'm sure there are many who could be described as beautiful."

Malcolm nodded. Jessica grabbed hold of his boots and pulled herself to her feet. Malcolm swung her up in his arms.

Suzanne stared at the blacking brush, then tucked it into its inlaid drawer. "I can't swear I didn't cross paths with him without knowing his name. But he'd have to have somehow learned the truth about me for that comment to make sense. And if I was that sloppy, I wouldn't have survived this long."

"A point." Malcolm pressed a kiss to Jessica's forehead. "But whomever he saw it wasn't just an agent. It was someone he knew had betrayed Britain. Or at least betrayed something or someone."

Suzanne nodded, carefully matter-of-fact. "Which would apply to me. But—"

"It could apply to others. It may be nothing to do with Whateley & Company and Coventry's death. But—"

Suzanne stared out the window for a moment. "Darling. Maria Monreal. I haven't seen her, but from Harry's and Oliver's responses I imagine she's quite beautiful."

"But not a traitor to Britain. Or—" Malcolm met her gaze. "Not that we know of."

"Precisely. If she had been playing both sides and Coventry knew and threatened to expose her now, when she's trying to build a life in Britain, that would give her a reason to have killed him."

Malcolm shifted Jessica against his shoulder. "According to Ennis and Sue Kettering, Coventry broke in alone."

Suzanne leaned forwards to scratch Berowne under the chin. "But it looks more and more as though a second person broke in. Maria broke into the Brook Street house two nights later." She got to her feet, shaking out her scalloped skirts. "Suppose, for all her denials, she also broke into Whateley & Company the same night Ben did. Perhaps on Carfax's orders." Jessica stretched out a hand to Suzanne. Suzanne laced her fingers through her daughter's own. "Perhaps she didn't kill him because of the papers, but because he recognized her."

Malcolm drew a breath. "I need to see Carfax. Not that I have a prayer he'll actually tell me anything."

31

"Oh, Malcolm, good." Carfax looked up from the papers strewn over his desktop. "I saw you much more in evidence at the ball last night than you generally are at a social engagement, so I presume the investigation is proceeding apace? Beyond your accusations about Whateley & Company and my role in it?"

Malcolm dropped into one of the straight-backed chairs. "We've made progress."

"Which you aren't prepared to share with me." Carfax pushed his spectacles up on his nose. "Fair enough."

"*Fair enough?*" Malcolm was wary of anything approaching reasonableness from the earl.

"I'm not precisely in a position to make demands. Provided you tell me in the end whatever concerns my family. Or the country."

"And you're confident I will?"

"You're still loyal to your country even if you're one of the last people I'd want to see running it. And you're enough of a father yourself to understand my feelings about my family." Carfax coughed and aligned a sheaf of papers. "Do you still think Maria Monreal was behind the Brook Street break-in?"

"It appears that way." Malcolm hesitated, aware of the pressure of the hard slats against his back. To voice the obvious next question seemed a betrayal of a trust that went back over a decade. But Oliver had already betrayed that trust by lying and refusing to explain himself. And Malcolm needed to know what Carfax knew. "Did you know Oliver knew Maria Monreal?"

"Oliver?" Carfax looked up at Malcolm in seemingly genuine surprise. Then his eyes narrowed. "Are you saying Monreal was Oliver's mistress? Is Oliver's mistress?"

"Oliver claims not."

Carfax gave a short laugh.

"And oddly, I'm inclined to believe him."

"You would. That's the romantic in you talking, Malcolm."

"I'm not in the least romantic. If you mean I love my wife, so do you."

A dry smile that held more regret than Carfax normally admitted to curved the earl's mouth. "I never had any illusions that Oliver was in love with Bel. It was one of the reasons I wasn't overjoyed when he offered for her. But Bel's always been practical. I thought they had a reasonable chance of making it work."

Isobel, Malcolm had sometimes thought, might be Carfax's favorite child. She was more of an intellectual than her sisters, but Carfax's relationship with her didn't have the layers of father-and-son and earl-and-heir that weighted his relationship with David. And Isobel might perhaps come the closest of all the Mallinson children to possessing some of Carfax's hardheaded pragmatism.

"Has Oliver had mistresses in the past?" Malcolm asked.

"My dear boy. Do you think I've had my daughters' husbands watched?" Carfax demanded.

"Yes," Malcolm said.

Carfax gave a faint smile of acknowledgment. "Keeping an eye on Trenchard and Craven was difficult enough. I may have made myself generally aware of Oliver's activities, but not to the point of knowing whose bed he shared." Carfax adjusted his right spectacle earpiece. "To own the truth, I'd prefer not to know that about my sons-in-law. Unless it has implications beyond the personal."

"Had you ever sent Oliver to meet with Maria Monreal?"

"Why on earth would I send any of you to meet with one of my agents?" Carfax's tone made it quite clear that the "you" referred to with mild contempt was Oliver, David, Simon, and Malcolm himself. "Yes, all right, I might send you, but only because you're so damnably good at your job. And I never even sent you to meet with Maria."

"Oliver's your son-in-law. Maria's your agent. And there's some connection between them."

"Former agent. But, yes. It's concerning." Carfax tapped his fingers on the ink blotter as though he could summon answers. "What's Oliver's story?"

Malcolm repeated the account Oliver had given him. Hardly sharing his friend's secrets, as he was quite sure the account was a lie.

Carfax picked up a pen and twirled it between his fingers. "If he's telling the truth, Maria could have set up her meeting with him at Somerset House."

"To get close to your son-in-law."

"Presumably."

"Why?"

"If I knew that, I wouldn't need you to investigate, would I?"

"Did she know anything about Whateley & Company?"

"Not to my knowledge. It was never essential to anything she worked on for me, and when have you ever known me to share information that isn't essential?"

"Do you think it's possible Maria was playing both sides in the Peninsula?"

Carfax's brows snapped together. "What makes you say that?"

"Two weeks before he was killed, Coventry saw a beautiful woman in London whom he recognized from the Peninsula. He said she had committed one of the greatest acts of treachery he ever saw."

"And you think Maria—"

"It's only a theory. One of several."

Carfax stared down at the ink blotter. "I'd like to say it's impossible. But of course one can never really be sure of one's agents."

"In which case, she might be working for your enemies now."

"An interesting theory." Carfax sat back in his chair, still twirling the pen. "Whom did you have in mind?"

"You tell me. Who are your greatest enemies now the Bonapartists are defeated?"

"I wouldn't say defeated. Held at bay."

"Sir, you can't seriously think there's a threat—"

"I think there will always be a threat. It's only a few months since there was an assassination attempt on Wellington."

"In Paris."

"Conspiracies can cross borders. And then, of course, there are the conspiracies at home. The machine breakers. The Radicals willing to go further than you. Not to mention foreign spymasters, many of whom would like to see a change in the French and Spanish governments, not to mention our own."

"Where's Fouché these days?" Malcolm asked, seizing on this opening.

"Fouché?" Was it his imagination, Malcolm wondered, or was Carfax's voice just a shade too casual? "In exile in Trieste, last I heard."

"Last you heard? You may not be tracking Oliver's every movement, but don't tell me—"

"Yes, all right. I get regular reports on Fouché."

"Surely if you think there really could be a plot to reinstate Bonaparte—"

"Or more likely a surrogate. Getting Bonaparte off St. Helena wouldn't be easy. But Fouché's a pragmatist who bends with the prevailing wind. A Bonapartist restoration would be a desperate gamble. Which doesn't mean it couldn't cause the devil's own havoc. But it would be the act of a burning idealist."

"If any enemy of yours is behind the break-ins, there's no reason to think it has anything to do with Bonaparte."

"True. But we never wrote down anything at Whateley & Company about our unofficial business. I fail to see what Fouché or some other enemy might have been after at either Whateley & Company or the Brook Street house."

"Yes," Malcolm said, "that remains the question."

Carfax leaned back in his chair. "Speaking of enemies, I saw Raoul O'Roarke come in with you last night. Is he staying with you?"

Malcolm leaned back in his own chair, mirroring the earl's posture. "Yes, as I'm sure you were well aware. He stayed with us when he was in London last April, as I'm sure you're also well aware. He's an old friend of my family's." There was no reason to think Carfax knew O'Roarke had worked for the Bonapartists in Spain. He considered O'Roarke an enemy based on the United Irish Uprising and O'Roarke's Republican principles. If Carfax knew anything more, it was most likely that O'Roarke was Malcolm's father. Which was tiresome, but not dangerous.

"A dangerous man, O'Roarke," Carfax said. "I always thought he was the most dangerous of the United Irishmen. Far more of a risk than that foolish idealist, Fitzgerald. Even when circumstances made him our ally in the Peninsula, I can't say I trusted him. And now he's working against the Spanish government—But I daresay you're in agreement with that."

"With the Spanish wanting their constitution restored and the Inquisition suspended? Can you doubt it?"

"Purely rhetorical. Politically you're a natural ally of O'Roarke's. Just remember that the things you spout off about in theory, he actually seeks to put into practice."

"So you're saying he's more effective than I am? Or braver?"

"Hmph," Carfax said.

"I assume you're having him watched in London?"

"Given his friendship with your family, not to mention the fact that he's staying with you, you can hardly expect me to answer that, Malcolm."

"I presume you aren't suggesting O'Roarke might be behind the break-ins and Coventry's death?" Malcolm said. It was a bold question, but bold moves were often called for with Carfax.

"I wouldn't put it past him," Carfax said. "Especially if he thought he could gain information about me. But as I don't know what information the thieves were after, it's impossible for me to say."

"Or at least impossible for you to share with me."

"If I thought O'Roarke was a creditable threat in this I'd tell you, Malcolm." Carfax sat forwards, hands on the desktop. "Acknowledge his friendship with your family. Have him in your house. Discuss your Radical views with him. But don't make the mistake of thinking your shared views equate to shared tactics. O'Roarke is far more ruthless than you'll ever be."

It was, Malcolm suspected, not unlike what his father would say. It was what he once would have said himself. He was no longer entirely sure it was true. "Are we done, sir? Or do you have more questions about my friends and domestic arrangements?"

Carfax frowned in the way he once would have when he called Malcolm or David "scamp." "By all means, get back to your investigating and make yourself useful."

Malcolm started to push himself to his feet, then said, as a seeming afterthought, "You did send Oliver to Whateley & Company to discuss Louisa's marriage settlement, didn't you?"

Carfax riffled through the papers on his desk as though looking for something. "Of course. Why else would he have been there?"

Malcolm couldn't always tell when Carfax was lying. But just then he was quite sure the earl had done so.

"Malcolm." Lucinda ran out of a downstairs parlor as Malcolm emerged from her father's study.

"Lucy." Malcolm masked his qualms to give David's little sister a quick smile. He remembered holding her when she'd been a baby, years ago, at the age of thirteen. She'd felt so fragile and wobbly and unbelievably tiny. Later, he'd got quite comfortable tossing her up on his shoulders. But the thought of ever being a parent himself had still seemed as distant as the moon.

"Can you come into the parlor for a few minutes?" Lucinda asked. "I have tea."

The youngest in the family by many years, not yet formally out in society, and the only young Mallinson left at home, Lucinda often seemed to make a plea for attention. But Malcolm read something more in her anxious gaze. "Tea would be welcome," he said, and let her pull him into the blue-papered parlor. A tea service stood on the satinwood table. Lucinda poured two cups, her hands jerky.

"What is it, Lucy?" Malcolm asked, perching on the scrolled arm of a sofa.

Lucinda's gaze darted over his face as she put a cup of tea in his hands. "I don't suppose you can tell me anything. And while part of me wants desperately to know what's going on—I mean how could I not be curious?—there's another part that would distinctly prefer not to know. But I know you're looking into the break-in at Whateley & Company and the one in Brook Street, and I daresay a great deal else. And I think you should know."

Malcolm took a sip of the delicately scented tea, which Lady Carfax had specially blended at Fortnum's. "Know what?"

Lucinda splashed milk into her tea and stared into the purple-flowered cup. "Last night. After the ball. We were all sitting in the small drawing room at Bel and Oliver's. Well, Mama and Bel and I were. Oliver and Papa were downstairs in the study, which was a bit odd because no one could call them confidants, but they do talk sometimes, and perhaps they wanted to discuss manly things after all the dancing. I realized I'd left my reticule downstairs when Rhys and I went into the library earlier in the evening." She colored slightly; Rhys was Lucinda's particular friend, and though she claimed there was nothing more to it, Malcolm sometimes wondered. "I went into the library, the door to the study must have not been closed properly. I heard raised voices that I couldn't make out and then Oliver must have moved closer to the door, because I suddenly heard him say quite clearly 'You may own me in most things, but my soul's still my own.' And Papa mumbled something back. All I could make out was something that sounded like 'illusions.' And then Oliver said, 'Leave Malcolm out of it.' And Papa said, 'My dear Oliver'—you know how he talks— 'Malcolm has been at the heart of it from the beginning.'"

Tea spattered against Malcolm's hand. The world as he knew it tilted in his mind. He tightened his grip on his cup and tried to hold on to his sanity.

Lucinda gaze darted across his face. "Do you know what it means?"

Malcolm forced a swallow of tea down his throat. It tasted more bitter than usual. "I'm not sure."

"I never thought how hard it must be on Oliver that most of their money is Bel's. I suppose that's what he meant about Papa owning him. But I can't think what he meant about you—"

Malcolm squeezed Lucinda's hand. "I'm not precisely sure either. But I'm glad you told me."

Lucinda's gaze clung to his face, at once seeking reassurance and acknowledging that she was old enough to know that reassurance might be impossible. "After everything that's happened, I just can't bear for anyone else in our family to be hurt."

And she trusted that confiding in Malcolm was more likely to save her family from hurt than to cause it. A frightening burden.

Malcolm gave Lucinda a quick hug. "Very often words overheard out of context don't mean what one thinks, Lucy. But I'm glad you confided in me."

Lucinda clung to him for a moment. "I know how difficult Papa can be, but he's fond of you, Malcolm. You're practically one of his children."

Which might be true. But considering the way Carfax treated his children, it wasn't much comfort.

Malcolm finished his cup of tea, hugged Lucinda again, and let her show him from the house. He accepted his hat and gloves from the footman with a smile, pressed Lucinda's hand, and went out the front door as he had countless times in the past twenty years. He paused in front of the half-moon forecourt. The wrought iron gate, worked with roses and acanthus leaves from the Mallinson crest, was elegant but always put him in mind of a fortress. He stared at the gilded tips of the metal, his own words to Harry the previous night playing in his head. *Carfax might have turned to Oliver for help with family matters, but it's hard for me to imagine him turning to Oliver for something involving his agents.*

Unless, of course, Oliver was one of those agents. The conclusion slapped him in the face. As obvious and unthinkable as when he'd realized his wife was the Raven.

He felt a spatter of damp against his face and realized a light rain had begun to fall. My God, you'd think he'd have learned his lesson. Less than an hour ago he'd said he assumed Carfax was watching O'Roarke. For all the people Carfax spied on, why had it never occurred to him his spymaster's efforts would have been turned on him?

32

Harry made his way down the rain-spattered pavement of Half Moon Street at a fast clip. He had very little expectation that Maria would reveal anything to him about her relationship with Oliver Lydgate, but he had to at least make the attempt. He might be able to read something into her silences, or into whatever fresh spin she put on her story.

Last night, home from the Lydgates' ball, Cordy had acknowledged that he'd need to see Maria again, in a crisp, bright voice that at once betrayed and defied concern. Was he a monster to feel a twinge of gratification? Not that he had any desire to cause his wife disquiet, but it sent a shock of wonder through him that she cared enough to feel it.

He slowed three houses down from Maria's, instincts tuned to a stir of movement. The door of Maria's house opened, and a woman descended the steps, a pale blue umbrella unfurled against the light drizzle. Not Maria. The ringlets escaping the brim of a sapphire satin were pale blonde. The bonnet, Harry knew thanks to his wife, was in the first stare of fashion, as were her sapphire spencer and muslin gown with flounces edged in blue ribbon. He stepped back into the shadows of a lamppost. As he did so, the woman paused to adjust a pale blue glove and turned in his direction. He wasn't sure she'd seen him, but he got a good enough look to know he should recognize her elegantly boned face.

Where—That was it. The opera. She'd been in the box next to theirs with her husband. It was Lady St. Ives. Sylvie de Fancot that was. Her parents had been French émigrés. And Malcolm had told him that Oliver Lydgate had been in love with her, but lack of fortune had put an end to any prospect of a match.

Harry stayed still as Sylvie St. Ives descended the steps and turned, heading away from the direction from which he had come. On foot, which was surprising. She was the sort of lady he'd have expected would always have her carriage waiting for her.

Was that the connection between Maria and Oliver Lydgate? Was Maria helping facilitate a liaison between Lydgate and his old love? Why? And what did it have to do with Whateley & Company?

Once Sylvie St. Ives was out of sight, Harry made his way to Maria's door and rapped sharply on the panels. The maid admitted him and took him up to the sitting room where he had seen Maria before, without first checking with her mistress. Maria must have known this interview was inevitable as well.

He found his former mistress seated at her marquetry-inlaid escritoire, a pen in her hand, a furrow between her brows as though she was searching for the right word. It must be less than ten minutes since Sylvie St. Ives had taken her leave. Had that interview sent Maria to her writing desk? Or was this a deliberate pose, designed to make Harry think her thoughts were elsewhere?

"Harry." Maria set the pen down. "Two visits in two days. I'm flattered."

"Gammon, Maria." Harry advanced into the room as the maid closed the door behind him. "You had to have known I'd be back."

"Because you couldn't accept my perfectly reasonable explanation?" Maria got to her feet and gestured towards the sofa and chairs. "Perhaps. You always were infernally stubborn and disinclined to trust. I thought perhaps your wife had changed that, but it seems not."

"My faith in Cordelia has nothing to do with my ability to see through a farrago of lies."

Maria gave a laugh that might have been acknowledgment or denial and moved to the sofa. "I don't really see what I can tell you that I didn't tell you yesterday. But it's very pleasant to see you."

Harry dropped down on one of chairs. "Yesterday you omitted to tell me of your friendship with Oliver Lydgate."

"Ah." Maria's hand faltered slightly settling the gauzy skirt of her gown. Surprise? Or the counterfeit of surprise?

"Did you really think I wouldn't find out?" Harry asked. "I thought you had more respect for my abilities."

"I have utmost respect for your abilities. But you couldn't expect me to simply drop information into your lap." Maria twitched her amber satin sash smooth. "It's not what it seems."

"I didn't think it was," Harry said. "Go on."

Maria proceeded to give the same story Lydgate had given Malcolm the night before. The chance meeting at Somerset House, Oliver's assistance with legal difficulties. "That's what Lydgate said," Harry said. "Almost word for word."

"That's because it's true."

"So if he's such a good friend, why didn't you ask him to search for your letter to Craven? He's in the Brook Street house all the time."

"My dear Harry. Oliver Lydgate is an able man, but he's no agent. He could scarcely have searched the Craven house without raising just the sort of questions I wished to avoid."

"A point." Harry stretched his legs out and crossed his feet at the ankle. "Was it Lydgate who introduced you to Lady St. Ives?"

Maria gave a sigh, fluttering the ruffle at the neck of her gown. "I should have known you'd have seen her."

"Yes, you should. Though I can quite see you not admitting it on the off chance I hadn't."

Maria gave a faint smile. "Oliver—Mr. Lydgate and Lady St. Ives were very attached when they were younger. The attachment endured. Or revived in recent years. I don't know the details, but Mr. Lydgate confided his feelings for Lady St. Ives to me. I offered to let them meet at my house and to pass the occasional message."

Harry folded his arms across his chest. "You were helping along their love affair simply out of the goodness of your heart?"

"I do have a heart, Harry, even if it's a bit bruised. And I know full well that marriage and love don't always go hand in hand. I know Oliver's wife is a friend of yours and the idea of someone seeking solace outside marriage probably carries a particular sting for you, but I assure you the attachment existed long before I met Oliver and Lady St. Ives."

"Whom Lydgate sleeps with is his own business." Actually, it was also Isobel's, but Harry was not going to have that particular debate with Maria. For an instant though, he saw Isobel standing at the head of the stairs last night. Was it his imagination that there'd been strain about her eyes when she greeted him and Cordelia? "But even granted your story about your friendship with Oliver is true, are you really asking me to believe you did all this simply out of friendship for a man you've only known a few months?"

Maria raised her brows. "Is that so hard to believe?"

"It is. Unless you got something else from him entirely."

"My dear Harry. You intrigue me. What are you suggesting?"

"I don't know. But I have every intention of finding out."

"Uncle Bertrand." Colin looked up from the burgundy felt of the game table in the library where he, Suzanne, Laura, Emily, and Blanca were engaged in a rainy day game of lottery tickets. "Did you bring Stephen?"

"Not today, I'm afraid. Next time. I need to speak with your mother."

Suzanne handed Jessica to Laura and took Bertrand into Malcolm's study. "You've learned something." It wasn't a question.

"Yes. Though I can't say what it means." Bertrand dropped down beside her on the sofa. "Patrice Rénard, a haberdasher I helped get out of Paris in 1816, spotted Germont in Bruton Street yesterday. Rénard had seen Germont once or twice in Paris, and is quite confident it was the same man. He said Germont was speaking with a fashionably dressed woman who looked so like him that he assumed she was his sister."

"Does Germont have a sister?"

"Not that I heard of. Certainly not that he had a sister in London. But there are the accounts of an aunt who settled here. It might have been a cousin. In which case, he could have sought her out for reasons that have nothing to do with the Phoenix plot. But Rénard said that while they weren't being obviously furtive, they seemed to be attempting to make their meeting appear casual. You've had no reports of a woman approaching anyone about the Phoenix plot?"

Suzanne shook her head. "Only the anonymous-sounding man. Who sounds as though he's disguised. I suppose—" She drew a breath, turning over possibilities.

"The anonymous man could actually be a woman?" Bertrand's gaze grew thoughtful. "I've donned the guise of a woman often enough. Or, I suppose, the woman Rénard saw could actually be a man."

"More likely it's two different people," Suzanne said. "But either way, if we can trace this woman, even if she isn't part of the plot, it could lead us to Germont."

And to the answers to numerous questions she wasn't sure she was ready to have resolved.

Malcolm sipped a cup of coffee at the Coffee Tree, off Piccadilly. Their excellent brew tasted unusually bitter today. Much like Lady Carfax's tea. He forced another sip down. He wanted nothing more than to stalk off and confront Oliver, but he knew prudence dictated that he wait for Harry and see if his friend had ascertained anything from Maria Monreal this morning. He'd only have one chance to confront Oliver unawares. He needed the best hand possible.

He drummed his fingers on the worn tabletop, scarred with the initials of numerous law students and undergraduates down from Oxford and Cambridge. He'd sat at this same table six months ago while Suzanne's former lover taunted him and inadvertently revealed the information that led Malcolm to put together the pieces and realize his wife was the Raven, a Bonapartist agent.

Perhaps he should have found another coffeehouse in which to meet Harry after that episode. But he'd be damned if he was going to let Frederick Radley disrupt his life. He tossed down another swallow of coffee. For that matter, he was damned if he was going to let Suzanne disrupt it.

A draft of air, damp with the day's drizzle, signaled the opening of the door. He looked up to see three young men clutching sheaves of foolscap push their way into the coffeehouse, arguing with the passion of the young. And behind them, sweeping a damp beaver hat from his head, Harry Davenport. He dropped into the chair opposite Malcolm. "You've learned something."

"I was waiting to see if you had," Malcolm said.

"I have, though from the looks of it yours is more surprising."

Malcolm's fingers tightened round his coffee cup. But were the situations reversed, he'd want Harry to be honest with him. "I think Oliver is working for Carfax."

Harry released his breath. "That—changes things."

"Quite."

Harry regarded him for a moment the way he might look at a comrade who's received a wound in the midst of a battle. "I'm sorry."

"I should have seen it sooner."

"The spy's mantra on discovering unexpected information."

"Fitzwilliam Vaughn. Louisa." His own wife. His father. "You'd think I'd be used to it by now."

"I don't think one can ever get used to it." Harry leaned forwards, arms on the table. "This puts a different complexion on my discovery. I saw Lady St. Ives leaving Maria's."

Malcolm drew a breath. He'd thought he was beyond surprise, but this was a fresh twist.

"Maria claims she was facilitating their love affair, out of sympathy," Harry said. "Which I didn't believe for a moment. But if Maria and Lydgate were both working for Carfax—"

"She'd have helped Oliver betray his wife, who is Carfax's daughter?" Malcolm shook his head. "Difficult to make sense of it. But it does make it look far more as though Carfax put Maria and Oliver up to both break-ins."

Harry met his gaze across the table. It didn't take words for them to acknowledge what crossing swords with Carfax meant.

Malcolm scraped his chair back. "I need to see Oliver."

"Malcolm—"

Malcolm managed a faint smile. "Don't worry, I won't throttle him or plant him a facer. I acknowledge the temptation, but I want answers too much to do anything that might interfere with getting them."

Malcolm set his shoulders against the door of a sitting room at Brooks's. "How long?"

Oliver, whom he had found alone in the room, looked at him in seeming bewilderment. "How long what?"

"How long have you been working for Carfax?" Malcolm advanced into the room and leaned over his friend, hands braced on the table in front of the wing chair where Oliver was sitting. "Before we met you? Was it his idea you audition for *Henry IV?*"

Oliver's skin drained of color. He was obviously far better at deception than Malcolm had credited, but Malcolm recognized the flash in his gaze of an agent who knows he's caught. "Malcolm—"

"Don't try to deny it. We'll just waste time. I'd have seen it years ago if I hadn't been almost willfully blind."

He saw the denial rise to Oliver's lips, saw the hope of it working smash in Oliver's eyes. "Malcolm—" Oliver pushed back his chair and sprang to his feet. "You can't think when I met you—"

"When, then?" Malcolm held his friend's gaze across the table as though he were holding him at sword's point.

Oliver drew a breath as rough as the cracking of illusions. "The autumn after I first visited Carfax Court. The summer after our first year. That was the first time I met Carfax. I scarcely thought he paid much heed to me. And I was busy trying to navigate my way in this strange world. You were helpful with that."

"Go on," Malcolm said, willing his voice to remain steady.

"Carfax sought me out at Oxford. I thought he was looking for David at first. He took me to dinner at an inn away from the university. In a private room. He was—" Oliver grimaced. "It sounds mad to say engaging—"

"No. He can be," Malcolm said.

"He painted himself as a concerned father more than a spymaster. He said he could see I had more sense than his son and his friends—even then, I could recognize it for flattery." Oliver stared at a hunting print on the wall opposite. "But it's still something at nineteen to receive such notice from one of the most powerful people in Britain. He said he wanted to make sure David didn't get himself in trouble. That he'd be grateful to me if I'd keep an eye on him and let him know if he fell in with the wrong people." Oliver dragged his gaze back to Malcolm's. "I knew what he meant. Though I wouldn't have called it spying. Not then."

"It's difficult to admit one's a spy," Malcolm said. He wouldn't have called himself a spy that first day Carfax engaged his services, or for months after. His wife and father were much more honest about their work. "I suppose I should be flattered Carfax took such notice of us."

"You have to admit some of our talk went a bit far in those days. There was that article you wrote advocating universal suffrage and the abolition of the House of Lords."

"Yes, I'm still rather proud of that one." It was one of the ones Raoul had mentioned. In some ways, what Carfax had done could be looked at as not so different from Raoul getting reports from Arabella and Frances. Save that Raoul had wanted reports on how Malcolm—his son—was doing, rather than trying to stifle his activities. Motive could make all the difference. That, and the fact that Raoul hadn't paid one of Malcolm's friends to spy on him. Granted he'd set Suzanne to spy on him, but by that time Malcolm had been a spy himself.

Oliver spun away and took a turn about the room. "I didn't—I didn't tell him everything, Malcolm. I didn't tell him about David and Simon. Once I figured it out for myself, that is. But—damn it, we weren't doing anything illegal. We weren't plotting anything. There was no reason he couldn't know most of our activities."

"No reason except that they were *our* activities. Which we believed to be private."

Oliver met Malcolm's gaze across the stretch of carpet, worn smooth by the well-made boot heels of countless well-heeled members of Brooks's. "You have no idea what it was like. The things you and David and Simon could do without thinking. Counting my coins before I agreed to go out to dine or letting one of you pay the reckoning. Sending my coats home to my mother to darn instead of ordering new ones. Not understanding the rules of the games played in your world, whether fox hunting or flirtation. Sharing dreams with you, but knowing that if I ever wanted to make a difference in the world I needed money. I saw what my father could do as a country lawyer. I knew I wanted to play on a larger stage."

"An alliance with Carfax would hardly help you make the sort of difference you wanted to make."

"It let me step onto the playing field. I told myself I could control how I played."

"Always a mistake with Carfax." Though one, Malcolm acknowledged, that he himself had made.

Oliver passed a hand over his face. "Even with everything I wanted, I think I'd have thrown his words in his face. If I hadn't met Sylvie on my visit to Carfax Court."

Malcolm remembered the Fancots coming to stay at Carfax Court for the midsummer ball, remembered Oliver unable to take his eyes off Sylvie. And Sylvie unable to take her eyes off him. It had left Malcolm the one unattached one in their little band. A state he'd rather expected would endure forever.

"I knew I'd never have a prayer with her without position and influence," Oliver said. "Ironic, given how things played out. I don't even know—But at the time, it seemed she held all my happiness. And I was mad enough to think we could have that happiness living in lodgings on a barrister's earnings."

Despite everything, Malcolm felt a flash of sympathy at the remembered yearning in Oliver's gaze. "St. Ives has a title and fortune. Difficult to compete with."

"Yes. Sylvie might have married him anyway."

"Anyway?"

Oliver swallowed hard. Malcolm knew that look. He saw it on his wife's face more often than he could count, of late. He knew he wore it himself. An agent calculating how much to admit. "Sylvie married St. Ives because Carfax ordered her to."

Malcolm stared at Oliver. "Carfax—"

Oliver raised a brow. "You hadn't worked that out? But if I hadn't told you, I daresay you would have done. I didn't know when I first met Sylvie. When I agreed to work for Carfax. It wasn't until that Christmas when I saw her at Carfax Court again and we—we confessed our feelings to each other. She'd been gathering information for Carfax for over a year. There's a lot to be learned from the prattle of young girls. Especially when they have powerful fathers. Sylvie may have been an outsider, but she moved in exclusive circles."

Malcolm had always known Carfax had a network of agents in London. He just hadn't realized how extensive it was. Or how many people it included whom he knew. "Sylvie would have needed the money as well."

"Yes, although—" Oliver's brows drew together. "It was more than that. Carfax has some hold on her. Something to do with her father. Which is why when he told her he wanted her to accept St. Ives, she couldn't stand against him." Oliver's hands curled into fists at his sides.

"That must have been hard to take," Malcolm said. "The more so as I imagine you trusted Carfax to a degree." He knew what it was to trust the spymaster and then have him turn on one.

"He told me I'd get over it." Bitterness twisted Oliver's mouth. "In some ways, he was right. In some, he wasn't."

"I understand now why Carfax consented to your marriage."

"You think—" Oliver stared at him. "Malcolm, no. Carfax didn't order me to marry Bel. In fact, I don't think he was best pleased with our betrothal, though perhaps he was more willing to accept it because he thought he had a hold on me. But— God, he's never controlled my votes. Do you believe me?"

"I'm not sure what I believe."

Oliver nodded. "I deserve that. You may not believe this either, but I stopped reporting to him after we all came down from Oxford. You went to the Peninsula. David stood for Parliament."

"Carfax thought we'd compromised."

"He didn't seem as worried. I went my own way in Parliament. But every so often he'd ask me for a favor. An errand. I was his son-in-law. But though he never said so, it was plain between us that he could tell Bel and David and you what I'd done if I refused."

"Yes. He's good at making his wishes known that way. You met Maria Monreal through Carfax?"

"He wanted her to recover some papers from the Spanish embassy two years ago. I'd been there, so he needed me to give her tactical advice."

"And then he tasked the two of you and Sylvie to recover papers Craven had left?"

"*What?*"

"Harry saw Sylvie leaving Maria's house this morning. Given that you all worked for Carfax, I assume he put the three of you up to this. The only thing I'm not sure of is what he wanted you to recover."

"Carfax didn't want us to recover anything. Malcolm, you've got it the wrong way round for once. We weren't working for Carfax. We were working against him. We'd made up our minds to be free of him once and for all."

Malcolm regarded Oliver. He couldn't afford to let betrayal befuddle his brain. "You and Sylvie and Maria Monreal were working against Carfax together?"

"Yes. That is—" Oliver scraped a hand over his hair. "It wasn't just the three of us. I don't think we'd have been mad enough to take on Carfax on our own. That's the secret of his power, in a way. No one would be willing to take him on on their own or even with one or two as back-up. He had us all trapped. Even you've said you don't feel you can walk away from him completely."

"True enough."

"But he doesn't have something on you or his other official agents like Tommy Belmont. It's different for the rest of us. The unofficial ones working in the shadows. The feeling of powerlessness—" Oliver shook his head. "I thought I'd always be under his thumb. Until a month ago."

"What gave you the idea you could challenge him?"

"Oh, it wasn't me." Oliver gave a twisted smile. "I'm not clever enough. Or brave enough. It was another of those he's entrapped into serving him. Apparently Craven had been in touch with him before he died, saying he had papers Carfax would give a great deal to keep from the light of day. He argued that if we all worked together, we could obtain our freedom. He contacted Sylvie before me. When Sylvie first told me, I said it would never work. But the more I thought about it, the more I realized how insupportable it was to continue at his beck and call."

"Who?" Malcolm said. "Who organized you?"

"I don't know."

"For God's sake, Oliver, having told me this much—"

"I'm not lying. I truly don't know. I don't think Sylvie does. That was part of the plan. A number of us were working together but we couldn't identify each other. My role was to call at Whateley & Company in the guise of talking to Eustace about Louisa's marriage settlement and have a look about.

Note any likely hiding places, the position of the door, learn what I could about when the warehouse would be empty."

"And this unnamed person engaged Coventry?"

"No, that was—" Oliver drew a breath. "That was Cuthbertson."

"Cuthbertson? William Cuthbertson?" Malcolm stared at his friend, seeing Cuthbertson waltzing with Laura the night before. "I didn't realize he worked for Carfax."

"Nor did I, until recently. But you can see why Carfax would want a source in the army, close to Wellington."

"And Cuthbertson was a comrade of Fitzroy Somerset. He's the one who asked Fitzroy to engage Ennis to engage Coventry, isn't he?"

"If you've already worked that out for yourself, I don't suppose there's any point in denying it. You know how Carfax has an ear to everything in London. We wanted to keep it as far away from ourselves as possible."

"No, it was clever. The trail led back to Fitzroy, which was enough to confuse anyone. Enough to confuse me for a time."

"Hopefully enough to confuse Carfax."

Malcolm regarded Oliver. "What happened? How did Coventry die?"

"I don't know." Oliver's gaze held seemingly genuine torment. "I had no idea he *was* dead until you told me. As far as any of us knew, he went into the warehouse alone."

"So someone else was after the papers?"

"Presumably. Perhaps the murderer recovered them, but we couldn't be sure."

"Which is why Maria broke into the Brook Street house."

Oliver nodded. "I wanted to search myself, but they said I couldn't search while David and Simon were there, and Maria would be better at doing it secretly. Which was right."

"Did she find anything?"

"No." The word was clipped, but fear haunted Oliver's gaze.

"You must have considered that the other person who broke into Whateley & Company, who killed Coventry, who may have taken the papers, could be working for Carfax."

"God, how could I not?" Oliver slumped against the paneling. "It's one of the things Sylvie and Maria and I were meeting about today."

"Have you seen any sign that he knows?"

"No. But you've actually spoken with him about the investigation. Have you seen any?"

"Merely denials. Which is what one would expect of Carfax, in any event." Malcolm regarded Oliver for a moment. "What did Carfax ask you to do last night—"

Oliver's eyes widened. "What—"

"Lucinda overheard you."

Oliver gave a slow nod. "And that's how you put the pieces together. Poor Lucy. She's been through more with her family in seventeen years than anyone should." He met Malcolm's gaze without flinching. "Carfax wanted me to report to him about your investigation."

"Did he say why?"

"Merely that you were clever, but he'd never been able to entirely trust what you'd do with your information."

"And you argued with him?"

"My God, of course. I always argue with him when he asks me to spy on you."

"Always?"

"Well, always since Oxford. Carfax of course reminded me I was hardly in a position to refuse."

"The fact that he asked you to watch me could mean he didn't know you had anything to do with the break-in."

"So I tried to tell myself. But you know as well as I do that if Carfax was behind Coventry's death, it's just the sort of thing he might do to keep watch on both you and me."

Malcolm met Oliver's gaze and nodded. When he walked into Brooks's, he'd never have guessed that after half an hour's talk, he and Oliver could be in such perfect agreement.

33

Raoul turned into Berkeley Square. The drizzle had let up. The air had the crisp freshness that follows rain. The gray skies had given way to white clouds that scuttered across an expanse of blue, and the green leaves on the plane trees in the square stirred in the breeze. He remembered his own trepidation opening the metal gate of the square garden at Colin's invitation and stepping inside to play catch with him. Was it really only six months ago? And only three months since he had sat on a bench in the same garden beside Laura and made a pledge that grew stronger by the day?

Laughter and the whinny of horses cut the air. Open carriages clustered round Gunter's. Footmen hurried from the confectioner's bearing ices to ladies in the carriages, while other fashionable patrons sat at the tables on the pavement. A flash of sunlight glinted off the bright curls escaping the bonnet of one of the women. Raoul turned to get a better view, saw the dark hair of the woman sitting with her, the unmistakable posture of both, the three children clustered round them. He hesitated a moment, but there was no reason now for him not to join them. And then, Colin looked up and waved, deciding the matter.

Raoul crossed the square. Mélanie had Jessica in her lap. Jessica was midway through a raspberry ice, managing very well with a spoon (she had her mother's dexterous fingers), though a considerable amount was smeared over her face. Colin and Emily were taking more restrained bites of their own ices.

Laura set down her lemonade and looked up at him with a smile. "When the rain let up, we couldn't resist. It seems so glorious after a gloomy morning."

"Absolutely. One must take advantage of the sunshine when one can."

Emily jumped up. "You can have my chair." She held up her arms to him.

Raoul hesitated a fraction of a second, the unreality of his present life washing over him. Then he said, "Thank you. A very generous offer." He scooped Emily up and dropped into the chair, settling her in his lap. He remembered the first time she'd taken his hand, getting into the carriage in an inn yard on the journey from the orphanage that had been the only home she'd known for most of her young life to the Berkeley Square house. Later that night, lifting her sleeping form from Laura's lap when they'd arrived in Berkeley Square. She'd been a boneless weight in his arms, but when he stepped down from the carriage, cradling her against him, she'd opened her eyes and blinked sleepily up at him. He'd thought she might be afraid to realize this man she scarcely knew was carrying her, but instead she'd given him a heart-stopping smile. Something had cracked open in him in that moment that he'd thought would remain forever closed.

It was only the following day that she'd first climbed on his lap. Laura had been talking with Malcolm, and Emily had seemed to be seeking reassurance in a household still reeling from the news of Louisa Craven's death. She'd clutched the fabric of his coat and looked about her with wide eyes. Now she snuggled against him with comfortable assurance and reached for the spoon for her ice.

"Were you Investigating?" Colin asked. "Daddy's Investigating."

"Something of the sort," Raoul said. "I can't say I learned very much."

"I'd like to Investigate." Emily took a bite of her white currant ice. "Like you and Uncle Malcolm and Aunt Suzanne. You help people."

Raoul exchanged a look with Mélanie. "That's part of it."

Emily licked currant droplets from her spoon. "You helped me. That's how you found me."

"That is how we all found you," Raoul said. "But mostly it was your mother."

Emily gripped her mother's hand. "Mummy's good at Investigating too."

"A bit." Laura wiped a trace of ice from her daughter's cheek. "I learned most of it from Uncle Malcolm and Aunt Suzanne and Uncle Raoul."

"Actually," Raoul said, subduing the impulse to reach for Laura's hand, "your mother was very adept before any of us met her. She always"—he leaned back in his chair and went on speaking, alert as always to his surroundings. Two ladies, a mother and daughter by the look of it, in a landau to their left, two young women flirting with two officers under the gaze of their chaperone, at a table to the right. A fair-haired man crossing the paving, juggling a trio of ices with dexterity as he—

Raoul's blood turned several degrees colder than the iced confections before them. For, as the fair-haired man crossed the pavement, Raoul caught a glimpse of his profile.

"What?" Colin asked. "What did Laura say then?"

Raoul realized he had stopped speaking. Rare for him to be so rattled. But then it was, thank God, a rare occasion to see anything as unsettling as the sight of that burnished blond head and that deceptively mild gaze. A gaze he profoundly hoped had not taken in their own group.

He met Mélanie's gaze across the table for only a fraction of a second, but knew she had seen it too.

"Laura said one should never forget a promise. Which I quite agree with. I distinctly remember I promised you a game of pirates when we got home."

"Pirates!" Colin and Emily exclaimed almost in unison.

"'Rats," Jessica said with enthusiasm.

The fair-haired man was standing beside a closed carriage a little removed from them to the right, delivering the ices to the unseen occupants. His back, thankfully, to them. Mélanie got to her feet, cradling Jessica perhaps a trifle closer than necessary. Raoul swung Emily up, which made her laugh. Colin held out his hand to help Laura up in a very grown up way.

Proceed as though all were usual. Don't make too much of it. Don't, above all, rush or look over one's shoulder. Standard operating procedure he'd followed dozens of times in similar circumstances. But not with three children in tow. How in God's name did Malcolm and Mélanie manage?

Mélanie carried Jessica. Raoul held Emily's hand, and Laura, Colin's. The children chattered enthusiastically. Carriages clattered by. Patches of rainwater glistened in the sunlight. The plane trees still rustled in the breeze. The white clouds still scuttered overhead.

And the unthinkable had happened.

Roth regarded Malcolm across the same table at the Brown Bear they had occupied the day before. "I'm honored. That's quite a confidence."

"It's part of the investigation."

"It's a secret about your friend."

Malcolm set his fingers on the scarred wood of the table. "You're my friend."

Roth returned his gaze. For a moment, the smoky air between them was thick with memories. Roth reached for the cup at his elbow, which today contained coffee, as did Malcolm's. "I should get you something stronger."

Malcolm shook his head. "I need my wits about me."

Roth took a sip of coffee. "Do you think Lydgate could have broken into Whateley & Company and killed Coventry?"

Malcolm curled his hands round his cup, as if the warmth of the pewter could still his instinctive recoil. Whatever he had learned of Oliver today, he couldn't see him as a killer. But then, there was so much he hadn't been able to see Oliver as until a few short hours ago. "I'm not sure. Despite today's revelations, it's true he's not a trained agent in the way Maria Monreal is. Logically, it's more likely Maria Monreal was the one who broke in. And then most likely killed Coventry." He took a sip of coffee, hot and bitter on his tongue. "But just now, I'm not sure how much of a grasp I have of logic. I still can't quite accept the idea that Oliver might have killed a man hours after he was playing on our drawing room carpet with his children and my own at Colin's birthday party."

Roth turned his cup between his hands. "It's an appalling betrayal. I can scarcely imagine it. And yet, at the same time a part of me can understand what it was like for Lydgate. It's not easy to be an outsider in your world."

"As my wife reminds me." Though until six months ago, he hadn't known how very hard it was or how very much she was an outsider.

"Easier for me, of course," Roth said.

"Easier?" Malcolm stared at his friend, a dozen past slights he had seen Roth endure running through his head.

Roth ran his finger over the initials scratched in the table-top. "Lydgate will always be an outsider in the beau monde, but he's just on the edge, married to one of their number, bumping up against an invisible barrier. Whereas I know I'd never have a prayer of belonging." Roth reached for his cup. "Not that there's a chance in hell I'd ever want to."

Valentin opened the door to admit Malcolm and informed him that Mrs. Rannoch was in the library with Lady Tarrington and Mr. O'Roarke. Malcolm handed his hat and gloves to Valentin, the acrid bite of the day's revelations still sharp in his throat. He did not relish sharing the news about Oliver with any of them. Yet there was much to discuss, and he welcomed all of their perspectives. Laura needed to know about Cuthbertson. He nodded to Valentin and opened the door of the library. "I'm glad you're all here. I've just learned—"

He stopped short as he stepped into the light from the windows. It fell across Suzanne's face, drained of color above the shiny rose-colored fabric of her spencer. Her eyes were dark, her lips bloodless. "Good God, darling." He crossed to her side in two strides and seized her hands. Despite the warmth of the sun spilling through the windows, they felt like ice. "You look as though you've seen a ghost."

"In a way, I have." Suzanne's fingers tightened round his own, as though in an unconscious plea for help. Which was at once oddly reassuring and bloody terrifying. His wife wasn't the sort to reach out for help. "Only, I had no illusions that he was dead. Men like St. Juste never die."

"Who?" Malcolm cast a glance at Raoul. His father's gaze was neutral as ever, but his face was set in unusually grim lines.

"Julien St. Juste," Raoul said. He was, Malcolm realized, standing closer than usual to Laura. "We caught a glimpse of him when we were sitting outside Gunter's an hour ago."

"Another former Bonapartist agent?" Malcolm drew Suzanne closer.

"Yes, though ultimately he was a freelancer who worked for the highest bidder," Raoul said. "You never crossed swords with him?"

"Not by that name."

Suzanne pulled her hands free of Malcolm's grip. "I met him on my first mission. Raoul sent me to retrieve a letter from him that the Empress Josephine feared would fall into the wrong hands."

Malcolm knew O'Roarke had been close to Josephine long before she married Napoleon Bonaparte. Their friendship went back to the early days of the Revolution, and they had been imprisoned in Les Carmes together, both a few days away from going to the guillotine when Robespierre fell. "St. Juste knew the empress as well?" Malcolm asked.

"When I first met him, he was her lover," Raoul said. "During the Directoire, before she came to Bonaparte's attention."

"And when you sent Suzette to recover this letter in"—Malcolm did quick mental calculations—"1809, you thought—"

"Josephine feared Napoleon was going to divorce her. She thought Fouché would use the letter to turn Bonaparte against her."

"And you retrieved it?"

"No." Suzanne's fingers locked together. "I failed. St. Juste caught me trying to take it."

Malcolm smiled despite the situation. He knew how much the admission of failure cost his wife. "It was your first mission."

Suzanne tugged at the lace-edged collar of her spencer, as though it choked her. "Then he gave me the letter. He said the empress was the one person he would never hurt. He's the last man on earth I can imagine ever trusting. But I believed him."

Raoul looked from Suzanne to Malcolm and inclined his head towards the sofa. Of one accord they all settled by the unlit fireplace, Malcolm and Suzanne on the sofa, Raoul and Laura on the settee beside it.

"Two years later, Josephine asked me to assist her daughter Hortense," Suzanne said. She looked between Malcolm and Laura. "The mission I told you about six weeks ago."

Malcolm nodded. Six weeks ago, Lisette Varon had sought refuge in their house, bringing a letter from Hortense Bonaparte, Josephine's daughter and the unhappy wife of Napoleon's brother Louis. The letter had been intended for Hortense's former lover, the Comte de Flahaut. When the letter had gone astray, Suzanne had told Malcolm and Laura about how she had gone into Switzerland with Hortense seven years earlier so Hortense could give birth to her child by Flahaut in secret. Malcolm was still shaken by how great a sign of trust it had been for his wife to share that confidence with a British agent. When he'd said as much to her, she'd simply said, "You wouldn't hurt a woman and her child."

Suzanne's hands locked together. "I still remember Hortense putting the baby in Flahaut's mother's arms and watching her carriage roll away. I don't know how she did it. And that was before I was a mother myself." Suzanne met Laura's gaze for a moment.

"Appalling," Laura said. "How society can interfere between a mother and child. Does Queen Hortense see the child?"

"Occasionally," Suzanne said. "So in that sense she's more fortunate than some."

It was much the story of Malcolm's mother and his illegitimate half-sister Tatiana. And of Tatiana and her own child, Pierre.

Suzanne turned her gaze back to Malcolm. "But what's pertinent now is that Josephine also asked Julien St. Juste to go with us into Switzerland as our escort."

Malcolm had a fairly shrewd notion of where Suzanne must have been to try to retrieve Josephine's letter from Julien St. Juste, and what she had probably done to get there. It shouldn't come as a surprise. He knew she'd employed seduction as a technique in her work as an agent. He'd faced the despicable Frederick Radley, who had been her lover. Still, there was something about her fear of St. Juste and the obvious importance he still had—"So you spent a lot of time with him," he said.

Suzanne gave a quick nod. "Though I can't really claim to have got to know him. But I do know him enough that I'm sure it was he who we saw today."

"So am I." Raoul's voice was grim.

"At Gunter's?" Malcolm asked. "Doing what?"

"Buying ices," Suzanne said. "Three. He carried them to a closed carriage."

Malcolm drew a breath. "You think he's part of the Phoenix plot? Could he be the man Lisette saw Louis Germont with?"

Suzanne exchanged a look with Raoul that told Malcolm they'd been discussing this. "I don't know that Lisette ever met him," Raoul said. "So it's possible."

"Flahaut knew him," Suzanne said. "So someone else would have to have called on Flahaut. Probably. St. Juste is a master of disguise. And Flahaut said the man who called on him looked familiar though he couldn't place him."

"He's far away from St. Helena if his mission is to free Bonaparte," Raoul said. "But he must be here on a mission of some sort."

"Has he worked for Fouché before?" Malcolm asked.

"On occasion," Raoul said. "They weren't natural allies, thanks to St. Juste's connection to Josephine and Fouché's antipathy to her. But it's a changed world since Waterloo."

"Do you know where St. Juste has been since Waterloo?" Malcolm asked.

"The last I saw him was at the Duchess of Richmond's ball," Suzanne said.

"What?"

"In a rifleman's uniform. He brushed past Cordy and me just after dinner. He had a girl in white on his arm. He could have been on a mission. Or he could have just found it amusing to shake Wellington's hand."

"He dropped out of sight after Waterloo," Raoul said. "As abruptly as he first appeared in the nineties."

"Did he see all of you at Gunter's?" Malcolm asked.

"I'm not sure." Suzanne folded her arms across her chest. "Not obviously, but with St. Juste one can never be sure."

"He'd recognize you." The threat of Suzanne's being exposed never failed to tighten Malcolm throat.

Suzanne nodded. "But he couldn't very well expose me without betraying his own cover." She hesitated a moment, fingers taut on the rose-colored silk of her spencer. "St. Juste is incalculably dangerous. But I don't think he'd betray me unless he was forced to it. In the end, we were comrades, and he has his own code."

Malcolm studied his wife, inches away from him on the sofa, tendrils of hair escaping round the fragile nape of her neck, pearl earrings swinging beside her face, shoulders pulling at the seams on her spencer, brows drawn. This man he had never met, had never heard of until a quarter hour ago, had obviously been an important presence in her life. "You trust him?"

"Dear God, no." Suzanne's fingers pressed into her sleeves. "To own the truth, I went cold at the thought of him being as close to the children as he was today."

"So did I," Raoul said.

Malcolm met his father's gaze. Coming from O'Roarke, it was quite an admission.

Laura was also staring at her lover. "I think that's the first time I've heard you confess to fear of anyone."

"Oh, I'm afraid of plenty of things," Raoul said with a quick smile. "I just manage to keep it to myself most of the time. But St. Juste is in a category all by himself. Not long after we first met, we were walking together in the boulevards after one of Josephine's parties. A man we passed fell dead to the ground. It took me a moment to realize St. Juste had stabbed him. St. Juste didn't even break his stride."

Malcolm stared at his father, remembering the confidences they had shared only this morning. He understood Raoul far better than he would have thought possible a few weeks ago. And yet, sometimes—"You sent Suzanne to face him."

O'Roarke's mouth tightened. "I trusted Suzanne."

"I didn't exactly live up to that trust," Suzanne said.

"On the contrary. We got the letter back. Fouché wasn't able to move against Josephine."

Suzanne turned towards Raoul. "Is that what you thought would happen? That St. Juste would catch me and give up the letter?"

"No." Raoul's eyes darkened. Malcolm couldn't read everything they contained, but he caught the bite of self-recrimination. "But it was one possible scenario."

Laura was staring at him as well, as though taking in the man he had been. O'Roarke met her gaze for a moment without flinching.

"We have to warn Carfax." Suzanne forced a smile to her face, though she was sitting with her arms folded in front of her, shoulders hunched, as though warding off an attack of ague. "And yes, those are four words I never thought would leave my mouth."

"Nor did I." Malcolm managed an answering smile. "But I think we need to find out what St. Juste's mission is before we warn Carfax."

"Darling, did you hear what Raoul said? Do you want a man like that running round Mayfair—"

"Of course not. But if St. Juste is working for Fouché in the Phoenix plot and the goal is to ferret out Bonapartists, we'd already decided Carfax would agree with Fouché."

"And if he's here for some other reason?

Malcolm frowned at the bronze tapers on the mantle. "You said St. Juste worked for the highest bidder. We have to at least consider the possibility that in this case the highest bidder was Carfax."

Suzanne sucked in her breath, but Raoul's gaze told Malcolm he'd already considered this possibility.

"Would St. Juste work for the British?" Malcolm asked.

"I don't think there's anyone St. Juste wouldn't work for," Raoul said, a knife edge in his voice.

"And there's no one I'd put it past Carfax to hire," Malcolm said.

Laura was frowning. "I'm not arguing with that, but what—"

"Any number of things," Malcolm said, "including a move against someone in the government."

Suzanne shook her head. "But—"

"Carfax has informants all over London," Malcolm said. "No matter how good St. Juste is, it's hard to believe Carfax has no idea he's here. One can't but wonder."

"And if that's the case—" Laura broke off.

"He could betray Suzanne without betraying himself," Malcolm finished for her. He reached for Suzanne's hand and gripped it tight. "Quite."

"He hasn't yet," Suzanne said.

"That we know of," Malcolm returned, a dozen possible scenarios, all equally grim, chasing themselves through his head. "Carfax would keep that sort of information until it was of use."

"There's someone else in England who might have hired him," Laura said. "The Elsinore League."

"I can certainly imagine them having use for a man of St. Juste's talents," Raoul said. "Did you ever hear Trenchard speak of him?"

Laura shook her head. "Not that that means anything. As you've often pointed out, the Elsinore League don't always work in concert. And even if Trenchard did know of St. Juste, he hardly confided in me."

Raoul's mouth tightened. Thinking of Suzanne's former lover, Frederick Radley, Malcolm could sympathize. And the late Duke of Trenchard made Radley look like a prince in a fairy tale.

Suzanne looked at Raoul. "You agree with Malcolm?"

"If Malcolm wanted to tell Carfax, I wouldn't try to stop him. But I think it's best that we're armed with data before we make any decisions."

Malcolm nodded. "In any case, I'm not much in charity with Carfax at the moment. I just learned he had Oliver spying on David, Simon, and me from when we were at Oxford."

Suzanne went still. "Darling—"

"Not the best news," he said. "Though it rather pales next to what you've told me."

"On the contrary." She reached for his hand. "We've seen an old enemy. You've learned you were betrayed by a friend."

"I'll live."

He saw the instinctive recoil in Suzanne's eyes, the brilliant smile that defied it. "You mean it can't be worse than being betrayed by your wife?"

"Of course not. That is—" He drew a rough breath. He'd scarcely had time to think it through for himself. "You did what you did for something you believed in. And it started before we met. Oliver did this for money. And it started after he knew us."

"He was at Oxford on a scholarship, wasn't he?" Raoul said.

Malcolm nodded. "And he desperately wanted to marry a woman without a fortune. Part of me can understand. But not—" He shook his head and told them, in as crisp and factual terms as possible, what he and Harry had learned, ending with William Cuthbertson.

Laura's eyes widened, but she merely said, "Well, that explains his presence in London and his renewed interest in me."

"It doesn't do anything of the sort," Raoul said.

Laura turned a level gaze to him. "He must have needed an explanation for his sudden arrival in London. I thought he was taking our past affair far too seriously."

O'Roarke reached for her hand. "Laura—"

"It's all right." Laura twined her fingers round his own. "I've been feeling guilty about Will. This means I needn't so much. But—" She turned her gaze back to Malcolm. "It's hard to credit him as a spy. He always seemed so open. That was one of the things I—He was working for Carfax?"

"So it seems," Malcolm said. "Or at least sending information to him, which isn't quite the same as actively spying."

"It's a blurry line." Laura cast a glance at Raoul. "Apparently I have a weakness for spies. Though I can't imagine Will was in your league."

O'Roarke had been frowning, but at that he gave a faint smile. "I'm not sure whether or not that's a compliment."

"Believe me it is," she murmured.

"I know you said you didn't have any idea," Malcolm said. "But now you know, thinking back—Is there anything that stands out?"

Laura frowned. "We'd talk about the political situation. It was one of the things I liked about him. I wonder if that was part of it even then. If he got close to me because my father was the colonel. Or because my father-in-law was an Elsinore League member on a diplomatic mission."

"No," Raoul said. "At least that certainly wasn't all of it."

Laura shook her head. "Objectively, you can't know—"

"Yes, I can. I saw the way he was looking at you last night."

"Being an agent doesn't stop one from having feelings," Suzanne said. "I think we can all testify to that."

Laura shook her head. "It scarcely matters. I wish I could remember more. I wish I could say I'd learned something dancing with Will last night. But he's obviously very good at concealing things."

"So is Sylvie St. Ives," Suzanne said. "I always rather avoided her because I was afraid as a real émigrée, she might see through my cover. I should have paid more attention."

"So should I." Malcolm's mouth tightened. "I've known her since I was in shortcoats. I knew she had a quick mind, but I never thought she had an interest in much beyond life in the beau monde. I remember once in the Peninsula—"

"Lady St. Ives was in the Peninsula?" Suzanne asked. "I thought St. Ives didn't fight until Waterloo."

"He didn't, but he was sent to Lisbon with dispatches once. In the autumn of 1810, before I met you. Sylvie came with him. I remember her saying she couldn't keep track of who was on which side, but at least it made for diverting parties."

"I've played roles like that," Suzanne said. "But I can't imagine keeping it up for so long."

"I was in and out of Lisbon that autumn," Raoul said. "I remember being at at least one party where the St. Iveses were present. I had no notion. Just as I had no notion Carfax's network in London was quite so extensive."

"Nor did I," Malcolm said. "And apparently he uses blackmail to control a lot of his agents. If not at the start, then to keep them from stopping working for him."

"Like Trenchard." Laura's voice was flat as scorched earth. Raoul reached for her hand.

"And to think I discounted Sylvie St. Ives as frivolous," Suzanne said. "I must be slipping. So we know part of what was behind the break-ins. But not who killed Ben Coventry."

"No," Malcolm agreed. "But if Carfax knew what his agents were doing, he'd certainly have wanted to recover the papers first."

"If that were true." Laura stared at her hands, spread over the cinnamon-striped fabric of her skirt. "And if St. Juste is working for Carfax. Could St. Juste be the other person who broke into Whateley & Company and killed Coventry?" She looked from Raoul to Suzanne.

Raoul met Suzanne's gaze for a moment, then looked at Laura. "A break-in, even one that leads to murder, is far beneath the scope of what a man like St. Juste takes on. But if he's working for Carfax on something bigger and if these papers are as important to Carfax as Lydgate made it sound—"

"A lot of ifs," Suzanne said. "We don't know that Julien is working for Carfax at all. Or that Carfax engaged whoever killed Ben Coventry."

"I need to talk to Cuthbertson," Malcolm said. "And try to learn who set up this plot to break away from Carfax." He looked at Raoul.

"You know far more about Carfax than I do," Raoul said.

"But you've been gathering intelligence against him for years. You must have sources. We need to pursue every angle."

Raoul inclined his head.

"We can find them at the Waterloo banquet tonight," Malcolm said. "It's a good thing Wellington invited you."

"It's amazing how an investigation can get complicated without taking one any closer to the solution," Suzanne said. "By the way, Bertrand was here earlier today. I almost forgot with everything else that's happened. A source of his saw Germont in Bruton Street with a woman who looked as though she was a relation. Bertrand and I speculated on everything from her being Germont's sister to actually being his anonymous-sounding colleague in disguise." She frowned. "Julien's coloring is similar to Germont's."

"And he's quite convincing disguised as a woman," Raoul said. "Interesting. Though hardly conclusive."

Suzanne drew a determined breath. "It's difficult to speculate more until we discover more information. Which Bertrand is endeavoring to do."

"And to think I once wondered if I would find life dull when I stopped working for the Elsinore League," Laura said.

"Not in this family," Suzanne said.

Laura didn't even seem surprised at the word family.

34

Laura watched Raoul as the library door closed behind Malcolm and Suzanne. The Rannochs had gone upstairs to dress for the Waterloo banquet. She and Raoul had lingered in the library, to give the other couple time alone, and because unlike Malcolm and Suzanne, they couldn't publicly share a bedchamber, so any talking they did would have to take place here. Raoul was frowning at the windows. Outside the leaded glass, the Berkeley Square garden was washed gray by the early evening light.

Laura moved to his side and slipped her hand into his own. "I was fond of Will. But it never meant more to me than a momentary escape. So I can scarcely be upset to learn that his feelings for me weren't all they seem."

Raoul turned his head to cast a quick glance at her. "One's reaction to such news isn't always rational. Quite the reverse, often."

"Perhaps if my feelings had been more engaged. Perhaps if I'd learned earlier. Before I"—she hesitated, then said it anyway—"met you."

He drew her hand up to his mouth and kissed her knuckles. "I'm honored."

"Mostly now I just feel foolish for not seeing the truth. To be intimate with a person and not realize—I don't think I properly appreciated how beastly it must have been for Malcolm—" She bit her lip.

"Quite," Raoul said. He looked down at their interlaced fingers. "It doesn't necessarily make Cuthbertson a bad person. Malcolm worked for Carfax."

"My dear. Are you pleading his case?"

"I'm endeavoring to be objective." Raoul's gaze moved back to the windows. "Much as my instincts may scream not to be."

"It doesn't change anything either way." Laura tightened her grip on his hand. "Malcolm took that better than I expected. Better than Suzanne feared, I think."

Raoul squeezed her hand but continued to frown at the window. "No. Sensible of him to suspect Carfax, though it can't be easy for him."

Laura leaned her head against his shoulder. "It's rather a relief to know you can be afraid of something."

Raoul turned his head and gave a bleak smile. "It's a dangerous life we live. But until this afternoon I was under the delusion that London was now more or less safe. I'm sorry."

Laura lifted her head to look up at him. "For what?"

"If it weren't for me, you and Emily wouldn't have to worry about St. Juste."

"You don't know that. We don't know for a certainty that he isn't working for the Elsinore League. And in any case Emily and I would be connected to him through Suzanne. We'd have been at Gunter's with her and Colin and Jessica today even if you were still in Spain."

"A point." He put his lips to her hair. "But I suppose it reminded me—"

She leaned in to him. "What?"

His arm slid round her. "I tend to live under the illusion that whatever risks I run don't affect Emily and you."

Laura moved to face him and gripped his arms. "Raoul. You can't think I'd worry—"

He smiled again. "I know full well that you don't."

"I should hope so. Especially given what I've been through. After Trenchard and the Elsinore League, Julien St. Juste doesn't scare me."

His gaze settled on her own. "But you must realize that I worry."

Laura released his arms and took his face between her hands. "My love." Odd that that word should come to her lips now. "You sound as though you're having what Suzanne calls Malcolm's 'Hotspur' moments. You can't seriously tell me that you're wasting your energies—"

"It's one thing for you to run risks on your own. It's another for you to be dragged into them because of me. And you have a right to be concerned for Emily."

For some reason, now was when panic closed her throat. "If you have any illusions that we'd be better off without you—"

"No. Or at least, I manage to be deaf to them. But I worry about what I've exposed you to."

"That's what it means to have people one cares about," Laura said, picking her words with care.

"Which is precisely why I've avoided doing so for most of my life, as much as I could."

"I think you've just avoided letting anyone catch on that you care about them."

"Perhaps." He took one of her hands and dragged it across his mouth. "Don't worry, my darling. I'm too selfish to let such qualms interfere with what we have."

"You're one of the least selfish people I know, Raoul O'Roarke." Which, at the moment, was worrying.

He pushed a strand of hair behind her ear. "I'd never before have said you were deluded, Laura."

"You sent Suzanne to face St. Juste."

"Which rather proves my point. It was an appalling risk."

"She was an agent. Everything she did was going to be a risk. She had to start somewhere. This was in Paris with you nearby. And because St. Juste was loyal to Josephine, it was less of a risk than sending her against the British."

His mouth twisted. "You're good at making excuses for me, sweetheart."

"I'm good at reading you."

"That too. All you say is true. It's what I told myself. But I paced the floor the entire night. Because there was no guarantee St. Juste wouldn't put a knife in her ribs if he caught her."

Laura put up a hand to turn his face towards her. "There's no guarantee for any of us."

"So I've told myself for most of my life. But it occurred to me today—"

She set her hands on his shoulders. "What?"

"That I'd very much prefer not to have Julien St. Juste know what you and Emily mean to me."

Laura's fingers froze on his shoulders. A chill went through her again. And yet, spoken in a level voice, it was an astonishing declaration. "My dear—"

To her surprise he pulled her into his arms. "For once it's as well you're a respectable widow and I have a wife. There's no reason for St. Juste to guess."

She didn't pause to examine precisely what that meant their relationship would be if he didn't have a wife. "Does St. Juste know what Suzanne means to you?"

"More than I tried to let on in the past, I think. For just this reason."

She pressed her face against his shoulder. "Does he know Malcolm is your son?"

"No." Raoul's arms tightened round her. "At least I hope to God he doesn't."

Laura lifted her head to look up at him. "My dear. I know how one's loved ones can be used against one. Trenchard controlled me that way for years. But if one lives that way, one lets the Trenchards of the world win."

Raoul pressed a kiss to her forehead. "I should have thought—You've lived these fears more than any of us. But you never asked to play this game. I chose it."

"I chose to stay in it." She touched his face. "I chose you."

Colin and Emily looked up almost in unison as Suzanne and Malcolm came into the day nursery where they were eating supper under Blanca and Addison's supervision. "You missed supper," Colin said. "Is something wrong?"

"Just some new information we had to discuss." Malcolm smiled at Colin, then exchanged a look with Addison.

"Is it to do with the man we saw at Gunter's?" Colin asked.

Suzanne drew a breath, aware of Blanca shooting a look at her. She hadn't yet told Blanca about their sighting of Julien St. Juste. "You saw a man at Gunter's, darling?"

"Right before Uncle Raoul said we all had to leave."

"I saw him too," Emily said. "He had yellow hair. Is he dangerous?"

Suzanne bent to kiss Jessica who was eating boiled carrots with great concentration. "He's just someone we were surprised to see in London." She almost said "an old friend," but in the disconcerting eventuality that the children encountered Julien, she didn't want them to consider him a friend.

"So he's not dangerous?" Colin said.

"We're going to make sure he isn't," Malcolm told their son.

"Nothing to worry about with your parents managing things, lad," Addison said. Blanca didn't say anything, but her gaze asked Suzanne myriad questions.

Suzanne sent her companion a look that promised later explanations and smiled at Emily. "Your mother will be up in a bit."

"And Uncle Raoul?" Emily asked.

"And Uncle Raoul," Suzanne said.

She and Malcolm promised to come back after they changed, and went down the passage to their own room. They had a brief window in which they could talk, and she wasn't sure where to begin.

Malcolm pulled the door to, stepped up behind her, and put his arms round her shoulders. Her impulse was to turn round and bury her face in his coat. But they didn't have time for that, and she couldn't afford an emotional breakdown. She put a hand over his, but said, "I'm all right. Silly to react so."

"You have a right to be shaken."

"By a chance encounter with a former fellow spy?"

"By an encounter with a man even Raoul O'Roarke fears. That's enough to make me go cold myself."

Suzanne pulled away from her husband before he could feel the chill running through her and turned to face him. "Julien St. Juste is one of the few men I know who could outwit Raoul. That's enough to make me grow cold at the thought of him. But it's no excuse to be missish."

"I would imagine your feelings are complicated when it comes to St. Juste."

Despite herself, Suzanne's gaze jerked to Malcolm's face. His gaze was at once gentle and ruthlessly neutral. "You spent a great deal of time with him," Malcolm said. "You said you became comrades."

Suzanne nodded. "I suppose you could call it that. We each saved the other's life on that journey. But I can't claim to have really known him." She met her husband's gaze, which offered to talk without demanding, and knew that he was aware of something else in her dealings with Julien St. Juste. "We weren't lovers. Not on the journey with Hortense. Not after—that first night."

His gaze remained steady on her face. "I didn't ask."

"No. You never ask." She searched Malcolm's face. Sometimes his gaze was as open as that of anyone she had ever known. And at others as armored as siege walls. "You have to wonder."

"Do you wonder?" he asked. "About my past?"

She swallowed, mind filled with memories of moments when a look or a touch would send questions racing through her head. The knife cut of her suspicions about Tatiana Kirsanova, which seemed so laughable now. The small bite of seeing him with a woman he'd grown up with, the sort of girl he'd been expected to marry. The questions that had run through her mind only yesterday, talking to Cordy. "Sometimes. But in my case—"

Malcolm leaned against one of the fluted walnut bedposts, arms folded, legs crossed at the ankle. "I hate what you've been through. I'd give anything to be able to go back and protect you. But of all the things you've done, I'd say whom you slept with before you married me has the least to do with me. You weren't married to me. You weren't betraying me."

"No one said it was logical, darling."

"This is no different from Frederick Radley. When you told me about him in Vienna, my only desire was to throttle Radley."

Odd now to think that at that point, early in their marriage, she'd been afraid the revelation that she'd had a lover before their marriage would destroy her husband's image of her. He was a British gentleman, but she constantly overestimated how much he was a prisoner of his upbringing and underestimated the flexibility of his thinking. She could still feel his arms about her that day in Vienna when she'd told him and his lips against her hair. "But my affair with Radley wasn't part of a spy mission. That is, it was, but you didn't know that then." She swallowed. "You didn't know I slept with men to get information." It was by no means the only technique she'd employed as a spy, but it had certainly been part of her arsenal.

"That's not—"

"In many ways I never stopped being a whore."

He crossed to her side in a quick stride and seized her wrists. "Damn it, Mel, I won't have you talking about yourself that way."

"It's a word. It describes what I did."

"I'm familiar enough with self-hatred to recognize it in someone else. And in that sense all agents are whores. Though I never—"

"No," she said. "I didn't think you would. Which rather goes to my point."

He released her wrists. His gaze moved to the watercolor she'd done of a stream at Dunmykel that hung over the chest of drawers, a misty idealized world of greens and blues and grays. A muscle twitched beside his jaw. She thought he wasn't going to answer, but after a long pause, he said, in a low, rough voice, "You were pretending. On our wedding night. That shouldn't bother me more than your other pretenses. But I can't deny that at times it does."

She swallowed. The memory of that night trembled through her nerve-endings. She'd thought a wedding night was the least she owed him. She'd realized, with a shock of surprise, that she wanted him. She'd gone into his arms conscious of the role she was playing. Which was nothing new for her. She was usually playing a role in the bedchamber, one way or another. But that night she had forgot her role, lost track of her masquerade, lost control of her own feelings in a way that could spell death for a spy. She'd wondered, lying with her head pillowed on his chest and his lips against her hair afterwards, if she'd betrayed herself. "It wasn't all pretense," she said. "You can't think it was."

"No? I love you, Suzette. But it's hard for me to be sure I can see anything when it comes to you. At least at that point in our marriage."

She turned her head away. "I deserved that."

"I didn't mean it that way." He put out a hand, then let it fall to his side. "I was being—"

"Honest." She forced her gaze back to meet his own. "I asked for honesty."

"You're very good at what you do," Malcolm said. "I can't but wonder sometimes just how good."

She looked into the gaze she knew so well and had hidden the truth from for so long. "I didn't have to pretend with you. Or if I did, it was only not to let you see—"

"The real you."

"No. Yes, in a way." Her fingers had locked together behind her back. "You'd better ask me what you need to ask."

The gaze he turned to her cut her in two. "I can't—"

"I wasn't a very good whore," she said. "I didn't understand—much of anything. All I could muster was a cheap pretense. But later. On missions. It was part of the job. But there were times I enjoyed it. Slipping into the skin of a fictional character, knowing it was just for that night. There's no other escape quite like it." With Malcolm, lovemaking was never an escape. He took it far too seriously.

"Is that what you found with St. Juste?" Malcolm asked. His voice was ruthlessly controlled, yet it held the tone of one who genuinely wanted to know.

"In a way. The sort of escape one finds in a bottle of rotgut."

Malcolm took a quick step towards her. "Did he hurt you?"

"No. He wasn't inconsiderate. He tied me to the bedposts—"

"What?"

"Oh, for heaven's sake, darling. You've read the Marquis de Sade. At least I assume you have. His books are in Alistair's library."

"And you *let* him—"

"I wouldn't have let him do it if I hadn't known I could get free in twenty seconds if I wanted to."

"Surely—"

"It wasn't the first time. Malcolm"—Might as well be blunt. Better for him to face it. Better for her not to worry about what she was holding back. "There isn't a lot I haven't done. Besides"—she glanced down, then forced her gaze back to him. She wanted honesty. They needed honesty—"it had a certain piquancy."

He drew a harsh breath.

"Don't look at me like that, Malcolm, it's not something I want you to do. That is"—she hesitated again; odd how one could share someone's bed for five and a half years and not be sure of certain things—"you could if you wanted to, but—"

"Thank you. No."

"That's a relief. It doesn't seem at all like us."

"So St. Juste liked to be in control."

"That's my Malcolm. Never let anything stand in the way of the mission. Yes, I'd say he liked to be in control. I got my hands free at one point, just in play, and he wasn't pleased." She thought back. Silk cords. Demanding lips. A compelling touch. A murmur that was close to a command. "I'd go so far as to say he needed to be in control."

"Which could be a weapon to use against him."

"Perhaps."

"And on the mission with Queen Hortense?"

"He never tried to resume our relationship, if that's what you're asking. Oh, he made it clear a few times that he'd find it an agreeable way to pass the time on our journey, but when I made it clear that I had no intention of indulging him, he was entirely professional. He's totally amoral, but he has a code of sorts."

"Would he really work for the highest bidder, regardless of their goal?"

"I never heard him express any political views. Except for a wry contempt for Raoul's and my Republicanism. So I don't think we can use politics or ideals as a guide to whom he might be working for."

"Even England?"

She wondered if Malcolm was looking for some reason not to think Carfax was involved. "He never expressed loyalty to any country. I'm not sure he was French by birth."

Malcolm's gaze sharpened. "Why?"

She forced herself to give it honest consideration. "His accent was flawless. Just as he could adopt a German or Austrian or British accent without betraying himself. But there was something—something about the way he'd look at the countryside or comment on things—He was detached in any case, but when it came to France he always struck me as an outsider." She paused again, turning over her memories of Julien St. Juste. For a moment, he was so vivid in her memory it seemed she could reach out and touch him. The mocking gaze. The gleaming hair. The smile at once dangerous and unexpectedly, deceptively sweet. "He liked danger. And risk. He got restless on that journey with Hortense, because, except for a few hair-raising moments, mostly we were traveling slowly through the countryside and stopping at unremarkable inns, with the complications of pregnancy the greatest risk we faced. He was doing it because of his loyalty to Hortense's mother. But in general, though he could be bought, he prided himself on only taking jobs that were worthy of his talents."

"So whatever's he's doing in Britain, it has to be something big."

Suzanne's fingers bit into her arms through the fabric of her spencer. "Yes. That's why, if he had anything to do with the Whateley & Company break-in, it's only as part of something larger."

Malcolm drew her into his arms. "We'll get through this. I don't care how brilliant he is, he can't be a match for all of us combined."

She laughed. "How uncharacteristically optimistic of you, darling."

He smiled down at her, his gaze alight. "I can be an optimist."

"Perhaps. You can take blind leaps of faith. Like insisting our marriage can work."

He bent his head and kissed her. "That's because it can."

Malcolm came into the library to find Raoul standing by the windows, not far from where he'd been standing when Malcolm and Suzanne left the room but now dressed for the Waterloo banquet. Raoul was frowning at the leaded glass as though the plane trees beyond held the answers to the mysteries facing them, but he turned round at Malcolm's entrance. Malcolm looked sideways at his father. "Mel thinks St. Juste might not be French. That he could even be British."

O'Roarke didn't appear surprised, but he gave the comment honest consideration. "It's possible. I always suspected he wasn't French. Mostly, his detachment from France's political conflicts was simply a function of who he was, but there was always something of the outsider about him. And then there's the fact that he appeared so abruptly. St. Juste was the sort who would make his presence felt, even as a very young man. And yet I heard nothing of him until he was twenty."

"Do you think he could have been in Britain since Waterloo?"

Raoul drummed his fingers on the sofa back. "I'd have said that the boredom of lying low for three years would drive Julien St. Juste mad. But he appears to have been lying low somewhere. I rather thought he'd taken his talents off to the East Indies or South America or the United States. I suppose it's possible that's what he did, and that now he's back."

"Mel also says he wouldn't come back for any job he didn't consider worthy of his talents."

O'Roarke's mouth tightened. "Quite."

"And I presume the Phoenix plot, whether a real plot or a creation of Fouché's to entrap agents, would qualify."

"So it would. Though I still have difficulty imagining St. Juste working for Fouché."

"Is it easier to imagine him working for Carfax?"

"Yes, actually. He'd appreciate Carfax's hardheaded pragmatism. I'm less sure Carfax would trust St. Juste enough to engage him."

"Carfax isn't squeamish about whom he uses. And he tends to assume he can control people."

Raoul regarded Malcolm for a moment. "As usual, your forbearance is remarkable, Malcolm."

Malcolm moved to the drinks trolley and picked up the decanter. "I don't know why everyone keeps expecting me to have some sort of extreme reaction. I have a healthy respect for anyone you and Mel think is so formidable. So I'm concerned. As a husband, as a father, as an agent. But I also think we're a match for St. Juste." He splashed whisky into two glasses.

"I think so." Raoul accepted a glass from Malcolm. "I don't deny my own concern. But what I meant is that the past has a damnable way of intruding for you and Mélanie."

Half the time now Raoul referred to Suzanne as Mélanie. Malcolm wasn't sure he himself always even noticed the difference. "I don't see why everyone keeps expecting Julien St. Juste to bother me so much. It's not as though Mel was in love with the man."

"No. Far from it, I'd say. But it serves as a reminder—"

"That my wife deceived me?" Malcolm reached for his own glass. "My dear O'Roarke, I could scarcely draw breath and not remember that."

Raoul set his glass down on the library table. "A palpable hit. She's—"

"Her own person with her own loyalties. Which don't always align with mine. It's the height of arrogance to expect her to always think of herself as my wife before all else. I understand that. If I were the sort of enlightened husband that Juliette Dubretton and Mary Wollstonecraft talk about, that I prided myself I was, I'd have understood it rather sooner." He took a swallow of whisky, deeper than he intended. "But—"

O'Roarke said nothing but stayed still, watching him intently.

O'Roarke was the most laughable choice for a confidant. But whom else could he share the crazy farce of their situation with? "I know it's folly ever to claim one can really know another person. And Suzette and I are still coming to know each other in many ways. That was true before—before last December. But now—I'm more aware than ever of the parts of her life I don't know. That she felt she had to keep from me in the service of her masquerade. There are moments when I wonder if I really know her at all."

"And St. Juste reminds you of that?"

Suzanne's words, just now in their bedchamber, echoed in his head. Along with the images those words could not but stir. In many ways, they'd always been at their closest in bed, defenses stripped away in a way neither of them would permit in the light of day. But despite her words less than half an hour ago, he could not but wonder how far the pretense had extended to their most intimate moments. Even now. He remembered her pulling him down on their bed last night, remembered the brush of her fingers, the heat of her mouth, the way she had clung to him. Had she lost herself in him as much as he had in her? Or—

Of course he could say none of that to Raoul. And yet— "Perhaps. A bit."

Raoul's gaze told Malcolm he saw more than Malcolm might wish. "For what it's worth, I've never seen her so happy as she is with you." Raoul reached for his glass and took a sip. "However gifted one is at deception, that can't be counterfeit."

"She has a gift for finding happiness in the moment, whatever her circumstances."

"I wouldn't argue with that. It doesn't change the fact that I haven't seen her as happy as she is with you. Because of you."

Raoul's voice had that rare quality of stripped-to-the-bone honesty. Malcolm gave a quick, defensive smile. "She's rather stuck with me. However suited or not we may be."

Raoul put out a hand and let it fall to his side. "My dear Malcolm. You can't possibly think you aren't suited."

"Not most of the time." Malcolm took a drink of whisky. "Not until something makes me remember—"

"That she deceived you?"

Malcolm's fingers tightened on the glass. He stared at the Rannoch crest etched into the crystal. "The woman I know, the woman I live with, isn't the woman she was before she went on that mission to intercept me in the Cantabrian Mountains. It's someone she tailored to suit my needs." In any number of ways.

"You're an agent, Malcolm." Raoul's voice was crisp and neutral, but beneath Malcolm caught a trace of warmth that reminded him of childhood, like the whiff of apples or the scent of the sea. "You know no one can play a role that completely."

"Of course not. I'm just not sure where the role leaves off and the real Mélanie Suzanne begins. I don't think she's sure, herself."

Raoul met his gaze with the honesty of one agent facing another. "I won't argue with that."

Malcolm managed another smile, though his defenses felt distinctly the worse for wear. "I don't mean to wallow. In many ways I'm fortunate."

"My dear Malcolm. Only you could call your situation fortunate."

"If it wasn't for the mission, I wouldn't be married to Mel."

"That's—"

"Undeniable, given that she was an enemy agent. Not to mention a number of other things. I'm not quite sure where I'd be without her, but I'm quite sure I'd be alone."

"Malcolm—" Raoul stared into the whisky in his glass. The light from the brace of candles on the table caught the tangle of emotions in his eyes. "Mélanie may not know precisely where her role leaves off, but she's also not the woman she was before she met you."

"You're saying playing a role changes one?"

"It certainly can. You must have felt that yourself. So, I would imagine, can being married, though my own marriage didn't last long enough to put it to the test."

Malcolm had only seen O'Roarke's wife once or twice, as a young child. He had a vague memory of a slender woman with brown ringlets. Quite lacking his own mother's vibrancy, though at the time it wouldn't have occurred to him to compare them. He hadn't even had suspicions about his own relationship to Raoul O'Roarke at the time, though he'd been fond of him. Now it occurred to him to wonder what had driven Raoul to matrimony, and what had gone wrong.

Raoul met his gaze and gave a crooked smile. "Margaret was—is—a clever woman. Brilliant, even. I think she saw a certain romance in my revolutionary views. Until the reality made her fear for her father's estates." He took a drink of whisky, hesitated a moment, as though he meant to leave it at that, then said abruptly, "Things weren't over between your mother and me at the time as it turned out, but I thought they were. After Arabella—I think I was looking for a haven. I mistook conventionality for stability. No one conventional would have a prayer of putting up with me."

Malcolm's fingers tightened round his glass. It was one of the most revealing speeches Raoul had ever made to him. Had Raoul been trying to level the playing field after Malcolm's own admissions? "Do you ever see her?" he asked.

"Not in years. She manages her father's estate now. Her childhood sweetheart has the neighboring estate. She should have married him. Probably would have if I hadn't appeared while he was at university. They've been lovers for years. He has an invalid wife. Easier all round if I don't show my face."

"I'm sorry."

Raoul shrugged. "It hasn't troubled me in years. Better for me to have as few known connections as possible."

"Hostages to fortune?"

Raoul drew a breath, brittle as old paper. "No sense in belaboring it, but we should all be on our guard. Laura and Emily as well. Because they live with you and Suzanne."

"And because St. Juste could know of their connection to you."

"Possibly." Raoul twisted his glass in his hand. "Laura and I've done our best to be discreet, but with a man of St. Juste's abilities—He might know. If he noticed us in Berkeley Square, he'd have seen Mélanie and me with Laura and the children. When I caught sight of him, I had Emily on my lap." He cast a glance at Malcolm. "I don't know how you and Mélanie have managed all these years, facing danger with Colin and Jessica."

"It's the only reality we've known as parents. And for better or worse we both think the children are better off with us than away from us."

Raoul passed a hand over his hair. "I confess I'm not accustomed to feeling this sense of responsibility."

"It took a ridiculously long time after I married Mel. To remember there was someone to worry when I went on a mission. Even sometimes to remember there was someone to notice if I came home to dinner. I remember a guerrillero commander who wasn't best pleased with me threatening to do his worst by me and my family three months after our wedding. The sort of bluster I'd dismissed countless times in the past. But it hit me like a punch to the gut that I actually had a family who could be affected."

"I can well imagine. Though my situation is hardly the same as yours was."

"No, I'd say you're much further along on admitting what Laura means to you than I was on admitting what Suzette meant to me at the time."

Raoul opened his mouth as though to argue, then gave a reluctant smile and shook his head. "I've been meaning to tell you—I saw my man of business when I was in London in April and made some changes to my estate. Margaret is well provided for with her father's properties." He hesitated a moment, then added, "And you—"

"Fortune is one thing I've never lacked. Quite. And I can provide for Colin, so you needn't worry about him."

Raoul met his gaze, a flare of surprise in his own at the implied connection in the words.

Malcolm looked back steadily. "Though I have no doubt you'd do so, were it necessary. Just as I have no doubt you'd have provided for me."

Raoul held his gaze a moment longer, unspoken words thick in the air between them, but merely said, "James Trenchard has seen to it Laura and Emily are well provided for. I haven't mentioned it to Laura, because she probably won't need it, but I've put everything I have in trust for the two of them as well. I'd like you to have copies of the papers."

"Of course." The decision didn't surprise Malcolm, though something about the seriousness with which Raoul spoke shook him.

Raoul took a drink of whisky. "I'm not anticipating anything happening. But between St. Juste and what's happening in Spain—"

It was a moment before Malcolm saw in Raoul the same painstaking difficulty choosing words he often experienced himself. And caught the full subtext beneath the precise words. "I'd do anything I could for Laura in any case," he said. "But the fact that, to all intents and purposes, she's my stepmother only increases the tie."

Raoul released his breath and met Malcolm's gaze for a long moment. "Thank you. It's not—There's no need for Laura to know."

"That you've put money in trust for her? Not necessarily. That you feel this deep a bond to her and Emily—I rather think she has a right to know that."

Raoul stared at him for a moment longer then turned away. "Laura would probably be far better off if I ran a mile."

"You don't mean that."

"I don't intend to act on it, which is a rather different thing."

Malcolm continued to watch his father. "Sometimes, emotional commitment isn't a demand. It's a gift. It's taken me years to realize that."

Raoul looked back at him. "I'm inestimably glad that you have. But for some of us, it's a dangerous gift."

Malcolm held that gray gaze that was no longer so inscrutable as he had once found it. "The last time you were worried about the safety of the woman you loved and your child, you sent them both away. Selfishly, I'm inestimably glad that you did. I'd even venture that it hasn't turned out badly for Mélanie and Colin. But as you say, it's not wise to play a hand the same way twice. For God's sake, don't do so again."

35

Malcolm surveyed the white-and-gold expanse of the Apsley House drawing room. Wellington's brother Richard, Marquess Wellesley, had bought the Robert Adam house a decade ago and had engaged James Wyatt to improve it. Though the grateful nation had planned to build Wellington a London house after Waterloo, the previous year the duke had instead purchased Apsley House from his brother, who was in financial difficulties. The duke had engaged Wyatt's son, Benjamin Dean Wyatt, to make repairs to his new home and had told Malcolm he was planning further improvements of his own.

"It's amazing how many of the players are here," Suzanne murmured.

His wife was right, Malcolm realized. Carfax was not present, nor Oliver and Bel, as none of them had been directly involved with Waterloo, but Sylvie St. Ives sat on a striped satin sofa by Robert Adam's exquisite marble fireplace at the far end of the room, surrounded by a crowd of admirers. Her husband was standing in one of the niches to the side with a crowd of his fellow Life Guards veterans, including

Cordelia's brother-in-law, John Ashton. Fitzroy and his wife, Harriet, were on the other side of the room, talking with two other couples including John Ennis and a slender dark-haired woman in a lavender gown.

Cordy and Harry slipped through the crowd to join them. "I always have mixed feelings at these," Harry murmured. "It's good to see old friends. And it's damnable to remember."

"If it wasn't for Waterloo we wouldn't be here," Cordelia said in an unusually quiet voice.

Harry turned and lifted his wife's hand to his lips. "True enough."

Malcolm smiled at his friends and then caught sight of the man he had been searching for. William Cuthbertson stood with some fellow officers in the middle of the room. He turned and smiled at Laura. Laura lifted a hand in acknowledgment and then turned to speak with the others, as though to signal to Cuthbertson that she was presently engaged. Malcolm squeezed Suzanne's hand and moved across the room towards Cuthbertson, who had already disengaged himself from his friends and was moving towards Laura, regardless of her signal.

"A word, Cuthbertson." Malcolm contrived to block the other man's way in the crowd. "Then you can seek out Lady Tarrington."

Cuthbertson met his gaze for a moment, then gave a crisp nod and followed Malcolm into an anteroom without protest.

"I understand what you're doing, Rannoch," Cuthbertson said, as Malcolm closed the anteroom door behind them. "And I honor you for it."

"You understand?" Malcolm regarded the other man in genuine puzzlement.

"You naturally feel it is your duty to protect Jane—Lady Tarrington. I assure you, my intentions could not be more honorable."

Despite the events of the day, Malcolm choked back a laugh. "I'm very fond of Laura, but if I acted protective she would no doubt laugh, or tell me to mind my own business, or both. Her life is her own to decide about as she chooses."

Cuthbertson frowned, then gave a smile. "I've been wanting to thank you for everything you've done for her."

"We're very fond of her," Malcolm said. "She's come to be like one of the family."

Cuthbertson shook his head. "I still can't credit her as a governess. But I'm glad beyond measure she found friends. Davenport always said you were a good man, but I had no notion how very true it was."

"Most people would do a great deal for someone who loved their children so well."

"You know that's not true. Or governesses would be treated far better."

"A point. But Suzanne and I hardly did anything but act on the call of friendship."

"I can never forgive myself for being so far away when she needed help."

Cuthbertson's blue eyes darkened with a concern that seemed genuine. Even to Malcolm, braced to look for deception. "You could have had no notion she was in need of help. Or even alive."

"No." Cuthbertson shook his head. "Waterloo changed a lot." His gaze moved to the door to the room where his comrades were gathered. "And I don't just mean the end of the war. Suddenly a different sort of future seemed possible."

Malcolm nodded. "It wasn't long after that I started thinking about returning to Britain."

"I saw men doing it all round me," Cuthbertson said. "Selling out. Proposing to sweethearts. Settling in the country. But I had no desire to come back. In fact I wanted to stay as far away and as busy as possible."

"You don't have family here?"

"A brother, comfortably ensconced in the country raising children. He'd like to see me settled. But I had no desire to settle. Until—" Cuthbertson drew a breath. "As soon I heard Jane was alive, I got leave to come to England."

"To see Lady Tarrington."

"Of course."

"Not so you could attempt to bring Carfax down?"

Cuthbertson went still. Scarcely a muscle moved in his face, but Malcolm caught a trace of the hardened agent in the flicker of calculation in the other man's gaze. "Why—"

"Spare me the protestations, Cuthbertson. Oliver told me. Not willingly. He's not the sort to betray his friends—" Malcolm drew a breath, for that was just what Oliver had done to him and David and Simon. "I learned enough that he didn't have much choice but to tell me."

Cuthbertson's gaze stayed steady on Malcolm's face. "What precisely did Lydgate tell you?"

"You worked for Carfax. So did he. So did a number of others. Carfax had holds on all of you. One of you learned Craven had information that could be used to counter Carfax's power over you. You asked Fitzroy to find someone to recover it from Whateley & Company."

Cuthbertson folded his arms across his chest. "That's quite a story, Rannoch. Can you prove any of it?"

"I could bring Fitzroy in here. He's determined to do the honorable thing, but for that very reason I don't think he could lie to my face if I confronted him with the truth." Malcolm watched the other man for a moment. "I'm not without sympathy. I work for Carfax myself, and though I wouldn't precisely say he has a hold on me, I also know I'll never entirely break free. If I'd known you were trying to recover these papers, I don't know that I'd have tried to stop you. But now a man is dead."

Cuthbertson drew a sharp breath. "That wasn't—"

"Part of the plan? No, I know it wasn't. But it changes things. You're a man of honor, Cuthbertson." Even as he said it, Malcolm could imagine Suzanne shaking her head over his word choice. To her, honor was a smoke screen used to cover a multitude of sins. But the wording would resonate with Cuthbertson.

"Can you say so?" Cuthbertson asked. "Knowing what you know?"

"That you worked for Carfax? Whatever else he may be, Carfax does serve his country. And I worked for him myself. Though one could make a fair case it's difficult to maintain any sort of honor in the intelligence game."

Cuthbertson's mouth twisted. "It began as an adventure. God help me, I loved the challenge. Each step seemed justified. Until I looked back suddenly and saw the lines I'd crossed, the impossibility of ever going back."

"I know the feeling. But one can still hold on to something of oneself. I've seen enough of you to know that you've managed to do that. A man was killed on a mission for you. You're the sort who looks after your own. You have to want justice for him."

Cuthbertson's gaze went dark with torment. "I didn't even know his name. I didn't know Ennis's name until later. The less we all knew, the better, that was the plan. No way to trace the plot back to us if we couldn't connect the dots ourselves.

God, I hate this sort of plot. I'd much rather be running the risks myself than hiding behind others."

"If you had, Carfax would have followed the trail straight to you. This was a clever way of going about it."

Cuthbertson grimaced. "But it cost Coventry his life. It wasn't his fight." He stared at Malcolm for a moment, almost pleading. "Do you know? Who killed him?"

"Not yet. Is there any chance Carfax was on to you?"

"With Carfax, there's always a chance." Something leapt in Cuthbertson's eyes. "Is that it? Do you think Carfax was behind Coventry's death?"

"Someone else broke into the warehouse. If Carfax knew what you were doing, he'd have had a motive to send someone to intercept Coventry."

Cuthbertson nodded. "Which would mean Carfax knows about us."

"Not necessarily who is involved but the group in general." Malcolm studied Cuthbertson for a moment. That open, honest gaze was probably one of his best assets as an agent. "Who was the ringleader for your group?"

Cuthbertson scraped his hands over his face. "I don't know."

"That's what Oliver said."

"Do you believe us?"

"I'm not sure. But I could see the ringleader's logic in keeping his identity secret. Or hers."

Cuthbertson's eyes widened slightly at that last. Which probably meant he really didn't know the ringleader's identity.

"Who asked you to go to Fitzroy?" Malcolm asked.

Cuthbertson drew a breath. "I can't say."

"Can't or won't?"

"You said I was a man of honor, Rannoch. As one yourself, you must understand."

Which meant he wasn't going to get anywhere with a direct attack. "What do you know about Eustace Whateley?" Malcolm asked.

"Not a great deal."

"But you knew Carfax was using Whateley & Company for his own purposes?"

Cuthbertson gave a curt nod.

"Could Whateley have been one of his agents?"

"Good God."

"Is it so surprising? Craven was."

"Whateley wasn't, that I know of. Which doesn't prove a lot." Cuthbertson stared across the room. "I've lied about a lot. I've taken information from people who trusted me. I've used friends for cover." He took a turn about the room. "But you've got one thing the wrong way round, Rannoch. I wasn't using Jane as cover for coming back to England. I came back because I heard she was alive. I agreed to be part of bringing down Carfax because I learned she was alive. Because for the first time in years, I cared what happened to me. I wanted to be free. So I could have a future." He gave a rough laugh. "And now that's smashed to bits."

"Not necessarily," Malcolm said. "For one thing, we still don't know where the papers are."

Malcolm left the anteroom mulling over ways to get Sylvie to talk to him before the company moved into the dining room where they'd be trapped at the table for multiple courses and lengthy toasts. To his surprise, Sylvie met his gaze across the room and moved towards him. "Oliver warned me," she murmured, brushing past him in a stir of gold tulle and Parisian scent. "We'd better get this over with."

Back in the same antechamber, Sylvie regarded him with the bright gaze he remembered from the Carfax Court dinner table all those years ago. Harder now, more discontented, but fundamentally still the same girl. "I knew it. I knew as soon as you started poking into Whateley & Company. I told Oliver you were going to come too close to the truth."

"I'm sorry," Malcolm said.

"Sorry you figured it out?"

"Sorry you came under Carfax's influence. It's not easy, as I know to my own cost."

Sylvie spun away, gloved hands locked together. "I thought it was exciting at first, God help me. Coming to the notice of one of the most powerful men in Britain."

"It can't have been easy living as an émigrée."

"No." She shot a look at him. "Despite your wife being one, I don't think you can have any notion of how hard it really was. How could you, with your name and your fortune and your grandfather's title behind you? You went to Harrow and Oxford with half the powerful men of your generation. Your father went to school with their fathers. How many times I'd find myself lost at the dinner table in the midst of stories that went back to before anyone in my family set foot in Britain. And we were constantly scraping to keep up appearances. Once I worked for Carfax I had enough pin money to keep my wardrobe up to date." She flashed a half-defiant look at Malcolm.

"I know my wife enough to appreciate the importance."

Sylvie gave a dry smile. "Oliver understood. What it was to be an outsider. And what it was to be Carfax's." She tugged at her glove. The gold embroidery on it flashed in the candle-light. "I don't know that Oliver and I could have made things work. I suspect I wouldn't have done well in lodgings, eating mutton five nights a week. But I wish we'd had the chance to try. We *should* have had the chance to try."

"Oliver said Carfax insisted you marry St. Ives."

"If I'd married Oliver, I'd have been a lawyer's wife scarcely even on the fringe of society. He wanted me well positioned to gather information among the beau monde." She tugged at her second glove. "He also dictated the men I dallied with after my marriage." She looked up to meet Malcolm's gaze, her own hard. "Shocked, Malcolm? It's one of the most effective ways for spies to gather information, after all."

Malcolm knew that. He certainly wouldn't have thought Carfax would cavil at seduction as a tool of information gathering. Was he surprised because he had known Sylvie since she was a girl? Because Carfax had?

Sylvie smoothed the fingers of her glove. "I don't know that my marriage to St. Ives would have stood much of a chance in any case. I'm the sort who grows restless, and St. Ives bored me from the first. But Carfax as good as ensured we didn't have a prayer. Not out of malice. I don't think he thinks of me enough for that. We were collateral damage."

And Carfax had always been ruthless about accepting collateral damage.

"Rather different from what he asked you to do, I suspect," Sylvie said. "His official agents like you and Tommy Belmont are the prized racehorses in his stable. And yet we both know what it is to do his bidding." She looked down at her fingers. "I don't know that you'll believe this, but while I may not be a faithful wife, I've never numbered Oliver among my lovers. Not out of any conviction on my side. God knows, not out of lack of caring. Some things haven't changed. But Oliver takes his marriage more seriously than I take mine." She regarded Malcolm for a moment. "I know or can guess how angry you must be at Oliver."

"Can you?"

"I know betrayal. Knowing what you and David and Simon mean to Oliver, I can guess what he means to you."

Malcolm gave a short laugh. "We obviously mean less to Oliver than I assumed."

Sylvie shook her head. "You would see it that way. But if you'd seen the way it's eaten at him all these years—"

"Not enough to stop."

"Oh, but he did. As much as one can ever stop working for Carfax. In some ways I think your friendship mattered to him more than anything. In fact—"

"What?"

"I think that was part of what drove him to work for Carfax. That he wanted to be part of your world."

Malcolm gave a harsh laugh.

"Not just the fine houses and horses and being able to hunt and belonging to the right clubs and the rest of it. That sort of thing has always mattered more to me than to Oliver. It was what the four of you shared."

Malcolm's mind shot back to an Oxford tavern. "Oliver didn't need a fortune to share it." His voice came out lower and rougher than he intended.

"Didn't he? What would have happened if he'd come down from Oxford and set up as a solicitor, while David went into Parliament and Simon wrote plays and you joined the diplomatic service? You wouldn't have consciously intended to drop him, but he'd have played on a different stage."

Scenes from the past hovered on the edges of his memory, but he wasn't ready to explore his feelings with Sylvie. "How much did you know about the Whateley & Company break-in?"

"As little as possible. Much safer that way. I didn't even know where we were looking for these papers of Carfax's. I didn't know the man killed at Whateley & Company had been working for us until Maria told me. I've made a lot of mistakes, Malcolm, but I'm good at self-preservation."

"You must be worried."

"That Carfax is on to us? How could I not be?"

Malcolm watched her for a moment, seeing the girl with blonde ringlets in a flounced white dress. Seeing her staring at Oliver across the dinner table. According to Oliver, she'd been Carfax's creature even then. "I know how hard it is to break away from Carfax, but I'm not his creature in everything. What does Carfax have on you, Sylvie?"

"My dear Malcolm. You can hardly expect me to answer that."

"I might be able to help you."

Sylvie shook her head. "Oh, Malcolm. I was far beyond help while you were still a starry-eyed undergraduate who had no notion of the word 'spy.'"

36

Lisette Varon stared up at the Rannochs' Berkeley Square House. The iron spikes of the area railings. The hard glass of the windows, which told of no fear of the window tax she had learned of since her arrival in Britain. Or the candle tax, judging by the amount of light glowing behind the drawn curtains. The bright, clean light of wax tapers. It had been one thing to climb through a window six weeks ago, in the company of comrades who called the Rannochs friends, driven by the needs of the moment. It was quite another to walk up to the front door. She had felt a jolt of trepidation the three times she had been to the house since her arrival in London. And those times, she had been invited. Now she was arriving unbidden, long past the hour for calling.

She drew a breath, climbed the steps, and rang the bell.

Valentin, the footman she remembered from her other visits, who spoke English with a Belgian-French accent, opened the door. "Mademoiselle Varon." He stepped aside to admit her to the house without question.

Lisette stepped into the entrance hall and stopped short at the sight of a tall man with disordered brown hair who stood by the console table, scribbling on a piece of paper. It was Jeremy Roth of Bow Street, she realized. She'd met him at a dinner the Rannochs had given not long after her arrival in Britain.

"Mr. Roth."

"Mademoiselle Varon." He inclined his head.

"I was looking for Mr. or Mrs. Rannoch."

"So was I. They're out. Wellington's Waterloo banquet."

Of course. How could she have forgot the anniversary of the day that had changed so much for so many of them? "Do you know if Mr. O'Roarke went with them?"

"Apparently. Lady Tarrington as well. I was just leaving them a note."

Odd to think of Raoul at a banquet to celebrate the British victory. Surely it would test even his skills at dissembling.

Lisette surveyed the man before her. She knew he'd come to the Berkeley Square house with a man from the Preventive Waterguard the night she and Raoul and Bertrand had sought refuge there. But she also remembered Malcolm Rannoch saying Jeremy Roth was a friend and a man he trusted. "The Rannochs undertake investigations with you."

He smiled. "It might be more accurate, at times, to say I undertake investigations with them, but yes, we've worked together on more than one occasion."

"And you're working together now. The murdered man at the warehouse by the docks."

"Not many have heard of him. Or are paying attention."

"Partly why it drew my notice." Lisette fingered a fold of her muslin skirt. A British officer of the law was her natural enemy, in many ways. But he was the friend of her friends. His gaze was shrewd and direct, and his smile showed welcome humor. Sometimes, Raoul had told her, one has to trust one's instincts. "I have a message I need to get to them. Time is of the essence."

Roth gave a quick nod. "I can escort you to Apsley House. I'm sure we can get someone to take a message in to them."

"You're very kind."

He gave a quick smile and held out his arm. "I'm well enough acquainted with the Rannochs to know that if a friend of theirs says time is of the essence, the situation is probably urgent indeed."

Reliving Waterloo would never be the same, Malcolm realized, before the first covers had been removed, the first speech started, the first glass of claret lifted. His memories of Waterloo were now bound up with the knowledge that his wife had been working for the opposite side. That his father had fought on the opposite side and had killed one of his own allies to save Malcolm's and Harry's lives.

Suzanne was seated across the table next to Fitzroy. A favored spot. Wellington had always been fond of her. Her smile was serene, the smile of a wife pleased at the victory but aware of what it had cost. Even now he knew the truth, it was almost impossible to find cracks in the veneer of her performance.

O'Roarke was further down the table, sitting back a little, as appropriate for one who had supposedly not fought at Waterloo. Harry's fingers were curled round the stem of his wine glass. Malcolm met his gaze for a moment. He knew his friend hated anything that verged on sentimentality. Cordelia was looking at Suzanne, as though sharing their memories nursing the wounded. Laura sat quietly. Cuthbertson's gaze was trained on her.

A footman slipped up behind Malcolm but not, as Malcolm thought, to refill his glass. "Forgive me, Mr. Rannoch, but there's an Inspector Roth of Bow Street below with a lady. He says he has an urgent message for you."

Malcolm met Suzanne's and O'Roarke's gazes. Of one accord, the three of them slipped from their seats. The commotion of the course being removed helped cover their departure. They met in the passage outside and went down to the ground floor sitting room where the footman had shown Jeremy Roth and the lady with him. Lisette Varon.

"I'm sorry for the interruption," Roth said. "I had called in Berkeley Square. To tell you that I've been ordered to stop the investigation into the break-ins at Whateley & Company and Brook Street."

"Damnable," Malcolm said, "but not entirely surprising. The wonder is Carfax let the investigation go on as long as he did."

Roth nodded. "I was leaving you a note when Mademoiselle Varon arrived. She has news that's more urgent."

"One of the coffeehouse waiters is a friend," Lisette said. "I had him watching for Germont and his friend to come back into the tavern. And listening." Lisette's gaze flickered from Malcolm to Suzanne to Raoul. "They were discussing some sort of meeting. Tonight at ten-thirty. By the stand of oak off Hyde Park Corner."

Malcolm exchanged looks with his wife and Raoul, then glanced at the clock. It was five minutes to ten.

"I don't have the least idea what this is about," Roth said. "But tell me what I can do to help."

"You're the best of friends, Jeremy," Malcolm said. "Can you see Lisette safely home?"

Lisette opened her mouth as though to protest, then slowly nodded. "I suppose I'd only be in the way. You'll tell me—"

"Everything we can," Raoul said.

"Which could be precisely nothing. But I appreciate the thought."

Apsley House stood at Hyde Park Corner. Suzanne could see the stand of oak as she and her husband and Raoul slipped from the house. "Almost as though they planned this with us in mind," Malcolm muttered.

Raoul cast a sideways glance at him, but didn't say anything.

Not knowing what the evening would hold, they of course hadn't dressed for blending into the shadows. Malcolm's and Raoul's dark coats did well enough, and fortunately her gown was black net over champagne sarcenet, not as well suited as a plain black silk but far better than coral lace or silver gauze.

The park was dark and mostly still at this hour, though the wind stirred the trees, the occasional owl called, and small animals rustled through the grass. Dark shapes beneath the trees also occasionally stirred. Hyde Park was a refuge for those with nowhere else to sleep. Many of whom, Suzanne knew, had returned home less than whole from the battle they had been celebrating in the candlelit house across the street.

Without the need for speech, they took up positions in the shadows on the edge of the stand of oak. They could adjust later as needed, depending on where Germont and his friend and whomever they were meeting positioned themselves.

Another owl hooted. A real one, she thought, though her senses were keyed for a call between agents. The wind whipped a branch against her cheek. And then the wind brought something else. The sound of soft footfalls on the grass. Somehow there was something familiar about that gait. But it was only when he stepped into the stand of trees and a shaft of moonlight fell across his profile and bounced off his spectacle lenses that she realized what.

Apparently, Germont and his confederate were meeting with Lord Carfax.

Beside her, Malcolm had gone absolutely still. She wanted to reach for him, but was afraid to do anything that might disrupt his concentration.

Carfax paced the clearing, then turned abruptly as another man stepped between the trees. His features were in shadow, but the moonlight caught his pale hair. And she'd know that posture anywhere.

The man Carfax was meeting wasn't Louis Germont. It was Julien St. Juste.

"Isn't this a bit overdramatic?" Carfax spoke in his familiar, incisive tones, but she caught the tension beneath.

"Neutral ground." Julien leaned against a tree across the clearing from where Suzanne, Malcolm, and Raoul were positioned behind the trees.

"We haven't needed neutral ground before."

"We haven't done this sort of exchange before." Julien folded his arms across his chest. The posture was casual, but Suzanne could read tension in the lines of his body as well. "Did you bring it?"

Without speech, Carfax reached inside his coat and drew out a sheaf of papers.

"I'll need to verify them," Julien said.

"Do you think I'd be fool enough to give this to you without seeing what you brought me? You're quite capable of sticking a knife through me."

"My dear Carfax. Tempting as that might be, I'm quite sure you've arranged for things to be exceedingly difficult for me should you meet with any sort of accident." Julien reached into his own coat (beautifully cut, as always) and drew out a slimmer sheaf of papers. From his other pocket he drew out a candle and a flint. "We both verify at the same time."

The two men approached each other with the measured caution of duelists. By the light of the candle Julien held, they each studied the papers the other held. Apparently—remarkably given the two men involved—what they saw pleased them, for after a minute or so, Carfax gave a crisp nod.

Julien's smile gleamed in the candlelight. "That wasn't so hard, was it?"

Carfax snorted.

Julien tucked the papers Carfax had given him into his coat. "Needless to say, that other business stops now."

Tension shot through Carfax's shoulders. "There's no need—"

"You can't possibly believe I'd assist your ridiculous plan now." Julien blew out the candle. "You should thank me, Carfax. You're too sensible a man to waste your energies in some ridiculous quest to ferret out Bonapartists. We're done."

Carfax held Julien with his gaze. "We're never going to be done, Julien. You must know that. But I agree we're done for the present."

Oddly, tension shot through Julien. Suzanne could almost feel the power shift in the scene before her, like the ground tilting beneath her feet. "For the present, then." Julien's voice was that of a man who won't cede ground but knows he is in check.

Carfax turned on his heel and strode back towards Park Lane. Julien looked after him but made no move to leave the park. At last, as Carfax's footsteps faded into the distance, Julien settled his shoulders against a tree trunk and cast a glance round the clearing. "You can come out now, Suzanne. And whomever you've brought with you."

37

For a moment, Suzanne stood rooted to the ground. Julien could have that effect on one. At the same time, a voice in her head screamed. *Of course.* It had been far too easy.

She felt the tension that ran through Malcolm. She squeezed his hand, willing him to understand, and stepped from the shadows.

"Good evening, Julien."

He turned his head. His gaze cut through the shadows. "Suzanne. You are still calling yourself Suzanne, aren't you?"

Suzanne was the name she'd used on their journey with Hortense. For long enough she'd grown quite accustomed to it, long before she became Malcolm's wife. "Don't tell me you don't know."

"I heard rumors. To own the truth, I wasn't sure until I saw you at the Duchess of Richmond's ball. I have to say, I'm impressed. I've never kept a mission going for so long."

"It's not a mission any more."

"You're an agent, Mélanie Suzanne. You'll always be on a mission."

"These days I work with my husband, rather than against him."

Julien raised a brow.

"Most of the time."

"Can't be easy. I hear he's quite formidable in his own right, though I can't imagine he's any match for you."

"Don't be so sure."

He gave a soft laugh that echoed off the stone. "You used to be made of harder stuff."

"Being married has changed me."

He shook his head. "How are the mighty fallen. I remember you swearing you'd never marry."

"We hardly had a happy example in front of us in Hortense, at the time. I also said I doubted I'd ever have children."

"And having children has changed you?" He sounded genuinely curious.

"Thankfully." She paused a moment. "I have a whole new understanding of how strong Hortense is."

For a moment, Julien's gaze went serious in a way it seldom was. "Even I have a glimmering of that. The more so since Waterloo. The perils of letting one's happiness depend so much on another person."

A gust of wind cut through the trees. She drew her shawl about her. "The alternative being to be alone."

"I see nothing wrong with my own company." Julien ran his keen gaze over her. "At least you haven't done badly for yourself after Waterloo."

"Nor have you, by the looks of it."

His grin gleamed in the shadows. "If that's an attempt at gathering information, you used to be subtler."

"You were working for Carfax." She could still scarcely credit it.

Julien cast a glance round the clearing. "I think we should all be present for this. I made sure you brought O'Roarke with you. I rather hope you brought your husband as well."

A few moments of silence followed. Just long enough for seasoned agents to make quick calculations. Then Malcolm and Raoul emerged from the trees.

Julien's gaze shot between them. "O'Roarke. It's been a long time. And you must be Rannoch."

Suzanne moved to Malcolm's side—half protection, half warning. "My husband, Malcolm Rannoch. Julien St. Juste. At least, that's what he calls himself most often."

Julien's gaze moved over Malcolm. "Since you're here, I assume you know the truth about your wife. I have to say, I'm impressed. You're a wise man to recognize that she's worth holding on to."

"Shut up, Julien," Suzanne said.

Julien continued to regard Malcolm. "And no, Carfax doesn't know about her. At least, not from me."

"But you were working for him." Malcolm's gaze was trained on Julien, though he dropped his arm round Suzanne.

"Not exclusively. As with most of my relationships, professional and otherwise. Carfax came to my assistance early on in my career. I won't go into the details, but suffice it to say I owed him. I've gone my own way since. But I've never quite stopped owing him. Not enough to break away completely."

"So you decided to take matters into your own hands," Raoul said.

"I encountered Craven on a mission last year. Not one of Carfax's abler agents, but one night over a bottle of brandy he confided in me about the papers that could be damaging to Carfax." Julien cast a glance round the company. "In the autumn of 1810, Carfax traded information about British plans with Fouché in exchange for information he thought would lead him to the Elsinore League."

Malcolm drew a harsh breath. "Until this investigation, I didn't realize how obsessed Carfax was with the League."

"Quite," Julien said. "For all his faults, he's usually rational. This verges on obsession. Fouché had been dismissed from the ministry of police at the time. Perhaps that made it seem less of a betrayal to Carfax. Still—" He turned his gaze to O'Roarke. "Did you know about it?"

"My God, no."

"But then, Fouché was almost as much your enemy as Carfax, wasn't he? I knew. My—a friend was the one who actually made the exchange, in Lisbon. But I didn't have any proof. Craven had got his hands on a letter of Carfax's that was quite damning. I don't think he quite knew what he had. I was the one who saw what use it could be put to. There were other papers Carfax had that Craven was worried about. That made him hesitate to do anything against Carfax. He was hoping to retrieve them."

"Yes," Suzanne said. "Craven asked me to steal those."

Julien whistled. "Did you?"

"What do you think?"

"Depends on what Craven had on you."

"You don't have enough faith in me."

"I have faith in your sense of self-preservation. If he threatened your life here—Oh, all right. You're such a good agent I forget about your tiresome ideals. In any case, the next I heard Craven had been killed. I more than half thought Carfax was behind it." He looked from Suzanne to Malcolm to Raoul.

"So did we," Suzanne said. "But he wasn't, as it happens."

"Interesting." Julien regarded her for a long moment, then turned his gaze to Raoul.

"No," Raoul said. "Though I can see why you'd think it."

"You and your tedious scruples."

"My dear St. Juste," Raoul said. "You wouldn't recognize a scruple if it bit you."

"But I can see them in others."

Suzanne bit back further speech. Louisa Craven's secrets were not to be shared, for the sake of any number of people, most especially her children.

Julien looked from Raoul to her to Malcolm. "So you know. And you aren't going to tell me. I can't say I blame you. In any case, with Craven gone, I began to wonder about recovering the information and putting it to use."

"But you wanted your hands clean," Suzanne said.

"I have a healthy respect for Carfax. Besides if one of us tried to break away, even I, he could come after that person and make an example of them. If we did it as a group—"

"The power of collective action," Suzanne murmured. "You've finally turned into a revolutionary."

"Whatever tactics work." Julien gave a faint smile. "So, I contacted another of Carfax's agents I know. No one knew the names of everyone involved. Not even I. I didn't even know who had been hired to actually break into Whateley & Company."

"What happened?" Malcolm asked. "How did Coventry die?"

"I don't know. Isn't that what you've been investigating?"

"We thought most likely an agent of Carfax's had intercepted Coventry." Malcolm watched Julien a moment. "You weren't there yourself?"

"Do you really imagine I'd go anywhere near a job like that?"

"You had the papers," Suzanne said. "Did Maria Monreal find them in Brook Street?"

"Obviously," Julien said.

"That's not what Oliver says," Malcolm said.

"Lydgate may be lying. Or Maria may not have told him."

"You wanted us here tonight," Suzanne said. "You deliberately let the waiter overhear you and Germont talking about the meeting."

"Oh, yes. And I let you see me at Gunter's, despite the fact that I've been running about London in disguise for weeks."

"Why?"

"Because of the reason Carfax summoned me to London. His pet project that gave me cover for the other project."

"The Phoenix plot," Suzanne said. "So called."

Julien's mouth curled. "I don't deny Carfax's abilities, but he's inclined to overestimate the reach of Bonapartists." His gaze moved from her to Raoul. "No offense to present company."

"He wanted to lure them out of the shadows," Raoul said. "See who still posed a danger. Get evidence to have them arrested or send them back to France to face the Bourbons."

"Worked that out, did you?"

"Yes, but I thought Fouché was behind it, not Carfax," Raoul said.

Julien laughed. "It's the sort of thing Fouché might think of."

"And Louis Germont?" Suzanne asked.

"I brought him in to work with me. He's the cousin of an old friend, and he wanted out of France in any case. Disguise is effective, but some of the people I needed to approach knew me too well."

"Did you mean me to meet him?"

"He was supposed to fake his injuries rather than really be wounded, but, yes. I didn't think you'd really fall for it. But I wanted you to know about the Phoenix plot."

"Why, in God's name?"

"So you'd know what Carfax was up to."

Malcolm drew a harsh breath.

Julien cast a glance at him. "Still had illusions about your spymaster, did you? That's why I wanted you here tonight."

"You wanted *me* here?" Malcolm demanded.

"I don't deny it's pleasant to see Suzanne, and I can put up with O'Roarke. But you're the one I wanted to learn the truth about Carfax. Because from what I know of you, you're the only one with a prayer of keeping him in check. Which is no more than he deserves, and may keep him out of my hair for a time."

Malcolm stared at him.

"To own the truth, I'm surprised you haven't left to confront him yet."

"Go." Suzanne gripped her husband's arm. "Raoul and I can handle Julien."

Malcolm's gaze swung to her.

"Julien's annoying," Suzanne said. "But he's not the one who needs dealing with now."

Three months ago, Malcolm had called at Carfax House late at night. That night had ended with Louisa Craven dead by her own hand. The memory of Carfax staring down at his dead daughter was still imprinted on Malcolm's brain. But it was not compassion that filled him now.

The Carfax House footmen were used to seeing him at odd hours, but John, who was on duty, hesitated when he opened the door. "Mr. Rannoch—"

"I don't care whether he says he's at home or not." Malcolm pushed past John and strode to the door to Carfax's study.

Carfax, of course, might not have gone straight home, but Malcolm suspected the earl would have wanted to stow away or destroy the papers St. Juste had given him, as quickly as possible.

He pushed open the study door to find Carfax at his desk, bent over a stack of paper, as he had found him on countless occasions.

"Malcolm." Carfax looked up with raised brows. "It's a bit late. And I thought you were at Wellington's dinner. News about the investigation?"

"You could say that." Malcolm pushed the door to. "I just overheard you negotiating with the man behind the Whateley & Company break-in."

Carfax's gaze settled on Malcolm's face. He knew Malcolm too well to deny it. "My compliments."

Malcolm stared at his spymaster. "You must have known what the thieves were after. Why in God's name did you have me investigating?"

"You were going to investigate in any case. And I wanted the thieves apprehended. Though as it happens, I've been able to come to an accommodation, as you apparently overheard. You can consider the matter closed."

"It's nothing of the sort. Leaving aside the fact that you were engaged in a plot to ferret out Bonapartists in London."

"My dear Malcolm. Even you can scarcely quarrel with getting rid of those actually plotting to restore Bonaparte."

"There are so many suppositions in that statement I scarcely know where to start. Beginning with the fact that anyone who fell for the ploy would only have been plotting because of you."

"But if they were even susceptible to the influence—"

"That's entrapment."

"Call it what you will, Malcolm, if it gets rid of a menace it's a worthwhile tactic."

"It's a bloody waste of time, sir. It's distracting you—and valuable resources—when we have people starving at home."

"People who might join with the Bonapartists if they aren't controlled."

Malcolm folded his arms across his chest. "And yet you sold information to Fouché."

Carfax's hands tightened. "I don't sell information."

"You traded it."

"I don't believe you have proof of anything, Malcolm. But I shouldn't have to remind you how dangerous the Elsinore League are."

"And that justifies—"

"They could do incalculable damage if they aren't controlled."

"That's your solution to everything, isn't it? Control. Just as you used Oliver to try to control David and Simon and me."

Carfax leaned back in his chair. "I had no illusions I could control any of you. I wanted to know what you were up to."

"You were spying on us."

"I was protecting my son—and you too—from what you might get involved in."

"Who the hell is Julien St. Juste?" Malcolm demanded.

"If you overheard even part of our discussion, you can hardly expect me to answer that." Carfax pushed papers together on his desk. "Let it go, Malcolm. It's what I'm endeavoring to do myself. You've done what you can."

"I still don't know who killed Ben Coventry."

"Who?"

"The man your agents hired to break into Whateley & Company."

"Oh, yes. You would care about that."

Malcolm regarded Carfax. "Someone else was in What-eley & Company that night and killed him. And unless we're dealing with wild coincidence, I think that person was hired by you."

Carfax adjusted his spectacles. "My dear Malcolm. You are quite at liberty to think whatever you wish."

38

To all intents and purposes, their interview with Julien should be over. They had learned what of substance they were going to get from him, and to linger merely risked discovery. And yet—

Suzanne hesitated. Raoul had moved closer to her when Malcolm left, but he hung back, leaving it to her to decide when to go.

"You involved Flahaut," she said to Julien without consciously deciding to speak.

"Carfax insisted. I think he suspects Flahaut's settling in Britain and marrying the lovely Miss Mercer is an elaborate charade."

"Carfax thinks Flahaut is working for Bonapartists?"

"Or Talleyrand. Or both. It can't surprise you that Carfax doesn't trust Talleyrand."

"Did you send Germont to him?" Flahaut's description had sounded more like Julien in disguise.

"No. That was one visit I didn't want to entrust to someone else. I flatter myself he didn't see through my disguise. But then you spent more time with him in Switzerland than I did."

Suzanne saw Flahaut sitting beside Hortense's child-bed, then remembered Julien, suspiciously white-knuckled, when she'd gone downstairs to tell him Hortense was safely delivered of a son. "I'd have thought Flahaut was off-limits."

Julien's mouth hardened into a thin line. "Hortense is off-limits. Flahaut rather took himself off the list by abandoning her."

"I think it was a mutual choice," Raoul murmured.

"You can't seriously believe Hortense is happy to have let him go."

Suzanne saw Hortense's drawn face when she'd managed to take Colin to see her in d'Arenberg, after Waterloo. "I think Hortense wants him to be happy. And safe." Oddly, for a moment she saw Raoul watching Laura dance with William Cuthbertson. She didn't let herself look at Raoul, but an unexpected chill went through her.

"Flahaut could have fought for her."

"Are you saying that's what you'd do?" Suzanne asked.

"In the right circumstances. With the right woman. You could come close."

"My dear Julien." Suzanne kept her voice level, though it took more of an effort than she would have liked. "I'm flattered. Though I don't believe it for a second."

He watched her for a long moment. His gaze was at once appraising and what, in another person, might be called concerned. "I don't understand this life you've built for yourself. I don't understand your being happy in it. But I haven't come to disrupt it. If you want to dull your talents playing society hostess, that's quite your own affair."

"Thank you." The words came out more honest than she intended.

Julien continued to watch her. "But I presume I need hardly remind you that you're living on a knife's edge. To own the truth, I'm amazed you've managed as long as you have."

"Is that your idea of a compliment?" She kept her voice level.

He reached out and touched his fingers to her cheek. "I trust you have an escape plan, *ma belle*."

She shivered, though she knew the words were meant as advice, not threat. Raoul hadn't moved a muscle, but she could feel him poised to intervene. "You can hardly expect me to confide it in you."

"I'm not asking you to confide it. Merely recommending that you have one in place."

Laura was keenly aware of the moment Raoul, Suzanne, and Malcolm had slipped from the dining room. And yet, she knew the most helpful thing she could do was pretend that nothing had happened. She went on conversing with the former major and colonel seated on either side of her, and gave the best impression she could of having her attention focused on an occasion at once joyous and solemn. She was, after all, a military widow, even if her husband had died before Waterloo.

When the company at last rose from the table, Harry moved to her side. "Malcolm sent me a note," he murmured, under cover of giving her his arm. "He said they were obliged to leave, and if they weren't back before the party breaks up, could we see you back to Berkeley Square and wait there until they return." He gave her a quick smile. "Damnable not to be in on it, but I wouldn't worry. They're all well able to take care of themselves."

The company moved back upstairs. As they stepped into the drawing room, Laura saw William Cuthbertson making straight for her. There was nothing for it. She owed it to him to listen. And she might be able to learn something. She smiled at Harry, released his arm, and went to meet Will.

"I must speak with you," he murmured.

"Of course," Laura said. "There's an anteroom through that door."

The moment he had closed the anteroom door, Will seized Laura's hands. "I wanted you to hear the truth from me, Jane. I'll understand if you can't forgive me. But I wanted you to know the truth. I was working for Carfax in India, but that had nothing to do with what was between us. And I'd never have let him know of it."

"I daresay Carfax could have known of it, if he wanted. There was certainly gossip. And I wouldn't blame you for seeking information. I hope I have enough understanding to know that can coexist with genuine feeling. And enough to know that at least some of what was between us was genuine."

"*Some*—"

"I was hardly free of encumbrances myself."

"I've lied. I've done things that are dishonorable by any compass. I can understand if you wouldn't want me to be part of your life. Wouldn't trust me to be a father to your daughter."

Laura bit back a rough laugh. Dear, sweet Will. Even with these new revelations, she very much doubted he'd done anything as morally compromised as her own actions. "I did my own share of lying." After all, he knew she'd betrayed her marriage vows.

"That can't compare with what I've done. But I swear to you, I came back to London because I heard you were alive.

I agreed to be part of this crazy plot because I heard you were alive. Because I wanted to be free."

"Will—" She pulled one of her hands free of his grip and put it up to touch his face. "I'm not the woman I was. And I'm not free." She drew a breath, because it seemed odd to verbalize it. And yet it lifted a weight from her shoulders.

Confusion filled his gaze. "I didn't think—And I hadn't heard—"

"No. I don't believe it's generally known."

"But you're betrothed? In secret?"

"No. And I doubt we ever will be."

"By God, he's not worthy—"

"You're a good man, Will. And so is he."

His gaze skimmed over her face. "You're happy."

Despite everything, she found herself smiling. "Yes. My life is complicated, but I am. For the first time in a long time."

Will gave a smile that was rough and bittersweet. "How can I argue with that?"

"Whatever you're involved in, Will, I hope it frees you to find happiness yourself."

"I thought—but that's no matter. We must pursue it to the end. But if I'd known when she first asked me—"

"She?" Laura took an involuntary step forwards. "Will, who was it who asked you to go to Fitzroy? Was it Maria Monreal?"

"Maria who?" Will shook his head. "No it, was Syl—" He bit the name back, but not soon enough.

"Sylvie St. Ives," Laura said.

Laura rushed towards Suzanne and Raoul as they came back into the crowded Apsley House drawing room. "Thank God you're back."

Raoul caught her by the shoulders. "What? What is it, sweetheart?"

"Will told me. Who embroiled him in the plot to find the papers. It was Lady St. Ives."

Suzanne went still, the pieces shifting in her head. She cast a glance round the room and saw Harry and Cordelia moving towards them. Excellent timing. "Harry," Suzanne said, before either of the Davenports could ask questions, "can you introduce me to John Ennis? Cordy, Raoul can tell you what's happened."

Neither of the Davenports blinked or asked questions. Harry gave Suzanne his arm and took her across the room to an auburn-haired man with side whiskers. John Ennis tensed visibly at the sight of Harry but didn't attempt to evade talking to him and accepted the introduction to Suzanne with a smile that was charming, if a bit strained.

"Captain Ennis," Suzanne said. "Did Ben Coventry ever mention a beautiful women he'd known in the Peninsula who had committed a great act of betrayal?"

Ennis stared at her. "Good God. What does that have to do with—"

"He told Sue Kettering he saw this same woman in London a fortnight ago," Suzanne said.

Ennis drew a sharp breath. "It was early in the war. The autumn of 1810. Ben and I were both in Lisbon. Ben came looking for me. Tracked me down all over the city." Ennis didn't say so, but from the somewhat abashed breath he drew, Suzanne suspected Coventry had found him in a brothel. "Ben had been in a tavern. The sort of dark, out of the way place we used to pass messages. He said he'd overheard a woman passing information to a man. They hadn't said much, but he'd heard enough he'd swear it was about British troop movements."

"Good God," Harry murmured. "That was before I got to the Peninsula, but I don't remember ever hearing anything about it."

"That's because there wasn't much to report," Ennis said. "I went to the tavern with Ben. Made some inquiries. But we couldn't trace the woman, and Ben didn't know her name. He'd moved closer to the couple to try to hear more, and he said as she was getting up from the table, she'd looked up and seen him and gone still. But he didn't recognize her, and she didn't recognize him. I passed the information on to Grant, but without identifying her or knowing more about the intelligence she'd passed along, there wasn't much we could do."

"Did Coventry describe her?" Suzanne asked. "Besides saying she was beautiful?"

Ennis frowned, as though in an effort of memory. "He said she was wearing a mantilla, but he could tell her hair was fair. In fact, he said she and the man she was meeting looked enough alike to be brother and sister."

Suzanne squeezed his hand. "Thank you, Captain Ennis. You've been very helpful. Harry can explain more." Which wasn't entirely fair to Harry, but he would manage. "There's someone I need to see."

She glanced round the room again. Bertrand wasn't present. But Rupert, a Waterloo veteran, was. Along with his wife, Gabrielle, Bertrand's cousin. Suzanne excused herself to Harry and Ennis and went across the room to Gabrielle.

Gaby turned from the two officers' wives she was conversing with to greet Suzanne. "Exciting to remember, isn't it?" she said. "And sad." She cast a glance about and lowered her voice. "Rupert and I may not have the marriage you and Malcolm do, but I don't think I've ever been more terrified than I was those days in Brussels."

"Of course." Suzanne put her hand on Gabrielle's arm. "No one seeing you and Rupert together could doubt that you care for each other."

"Life's odd, isn't it?" Gabrielle said. "I don't think on that day three years ago it ever occurred to me I could be as happy as I am today. Or that Rupert could be."

Suzanne realized she could say the same. So much had gone wrong for her and Malcolm in the past three years and yet so much was better than she ever could have imagined. "Gaby," she said. "The Brillac family. Do you know if they could be connected to Sylvie St. Ives?"

Gabrielle's eyes widened. "How odd," she said. "Bertrand was asking me about the Brillacs yesterday, and I couldn't remember where I'd heard the name. But then tonight I saw Sylvie St. Ives, and I remembered hearing her mother and Tante Amélie talking. Sylvie's mother was a Brillac." Her gaze skimmed over Suzanne's face. "Is it part of your investigation?"

"I think it's the puzzle piece we've been missing."

Sylvie St. Ives was surrounded by four of her husband's fellow Life Guardsmen. But Suzanne had long since mastered the art of slipping into a crowd of gentlemen and breaking up the conversation. Two minutes and she had them laughing at a reminiscence of a moonlight picnic in Brussels in the weeks before the battle. Five minutes and she had extracted Sylvie and was moving towards the anteroom with her arm in arm. "I know my husband spoke with you earlier this evening, Lady St. Ives," Suzanne murmured. "So I'm sure you'll appreciate why it's imperative that I speak with you now."

Sylvie's mouth tightened, but she made no protest. In the privacy of the anteroom, Suzanne leaned against the closed door and turned to survey the other woman. She could see a pronounced resemblance now, in the cheekbones and about the mouth. "I should have seen it from the first. Louis Germont is your cousin."

Sylvie smoothed her glove. "Who?"

"I imagine you introduced him to Julien St. Juste. How long have you known St. Juste?"

"Yet another name that's new to me." But this time there was a definite edge beneath Lady St. Ives's well-modulated voice.

"We overheard St. Juste tonight making an exchange with Carfax." Julien had given her a gift with that overheard meeting. An excuse to know of him without revealing their true past connection. "The papers you stole from Whateley & Company."

"*I* stole— My dear Mrs. Rannoch, I'm sure Malcolm has told you I was part of a group attempting to recover papers from Carfax, so I won't fence with you about that. That group hired Coventry—"

"Cuthbertson went to Fitzroy Somerset who went to Ennis who hired Coventry—"

"Precisely. How—"

"But you were the one who went to Cuthbertson."

Sylvie St. Ives sighed. "I suppose there's no sense in denying that, but you must see that that doesn't mean I had any notion of Coventry's identity."

"I'm quite sure you didn't or you'd never have risked meeting him."

"I beg your pardon?"

Was it her imagination, or had Lady St. Ives gone still for a fraction of a second? "I don't know all the details," Suzanne said, "but for some reason you decided to be present for the break-in."

"Why would I risk that?"

"I suspect because before anyone else saw this letter of Carfax's, you wanted to see if it revealed the role you had played in the information he traded with Fouché. What you hadn't bargained on was the thief who had been hired through the elaborate chain you set up to create distance being someone who recognized you."

"What on earth makes you think—"

"Coventry told his mistress he'd seen a beautiful woman in London who had committed one of the greatest acts of treachery he'd ever witnessed in the Peninsula"

"I don't see what that has to do with me—"

"I don't think you were aware he'd seen you in London. Not then. He probably saw you passing in the street. Coventry didn't know your name, but he recognized you as the woman he'd overheard passing information to a man in a tavern in Lisbon in 1810. Carfax had one of his agents offer information to Fouché then. An agent known to Julien St. Juste. I think it was you. I expect you coordinated with Louis Germont, who worked for Fouché. Coventry said the woman and the man she was giving the information to looked enough alike to be brother and sister. Carfax probably chose you for the mission at least in part because Germont was your cousin."

"You can't prove—"

"I may not be able to prove it, but I'm quite sure the night of the break-in Coventry again recognized you, and this time you recognized him as well, and you killed him. And then took the papers. St. Juste implied Maria Monreal found them in Brook Street, but Maria denied that. It makes much more sense that you found them and gave them to St. Juste. But of course you wouldn't tell the rest of your network. So Maria broke into Brook Street thinking the papers were still at large."

"That's a fantastical story, Mrs. Rannoch."

"It's a story that makes sense of the facts. Though it leaves a lot unexplained. Such as what hold Carfax had on you and Julien St. Juste. And how you met St. Juste in the first place." Not to mention who Julien really was.

Sylvie regarded her for a long moment. "I'm not admitting a word of it, Mrs. Rannoch. But when you tell your husband, as I have no doubt you will, make sure you make it clear that whatever I did, Oliver knew none of it."

39

Suzanne hurried down the gilded Robert Adam staircase in search of Raoul and Laura. At the base of the stairs stood the naked Canova marble statue of Napoleon Bonaparte, which Wellington had had Benjamin Dean Wyatt install. Suzanne's hand tightened on the polished stair rail. She found herself averting her gaze. She was the furthest thing from a prude, but there was something about seeing a naked statue of someone one had actually met . . .

She drew up short at the base of the stairs at the sight of her husband. "Thank God you're still here," he said, coming forwards to take her hands. Without further speech, they went into an empty ground floor sitting room.

"Carfax didn't say much," Malcolm said, pushing the door to. "Though he said enough to confirm St. Juste's story. He denies he had an agent break into Whateley & Company and kill Coventry, but it's the obvious explanation—"

"Darling, no." Suzanne gripped her husband's hands and told him about Sylvie St. Ives.

Malcolm stared at her, not with disbelief but with the weary certainty of one putting the pieces together even as she laid them before him.

"Dear God."

"There's no reason to think Oliver knew any of it, Malcolm. Sylvie says no, and in that, at least, I think she's telling the truth."

Malcolm's brows drew together and she was sure he was remembering Sylvie as a girl, as a debutante in love with Oliver, as a young wife. "What the hell hold did Carfax have on her? And on St. Juste?"

"I don't know. The connection between Julien and Lady St. Ives obviously goes far back."

"Which could support your idea that St. Juste might be English. Someone Sylvie knew here as a girl."

"Perhaps. Or he could be connected to her family still in France. Louis Germont is, and she's obviously still in touch with him."

"And no way to prove any of it." Malcolm passed a hand over his face. "We'll have to decide what to tell Harry and Cordy."

In the end, they took the Davenports back to Berkeley Square with them, along with Laura and Raoul, and told them the whole. Rather amazingly, they could do so without mentioning her own and Raoul's prior connection to Julien St. Juste.

Cordelia shivered. "I never considered Sylvie St. Ives a particular friend, but—"

"I don't suppose there's any way to prove any of it," Harry said.

"No." Malcolm's voice was grim. "And if we could, Carfax would shut down an attempt to bring Sylvie to justice, as he's already shut down the Bow Street investigation. He'd be too concerned about the secrets that might be revealed."

"I can't say I'm much bothered by the thought of agents being able to break away from Carfax," Harry murmured.

Malcolm met his friend's gaze. "Nor am I. Though it appears Carfax still has some influence over St. Juste and Sylvie. I'm quite sure losing some of his agents won't slow Carfax down for long. And there's no way to bring him to account for the plot to entrap Bonapartists."

"You stopped it," Raoul said in a quiet voice. "That counts for a lot."

Cordelia curled her fingers round Harry's arm. "Maria was just trying to break free of Carfax. Difficult to blame her for that."

"I never had a great many illusions about Maria," Harry said. "But I confess I'm relieved to find she isn't a killer." He looked down at his wife. "All right?"

"How could it not be?" Cordelia pressed her face against his shoulder. "Especially since you're going home with me."

David watched Jamie launch himself across the Carfax House drawing room carpet at Lucinda.

"It's all right," Lucinda said, catching her nephew with a grin. "I've got him."

David cast a glance round his parents' drawing room. Amy was sitting on the sofa beside his mother, nibbling a biscuit, the toes of her shiny black shoes peeping neatly from beneath her ruffled skirts, making an obvious effort to mimic Lady Carfax's posture. Teddy and George were on the floor playing with the lead soldiers that had once been his. When Amy finished her biscuit she was going to want to abandon being ladylike and join them, which would make his mother raise her brows. But all things considered, it was going reasonably well. David bent to ruffle Jamie's hair and sent Teddy a grin, a "you're the eldest, you're in charge" look. Teddy received it and grinned back. David turned and followed his father from the room.

These visits were getting easier, but it would be good to be home. David paused at the door to Carfax's study. Odd. When had Brook Street, rather than the Albany or Carfax House, become home? It helped, of course, that Simon was spending more time there.

"Sit down, David." Carfax moved to his desk and waved David to a chair. "How much has Malcolm told you?"

"I haven't seen Malcolm since Bel and Oliver's ball." David dropped into a chair. "Is there news?"

"You could say so." Carfax tapped his fingers on the desktop. "You needn't worry about further break-ins at Brook Street."

"They've caught whoever was behind the break-ins?"

"In a manner of speaking. The matter has been taken care of."

"Thank God." No sense in even trying to get his father to tell him more. David knew Malcolm would tell him as much of the truth as he thought he could. Though he also knew that wouldn't be anything approaching the whole.

"There's another matter I need to discuss with you." Carfax aligned his pen on the desktop.

"If it's about Teddy—"

"It isn't. I'll grant that you've earned the right to decide what you think is best for him." Carfax moved the inkpot beside the pen. He seemed to be delaying coming to the point, which wasn't like him.

"Thank you," David said. His gratitude was genuine, but unease coiled within him.

Carfax moved a box of sealing wax beside the inkpot, then laid his hands flat on the inkblotter and regarded David for a moment. Behind his spectacle lenses his gaze was tinged with an unwonted compassion.

A jolt of terror shot through David.

"I'm sorry, David," Carfax said. "This isn't going to be easy to hear. But there's something you need to know."

Oliver stared at Malcolm across the same sitting room at Brooks's where they had spoken the previous day. "Sylvie—"

"Lied to you? A bit ironic if you find that surprising."

"She never told me—"

"You didn't know she knew St. Juste?"

Oliver shook his head. "I never even heard of Julien St. Juste. Who the hell is he?"

"An excellent question. But Sylvie has evidently known him for a long time. And they both worked for Carfax."

"She didn't—" Oliver broke off, a dozen unvoiced questions lurking in his gaze.

"It's hard," Malcolm said. "Facing betrayal. Even when one is familiar with it oneself. Perhaps worst of all from the woman one loves." Dangerous to say that, perhaps, but he hoped Oliver would think he was talking hypothetically.

"She's not—" Oliver stared at him for a moment. "I loved Sylvie. A part of me will always love her in a way, I suppose. Even—after this. But Bel's the mother of my children. How could I not love her after everything we've shared?"

"Does Bel know?" Malcolm asked in a quiet voice.

"I'm not sure. I think it might have made a difference to her once. I'm not sure it does now." Oliver ran a hand over his hair. "I'm going to tell Bel the truth. About my working for her father. If you'll—I'd like to do that before you tell David and Simon."

Malcolm regarded his friend for a long moment. "I'm not going to tell David and Simon."

Oliver's head snapped up. "You're not—"

"What you say to them is up to you."

Oliver gave a slow nod. "Thank you."

"There's little enough reason to thank anyone in this whole mess."

Oliver drew a breath as though he might say more, then gave a quick nod and turned to the door. He was reaching for the door handle when the door opened and David came into the room and nearly collided with him.

"Oliver." David drew up short, as though scarcely aware of where he was going.

Oliver scanned his brother-in-law's pale face. "Are you all right?"

David gave a curt nod. "I need to talk to Malcolm."

"I'm just on my way out." Oliver cast a quick glance between David and Malcolm, a different sort of concern in his face, then gave another nod and left the room.

David pushed the door to and leaned against the panels. He was paler than usual, his hair uncharacteristically disordered, as though he'd been running his fingers through it.

"What?" Malcolm took a step towards his friend. "What is it? The children?"

"Father." David's voice was rough. "He told me the most unbelievable story. He's never been above embroidering the facts, but this went overboard even for him. He said—" David pushed himself away from the door, took a turn about the room, as though the words stuck in his head.

Malcolm went numb, though he couldn't quite believe that what he feared was about to happen.

David turned to face him. His gaze held disbelief and apology for the outlandish thing he was about to say. "He claimed Suzanne was"—the words seemed to catch in David's throat—"a spy."

"Of course she was a spy." Malcolm forced normalcy to his voice. "We both were."

"That's not what Father meant." David's gaze locked on Malcolm's own, twisted with torment. "He said she was a spy for the French."

40

There it was, put into words, the thing he had feared almost from the moment he learned the truth about Suzanne. Every fiber of his being seemed to have gone cold. A part of his mind had never believed this would happen. Yet another part had always seemed to know this moment was inevitable.

"Is it true?" David's words were a hoarse plea.

"If it was, you can't imagine I would admit it, can you?"

"But you aren't denying it." David's gaze raked his face.

Malcolm looked into the eyes of his best friend of twenty-three years. The weight of a friendship hung between them, but as so often in the espionage game, the decision about whether or not to lie came down to practicalities. He could insist Suzanne hadn't been a French agent. He could probably convince David. David might not even revisit the topic with his father. But Carfax would. Carfax would use God knew what evidence and tell God knew whom else.

Yesterday Carfax had seemed, if not checkmated, at least put in check, his agents breaking away, his efforts to ferret out Bonapartists in London foiled. Now, with the shock of a deluge on a seemingly calm day, Malcolm was reminded how very dangerous his spymaster could be.

"Malcolm?" David's voice held an edge of desperation. "Did someone blackmail her? She's never mentioned family she still has in France, but did they use that as a hold on her?"

Malcolm's guts twisted at the longing and certainty in David's gaze. Longing for an explanation, certainty that there must be one. He'd felt that himself when he first realized Suzanne had been working for the French. "Suzanne is loyal," he said. "To the things she believes in. To the country of her birth."

David's eyes widened. Had his own gaze, Malcolm wondered, ever held such horror? "What about loyalty to her family?" David asked. "To her husband?"

"She was loyal to her cause and her comrades before she met me," Malcolm said.

"She married you knowing—"

"Most of what we both did in the Peninsula was a mission, one way and another." Malcolm kept his voice level. Part of it was an effort. But part was the situation as he'd come to accept it.

David stared at him as though he had transformed into another creature. Belle's prince changing back into le Bête. "She married you to spy on Britain. To spy on *you*."

"Among others. She didn't plan it. I played into her hands when my chivalry drove me to propose."

"My God." David took a stumbling step backwards. "How can you sound so calm?"

"It wasn't easy at first. I was rather inclined to see the whole situation through my own lens."

"You—How long—Malcolm, did you—" David broke off, not able to put what he feared into words.

But Malcolm took the meaning. It was like a blow to the gut. "Did I work with her? David, how can you ask that of me?"

"You're the one who's always saying we can't know what a person will do under any circumstances. That I don't understand the espionage game."

"Even I have my limits."

"And Suzanne doesn't?"

"No. It's not the same." Malcolm took a half step forwards. "You know me, David."

"I thought I knew you." David's voice was low and rough, unlike anything Malcolm had heard from his friend before. "I thought I knew Suzanne."

David's face was that of a man cut loose from his moorings. Malcolm remembered feeling the same way himself, though his work had given him a framework to grasp hold of. "I have no right to ask you to take my word for anything just now, David. But I wouldn't betray my country."

David's gaze hardened, like a devastated stretch of ground freezing over. "What do you call protecting a woman who did?"

"She'd stopped," Malcolm said. "Long before I learned the truth. She stopped after Waterloo."

"And you believed her?"

"Yes. I know it may sound mad to you, but I know her. And we're honest with each other. Now."

David gave a short laugh. "And if she hadn't stopped before you learned the truth?"

Malcolm swallowed and felt as though he'd downed shards of glass. If he'd been quicker, better at his job, more insightful, a better agent, less in love—He'd have figured out the truth while Mel was still working for the French. And then? He'd wondered about that obliquely but had always shied away from examining the question too closely. Unthinkable to have turned the mother of his child over to British intelligence, even before he'd admitted the depths of his own feelings for her. Would he have confronted her and given her the chance to escape? And take Colin with her? Equally unthinkable. Demanded she stop? He doubted she'd have agreed. With a shock like cold fire, he realized he wasn't even sure he'd have wanted her to.

"You aren't sure, are you?" David said. "My God, Malcolm."

"When I first learned the truth"—Malcolm's voice was rough as he picked his way over uncomfortable terrain. "I couldn't imagine that I could ever trust her again. Let alone"—his voice caught on a word he rarely used about his wife, even to his best friend—"love her."

"But you do."

"I'm a spy myself. I can understand why she did what she did. I can recognize it's something I might have done myself—"

"You'd have married a woman simply to steal information—"

"I'm not sure. I don't think I'd have gone that far. But God knows I know what it is to use people's trust. To betray and tell oneself it's for a good cause. Difficult to draw lines and judge. The part of me that's an agent can even admire the sheer craft of what she pulled off. I'm quite sure I couldn't have done it myself."

"You can admire—" David choked. "You can admire someone stealing information from you? Christ, Malcolm. British soldiers died because of her."

"And French soldiers survived."

"You can't." David shook his head. "You can't balance the scales that way."

Malcolm took a step forwards, instinctively reaching out for something he feared was already out of his reach. "Do you remember when we slipped out of Carfax House and went to that lecture by William Godwin? We thought we were so daring. And afterwards we sat in a coffeehouse, feeling ridiculously grown up, and said how amazing it was how logical his arguments were? That it was difficult to refute them? Those are much the same arguments Suzanne would make about the world."

He caught a spark of the past in David's gaze for a moment. And then the same shutter slammed closed. "Don't, Malcolm. Don't claim that even thinking about remaking our country is the same as being a Bonapartist agent. That puts you on a footing with my father."

"Fair enough. I didn't say Suzanne and I agreed on tactics. But then, we didn't start from the same place."

"You started from a place of working for your country."

"So did she."

"Malcolm, I know you. You'd never have let being a spy justify anything you did."

"No, not anything. We all have to make choices and draw boundaries. The question is what boundaries and how to draw them. I know enough to know that's not an easy question for anyone to answer."

"My God you sound coldblooded about it."

"I wasn't at first, believe me. It still takes work, at times."

David took a turn about the room, feet pounding against the Axminster carpet. "I want to believe you. I want to believe in the Suzanne I thought I knew. But if I let go here—" He stopped and turned to Malcolm again. This time the stretch of carpet between them was seemingly uncrossable. "Yes, our country isn't ordered as it should be. Yes, there's intolerable injustice. Yes, we could and do write treatises on what we'd change. But in the end, it has to mean something."

"What?"

"England. Britain. What it stands for. What we were fighting for. Otherwise, the whole thing just becomes a game."

"If it is, it's a game with life and death stakes. But not just for British men and women. And it's arguable what's best for those in Britain as well."

David shook his head. "She deceived you. She married you to gain information. She's the mother of your children. I can see how you have to go on living together. But how can you believe anything she says?"

"I suppose it would be more accurate to say I choose to believe it."

David stared at him as though looking at a stranger. "Father was right."

"About what?"

"That you're besotted."

"I suppose I am. But I think I see Mel more clearly than I ever have."

"Mel?"

"It's her real name. Mélanie Suzanne."

David's mouth twisted. "Nothing about her was true, was it?"

"Except the woman she is."

"Malcolm, as someone who loves you, I can't bear to see—"

"Think what you will of me, David. But I've made my own choices as well.

"In Vienna," David said. "Christ, at Waterloo. When I remember her nursing soldiers—"

"Many of whom survived because of her efforts. Waterloo was particularly hard for her. I can't imagine quite how hard. I wish I'd known at the time."

"You wish—Jesus." David turned on his heel and strode to the door.

"David—" Malcolm crossed to his friend's side in two strides.

"Don't, Malcolm." David put out a hand to forestall him. "We have nothing more to say to each other."

"Darling." Suzanne looked up with a smile as her husband came into the drawing room, then went still at the sight of his face. It was set in a tight, pleasant mask. But beneath the easy smile for the children, his gaze had the controlled focus he wore in the midst of a mission. All else subsumed by the task at hand.

He stopped to admire the arrangement of the castle in the center of the room and the doll table that had been transformed into the Round Table, then drew her over to one of the windows. She knew Raoul and Laura, who stayed kneeling beside the children, were both aware something was wrong, though both gave an excellent impression of not having the least idea anything was out of the ordinary.

He took her hands. His fingers were cold, but his gaze, oddly, was warm with compassion. "We have to leave, Mel. Tonight."

"For where? Dunmykel? Have you heard from Andrew and Gisèle—"

"Italy." His voice was flat and even, his gaze steady on her own. "Carfax knows. He told David."

She heard the words, but her brain refused to comprehend them. A roaring filled her ears. The blood rushed from her head, leaving cold, dizzying horror. And comprehension. For the second time in six months the unthinkable had happened. Her world had cracked open. The sword of Damocles had fallen. And all she could think was that she had been a fool not to see it coming.

"Sweetheart." His fingers tightened over her own. "I don't know how long he's known. I don't know whom else he's told. But I'm not sure David can keep it to himself."

She scanned his face. "Was it—?"

For an instant, beneath the control, she caught a glimpse of a pain he probably didn't even realize he was feeling. Yet. "Everything I feared."

"Darling. That's—"

"Between David and me." Whatever he was feeling, he wasn't, might never be, ready to share it with her. "I've sent word to Bertrand," he continued. "He'll have a boat meet us at the docks at midnight. Pack—"

"Only necessities." It was a mission, after all. Not the first time she'd been off at a moment's notice. She could do this. She had to focus on practicalities and forget that life as they knew it was falling apart. She glanced across the room at the children, subduing the impulse to snatch them up in her arms. "They'll think it's a great adventure. Thank God they're good travelers."

It was Malcolm who looked across the room at Raoul and Laura and inclined his head. When the other couple joined them, he merely said, "Carfax knows. We're leaving for Italy tonight."

Raoul's gaze told Suzanne he had already guessed. His mouth was a taut line, his shoulders tensed as though braced to go into battle. "What can we do?" he asked in a clipped voice.

"Everything's already prepared," Malcolm said. "We only have to put the plans in motion. I've already seen Bertrand."

"I've always wanted to see Italy," Laura said. "I can be ready in an hour."

"You don't need to come," Suzanne told her friend. "You didn't ask for any of this. The house is yours—"

"Stay in London without you? No thank you. Italy sounds much more interesting." Laura glanced at the sofa where Emily was helping Jessica arrange some of the dolls while Berowne rolled on his back and batted at the dolls' skirts. "And I wouldn't separate the children."

"Nor would I," Suzanne said, "not willingly. But your parents—"

"I'll write to them. Surely there will be a way for them to visit. Or for Emily and me to come back."

"You have to consider—"

"Mélanie." Laura took a step closer to Raoul. "I would go with you in any case. But if Carfax knows about you, he almost certainly knows about Raoul. Which means that if Raoul has a scrap of sense"—she cast a glance at her lover that indicated she wasn't entirely sure this was the case—"he won't show his face in Britain for some time either. So you see, I don't really have any choice about it."

Raoul opened his mouth to protest. Laura gripped his arm. Suzanne met her friend's gaze and nodded.

"I have travel documents for you, as it happens," Malcolm said. "Though at the time I put them together, you were still our children's governess. You're traveling as my sister. I used my great-grandmother's name. Fraser. You're Laura Fraser." He glanced at Suzanne. "I used Mélanie for you, so that's easy enough to remember. And I used my middle name."

"Not Alistair?" Suzanne said.

"No, my other middle name. Charles. Blessedly free of associations. Everything's in place. I need only leave a few letters to be posted once we're gone."

"I'll come with you on the way back to Spain," Raoul said.

"It's very out of your way," Malcolm said.

"My dear Malcolm, if you think there's a chance in hell I'm going anywhere until I've seen all of you safely settled in Italy, you are very much mistaken."

To Suzanne's surprise, Malcolm touched Raoul's arm. "Thank you."

The necessary words spoken, silence gripped them. The silence of realization. Suzanne looked at the wall hangings she had chosen. The furniture she'd had recovered. The corner of the wall she'd had moved to enlarge the room. Images shot through her mind. Walking through the house with Malcolm after Alistair's death. Conferring with the builders. Visiting a silk warehouse with Cordy and the children. Testing paint samples in the light. The children playing in the square garden. Colin and Emily sliding down the stair rail. Standing at the head of the stairs for their first party.

Like a slap it hit her. What they were leaving. This house. The square garden. London. Dunmykel. Britain. A country she had hesitated to come to. That she had fought against. A world in which, in many ways, she was still an outsider. And yet, in many ways, it had become the closest she'd had to a home since her father's death.

Malcolm squeezed her hand. "I need to write some letters. I've sent word to Harry. He should be here soon. Probably Cordy, as well, if you want to talk to her."

Suzanne nodded. Cordy was going to learn the truth now. She wanted her friend to hear it from her.

Malcolm glanced from Raoul to Laura. "Make sure she's ready to get on the boat."

"Really, darling." Suzanne managed a tone approaching normalcy. "It's not the first time I've made a middle-of-the-night departure."

"But never in these circumstances." He leaned in, heedless of Raoul and Laura, and kissed her.

As he drew back, there was a rap at the door, and Valentin entered the room. "I'm sorry to interrupt, sir. But Lord Carfax is below."

41

Malcolm always tensed with wariness at the sight of Carfax. Today he felt as though he were approaching a coiled snake. No, a dragon. The fiercest dragon from Colin's storybooks.

Paradoxically, when Malcolm opened the door of the study, Carfax turned to him with a look that held more compassion than Malcolm had ever seen on the earl's face. "You needn't reach for your pistol. I haven't brought soldiers. Or an order from Bow Street. In fact, I can promise to hold off the dogs until you put into effect the escape plans I have no doubt you made long since. I just wanted to see you first."

"What do you want?" Malcolm pushed the door shut and set his shoulders against the panels. As if somehow by keeping Carfax in the room, he could protect Suzanne and the children. Laughable.

"To apologize." Carfax began to tug off his gloves. "I hoped it would never come to this."

"Have you known from the first?" Better not to have said anything, but the question came unbidden.

"Oh, no." Carfax pulled the second glove from his fingers. "Suzanne did real damage. There's no letting any of us off the hook so easily. My lack of perspicacity remains on my conscience, as it does on yours. I should have seen the truth far sooner. So should you." He slapped the gloves down on the table.

"I don't deny it."

"Don't be too hard on yourself, my boy. She's very, very good at what she does. And you were in love with her, which doesn't help. I didn't have any such excuse. In the end, I didn't learn about her activities until after Waterloo, and only then through an agent of mine."

"Julien St. Juste."

"No, as it happens. He has an odd loyalty to her himself. But he told Sylvie St. Ives. And she told me after Waterloo when she needed something from me."

"You've known for three years?"

"Give or take."

"You didn't—"

"Consider moving against her? It would have been different if the war were still going on. I'd have been obliged to take action, like it or no. Perhaps even have her removed. But I had it on good authority that she'd stopped spying."

"And you believed it? That doesn't sound like you, sir."

Carfax coughed. "I confess that even I am not immune to the influence of having seen someone play with my grandchildren. It seemed enough to watch her. That's part of why I had Oliver keeping an eye on you."

"My God, are you saying Oliver—"

"No, he didn't have the least idea about that. Credit me with some sense, Malcolm. But I was confident it was safe merely to watch you both."

"And you had a valuable bargaining chip."

"Which I hoped I wouldn't have to use." Carfax dropped into a chair. In the light from the windows, he looked tired. "I said Suzanne had done incalculable damage. She's also a brilliant agent. I can admire her. And I'm quite fond of her. She's undoubtedly been good for you. I'd have been quite happy to have her continue to write outrageous articles and charm everyone at parties and you make impossible arguments in Parliament. Except for—"

Malcolm stared at Carfax. His spymaster. His best friend's father. "David. You told David because you wanted us to quarrel."

Carfax met Malcolm's gaze. His eyes held apology but no regret. "I needed my son back. Something drastic was called for."

"Because you know David will tell Simon. And you know which side Simon will take."

"I think I do. I hope I do. I'm generally rather good at reading people."

"That's like saying a dragon is generally good at breathing fire."

"It's not the way I'd have liked it to happen, for any of us. But it became clear to me in recent months that it would take something drastic to bring David to his senses."

"And we were collateral damage."

"In a sense," Carfax said without hesitation. "You should understand, Malcolm. I think you, more than anyone, should know what it means to protect one's family. I've been all too inclined to put the needs of my country ahead of those of my family. If nothing else, the unfortunate events of last March reminded me of the need not to neglect my obligations to my family."

Impossible not to feel for the pain in Carfax's gaze. Malcolm knew what it was to feel regret, but he could scarcely imagine the weight of regret the earl lived under. When he spoke, he heard more concern than anger in his own voice. "I would have hoped the events of three months ago would have shown you the importance of letting your children find their own happiness."

The gaze Carfax turned to Malcolm was stripped surprisingly honest. "You've been a good friend to David, Malcolm. I have no doubt he shares things with you he doesn't with his parents. But as a father yourself, you'll have to allow that I know my son in a way others can't. Ultimately, David won't be happy if he doesn't do his duty. I think the same thing is true for you, though you define your duty very differently."

"I also wouldn't be happy without the woman I love."

"But you aren't David."

For all the risks to his family, in that moment the fear that shot through Malcolm was for his friend. And perhaps for Carfax himself. "You'll break him."

"You're a good agent, Malcolm. And an undeniably brilliant man. But you've always been inclined to overemphasize the personal. David knows what matters for his country and his family. Let me see to my son. Look after your own family."

The threat to his family washed back over Malcolm like a deluge. Whatever else he had been to Malcolm, the man standing across the room from him had the power to destroy his wife and children and everything that mattered to him.

"I have no intention of spreading this further," Carfax said. "But you're right. Now the news is out, you can't be sure who will hear of it. I can think of a number of people who'd be only too happy to use it to bring you down. I can't protect you. But as I said, I can hold the dogs off long enough for you and Suzanne and the children to get out of England."

"Why on earth should I—"

"Trust me? You're far too good an agent to do that. But as it happens, I am telling the truth in this case. It's the least I can do for you."

"And you want me away from David."

"That too."

Malcolm gave a curt nod and turned to the door. Carfax could see himself out.

"Malcolm," Carfax said.

Malcolm turned back to the man who had shaped so much of his life. "There was a time when I would have been afraid something like this would break you. I'm not anymore."

"At least it will be warm in Italy," Blanca said in a bright voice. "Not like a gray English summer." She bit her lip and cast a quick glance at her husband.

Addison took her hand and smiled, though myriad questions darted through his gaze. "We've known this might happen for some time."

Concerned as she was about what might be transpiring between Malcolm and Carfax, Suzanne had used the time to tell Blanca and Addison about the need for their imminent departure. They sat with Suzanne, Raoul, and Laura at one end of the drawing room while the children continued to play at the other end. The sight of the three small figures grouped round the castle anchored Suzanne to reality. At the same time, it tore at her with the reminder of all they were about to lose.

"I have everything in readiness, Mrs. Rannoch," Addison said. "I'll begin to pack at once. It shouldn't take long."

Suzanne met Addison's steady gaze. He never blinked when drawn into a mission. Yet this mission would upend his life through no choice of his own. No choice but loving Blanca and working for Malcolm. "If there's anyone you need to see—"

"Thank you, madam. I already have letters written to my parents."

Blanca bit her lip. Her hand curved over her abdomen. So often it seemed impending parenthood made one truly aware of the bond with one's own parents. "*Querido*—"

Addison lifted her hand to his lips, a rare, public gesture of affection. "It's all right, sweetheart. Mr. Rannoch has promised to bring them to Italy, should it come to that."

Suzanne's nails curved into her palms. How often had she grimaced at the way the beau monde, including Malcolm's family, including sometimes Malcolm himself, took for granted the presence of servants in their lives. And yet she, the Republican revolutionary, had smashed Addison's life as he knew it to bits in the wake of her own betrayals. When she went into her marriage she'd scarcely considered what she was doing to Malcolm, let alone to his valet. And she certainly hadn't considered Addison's parents.

"The fewer people we speak with before we leave, the better," Raoul said in a level voice. "For their sakes."

Addison met Raoul's gaze. They all knew Carfax's power. If they had ever doubted it, today's events had reminded them. "My thoughts precisely, Mr. O'Roarke."

"I'll pack for the children," Blanca said.

"I'll see to it," Laura said. "Perhaps you could try to keep them occupied. I don't think we should tell them we're leaving just yet." She forced a smile to her lips. "And if anyone really wants to be helpful, try to figure out how we're going to pack the castle."

Malcolm returned to the drawing room to find Addison had joined Suzanne, Laura, and Raoul. Addison looked pale but determined. Blanca had taken the children up to the nursery. "She was the most matter of fact of any of us," Suzanne said.

"She's used to upheaval," Addison said. "She won't blanch at leaving Britain, provided she can take the people she cares about with her."

His gaze was on Malcolm as he spoke, dark with concern. Malcolm sent his valet a look intended to be reassuring and briefly recounted the pertinent parts of his interview with Carfax. Not Carfax's motivation regarding David, but Carfax's promise to hold the dogs off until they got out of the country. Addison gave a crisp nod and said he would see to the packing. Suzanne, pale, shoulders ramrod straight, hands locked together, said she should do so as well. Malcolm squeezed her hand and then kissed her again. Her lips were cold, but she returned the pressure of his hand and gave him a quick smile.

Laura went upstairs with her. Malcolm looked after them, then turned to Raoul, who had lingered in the drawing room. "Watch her," Malcolm said to his father in a soft voice.

Raoul's gaze darted over Malcolm's face. "You think she'd try to run on her own?"

"No. But I can't entirely rule it out."

Raoul nodded. "Mélanie's a survivor. And not the self-sacrificial sort."

"So I keep telling myself. But we've never been in these circumstances before. And she'll go a long way to protect those she loves. You should understand that."

"That may be the very thing that stops her from running. Mélanie doesn't really believe her children would be better off with anyone but her." Raoul drew a breath, rough with unspoken words. "Malcolm—"

Malcolm looked into his father's dark gaze. "It's not your fault, O'Roarke."

"That's highly debatable."

"The only way I'd be in a position not to run is if I didn't have Mélanie or my children. Which I can't imagine. And in the end this wasn't really about me or Mélanie or you."

"Carfax wanted to separate you from Worsley and Worsley from Tanner?"

Malcolm stared at his father. "Don't tell me you saw this coming."

"My God, do you imagine I would have stood by if I had? But as soon as I heard I cursed myself for a fool."

"So did I." Malcolm stared out the windows at the branches of the plane trees in the Berkeley Square garden, thick with leaves. He had forgot how dangerous a wounded lion could be. He and Suzanne had spent the past four days investigating a case that had come down to Carfax's agents trying to break free of his influence. And now that same influence was driving Suzanne and him from Britain. "Not the first time I've underestimated Carfax."

Raoul watched him for a moment. "If Carfax was determined to intervene between Worsley and Tanner, he'd have found something else if not this. It's up to Worsley and Tanner how they respond. From what I've observed, they both have considerable strength of will."

Malcolm nodded, though the searing bitterness in David's gaze burned in his memory. "I should start on my letters." That was all one could really do now, hold on to what needed to be done, one step at a time. But at the door, he turned back to his father. "Raoul? Thank you for coming with us."

Raoul's hand gripped his arm for a moment, steady and warm. "I wouldn't be anywhere else."

Malcolm went out onto the landing, but at the stairhead he paused for a moment, drinking in the smells of lemon and walnut oil, the curve of the stair wall, the way the girandoles on the wall sconces danced in the candlelight.

Damn it. As a boy, he hadn't even liked this house. His hand closed hard on the stair rail. Then he went quickly down the stairs to do what needed to be done.

Simon dropped down on the sofa in the Brook Street library. "Well. This explains a lot."

David stared at his lover. "Don't tell me you *knew?*"

"That Suzanne was a French agent? Not in the least. That Suzanne wasn't quite what she seemed to be? That was obvious from the first. That she had secrets? Which of us doesn't?"

David clenched his hands at his sides. Rage and disbelief still roiled through him. But Simon's voice was even, contemplative. He might have been analyzing the characters in one of his plays. "You never said anything."

"What was there to say? I didn't know anything for a certainty. I didn't even have any definite suspicions. I'm not given to speculating about other people's most intimate secrets."

"Simon." David dropped down on a chair arm, gaze level with his lover's. "She gave information to the French."

"Yes, you said she was a French agent. I would assume that's what you meant."

"She sold the French information—"

"I wouldn't say sold. It doesn't sound as though she was doing it for the money."

"Information used against us in the war."

"A war that was never mine."

Echoes of their quarrel when Bonaparte escaped Elba and David, who had initially opposed war, supported the Government once war had been declared, hung in the air. "Englishmen died because of her."

"A point. But I'm sure there are Frenchmen who survived because of her."

"Are you saying it's the same thing?"

"Rather depends on one's perspective. Suzanne's French, after all. Even granting I should have some bone-deep loyalty to England, shouldn't she have the same loyalty to France?"

"Damn it, Simon, you always do this. You deliberately take positions even you don't agree with, just to provoke me."

"I don't—"

"You like to raise questions. You like to poke and prod at things. But these are our friends."

Simon slumped back against the sofa cushions and passed a hand over his face. Even in the warm candlelight, his skin looked ashen. "You're right. Not that I don't agree with what I'm saying or that I'm deliberately quarreling. But I'm not thinking about our friends properly. My way of dealing with the news, perhaps."

"She's Malcolm's wife."

"Yes." A shadow crossed Simon's face and settled in the depths of his eyes. "This must have been hell for Malcolm."

"I can scarcely imagine."

"But he told you he still loves her, didn't he?"

"How can you—"

"Thinking back, I'd hazard a guess he discovered the truth round last Christmas. It was obvious something had happened between them then. But they're still together. And things seem easier between them."

"Malcolm—" David squeezed his eyes shut, recalling his scene with his friend. "It's as though I was talking to a completely different person."

"It can't be a revelation that Malcolm has always seen the world a bit differently from you."

"She lied to him. She stole information from him. Everything between them is built on lies."

"Not everything."

"You can't possibly be sure of that."

"You've seen them together. How can you possibly doubt it?"

David winced. He had a keen image of Suzanne running down the hall of the Rannochs' house in Brussels and flinging her arms round Malcolm, returned from the field the night of Quatre Bras. David's undemonstrative friend had kissed his wife and spilled half the glass of whisky he carried over both of them, heedless of their other friends standing in the hall. David didn't know if he'd ever seen two people so seemingly in love. "Suzanne is obviously brilliant at deception."

"Some things can't be manufactured."

David looked at the man with whom he'd shared more than anyone on earth. "You're a playwright and an actor, Simon. You see every day how love and other emotions can be convincingly manufactured on stage."

"A point. But close up, one can tell the difference."

"Can you?" David shot a hard look at his lover. "In a way make-believe and deception are your stock in trade just as they are an intelligence agent's."

Simon leaned forwards, hands between his knees. The mockery was gone from his gaze. "Think, David. The care she shows for Malcolm round his family. Her kindness to the children. The way she nursed the wounded after Waterloo—"

"Wounded men she helped put there."

"My God, David, you remember what it was like. Wounded slumped in the streets, blood on the hall tiles, sleepless nights spooning water into their mouths to keep them alive. Suzanne worked harder that anyone."

"And that excuses that she was a Bonapartist agent?"

"No, but I think the fact that she was a Bonapartist agent makes her actions all the more remarkable."

David shook his head, disbelief sharp within him.

"Could you have done the same for French soldiers?" Simon asked in a soft voice. "Knowing they were fighting your countrymen. Knowing you might be patching them up to go on fighting against your own people?"

"I don't know." David passed a hand over his hair. "I'd like to think I could. I'm quite sure you could. And I mean that as a compliment."

Simon gave a faint smile that didn't quite reach his eyes. "I'll take it as one."

"But it doesn't change—" And yet—David saw Suzanne, kneeling beside a Highland private, holding young Henri Rivaux to life by sheer force of will. The bonds that had formed between them in that house in the Rue Ducale in those days had seemed unbreakable.

"I saw her face when Malcolm left," Simon said. "And her relief when he returned. If all that was play-acting, she's an actress on a level I've never encountered. And I've worked with some of the finest actresses on the stage today."

"What Malcolm must have gone through—"

Simon nodded. "Betrayal would hit him particularly hard. Thank God they've found a way to go on together."

"Thank God?"

"Would you rather have them separate? Divorce? Live together in icy silence? Shatter their own lives and those of their children?"

"No, of course not. That is—" David's hand curled into a fist. Difficult to envision a happy solution to any of this.

"More than five years of deception," Simon said. "It must have been an unbelievable strain on her."

David stared at his lover. "You sympathize with her."

"I suppose I identify with her, in a way. I know what it is to have to live a lie."

"Don't you dare." David felt anger shoot through him again. "Don't you dare compare our loving each other with—"

"I'm not. I'm comparing our being compelled to live in deception because we love each other with how Suzanne had to live."

"Suzanne wasn't compelled to do so."

"Not at first. Once she fell in love with Malcolm, I don't suppose she had much choice." He watched David for a moment. "Have you thought about what it's going to be like for them now?"

"Now, what?"

"Your father knows, David. I can't imagine Malcolm was aware of that or he wouldn't have been so sanguine. I can't imagine he'll feel safe staying in Britain now."

"It's not as though I would—"

"Expose Suzanne as a traitor?"

"I couldn't do that to her. To Malcolm's wife. To Colin and Jessica's mother." He drew a breath. "To the woman we went through Waterloo with."

For a moment the air was so still he could feel Simon's indrawn breath. "So that means something."

"Whoever she is, whyever she did what she did then, you're right the memories won't go away."

"Her politics are probably closer to yours than your father's are."

"I'm English, Simon. I have to believe that stands for something."

"You have to believe being an English gentleman stands for something."

"What's that supposed to mean?"

"Suzanne's not just a spy for a foreign power. She's a revolutionary."

"I live with a revolutionary."

"Only in a very theoretical sense. That is, I'm a revolutionary in theory. But it's true I don't want a world run by people like your father. I don't think Suzanne does either. I'm not sure I'd do what she's done to try to change that world. But I can understand why she did what she did."

David met Simon's gaze again. The first rush of anger had drained from him. And yet, Simon, a few feet from him across Louisa's claret-and-blue library carpet, seemed an incalculable distance away. "I suppose that's the difference between us," he said.

"Quite," Simon said.

David started to lift a hand, then let it fall. "I never thought—"

Simon watched David. They were both standing stock-still, but he looked at David as though his lover were retreating into the distance. "It's a difference that's always been there, David."

42

Raoul rapped at the door of Laura's bedchamber and strode into the room the moment she answered. It was, Laura realized, the first time he had come into her bedchamber without climbing through the window, slipping in in the middle of the night, or otherwise disguising his visit. They were rather beyond considerations of propriety at this point.

"Suzanne said she wanted to be alone," she said, turning from the wardrobe. "But I think you should talk to her."

"Laura." He pushed the door to. "Don't think I don't appreciate the solidarity. On the contrary." He drew a rough breath. "It meant more to me than I can say. But you have to consider—"

"I have considered." Laura pulled a valise from the bottom of her wardrobe.

Raoul set his shoulders against the door. "You could—"

"Pretend to be shocked I'd been in a nest of Bonapartist spies, marry William Cuthbertson and become an officer's wife?" She grabbed her nightdress from behind the pillow and threw it in the valise.

She saw the recoil in his eyes, but when he spoke his voice was even. "Among other things. You have options."

She picked up two gowns and a spencer she had laid out on the bed. "I don't care about commitments or vows or the lack of them." She folded the clothes automatically, as she once had schoolroom laundry. "I don't care that you disappear half the time and can't tell me where you are. I'm not leaving you." She put the spencer in the valise on top of the gowns. "My options were severely narrowed one night in Maidstone." She looked at him over the valise, breathing hard. "You have to know that by now."

This time the flash in his eyes was anything but a recoil. He crossed to her side in two strides and seized her by the shoulders. "You have to know it was the same for me, sweetheart. Perhaps even before that night."

"Well, then." She looked up into his eyes. "Besides, I promised I'd look after them for you. I can't very well do that if I stay in England." She pulled away towards the door to the night nursery. "I should pack for the children. Suzanne's good at it, but she's scarcely in the most stable state and there are things she's used to me remembering."

He dragged her back to him and covered her mouth with his own. "I don't deserve you. I just want you to be happy."

She tangled her fingers in his hair. "Idiot. I am."

Suzanne paused at the door of her wardrobe, a pomegranate gauze and sarcenet dress in one hand, a coral lace in the other. She wouldn't need as many evening gowns. But she should take at least one, and both of these would travel well and were favorites. She'd worn the pomegranate on Colin's birthday, and the coral lace to the ball they'd given six weeks ago, their first since Malcolm had learned the truth of her past. She could remember him clasping the garnet pendant he'd given her that night round her throat—

She dropped the gowns on the bed and closed her arms over her chest. She was shaking. She couldn't remember when she'd been so cold inside. She paced across the room, dropped down on her dressing table bench, gripped the edge of the table to keep herself from smashing her fist into the looking glass.

She jerked at movement in the looking glass.

"I knocked," Raoul said. "You didn't answer."

She met his gaze in the looking glass. "Let me guess. Malcolm asked you to make sure I don't make any mad sacrificial gestures. I hope you told him I'm not the self-sacrificial sort."

"Yes, but even I can't be sure."

She pressed her fingers against her temples, then spun round on the bench to face him. "I know what I owe to the children. I know what I owe to Malcolm. I'm not going to do anything crazy."

Raoul crossed the room and dropped down in front of the dressing table. "*Querida*—"

"I can handle this." She dragged her hands from her face to prove she could do it and locked them together in her lap. "I've always known I might have to."

"Knowing isn't the same as confronting the reality." His voice was steady but his gaze held a bone-deep fear that shook her to the core.

"Isn't confronting hard realities what we've always done?" She put her hands on his shoulders, though she could not have said which of them she was trying to comfort. "It's all right, I won't break. You trained me well."

Harry leaned against the desk in Malcolm's study, arms folded, gaze stripped of its usual irony. "She's the Raven, isn't she?"

Malcolm stared at his friend. "My God. How long have you known?"

"I didn't know anything until just now. Despite speculating that the Raven might be a woman, I didn't even suspect it could be Suzanne until we were in the midst of the *Hamlet* investigation and looking into the Raven's identity. There was a night at the theatre when it was suddenly obvious something had gone wrong between you and Suzanne. At first, I was merely worried. It was so unlike anything I'd ever seen between the two of you that I couldn't help but wonder what had happened."

Every moment of that night was vividly imprinted on Malcolm's memory. He'd been too overwhelmed by his own feelings to take much note of other people's. Still, he'd noted Harry's conversation that night. "You started talking to me about betrayal. *You knew then?*"

"It occurred to me. I was shocked at my own thoughts. But there was a certain logic to the way the pieces fell together."

"And so you—"

"If I was right—and half the time I couldn't believe I was—it was for you to decide what to do about it. I can't tell you how relieved I was when things started to seem easier between the two of you."

Malcolm studied Harry, recalling dozens of moments in the past six months, Harry and Cordelia dining with them, sharing a glass of whisky after an evening out, playing on the hearthrug or in the park with the children. Harry waltzing with Suzanne, handing her a glass of wine, taking Jessica from her arms, putting Drusilla into them. "Did you decide you were mistaken?"

"I decided whatever had happened, you were a man who knew what was important in life."

Malcolm drew a breath and felt it cut through him. "Does Cordy know?"

"Not from me. I tell my wife a lot—more now than I'd have ever thought possible—but these speculations weren't mine to share."

Malcolm looked into Harry's dark blue eyes, at once veiled and yet more open than he had ever seen them. "Thank you."

"My dear fellow. I owe you an abject apology. When I think of the times I've blathered on about my concerns about my wife's past infidelities or whether she might grow bored—"

"You couldn't blather on if you tried, Davenport. And I'm glad you can talk to me about Cordelia."

Harry gave a twisted smile. "I just wish you could talk to me about Suzanne."

"I am. Now. It means a great deal."

"I always knew Suzanne was a brilliant agent. I didn't realize just how good."

Malcolm understood the appreciation in his friend's voice, though it had taken a while for him to get to that point himself. Still, Davenport had fought on the opposite side for over four years. "It doesn't—"

"My dear Malcolm. Given my attitude to Uncle Archie's activities, did you expect me to go Crown and country over this? Unlike Archie, Suzanne was working for her own country." Harry was silent for a moment. "It's a dirty game. I went into it out of boredom and desperation. I can't help but rather admire someone who went into it out of conviction."

"You're remarkable, Davenport."

"Easier, I think, to look at it from a distance. I'm not married to her." Harry drew a breath, as though debating whether to say more. "That I understand it—even that you understand it—doesn't change the hell this must have been for you."

Malcolm looked at his friend. Who, when Malcolm had first met him, had claimed not to believe in feelings. Who even now would raise an ironic brow at the idea of emotional display. Yet his keenness of understanding about the feelings of others never failed to amaze Malcolm. "I confess at the beginning, I was rather inclined to see it all from my perspective."

"Understandable."

"It took a while to realize she'd done something I might have done myself. Though I doubt I could have pulled it off."

"I expect you could have pulled it off. But you'd have had qualms."

Malcolm picked his way through the verbal landscape. Except for a bit with Addison and Raoul, he'd discussed this with no one, save for today with David, in the midst of anger. He was picking his way through feelings he'd barely even sorted out for himself. "Seeing the human element. Carfax always said it was my weakness."

"I think it was your soul's salvation," Harry said in a quiet voice.

Malcolm shot a quick look at him.

"Speaking as one sorely in need of salvation myself," Harry said.

Malcolm held his friend's gaze for a moment, recalling the embittered Davenport letting a young French ensign escape back to the lines in the Peninsula. "You're not bad at seeing the human element yourself, Davenport."

Harry gave a short laugh. "I was detached. That probably saved me from getting too involved. But then, neither of us shared Suzanne's level of commitment."

"She had commitments that went back to before she met me," Malcolm said, gaze on the circle of light the lamp cast on a patch of carpet, gray fading into indigo. "I always prided myself on being a modern husband. I thought the fact that I'd read Mary Wollstonecraft made me enlightened. But when I learned the truth, my first reaction was to think of Suzanne as my wife."

"She is your wife."

"But she has other commitments, other loyalties. We neither us of came into the marriage unencumbered. I didn't know that, of course. I was amazed at how quickly she took to espionage. I counted myself fortunate that she shared my adventures. But they were *my* adventures."

He half expected a quip from Harry, but his friend nodded. "You're a wiser man than I, Rannoch. If I'd seen earlier that Cordy needed her own life—" He shook his head. "Folly to refine upon it."

Malcolm nodded, started to speak, then hesitated. Some wounds were still too raw. And yet—If anyone understood raw wounds, it was Davenport. "I knew almost from the first that we had to find a way to go on for Colin's and Jessica's sakes. I realized that in—betraying—me she'd been holding fast to other commitments. That given my own actions, I could hardly get on a high horse about betrayal. I even believe—"

Harry gave a faint smile. "She loves you, Rannoch. I've never doubted that."

"Yes, I—" Feelings still had a way of getting bottled up in Malcolm's throat. Suzanne's feelings for him were still difficult for him to articulate. "Whyever she went into the marriage, I don't think she's sorry for it now. But—"

Harry leaned back, arms folded across his chest, and watched him for a moment. "It's probably the worst thing a spy can go through."

"It?"

"Being outwitted."

Malcolm released his breath. "Damn you, Davenport. Right as usual."

"I'll own I'm cursing myself a bit," Harry said. "I knew Suzanne in the Peninsula. I worked with her. I didn't have the muddying effects of being head over heels in love with her to dilute my perspective. I was cynic enough to wonder sometimes at the seeming strength of your marriage. But until six months ago, I never—"

Malcolm could see his friend recalling moments, sifting through the past, turning over memories. "I know," he said. "I did the same thing. She's good."

"And you're too sensible to let your bruised ego stand in the way of your marriage."

"I'm attempting to be." Malcolm moved to the desk. "If you can, there are things I'd appreciate your help with."

"Anything."

Malcolm picked up a stack of letters, most of them long since written, now sealed and franked. "This is for my sister and brother-in-law in Scotland. They're eminently capable of running Dunmykel, thank God, but this will give them further authority should they need it. This is for Rupert. Notes for the next parliamentary session and some advice on strategy. These are for Aunt Frances, and Allie and Geoff, and Paul and Juliette."

Harry took the papers. Questions flickered in his gaze, but he merely said, "You aren't going to try to see any of them?"

"There isn't time. And I don't want to burden them with the risk."

Harry nodded, taking his meaning. If the truth came out, anyone they'd seen tonight might be accused of assisting the escape of traitors.

"I'm burdening you," Malcolm said, "but you're an agent. You'll know best how to handle it."

Harry waved a hand. "Neither Cordy nor I would forgive you if you'd left without seeing us."

Malcolm reached for a letter he had just written and a bank draught. "This is for Sue Kettering. I meant to do more, to try to arrange employment for her—"

Harry took the papers. "I'll arrange it. And tell her what I can about Coventry's death."

"Thank you." Malcolm picked up one last paper from the desk. "This is for you. In case I wasn't able to see you before we left. And to give you and Cordelia power of attorney to handle anything else relating to our affairs or property."

Harry's eyes widened.

"I can't imagine anyone I'd rather trust with it." Malcolm clasped his friend's hand as he gave him the paper.

Harry's gaze met his and his fingers tightened briefly round Malcolm's own. For a moment they were standing on a sunny, rain-drenched ridge on a June morning, the smell of cooking fires and practice shots sharp in the air, the French army drawn up in glittering array across from them. Harry had clasped his arm then, knowing neither of them might live to see the other again.

"It's only just sinking in," Harry said. "You're really going."

"It's barely sunk in on me," Malcolm said. "I imagine we'll be in Italy before I can fully comprehend it."

Harry tucked the papers into his coat. "I'll do everything, I can, of course. I may not have your knack for running large properties, but between us Cordy and I should be able to manage. But don't count on our remaining in Britain indefinitely. Cordy and I've been wanting to take the girls to Italy. This makes it all the more likely we'll plan the journey as soon as possible."

Malcolm swallowed. Even Harry hadn't fully grasped what exposure meant. "Harry, once the truth comes out—"

"If you're going to say association with you may make us ostracized, then I'd cheer the prospect of no longer having social obligations. But I very much doubt it will happen. More's the pity."

Malcolm knew he should protest further, but he knew with Davenport it would be of little use. And he found there were some things he couldn't bear to give up. He felt his face relax into a smile. "You're the best of friends, Harry."

"I don't make friends easily. You'll pardon me for trying to hold on to those I have."

Malcolm studied his friend. Harry was many things. A brilliant scholar, a loving father, a man desperately in love with his wife, a loyal friend beneath the caustic tongue. He was also one of the best agents Malcolm had ever encountered. "I knew at the start of this investigation that we might cross swords with Carfax. I just didn't realize how. Yesterday I was rather glad Oliver and Maria and St. Juste and the others had broken free of Carfax. I still am. But I've never been more aware of how ruthless Carfax is. For all his offer to let us escape, he may try to find us. So may others."

Harry nodded. "To own the truth, I rather relish the prospect of the battle."

"I don't doubt you're equal to it. But neither of us quite has experience of having Carfax turn his full powers against us."

Harry nodded, with the hard gaze of an agent assessing a mission. "I still have friends in the army. That should help. Often the disagreements between different intelligence branches are tiresome. But sometimes they can be put to good use."

Colquhoun Grant, who had been head of Wellington's intelligence in the Peninsula and the Waterloo campaign, had a great deal of respect for Harry. He'd support Harry and perhaps even Malcolm himself. But—"If Wellington learns the truth—"

Harry gave a wry smile. "Hookey's a lot of things, but he's not precisely broad-minded when it comes to divided loyalties or the rights of the dispossessed, is he? On the other hand, there's not much love lost between him and Carfax. I can put that to good use."

Malcolm nodded. It was what he would have done himself, but he wasn't used to leaving such decisions in the hands of others. He saw Wellington, brows drawn as he ordered Malcolm on a mission, thrusting a dispatch into Malcolm's hand in the smoke and chaos of Waterloo, smiling with rare approval.

"Malcolm." Harry's face had gone serious. "Wellington values you. He knows your worth. This won't change that."

Malcolm gave a smile that he could feel twist his mouth. "You're a master at deception, Davenport, but not quite masterful enough to make me believe that. It's all right. Difficult to get through a day, let alone a lifetime, without incurring Hookey's disapproval."

"As we both have cause to know." Harry watched Malcolm for a moment, then gripped his arm again. "But I think his approval matters more to you than it does to me."

"My dear Davenport. I'm the last man to be sentimental when it comes to Wellington."

"But you take your duty more seriously than just about anyone I know. You were loyal enough to Wellington, and to Castlereagh, that you went on serving them long after the conflict between the positions they advocated and your own became untenable. It can't but be difficult to have them both see you as—"

"A traitor?"

"They won't see it that way."

"No? I rather think that's precisely what they'll think. They'll give me too much credit and Suzanne not enough, and think she couldn't have deceived me all these years. At the very least, they'll always wonder. It's all right, because they're right, in a way. My loyalty to my wife comes first."

Though the question flickered in his gaze, Harry didn't ask the obvious corollary. What would Malcolm have done if he'd learned his wife was a Bonapartist agent while she was still actively spying?

Which was a good thing, because Malcolm didn't have the least idea how he would answer it.

43

Cordelia dropped down on the edge of the bed. "Dear God. And yet in some ways, I feel as though I should have known."

"I don't see how you could have envisioned this level of deception," Suzanne said.

"I knew—"

"That I wasn't what I seemed?"

"Yes. But I never imagined." Cordelia rubbed her arms. "In a way, I'm relieved."

"Relieved?"

"I was afraid it was something between you and Malcolm."

Suzanne gave a short laugh. "This is definitely between me and Malcolm."

"Yes, but it's—work, I suppose. Not a personal betrayal, if that makes any sense. Malcolm is a spy. I think he'd understand."

"He does, in a way. More than I ever thought possible. But it's still a betrayal."

Cordelia's gaze moved over her face. Suzanne knew that look. Recasting the past. "Waterloo must have been unspeakably awful for you."

Suzanne saw them, raindrenched in the street, bent over the wounded, the flounces of their gowns stained with dirt and blood. Bent over the pallets of the injured men who lined their hall. Hunched over cups of tea in the kitchen, sharing their raw fears for their husbands. "You're kind to put it that way. You'd be pardoned for seeing it as my worst betrayal."

Cordelia shrugged. "I'm the last person to blame anyone else for betrayal. To own the truth, I think it's all the more remarkable that you did what you did supporting the other side."

"Would you have refused to tend French soldiers?"

Cordelia shook her head. "Anyone who was wounded deserved attention. At that point I don't think I cared much who they were fighting for. I don't see how one could look at any fellow creature in that state and not feel compassion."

"You're a remarkable woman, Cordy."

"I was going to say the same to you. I always knew you had a sense of purpose greater than mine. I never realized to what an extent."

"Cordy—" Suzanne hesitated. But Cordelia was going to think of it at some point. Better now than when they were apart. "It was the people I was working for who wounded Harry."

Cordelia's gaze froze on her face for a moment. "Of course. That's obvious, isn't it? Though I didn't think of it that way. I suppose—" She fingered a knot of ribbon on her sleeve. "I can't say how I'd feel if Harry had died. But he didn't. I saw you nurse him. He would have died if it hadn't been for Malcolm. He might well have died if it hadn't been for your care. If it weren't for you and Malcolm, I don't know where Harry and I would be today."

Suzanne released her breath. In a sense, she felt as though she'd been holding it since Waterloo.

"What did you think I'd do?" Cordelia asked. "Say I never wanted to see you again?"

"I thought it was a possibility. You could certainly be pardoned for doing so."

"How could I?" Cordelia said. "After what we've shared? How could you think I'd be anything but concerned for you?" She swallowed hard. "How soon are you leaving?"

"Tonight."

"So soon?"

"We can't afford to delay. We don't know—"

"You think you'd be arrested?"

"It's possible. I have information people would like to get their hands on. Malcolm has people who would like to bring him down. We can't risk what would happen if we were detained."

"No, of course you'd have to leave at once." Cordelia gave a brisk nod and smoothed her skirt. "The consolation is we've always wanted to go to Italy. Harry's been itching to get a look at real Roman ruins instead of the bits and pieces left in Britain. It's just the thing he needs to turn his monographs into a book. And the girls are a good age to travel now. It will take us a few weeks to make arrangements, but you've given us the perfect excuse for a long journey abroad. You can tell me what you want me to bring, because I'm sure you won't be able to manage all of it tonight."

Suzanne swallowed. "Cordy—"

"I promise we won't descend on you until you're ready for us. And we can find our own lodgings."

"It's not that."

"Livia and Dru are going to miss Colin and Jessica and Emily dreadfully. Damn it, Harry and I are going to miss all of you."

"Cordy, you have to consider—if this becomes public, associating with us—"

"Do you think I give a damn about that? With my reputation? It's not as though Harry would be blackballed by other classical scholars. Or even care if he was."

"You have two daughters."

"Whom I want to grow up understanding that one stands by one's friends."

Suzanne put a hand to her cheek. It was damp. "I don't deserve you, Cordy."

"That's nonsense." Cordelia pushed herself to her feet. "I've always thought you were harder on yourself than I am on myself. Well, the truth is, if I really dwelt on my own actions, I don't suppose I could go on at all. But you acted out of a commitment. To something that mattered to you before you ever met Malcolm. I married a very decent man who loved me, and threw that love back in his face."

Suzanne looked into her friend's troubled blue eyes. Odd, tonight of all nights, to find herself the one offering comfort. "You acted out of a commitment to George."

Cordelia gave a short laugh. "I can only hope your ideals are less tarnished than mine. Even the most disillusioned revolutionary could scarcely feel as betrayed as I do by George."

"I wouldn't say I'm disillusioned. More of a realist perhaps, though I went into this with my eyes fairly open. But disillusionment doesn't change the reality of the commitment one feels at the start. And you didn't marry Harry planning to betray him."

"No, I married Harry without giving much consideration to his feelings at all."

"I did much the same with Malcolm. I was almost entirely focused on tactics."

"You didn't consider your own feelings, so why consider anyone else's?"

"I suppose so, in a way." She'd never talked about her deception of Malcolm in this way before. She'd never, she realized, talked to anyone about it, save Malcolm and Raoul, to both of whom there was obviously a great deal she couldn't say, and a bit to Blanca, though she always feared that if she expressed too much guilt she would stir Blanca's own. "I'm not sure I acknowledged the power of feelings at all at the time."

"I was doing my best to numb my own," Cordelia said. "I either thought other people should do the same or I was completely blind to the fact that they had feelings at all. It's a bit of a muddle, looking back, but there's no way I come out of it seeming halfway decent."

"Malcolm was a means to an end for me." She wouldn't have been able to admit that to anyone else.

"So was Harry. I needed to be married. I didn't want to fall in love again. I was sure I never could fall in love again. He was there, offering me marriage, and not completely boring."

"And yet, look where you are now."

"I could say the same to you."

Suzanne pushed her fingers into her hair. "Nothing you did could ruin Harry if it became public knowledge."

"No, that's true. Embarrass him, perhaps."

"I haven't really been able to think about it," Suzanne said. "What it's going to do to Malcolm to give up the House of Commons. Dunmykel. The people he's known all his life. There's more than I ever dreamed possible that I'll miss in Britain, but for him—"

"Darling, you've only had a few hours. Don't try to think about it now. You'll have plenty of time in Italy—"

"For us both to realize the full implications, and the bitterness to set in?" She meant the words to sound ironic, but she couldn't keep the bite from her voice.

"Suzanne! Malcolm adores you."

Suzanne checked the retort that she would have used to deflect the conversation. She sank down on the dressing table bench, arms hugged over her chest. "I didn't believe in love when I married Malcolm. Or if I did"—she thought of Raoul for a moment and her tangled feelings for him—"I didn't believe in it as something one could build a life on. That's not true anymore. But I don't believe that it lasts invariably. Even steel has a breaking point."

"If what Harry felt for me could endure—"

"It's not the revelations. I thought Malcolm couldn't get past those, but somehow he has. But I think the numbing day-to-day reality of realizing, a bit at a time, what he's lost is what could destroy us."

"I thought that about Harry. That he'd look at me across the breakfast table and remember something. That he'd meet one of my ex-lovers or hear a bit of gossip and each one would be a cut that would make our marriage bleed a bit more. But so far, it doesn't seem to have happened. Despite the fact that my former lovers have a distressing tendency to become entangled in our adventures."

"You and Harry are remarkable. But you aren't isolated. I'm afraid of what boredom will do to us."

Cordelia's gaze had darkened with concern, but she smiled. "I don't think the two of you could be bored if you tried. I'm sure there are things to investigate in Italy."

Suzanne managed a smile. "Perhaps. In any case, there's nothing for it but to forge ahead as best we can."

Cordelia paused on the pavement in front of the Berkeley Square house, her fingers curled round her husband's arm. "I still can't really believe they're going."

"Nor can I," Harry said. "I don't imagine it will sink in until tomorrow or the next day, when we realize we aren't seeing them."

Cordelia looked up at her husband. "You knew." It wasn't quite a question.

"Suspected." He met her gaze. "I couldn't—"

"No, I quite see that. It wasn't your secret to share." She swallowed. Her chest was hollow with a loss she hadn't quite accepted yet. "Their marriage used to give me faith that ours could work."

Despite everything, the ghost of a smile lifted Harry's mouth. He put his lips to her hair. "Well, perhaps that's more true than ever."

Cordelia pressed her face against her husband's shoulder. "Let's go home, darling. I have the most absurd desire to hug my children."

Suzanne closed her valise. She'd found room for both the pomegranate and coral dresses. Not practical, perhaps, but comforting. Cordelia's farewell hug and Harry's kiss on her cheek lingered in her memory. Not the time to think about when she'd see them again. Not the time to think about the last time she'd seen Livia and Drusilla, or what questions Colin and Jessica and Emily would ask.

She looked up at the creak of the door. Her husband stepped into the room. Suzanne got to her feet and met his gaze. They'd both talked to nearly everyone they needed to since their world fell apart, she realized. Except each other. But then, of course, they'd have a long time for that.

"I've written out letters for the servants," Suzanne said. "I thought we'd gather everyone together and talk to them before we leave."

Malcolm nodded. "Do you have any more letters to post? Valentin can see them delivered."

She gestured towards her dressing table. "I've written to Manon and Bel." Poor Bel, her marriage in a crisis and Suzanne wouldn't be there to offer support. Or to see Manon's baby.

"We'll be able to write from the Continent," he said. "It's not as though—"

"We'll be completely cut off? Of course not." She folded her arms, gripping her elbows.

Malcolm took a step forwards. "Suzette—Mel—"

"No, don't." She put out a hand to forestall him. "Wait until we're on the boat. Plenty of time then."

And she really, really couldn't afford to break down before they left. Couldn't let herself think about what she'd brought him to. "The life of an agent," she said. "A mad rush and then interminable waiting. If—"

Malcolm crossed to her side and put his hands on her shoulders. "I love you. More with every day that passes. Whatever's to come, never forget that."

Tears stung her eyes. Unvoiced feelings choked her throat. "Darling—"

He bent his head and kissed her, the way she had kissed him before Waterloo. As though imprinting a memory against what the future might hold.

A rap fell on the door. "It's me," Simon said.

Malcolm drew back. "My dear fellow. Come in."

Simon came quickly into the room. "I saw Laura. She told me to come up. Thank God. I was afraid I wouldn't catch you before you left."

Malcolm turned to face his friend. Suzanne could feel the echoes of the past between the two men. "David's talked to you?"

Simon nodded. Then his gaze went to Suzanne. He crossed to her side in two strides and pressed a kiss to her forehead. "You're a marvel. I always knew it, but never more so than tonight."

"Simon—" Suzanne's voice caught. She turned her head away.

Simon pressed her head into his shoulder for a moment, his fingers gentle on her hair. "I won't keep you long. I know you must have preparations to make. I wanted to be sure I got to say goodbye."

"You knew we'd be leaving?" Malcolm asked.

"I know how your mind works," Simon said. "It's all right, I won't ask where you're going. Probably safer if you keep it to yourselves. But I hope you can write eventually."

"You couldn't stop me," Malcolm said.

"For what it's worth, David's seen sense enough to admit he doesn't want to destroy your lives. You needn't fear he'll try to stop you."

Though her face was still pressed against Simon's shoulder, Suzanne could feel the relief that ran through her husband.

"You weren't sure, were you?" Simon asked. "My God, what we've come to. I tried to reason with him. I tried every argument I could think of—"

"Simon." Suzanne stepped out of his arms to look at him. "David's right. I did betray Britain."

"Because you were doing your job. In the service of your own country."

"Which was at war with his. I don't agree with David, but I can understand why he sees it this way."

"Then you're more tolerant than I am, Suzie."

"Simon." Malcolm took a step towards his friend. "That's why Carfax told David. To drive a wedge between the two of you. He admitted as much to me."

Simon's mouth tightened. "I guessed as much. I'm sorrier than I can say that the two of you were tangled in Carfax's war on David's and my relationship. If it weren't for this investigation—"

"Something else would have brought it to a head. Simon." Suzanne gripped his arms. "If you let this come between you and David, you're playing right into his plans. Don't let Carfax win."

Simon gave a twisted smile, though his gaze was a wasteland. "In general, I'd be willing to go to almost any lengths to keep Carfax from winning. But the man is damnably perceptive. He hasn't created a rift, he's opened up one that was already there. David and I view the world differently. We always have."

Suzanne saw Simon and David the night she'd first met them at Lady Frances's house. So effortlessly in tune with each other. "You and David share more than any other couple I know."

Simon shook his head. "There are different types of sharing. Different types of love. And relationships change."

Those quiet words were like a knife thrust. She'd thought there was nothing worse than seeing her actions threaten her own family. But to see another family begin to unravel because of her—

Malcolm had gone still. Every emotion held in check. For Simon. Or perhaps for her.

"Simon," she said, her voice dry, "you wouldn't—"

"Leave him?" Simon's voice had the blunt edge of the flat of a sword. "I would have done, once. Before we had the children."

Amazing how his reaction echoed her own. "Children change everything," Suzanne said.

"Of course," Simon continued in the same voice of hammered steel, "that doesn't mean he won't leave me."

"He won't," Malcolm said with assurance. "If I know him at all. David's loyal. And the person he's really angry with is me."

Malcolm met Simon's gaze. The past hung between them. Something had smashed in the past hours, something older than her and Malcolm's relationship or even David and Simon's. Something that had sustained all three men since they were little more than children. A cry nearly tore from Suzanne's throat.

"It's our lookout," Simon said. "Our efforts to find a way to go on, after a fashion. You need to look after yourselves."

Colin peered over the prow of the boat. Moonlight shimmered against the dark water, hiding the greasy patches, turning it into a thing of magic and mystery. Lamplight glowed along the edges of the river. "Are we escaping?" he asked.

"Nonsense." Suzanne shifted Jessica against her shoulder. It was past midnight, but things like bedtimes seemed singularly unimportant just now. Eventually, somehow, they would get back to some sort of routine. Not that there was ever much of a routine in their household. "We're going on a journey."

Colin twisted his head round to look up at her. "In the middle of the night."

Malcolm put a hand on his son's back to steady him. "Not the first time we've done so, lad."

"I know. We've escaped before." Colin looked between his parents as though to offer reassurance. "It's all right. I like escaping. So does Jessica. Emily doesn't mind, do you, Em?"

"No. But I can't see." Emily gripped the ship's rail and pulled herself up onto her tiptoes.

Raoul swung her up onto his shoulders. "Better?"

Emily gave a crow of delight, then looked down at Raoul. "Are you coming all the way there with us?"

"All the way," he assured her.

Further along the rail, Addison slid his arms round Blanca's waist, above the curve of her abdomen. "I have fond memories of the Italian villa."

They'd gone there, all of them, on a holiday when they were living in Paris. Watching Blanca lean back against Addison, Suzanne wondered if that trip might have been a key turning point in their relationship.

On Raoul's shoulders, Emily cast a glance back in the direction from which they had sailed. "I miss our home," she said in a small voice.

"We'll be back," Laura said in a firm voice, reaching up to touch her daughter's hand.

"I've had lots of homes," Colin said. "Some I don't even remember."

Suzanne touched her son's hair. "We can always make a home as long as we're all together, darling."

She pulled Jessica closer and looked from her son to Raoul, Emily, and Laura, to Blanca and Addison, to Malcolm. And back to the cabin where Berowne was curled up on a cushion with the ease of a seasoned traveler. It was the sort of thing a mother said. The sort of thing she'd once have dismissed as trite. Yet oddly, as she framed the words, her fingers in her son's thick hair, she found she believed her own reassurance. The pressure of unshed tears stung her eyes. Her throat ached from unspoken words and unvoiced cries. They hadn't any of them really begun to mourn what they had lost. She wasn't blind to the risks ahead, to her family, to her marriage. But they still had their foundation. Colin was right. They had had a home long before they came to Britain and would have one after they left.

Malcolm took a step closer and dropped a kiss on her hair. "It's what lies ahead that matters."

HISTORICAL NOTES

I have taken some liberties with the Duke of Wellington's Waterloo banquet. Wellington probably did not give his first banquet for Waterloo veterans at Apsley House until 1820, and the first of his banquets took place in a dining room that could only seat 35, so the guests were limited to senior officers. After the Waterloo Gallery was completed in 1830, up to 85 guests could attend, including guests who had not been present at the battle, but the guest list was limited to men.

Wellington's brother Richard, Marquess Wellesley, purchased Apsley House in 1807 and engaged James Wyatt to improve it (with the assistance of Thomas Cundy). Wellington bought Apsley House from his brother in 1817 (to help Richard out of financial difficulties). In 1818 Wellington engaged Benjamin Dean Wyatt to make repairs to the house. Wyatt installed the nude statue of Napoleon by Antonio Canova, which Wellington had acquired. But Wellington was still British ambassador to France in 1818. Because echoes of Waterloo reverberate through *London Gambit*, I have taken the liberty of having Wellington in London for the battle's third anniversary and having him give a banquet at Apsley House with a guest list that accommodates most of the key characters in the book.

I am indebted to a wonderful research visit to Apsley House and to the Victoria and Albert Museum's excellent publication *Apsley House: Wellington Museum* (London: Victoria and Albert Museum, 2001).

Fitzroy Somerset was still Wellington's secretary at the British embassy in Paris in 1818, though he did stand for and win a parliamentary seat at Truro in the general election in August of 1818, and he was in Truro for the election.

Hortense Bonaparte did travel into Switzerland in 1811 to give birth in secret to her child by the Comte de Flahaut (who joined her for the birth). Mélanie Suzanne Lescaut and Julien St. Juste did not accompany her. But if they had . . .

A READING GROUP GUIDE

LONDON GAMBIT

Tracy Grant

About This Guide

The suggested questions are included
to enhance your group's reading of
Tracy Grant's *London Gambit.*

DISCUSSION QUESTIONS

1. The book ends on the anniversary of the battle of Waterloo. Discuss how echoes of the battle reverberate through the book and influence the various characters.

2. Do you think Suzanne was right to keep the Phoenix plot from Malcolm at first? What do you think would have happened if she'd kept it from him longer?

3. Suzanne worries about the dilemma Malcolm would face if Raoul were involved in the Phoenix plot. How do you think Malcolm would have handled that situation?

4. Malcolm says Laura and Raoul's future "rather comes down to what Laura decides she wants as she comes back to herself. And if O'Roarke can give it to her." What do you think Laura will decide she wants? And can Raoul give it to her?

5. The end of *London Gambit* sees a major change in the Rannochs' circumstances. Some of Suzanne's worst fears have come to pass. How do you think Suzanne and Malcolm will cope with their new circumstances individually and as a couple?

6. What do you think lies ahead for David and Simon?

7. Do you think Malcolm and Suzanne really were "collateral damage" to Carfax?
8. Who do you think Julien St. Juste really is?
9. Oliver and Isobel Lydgate both seem to have had stronger feelings for each other than the other realized. Do you think they can salvage their marriage?
10. Do you think the revelations about Maria Monreal strained the Davenports' marriage or left it stronger?
11. Discuss how Harry and Cordelia reacted to the revelations about Suzanne. How might some of the other characters who haven't learned the truth yet react? Lady Frances? Rupert? Isobel?
12. Carfax tells Malcolm that David couldn't be happy if David didn't do his duty. Do you think that is true?
13. Harry and Malcolm both say that they choose to believe their wives won't betray them again. Do you think the marriages could survive new betrayals?

MORE BY TRACY GRANT

Rannoch / Fraser Series
Incident in Berkeley Square
The Mayfair Affair
London Interlude
The Berkeley Square Affair
The Paris Plot
The Paris Affair
His Spanish Bride
Imperial Scandal
Vienna Waltz
The Mask of Night
Beneath a Silent Moon
Secrets of a Lady

Traditional Regencies
The Widow's Gambit
Frivolous Pretence
The Courting of Philippa

Lescaut Quartet
Dark Angel
Shores of Desire
Shadows of the Heart
Rightfully His

ABOUT THE AUTHOR

Tracy Grant studied British history at Stanford University and received the Firestone Award for Excellence in Research for her honors thesis on shifting conceptions of honor in late-fifteenth-century England. She lives in the San Francisco Bay Area with her young daughter and three cats. In addition to writing, Tracy works for the Merola Opera Program, a professional training program for opera singers, pianists, and stage directors. Her real life heroine is her daughter Mélanie, who is very cooperative about Mummy's writing time. She is currently at work on her next book chronicling the adventures of Malcolm and Suzanne Rannoch. Visit her on the Web at www.tracygrant.org

© Raphael Coffey Photography